LIBERATING THE LADY OF LOUGHMOE

The Ladies of the Keep, Book One

(Connected to The Lords of Vice Series and The Duke's Guard Series)

C.H. Admirand

ARE YOU SIGNED UP FOR DRAGONBLADE'S BLOG?

You'll get the latest news and information on exclusive giveaways, exclusive excerpts, coming releases, sales, free books, cover reveals and more.

Check out our complete list of authors, too!

No spam, no junk. That's a promise!

Sign Up Here

www.dragonbladepublishing.com

Dearest Reader;

Thank you for your support of a small press. At Dragonblade Publishing, we strive to bring you the highest quality Historical Romance from some of the best authors in the business. Without your support, there is no 'us', so we sincerely hope you adore these stories and find some new favorite authors along the way.

Happy Reading!

CEO, Dragonblade Publishing

Additional Dragonblade books by Author C.H. Admirand

The Ladies of the Keep Series
Liberating the Lady of Loughmoe (Book 1)
Bargaining with the Lady of Merewood (Book 2)
Rescuing the Lady of Sedgeworth (Book 3)

The Duke's Guard Series
The Duke's Sword (Book 1)
The Duke's Protector (Book 2)
The Duke's Shield (Book 3)
The Duke's Dragoon (Book 4)
The Duke's Hammer (Book 5)
The Duke's Defender (Book 6)
The Duke's Saber (Book 7)
The Duke's Enforcer (Book 8)
The Duke's Mercenary (Book 9)

The Lords of Vice Series
Mending the Duke's Pride (Book 1)
Avoiding the Earl's Lust (Book 2)
Tempering the Viscount's Envy (Book 3)
Redirecting the Baron's Greed (Book 4)
His Vow to Keep (Novella)
The Merry Wife of Wyndmere (Novella)

The Lyon's Den Series
Rescued by the Lyon
Captivated by the Lyon

Dedication

This book is dedicated to Kathryn Le Veque, CEO of Dragonblade Publishing, Inc., author extraordinaire and friend. You gave me a reason to carry on when my life fell apart and helped me keep my promise to my Heavenly Hubby to finish the Lords of Vice series and continue to promote my books.

I will be forever grateful for your compassion, understanding, and a place within the Dragonblade Family. You helped me to find a purpose in my life again, and a place where I can imbue my hardheaded Dragonblade heroes with some of DJ's best qualities: his honesty, his integrity, his compassion for others, and his killer broad shoulders—and introduce them to my feisty Dragonblade heroines. Thank you!

PROLOGUE

1071 Northumbria

L ADY JILLIAN STOOD atop the curtain wall of Sedgeworth Keep, grateful for the new moon, for it would shield her from the guard patrolling the battlements. The darkness allowed her to move like the wraith she was forced to become…a mere shadow of her former self.

The midnight hour was solely hers. A time where she could escape her life of servitude without the worry that she would be late answering the impatient summons from the lady of the keep. A lady whose punishments were meant to degrade Jillian and break her spirit. Determined, she clenched her jaw and curled her hands into fists.

She would not be broken!

A gust of damp, bone-chilling air tugged at her mother's cloak. She pulled the worn material closer. A lump filled her throat when she snagged her chapped and callused hands on it. Jillian did not mind the work that roughened her hands and put an ache in her back. But she did wonder, would the rest of her body become hard and callused over time? It was through no fault of her own that she had been forced into this mean state. She used to wear lovely gowns and have the soft hands of a lady.

So much of her life and very existence had changed quickly—

too quickly. Word of the Norman conqueror's victory at the Battle of Hastings struck terror in the hearts of the Saxons. When news of the Lord of Loughmoe's death at Hastings reached them, she and her mother had had no choice but to flee their home.

They thought they'd found their savior in Owen of Sedgeworth, but he'd offered his protection and opened his holding to them under false pretenses and the guise of neighborly concern. His black heart shielded the truth from them: he lusted after their fertile keep—Loughmoe!

Jillian poured every ounce of her being into taking care of her mother, but she had been unable to turn back time or heal her mother's broken heart. Mother no longer had the will to live without the strength of the other half of her heart—Jillian's father. Two months after her father was slain at Hastings, Jillian was alone, with no one to turn to. She was no longer the cossetted daughter of Loughmoe Keep, with a loving father and mother, but a slave to the lady of a nearby holding. Accepting the harsh words and beatings as her due for failing to perform her duties to the Lady of Sedgeworth's satisfaction, she resigned herself to the life she now led.

Had she been able to return to Loughmoe Keep, she would have nothing to offer the people her parents had given their lives to protect. She had nothing of value—even after five years of servitude—save her indomitable will to survive and her callused hands. But of what use would she be without a warrior able to defend her keep standing beside her? A knight of renown who had the strength and cunning to retake Loughmoe Keep from those that had stolen it from her family.

The warrior of her dreams would help her and would have the means to see that the good people of Loughmoe not only survived—but thrived! With his aid, she *would* reclaim her birthright!

"Lord, how much longer will I have to wait for him to come?"

CHAPTER ONE

1072 Northumbria

"H E SAID NO, milady."

Lady Jillian's heart skipped a beat. "Did he say why, Stephan?"

The stable lad gripped the hem of his dirt-brown tunic and started wringing it.

When he remained silent, she prodded the young man, "Did you tell him Owen of Sedgeworth has imprisoned his brother?"

Stephan looked up at her. "'Xactly like you said, milady."

She could not believe it. "He's not going to help us?"

What would she do now? Her plans of escape evaporated. The man she'd thought to be her savior was refusing to help. Struggling to keep her composure, she dug deep for a calm she didn't feel.

A horse whinnied from the stall behind them, startling them both. To cover the way he jumped at the sound, Stephan kicked at the dry straw covering the stable floor.

Mayhap he spoke to the wrong man! "This man you spoke to," she began, "was he tall with light hair?"

Stephan nodded, and she asked, "Fierce looking? Built like a warrior?"

The young man grabbed her hand. "I spoke to the Lord of

Merewood Keep."

"You're sure?"

"He's every bit as tall as MacInness the Scot...just as broad through the shoulders."

The look of awe in Stephan's eyes convinced her. Garrick of Merewood was reputed to be a giant, like the tall Scots mercenary who'd befriended her. "Did he speak at all?"

Stephan looked down at the hard-packed earthen floor and the bare spot he'd made in the thin layer of straw. "Aye."

"What did he say?"

His shoulders slumped. "He laughed."

Jillian stepped closer to him and placed her work-roughened hands on his bony shoulders. "But not at you?"

He refused to meet her eyes and her stomach clenched. A tight knot of fear began to form as a grim thought took hold. "Did he try to hurt you?"

He looked up at her then. "Nay, he said seeing's how you knowed so much 'bout his warrior skills, you'd know he don't need no help. 'Specially from no lady."

Her hands tightened reflexively on his shoulders. Every word was true. Garrick of Merewood's reputation with sword and axe were a vital part of her plan to regain her family's holding. Without the Lord of Merewood Keep, she would be doomed to fail.

But what he didn't know terrified her. If her guardian followed through with his threat ... she caught herself starting to grind her teeth. In a bid to stop the damning habit, she closed her eyes. Immediately, the face of Garrick of Merewood's youngest brother appeared in her mind's eye. So handsome, yet arrogant while kissing her hand. But his arrogance dissolved into a look of stark terror as the hammered tip of a claymore hovered at the base of his throat.

Fear sprinted through her heart. Her guardian had threatened the young man's life right before imprisoning him. Her eyes shot open. "Garrick doesn't know how badly Lord Owen wants the alliance."

She paced back and forth, stirring up tiny motes of dust with each step. "He'll not stop until he can sink his greedy fists into Merewood Keep's revenues."

"Lord Garrick's smart," the young lad said. "He don't need to worry 'bout Owen."

Jillian stopped dead in her tracks; took a look around the stable to make certain they were alone. "Shhh…lest someone hear you. I'll not have Lady Haldana use her switch on you, too."

Unconsciously, she rolled her shoulders to relieve the constant ache in them. The newly healed layer of skin across the top of her back pulled. She stopped before it could split open again.

Stephan put a hand on her arm, "'Tis not right that she beats ya."

Staring down at her self-appointed protector, Jillian's eyes filled with tears. Orphans no one wanted, they'd looked out for one another for the last three years.

Smoothing a fat blond curl back off his dirt-smeared forehead, she rasped, "You're a brave lad to watch over me. But you must understand, we don't always have a say in how our lives turn out. 'Tis the will of God."

Her thoughts drifted back to a time when her life was far different. If she concentrated hard enough, she could almost see her parents walking arm in arm across the bailey as they stopped at the keep's well where her father always snuck a kiss.

Lost in the past, Jillian tilted her head to one side. If she listened hard enough, she could hear a whisper of her mother's soft laughter. The memories made her smile.

"Milady?"

"Hmmm?" Small hands were grabbing her arm, shaking her. "Oh! Sorry, I was just thinking…"

"Why does the mistress beat ya?" His face was lined with worry.

"I do not know. Mayhap I don't work fast enough to suit her."

"But you're always breaking your back toiling over some such—"

"Hush now." She placed a finger to his lips. "It matters not why she does, it just is. If I could just meet with Lord Garrick and convince him…" Her voice trailed off.

"That's it!" She grabbed the boy and hugged him hard. If she could meet the Lord of Merewood Keep face-to-face and explain the dire situation, mayhap he'd have a change of heart.

Hope speared through her. *There was still a chance.*

⤞⥲⥲⥲⥲⤝⤝⤝⤝

JILLIAN CROUCHED LOW behind an ancient oak tree, the last hiding place between the edge of the forest and the curtain wall surrounding Merewood Keep. Her body was stiff with tension from waiting.

Lifting her shoulders to ease the pressure sent shards of pain slicing through her. Her vision grayed as the skin pulled and stretched. Inhaling a deep, cleansing breath, she waited for the pain to subside.

She looked up. A cloud was inches away from the moon. Gauging the distance one last time, she rose up on the balls of her feet and prayed her stiff muscles would obey.

"Now or never," she whispered into the darkness.

The moonlight faded as she ran toward the curtain wall. Fear had her heart pumping in her breast, giving her feet wings. This would be her last chance to change her life and put an end to the beatings. *She was taking it.*

Thin rays of moonlight silvered the ground around her as she dove through the break in the curtain wall. Crawling forward she felt each and every twig snapping beneath her sweat-slickened palms, felt tiny stones bruising her kneecaps. Panting from the exertion, she stopped, straining to listen. Finally, she heard what she waited for.

Footsteps. "Castle guard…south corner…right on schedule. Bless you, Stephan." His information was accurate. Watching from her hiding place, four knights met and passed one another, continuing two-by-two on their midnight sweep of the southern perimeter. Once they'd gone, she stood up, brushed her skirts, and searched the night sky.

"Not a cloud." She would be out in the open now. Fear sprinted through her. With ice-cold hands she gripped the amber pendant hanging between her breasts. Fingering the flat side, she sought the etched Celtic cross. Finding it, she offered up a quick prayer to God. Slowing her breath, she inhaled deeply and instinctively sought the Runic inscription on the slightly rounded face of the pendant. Saying another prayer to the ancients, she felt the familiar warmth begin to surge through her hand where she held the amber, flowing up her arm to her heart.

Her fear dissolved. With one last fortifying breath, she ran across the bailey, shadow to shadow. Up ahead a faint flicker of light beckoned her closer.

A feeling of dread snaked up her spine, chilling her to the very marrow of her bones. She stiffened to control it, reaffirming her resolve to secure her future. There was no one else to do it for her.

"Do not fear him, he's just a man…well, warrior," she qualified. "I can do this!" 'Twould be like talking to Winslow MacInness—vassal to her guardian.

Heading toward the beacon of light, she heard the deep rumbling of a male voice and answering whinny. *Was the warrior she sought in the stable?* Uneasy in the dark, uncertain of her welcome, she changed direction, following the comforting sounds of man and beast.

Three steps from the open doorway to the stable, someone grabbed her from behind, spinning her around. Before she could draw a breath to scream, she was roughly hauled up against the rock-hard wall of a man's chest. His hand tipped her head back before tangling deeply in her waist-length hair.

"Who are you?" he demanded.

The depth of his voice resonated through her. Fear robbed her of her voice.

"What do you want?" he asked, shaking her. The voice and hands belonged to a very powerful man, one she imagined could crush the breath from her lungs and the life from her body. Her gasp of fright had him loosening his hold. His hand found its way free of her hair to gently toy with the curl brushing against her temple. His tender touch warred with his rough demanding actions, confusing her.

She strained to see in the dark, but could not quite make out more than the outline of a very large man. *He could be the one she sought.*

He let go of her hair, but the grip on her arms tightened. She sucked in a breath, hoping he wouldn't guess how badly he frightened her, saying, "I need to speak to Lord Garrick."

In the silence that followed, her fear compounded and grew to epic proportions until she started to tremble and could barely draw in a deep breath.

"Why?"

She struggled with her fear and overcame it, "I have news of his brother, Roderick."

His grip was punishing. As he dragged her closer to the lighted torch he'd left in the stable, she would later swear she felt each one of his fingers biting into the flesh of her arms through the coarse wool of her cloak. She cried out in pain, and his grip immediately loosened.

"I'll take him a message," the man offered.

Jillian shook her head, "What I must say is private." Fear snaked through the pit of her stomach at the low, almost feral sound he made in reply.

"Garrick?" A low-pitched male voice called out. *Someone was looking for the lord of the keep.*

Her captor tensed and she knew then, he was the man she sought. Her temper spiked. "Dare you play games with your brother's life?"

Not waiting for his answer, she brought her left foot down on his instep. He hissed, drawing in a sharp breath, but straightened his arms as she had hoped. *Just enough room.* She kicked out with her other foot, connecting solidly with the bone of his shin.

The arms holding her loosened. Struggling, she sprang free only to be grabbed again and brought back against the warrior's chest.

"Hold, wench." He cursed, bending to rub his shin.

Her anger gave her courage, "'Tis Lady Jillian to you."

"Ahhh." He relaxed his hold on her. "Did you not get my message?"

She stiffened. He knew who she was? "Aye, but Owen has plans for you. If you would but agree to my plan—"

"To marry you in exchange for my brother's life?"

Somehow when this powerful warrior gave voice to her plan, it sounded impossible. And yet, she couldn't give up now, "But Owen's guards—"

"Are not worth the time it takes to train them," he finished for her.

"He'll hang your brother." *How could he refuse her offer of help?* "I can free him." *Surely he would not let his brother hang!*

"Your price is too steep."

"His life is not worth marrying me?" A wave of dizziness swamped her as she realized he would refuse.

"'Tis not that. I have other plans for marriage. Besides, I need no help freeing my brother."

For one heart-breaking moment Jillian imagined how pitifully insignificant she must seem to a warrior of his skill and renown. But her future lay in this man's hands; she had placed it there.

She had to try to sway him, "Lord Garrick, please … I can offer Loughmoe Keep—"

"You are propertied?" he interrupted.

"Aye. Well, that is to say…" She fumbled over the words, and the truth.

"Aye or nay?" The harsh tone of his voice demanded the truth of her; she would be a fool not to give it to him.

"With a strong husband at my side, I could persuade King William to restore it to me." She hated pleading.

When he remained silent, she decided to prod him a bit. "My mother trained me well, I can manage a keep this size—"

"What do you gain from this bargain?"

Face flushed, eyes bright, she looked him dead in the eye, wishing it were brighter so she could see his expression. "My freedom."

"Freedom from what?" He sounded surprised.

"'Twill not be your concern unless you agree to my bargain."

She felt his gaze on her and wondered if it softened for a brief moment before the steely resolve she sensed would be there returned. His silence gave her pause. *Is he thinking about it?* Hope blossomed in her breast.

"I cannot agree to your bargain."

"But Roderick—"

He didn't wait for her to finish. He walked away, melting into the darkness from whence he came. The breath she drew in caught and held as she watched her last hope disappearing into the night.

Her limbs felt leaden. It was an effort placing one foot in front of the other, retracing her steps. With all hope lost, her spirit weakened. Past indignities and humiliations swamped her, crushing the tiny spark of hope inside of her until it flickered and went out.

She was truly alone. Other than young Stephan, no one cared what became of her. Her soul felt hollowed out, like a well-chewed nutshell, with nothing left inside.

Blinded by the force of her despair, she stumbled back through the opening in the curtain wall. When she reached the gnarled oak where she'd left her horse tied, she fumbled with knotted reins. But her fingers were numb with shock, making it impossible to untie the leather. Finally, the tree branch snapped, releasing the reins to the sway-backed mare.

As she slowly followed the path that would take her back to her prison, she no longer cared what would become of her. Her reasons for surviving under intolerable conditions no longer existed.

With each mile, she could feel the walls closing in on her, suffocating her. She neither saw nor heard her young protector guide his pony into step behind her horse.

By the time she reached the overgrown gate in the wall surrounding Sedgeworth Keep, she had resigned herself to her fate. Her family holding was lost to the Norman king, and she would be servant to the mistress of Sedgeworth until the day she died.

CHAPTER TWO

G ARRICK'S MIND WAS filled with fragments of the strange visit from one of Sedgeworth's stable lads and more recently, his midnight encounter with the stubborn woman who insisted she could help him free his brother.

The urgency behind her words could not be denied, but he wasn't about to let a mere woman dictate the course of action he would take.

His gut told him Roderick was in trouble. *Grave trouble.* His mind raced. Could he risk the life of another of his family, entrusting his brother's life to the whims of a woman? *No. The price was too dear.*

His boot heels echoed on the hardwood floor as he strode into the near-empty hall. Gertie had left a pitcher of ale and a loaf of dark brown bread on the table for him. The gesture made him smile.

She still thinks I'm a green lad, hungry at all hours of the night.

"Dunstan!" he shouted loud enough to be heard across the bailey where he'd last seen his brother.

While he waited for his brother to show himself, he poured a flagon of dark ale, watching the doorway. His brother should have heard his call. His stomach rumbled. Hungry, he broke off a hunk of still-warm bread. Placing it in his mouth, he slowly chewed and swallowed.

A few moments later, he was still waiting. Sighing, he lifted his ale and sat down. "Never around when I need him," he grumbled into his drink. "Probably got his head stuck in the keep's accounts." His drink was half gone before he heard footsteps descending the stair.

"You bellowed, brother?" Dunstan asked, entering the hall.

"Aye, we've a problem—Roderick."

Dunstan grabbed the loaf of bread. "What's the lad done this time?" Ripping off a large chunk, he popped into his mouth, straddled the bench, and sat down.

"If I heard a'right, he is to pay the piper this time."

"Was he caught with Lady Gwendolyn again?"

Garrick shook his head.

Dunstan slapped the heel of his hand to his forehead in mock disbelief. "Can our brother not find a woman of his own? Must he insist on sharing other men's wives?"

"Our brother has a healthy appetite," Garrick replied, "one that may cost him his life."

"Go on," Dunstan urged.

"He's being held captive at Sedgeworth Keep."

The brothers locked gazes. No other words were spoken, but each knew the other was thinking about the rumors running rampant through their keep and the surrounding area.

"How did you hear?"

Garrick rubbed his index finger across his forehead with enough force to leave a dark red smudge behind. "'Tis the one part of the puzzle that does not fit."

Dunstan waited.

"First a stable lad, then one of Roderick's women—"

"Married, titled, or serving wench?"

"I'm not certain, it was too dark to tell." Garrick paused, trying to remember. "But she spoke like a lady, in soft cultured tones."

Unable to sit still any longer, he braced his hands on the table, pushed back and stood up. The movement helped; at least he was doing something. Walking over to the brazier, he stared into the remains of an earlier fire. "If he's at Sedgeworth," Dunstan said, "there is no time to wonder which woman."

Garrick turned around to face his brother. Their eyes met and held; and he knew his brother understood what he was thinking.

They spoke at the same time, "The Lord of Sedgeworth is not to be trusted."

Garrick nodded. "We may need help getting into the keep."

Dunstan squared his shoulders as if ready for action. "I know of a knight who feels as we do about Owen. But I warn you, we may not be able to convince him to aid our cause."

"What is his name?"

"MacInness."

"A Scot?" Garrick hadn't expected to enlist anyone's help, let alone that of a Scotsman.

His brother nodded. "A mercenary with skills enough to match your own."

Emotions battled within Garrick as he fought to choose the right words, "Not everyone can wield a blade." Looking up he met his brother's direct gaze. "Some are more content counting barrels of grain and salted meat, brother. Our people would starve without someone keeping track of our stores."

He wished he could tell his brother how proud he was of Dunstan's ability to keep track of which field to plant, which grain needed to be resupplied, but had learned to keep his own counsel after their father died.

'Twas his fault their father was dead.

Unaware of the turmoil rioting within Garrick, Dunstan grinned. "'Tis the truth, you've no stomach for the task."

Garrick set aside his dark thoughts and concentrated on the problem at hand.

When he didn't speak Dunstan prodded, "You have a plan?"

"Aye," Garrick bit out. "Marriage."

His brother accepted his words without question; they had had this conversation before. "Beatrice is the one, then?" Dunstan asked.

"Nay." Garrick was sorry he'd not have the chance to offer marriage to the wealthy heiress his brother referred to. She'd be the perfect choice. "I've yet to offer for her."

"Then who?"

"If we cannot breach Sedgeworth's walls," Garrick said, "I must try to convince the lass to ask me again."

"Again? Which lass? Who asked?"

"Her name is Jillian."

Dunstan scrubbed his hands over his face. "Who is she?"

"The one who brought news of Roderick's capture."

"But I thought the stable lad told you," Dunstan said.

"We shall talk later."

The brothers walked to the doorway. Dunstan stopped before going through, placing a hand on his brother's arm. "What of your plans for Beatrice? Did you not love her then?"

"What has love got to do with marriage?" Garrick hated the thought of spending his life with a woman he had yet to meet, but he'd been prepared to offer for Beatrice. He'd simply switch intended brides. After all, the only thing he knew about Beatrice was the sum total of her dowry.

"It makes the marriage bed—"

"Not important." Garrick glared at his brother. "Marriage is a simple agreement," he said. "A merging of households and land. Mayhap a promise of protection."

Dunstan stared at him expectantly, but Garrick could not bring himself to confide the underlying reason he pushed to rebuild Merewood Keep and for marriage to the wealthy heiress.

He never would tell Dunstan. Besides, the curtain wall was almost complete. *I have to finish.*

"'Tis not my goal to rebuild," Dunstan interrupted Garrick's thoughts as if they'd been had spoken aloud. "Nor is it my plan to marry some faceless lady. What if she is the size of a cow? What if she has the face of a hag?"

Dunstan's words hit home, with alarming accuracy. But

Garrick had already asked himself those questions. "You worry like an old woman."

As they walked through the doorway and outside, Garrick added, "We've strength and cunning enough to breach the walls of Sedgeworth Keep."

Dunstan's face showed his concern. "Garrick—"

"Leave it." He couldn't let anyone or anything sway him from his noble cause. "We must find MacInness."

GARRICK NUDGED HIS horse closer to his brother's mount and asked, "You are certain he will help?"

His brother grunted, "He has no liking for his overlord."

"Why does he pledge allegiance to Owen?"

"MacInness is a mercenary. He serves his forty days, collects his gold, and moves on. I'm certain we can come up with the coin to convince him to aid our cause."

A drizzle of rain softened the dirt on the road before them, muffling the sounds of their approach. The lateness of the hour cloaked them in velvety darkness.

"Why should we trust him?"

Dunstan's sigh was heartfelt, "Because we have to."

All will be well, Garrick tried to convince himself. *Now if the damned Scot would agree to help ...*

He followed his brother to the wattle and daub hut at the edge of the wood. Dunstan dismounted first and strode to the door. Coarse laughter and crude suggestions reached their ears.

Dunstan turned back and grinned at him. "I'd like to see that one tried."

Garrick shook his head. "'Tis the mead talking," he said quietly. "'Tis not possible to—"

Dunstan nearly choked on his laughter, "Nay?" Shaking his head, he knocked twice before opening the door. The sounds of revelry immediately died away.

"MacInness," he called out.

"Aye," a deep voice answered back.

Garrick saw a redheaded man rise up from a bench by the far wall and begin to make his way across the crowded room toward them. Fighting the urge to wade through the crowd and meet the man halfway, he stood beside Dunstan and waited until the man stood in front of them.

Dunstan nodded at him. "MacInness." Turning back to his brother, and as an introduction, mumbled, "Garrick."

The two men greeted one another warily while the room grew quiet. Garrick noted MacInness was not the only warrior present. He glared at the group closest to them, satisfied when they quickly lost interest and went back to their pitchers of mead and ale.

The Scot was half a head taller and wider through the chest and shoulders than himself. Few men were. Searching the man's face for a clue to his thoughts, Garrick was more than satisfied when MacInness's eyes gave nothing away.

Garrick found his first smile. God's teeth, the warrior impressed him.

"We need your help," Dunstan said simply.

MacInness nodded and led the way outside, crossing the yard toward the stable. "Ye've come aboot yer brother."

"Aye," Dunstan agreed.

Garrick was impressed the man already knew the situation they faced. He may be the right choice after all. "Can you get us inside the keep?"

The Scot scratched his shaggy head and answered, "Aye, but I canna get ye in to where they've got yer brother. I dinna have the keys. 'Twould take a batterin' ram or a miracle to open that door."

Garrick thought of the midnight woman and her offer, the one with the hefty strings attached, and whispered her name, "Jillian."

"Do you ken the lassie?"

"We've met."

"She could help ye if she's of a mind," MacInness said, "but I canna ask her. Lady Jillian's suffered enough."

"Lady?" Garrick's voice strangled out the word. *So her voice matched her station in life.*

"Aye, she is ward to Owen. Before the Normans came into power, she was an heiress in her own right."

More and more pieces of the puzzle that surrounded Jillian fell into place. "She offered to help."

"Weel now, 'tis her choice," MacInness said slowly. "Ye'll no' be sorry."

Garrick cleared his throat. "I turned her down."

"Are ye daft, mon?"

"Nay, but I didn't think I would need her."

MacInness scowled at him. "Ye do. Dunstan, go to the third hut down, the one badly in need of a thatchin'. Tell the mistress we need Stephan to get a message to the lass."

"Aye." Dunstan met Garrick's questioning look with a shrug before hurrying off into the night.

Garrick turned back to the Scot. "How can you keep the guard from skewering us with their arrows?"

"Didna yer brother tell ye aboot my Irish Contingent?"

Garrick shook his head. He couldn't put into words exactly what it was about the warrior, but his gut said to trust him.

"Wait here," MacInness ordered.

Stunned by the quiet force behind the command, Garrick did just that. Before he could mull over his instinctive reaction to obey, the man returned with a flagon in each hand.

MacInness smiled. "We canna talk wi'out a wee bit o' mead." He motioned toward a fallen log and sat down.

Garrick hesitated; not taking the mead, his overwhelming need to find and free his brother ate at him. "I don't have time."

"Aye, ye do," MacInness said pleasantly. "Let me tell ye aboot my men."

"Your men? But I thought they were Owen's."

"Oh, aye." the Scot grinned then drank deeply. "He thinks so, too." He licked his lips, "Ahh … eases the throat."

"We're wasting precious time," Garrick bit out.

MacInness bent toward him and whispered, "Keep yer voice down, mon, or ye'll have the guard on us."

Defeated, Garrick knew he would have to wait until the damned Scot was ready to talk. He took the mug offered, downed a healthy gulp, and glared at the man.

When MacInness emptied his flagon, he started to talk. "I've four men I'd trust my life with, ye ken?"

Garrick understood and nodded.

"O'Malleys—two brothers, two cousins. They head up the reinforced guard atop the curtain wall."

The Scot was crafty.

"I dinna think Owen knows aboot the others though."

"Others?"

"I've recruited twenty others who've seen the kind of mon the Lord of Sedgeworth truly is. He's no' to be trusted. The mon has no honor."

Garrick had heard rumors about the Lord of Sedgeworth, but hearing one of Sedgeworth's men speak of them convinced him.

"What of Jillian?" Garrick asked. "What has she suffered?" He watched the now-silent warrior beside him closely and noticed MacInness chose his words with care.

"She's a bonny wee lass, a true lady, but—"

"But?" Garrick prompted.

"There're rumors the mistress beats her."

Garrick's blood ran cold at the thought. He half-rose before a meaty hand pulled him back onto the log.

"Think first, mon."

Recognizing the wisdom in the other man's words, Garrick settled back down. Raising the mug to his lips, he drank deeply.

"Tell me why she came to see ye." MacInness kept his voice pitched low.

As Garrick related the story, he remembered her scent vividly. Taking a deep breath to clear his head, he set the mug aside.

MacInness listened, nodding every once in a while, then told Garrick about Lady Jillian. By the time Dunstan returned, Garrick had a clearer picture of her life at Sedgeworth.

Garrick and MacInness stood together. "Well?"

"'Tis done," the younger man answered.

Garrick took MacInness's hand in his. "My word is my bond."

The burly Scot nodded. "Ye've mine as well."

THE WIND WHIPPED the lone figure silhouetted against the pre-dawn sky. Jillian raised her face, welcoming the turbulence buffeting her. It more than matched the unease clawing at her from within. Garrick would come; he had to. His brother's life lay in the balance.

Young Stephan had roused her from a dead sleep just hours ago to tell her Garrick sent word he was ready to bargain.

What had changed his mind? He had been so sure he did not need her help he hadn't stayed to listen to the whole of her plan. *Was he really willing to believe she was his only hope of freeing his brother in time?*

If he kept his part of their bargain, would he gentle his warrior's strength on their wedding night, the way he'd brushed the hair from her eyes, or would his grip be bruising as it had been when he questioned her? Dear God—her scars! How would he react to the marks crisscrossing her shoulders and back?

She drew her black woolen cloak tighter. *Too late to worry now.* The plan had been put into action. *Garrick was her only way out. He wouldn't change his mind again. Would he?*

She paced the wooden platform running the length of the stone wall surrounding Sedgeworth Keep. She paused, desperate for a glimpse of him, but the empty horizon offered nothing. "He's late."

Gray clouds drifted together, while vibrant strokes of orange and pink slashed through the misty gray of morning.

She drew in a breath, she was not afraid. He'd given his word, he would come.

From within the keep, her guardian's voice exploded in anger, sending a jolt of fear through her.

"At least 'tis not my clumsiness he has endured this time." Three years spent serving the lord and lady of the keep had taught her to guard her tongue and mind her ways. But even that had not spared her from the wrath of her mistress; she had the scars to prove it. But it was the marks that could not be seen that bled slowly, draining the very spark of life from her.

If she did not get away soon, she'd die...on the inside ... where the true Jillian still lived and breathed. She closed her eyes remembering running through Loughmoe's southern meadow, stopping to let her father catch up to her.

He'd lift her up and swing her around in a circle before setting her back down on the ground to teasingly scold her for soiling the hem of yet another gown.

"*'Twould make your mother frown, Jillie lass,*" he'd say. He knew her all too well, knew how she hated to see her mother's pretty face do that. As their faces blurred into the mist of her memories, she vowed not to forget the lessons learned. They were all that she had left of her parents. "I won't forget you." Her voice broke, and she opened her eyes.

Roderick's imprisonment changed everything. Instead of having to face another year of humiliation and servitude, she had a chance to escape, to start her life over, mayhap as mistress of Merewood Keep. She had the skills; they were just a bit rusty.

Owen's voice rang out sharply followed by a resounding crash. A pang of kinship for the servant unlucky enough to incur the wrath of her guardian swept through her tumultuous thoughts.

Pulling the edges of her cloak tighter around her, she felt the work-roughened skin on her hands snag in the coarse fabric. Lifting her once-smooth hands to the early morning sunlight, she grimaced. They were no longer the hands of a lady.

What would Garrick think of them? Yet another imperfection; she had so many now. Tears filled her eyes, but she blinked them away, refusing to cry. Her once graceful hands were no longer fit to strum a harp or sew fine linens. They were rough and clumsy. *She was clumsy.* Her mind mimicked the daily taunt she had learned to live with.

Jillian stiffened her spine, recalling with sadness the words her mother so often used: There is no shame in hard work. But where did one draw the line between honest work and servitude, duty, and blind obedience?

Her mother had not slaved on her knees for hours scrubbing the stains of food and dirt from the soiled linens of the temperamental Lord and Lady of Sedgeworth Keep. She had. In her heart she knew her mother would not have wished her daughter to either.

"'Twould never have been Father's wish to see us as servants to a man with no more honor than a goat!"

Us. The word stuck in her throat. They'd had only two short months before her mother had slipped away to join her father. She could almost hear the sound of her mother's bright laughter and her father's deep rumbling chuckle. *Lord, she missed them.*

The sudden glare of the sun intruded, reminding her of the hour and the events about to transpire. Events she had bargained with her life to alter.

Her gaze swept the horizon one last time. Sharp pain arrowed through her heart while a dull ache throbbed at her temples. *There was no time left.*

"God help us, his brother is as good as dead."

A flicker of movement off to the north caught her eye. Two mounted riders came into view. *Garrick!* She took the stairs down two-at-a-time, nearly pitching headfirst down the last few.

Behind her she heard the cry go up to open the gates. Looking over her shoulder, she saw Winslow MacInness and half a dozen men make short work of hefting the massive wooden bar that secured the gate. The immense structure creaked and groaned as it swung open and two grim-faced warriors spurred their lathered mounts past her, toward the lifeless form that swung from the hastily constructed gallows.

23

CHAPTER THREE

G ARRICK'S ANGUISHED CRY was echoed by his brother. He reined in his destrier one-handed. It reared up on its hind legs. In a fluid motion, he swung his legs over the saddle, landed on his feet, and broke into a dead run.

As he took the steps to the platform two at a time, anger and fear pumped through him, enabling him to wield his broadsword one-handed. He could hear Dunstan clamoring up behind him. His only brother now that Roderick—he couldn't finish the thought—shook his head to fight against the white-hot rage burning deep within him.

The second his boots hit the platform, he cut through the knotted rope in one smooth slice. *Dear God, first Father, now my brother?* Tilting his head back, closing his eyes, Garrick's already frayed emotions snapped. His eyes opened to a vision of death washed in crimson. The stench of it clung to the unwashed body cradled in his brother's arms.

Pain lanced clear through to his soul. He could not bring himself to look upon the contorted face of his youngest brother. For the first time in his life, he grew weak headed, the thought of his brother gasping for air…the strength of the rope…

He pushed the grim thought aside. His mind clung to the past, not willing to let go of the well-remembered vision of a young adoring face with laughing gray eyes. He held fast to the memory, tucking it away. It was all he had left.

Acute agony left a gaping wound in Garrick's already bleeding soul. He'd avenge his brother, as he'd not been able to avenge their father. Throwing his head back, he bellowed the ancient Saxon battle cry that had echoed through the hills for centuries.

He vaulted from his high perch and hit the ground running. Eyeing a group of surprised onlookers, he grabbed the only well-dressed man among them. Holding the tip of his sword to the wildly pulsating skin at the base of the man's throat, Garrick demanded, "Where is he?"

The poor man shook with terror as he bravely asked, "Who?"

Garrick pressed the tip of his blade with enough finesse to prick the man's skin, until a drop of blood welled up. "Owen of Sedgeworth, Lord of this Keep. By all that is holy, if you do not tell me, I'll kill you where you stand!"

Garrick heard the commotion behind him, but ignored it, focusing on the man beneath his blade.

Shakily pointing, the man blurted out, "My Lord Owen is in the great hall breaking his fast."

Garrick lowered his blade sprinting toward the timbered building, bellowing Owen's name.

"Wait," Dunstan called out. "It's not him! It's not Roderick!"

Garrick held his sword to an overweight, richly dressed man's belly. His mind registered the fact that the man's family and an entire household of servants watched. The pain of Roderick's death blocked it out.

Keeping tight control of his battered emotions, he concentrated on the Lord of the Keep. *He could grieve later. He would have revenge now.* "If I do not get the answers I seek, I'll run you through."

"Garrick." The tone of command in Dunstan's voice cleared the red haze engulfing him. He looked blindly toward the sound of his brother's voice.

A sobbing woman fell to her knees in front of Dunstan. "Please, milord, don't let that man kill my husband!" Pointing an accusing finger at Garrick, she continued, "My husband is a good man, a fair man."

"Fair?" Garrick shouted, "Do you call hanging an innocent man fair?"

"As overlord of these people and the land surrounding it, I deliver justice daily," Owen said. "I caught Delbert stealing my prized stallion and two of my brood mares!" His face visibly tightened with anger. "He has stolen from me for the last time."

Garrick slowly turned to face his brother. "Delbert?"

At Dunstan's calmly controlled look, Garrick froze and looked behind him, knowing something was not as it should be. Owen's guard had surrounded him without him realizing it. One face stood out among them. Though MacInness gave no outward sign of recognition, Garrick read it in the man's fierce gaze.

Unanswered questions churned within him. Had MacInness changed his mind, or would he still aid their cause to free his brother? But a more important question had his stomach flipping over: *Had he let his emotions rage out of control, feeding his thirst for revenge?*

Damn my mother's people and their unwanted curse—a Viking's bloodlust—a Berserker, one so caught up in the killing that he is blinded to it...

God's blood! Had he almost exacted revenge without cause? His gaze quickly scanned the room. He almost killed the man who stood before him ... an innocent man. Garrick's blood froze and his stomach bottomed out. A quick glance at Dunstan and Garrick knew what his brother was thinking. A shared memory of father pitted against son mirrored their pain. Once again it was the younger brother silently questioning the elder with a look of agony. *God, would he never be freed from the past?*

Pushing those memories aside, Garrick watched the Lady of Sedgeworth, kneeling before his brother. Her face lined with pain. He remembered well the look. It had been on their mother's face the day she had stood waving good-bye to their father. Had she known it would be for the last time?

He watched Dunstan help the woman to her feet and pry the linen square from her tightly clenched hands in order to dry her eyes. Gratitude replaced the look of fear in her eyes. Lady Haldana graced his brother with a smile that lit up her rather pale features transforming her to a woman of rare beauty, not unlike their mother. *Had his brother been reminded of their mother as well?*

A movement out of the corner of his eye caught his attention. As the guard closed in on him, Garrick noted all of the warriors had their hands on the hilt of their swords. *Would MacInness tip his hand now, or would Garrick be taken prisoner as well for show?*

Owen cleared his throat to speak, and Garrick decided to let the other lord think the warriors surrounding Garrick intimidated him. He sheathed his sword and with it his Viking's rage. The sound of steel brushing against leather broke the silence. Brother looked to brother; their bond unbreakable.

Ignoring the ten grim-faced warriors surrounding him, he spoke quietly, "I am Garrick of Merewood." He turned and nodded in his brother's direction, "My brother, Dunstan. We have been summoned here with news that our brother was to hang this day. Mayhap we were misinformed."

Owen's stance relaxed and he waved his guard aside. They moved to flank MacInness, and he saw a brief glint of triumph in the Scot's eyes.

A soft sound from behind Garrick distracted him while the familiar wisp of wildflowers beckoned to his already heightened senses. Breathing deeply, he spun around and felt the heart stop in his chest. Auburn tendrils curled against cream-colored skin. His hands itched to reach out and capture an errant curl, trace the line of her jaw. *Would her hair feel soft, her skin feel of silk?*

The woman was too beautiful to be real. He blinked, but she did not vanish. Her full lips were parted as if to speak. The wood sprite's eyes were wide, but was it fear he saw in their warm brown depths?

She flushed, her skin resembling a ripe, sweet peach. He wanted to press his lips to hers. Pinpricks of awareness blossomed into a fiery arc that flashed back and forth between them.

Their gazes locked and held. His, clear and bright with challenge, bore into hers, wary and dark with uncertainty. She captivated him.

Her gaze turned from rapt to haunted, and it was then he recognized the depth of his own pain mirrored back at him. His aching heart reached out to hers, and their tattered souls connected, joining them with invisible strands of hope. As his eyes focused, he saw fiery curls cascading down her back as the vision tilted her head up to look at him.

"You came!" Her voice was low, husky.

His mind reeled. *Who was she? How did she know him?*

Whoever she was, she was definitely a temptation he could ill afford. There were debts to be paid, and a lady to find, before he could give into the weakness that suddenly burned within him.

The lady of the keep called out to the young woman, "Jillian!"

Stunned, he stared down at her. "Lady Jillian?" *He agreed to marry her?* Desire's heat intensified as he imagined sealing sacred vows with the exquisite beauty standing before him.

Lady Haldana's voice turned shrill. Snapping back to attention, he wondered what the lass had done to cause the elder lady such displeasure. He was not left to wonder long.

"You will see to the preparation of our midday repast. When you are through, you may continue with your duties." With the wave of a milk-white hand, the lady of the keep dismissed her.

Without another word, Lady Jillian turned to do as she was bid. Left with no other choice but to follow their plan, he cleared his throat, and his mind. Turning to Owen, he asked, "May we have a word with you in private?"

The man studied Garrick and his brother before agreeing, "This way."

When MacInness moved to follow, Owen shook his head. "I can handle this alone."

Garrick watched the tall Scot and his men file out of the hall and a thought occurred to him as he remembered the daughters of the keep. Turning back around, he saw a knowing smile simultaneously light the five rather pretty faces that now surrounded him and his brother. "You're Roderick's brothers?" the shortest one asked.

"Oh, doesn't he look just like them?"

"That one is so handsome," another added.

"They are all so handsome."

Garrick's head began to swim.

"I rather like the quiet one, then again—"

"*Silence!*" Owen's tone held a warning note, but his daughters completely ignored him. "See to your mother," he ordered them. This time they obeyed, though not without muttered protestations.

"Garrick, Dunstan, if you would join me in my chamber, we can speak privately there."

Garrick followed only to stop at the sound of high-pitched feminine laughter. Turning around, he realized his brother hadn't moved. Dunstan stood surrounded by the five fair daughters of the keep. In that moment, Garrick envied his brothers and decided there would be no marriages of convenience for them. Once he had secured their future and rebuilt their family's fortune by marrying the well-propertied Lady Jillian, they could marry whomever they wished, whenever they wished.

Duty sharpened his voice, edging it with steel. "Dunstan."

His younger brother gave a heart-melting smile to all of the lovely ladies before following.

A glance over his shoulder confirmed his suspicion. Five adoring pairs of eyes stared at them as their confident strides ate up the distance between the great hall and the massive staircase.

LADY HALDANA SMILED at her daughters. "I'm pleased to note you all have the good sense the Lord granted you, recognizing men worthy of your stature in life." She paused, staring after the men. "Now if I could only convince your thick-headed father of young Roderick's value."

Tapping her fingers to her lips, she added, "His brothers would be ideal sons-in-law. Although Roderick's not wealthy enough, in these troubled times, a strong warrior must also be considered."

Walking toward the circle of young women, she added, "Mayhap, your father could be persuaded to let Roderick's indiscretion be forgotten." She narrowed her gaze at them, "If in the bargain we gain two powerful husbands."

Lady Haldana motioned her daughters toward the long oak table. When they finally seated themselves after the flutter of feminine primping, she began, "Now, you all know how unreasonable your father can be. As I see it, none of my darlings are ready to admit who encouraged Roderick, are they?" *Silence.*

"Then I am forced to either agree with your father or bargain with him. Whom shall I suggest to him as brides for Garrick and Dunstan?

SHOCKED BY LADY Haldana's announcement, Jillian's breath whooshed out. She clamped her hands over her mouth. Haldana would beat her if she caught her eavesdropping.

"She cannot get away with it. Garrick and I made a bargain!" She nearly choked on the words.

Thinking back to their first meeting, she frowned. Now that he was within the keep's walls, would he still need her help? *Could she trust him to keep his word?*

Her stomach roiled. If she could not help him, she could not expect Garrick to keep his bargain with her. Clenching her hands into tight fists, she resolved to take matters into her own hands and free Roderick now, before Garrick had a chance to fall prey to the machinations of the lady of the keep.

CHAPTER FOUR

O WEN MOTIONED FOR the warriors to be seated. Sedgeworth's lord had no clue his own vassal plotted against him. He was either blind, stupid, or arrogant. MacInness was right about his overlord; the man had no honor. 'Twas a black sin as far as Garrick and his brother were concerned.

Owen poured wine into two jeweled goblets and offered one to him and the other to Dunstan. The gesture was not lost on Garrick, the man appeared overly confident that Garrick and Dunstan were no longer a threat. For the moment, he was content to let Owen think so.

Garrick fingered the jewel-encrusted goblet, trying to assess its value while Dunstan sipped before drinking deeply. At Dunstan's nod, Garrick grew thoughtful. 'Twas as suspected, an abundance of wealth surrounded them at Sedgeworth Keep. But would some of that wealth come with Jillian when she came to Merewood as a bride? More importantly, would he be able to convince the king to reinstate her family's holding? For the sake of his family and their people, he prayed it would be so.

His thoughts turned once again to the daughters of the obviously wealthy keep. Perhaps a marriage could be arranged for Dunstan or even the wayward Roderick. He'd ask his brothers once Roderick was safe.

Sipping his wine, he watched Owen out of the corner of his

eye. The man appeared relaxed, at ease. Time to put their plans into action.

"Where is Roderick?" Garrick asked, startling the man.

"What have you done with him?" Dunstan demanded.

When Owen spoke hastily, as if to reassure them, Garrick knew they'd unnerved the man.

"He is secured below stairs, where he shall remain until we have completed our business."

"You have him tied up?" *He'd beat the pompous lord's smiling face to a bloody pulp once Roderick was free.* "Where?"

Owen evaded, asking, "Do you want to know how your brother came to be in my dungeon?"

That last remark caught the undivided attention of both brothers. Garrick sensed his brother's turmoil. It matched his own. "Aye, continue," Garrick growled.

Owen smiled and Garrick frowned. Why was Owen amused?

"Your brother was caught in the upstairs hallway after scaling the walls of my keep. I know he attempted to slip unnoticed into one of my daughter's rooms, but so far none of them will admit whom he was trying to meet."

Garrick looked at Dunstan. As he and his brother tried to digest this latest bit of information, Owen continued, "My manservant caught him sneaking in through the window. Why my darlings would keep this information from me is beyond me."

Looking each man directly in the eye, Owen admitted, "I overreacted when I told them if no one came forward by this afternoon, Roderick would hang from the same gallows that the horse thief had."

Garrick's hands fisted at his sides as he cleared his throat to speak, "Did you truly mean to hang our brother?"

Sighing loudly, Owen shook his head, "I believed that the guilty party would come forward out of love for your brother. I had no intention of hanging a man for lusting after my daughters. How could I blame a man for that?"

His black eyes narrowed, and his voice took on an edge of

steel, "However, my family's name has been besmirched. It must be redeemed." Owen's stare grew colder. "I intend to use Roderick as a means to an end, profitable for all." The look he turned on Garrick was calculating. "Mayhap for most concerned."

"What is to be done now?" Garrick demanded. "None of your daughters have come forth."

Owen's sneer could have been misconstrued as a smile. "How old are you, Garrick?"

Garrick's gaze raked over the man. Why in the name of God would Owen ask that? His brother gave a slight shake of his head and Garrick answered, "Eight and twenty come winter, why?"

"Dunstan?"

Garrick's gaze met his brother's. Again Dunstan shook his head. "Five and twenty, why?"

"Do you still own Merewood, or are you vassal to a Norman baron? Are you pledged in service to anyone?" Owen's rapidly fired questions fueled the surge of fury Garrick fought to suppress.

Rising to his feet, Garrick towered over the man. "Why do you ask? What is your plan?"

"I'll have your answer first, Garrick." Owen's smile hardened into a look clearly meant to intimidate. Raw power held Owen enthralled.

Garrick recognized the look well, he had used it often himself. The coarse insult, burning the tip of his tongue, slid down his throat, unuttered. It was too soon to wrest control of the keep from Owen. He had yet to receive word from MacInness—Roderick was not free. Without the Scot and his men to back him up, an open show of hostility would gain them nothing. Garrick had to appear agreeable until he knew for certain Roderick was safe.

Quickly weighing their options, he knew the success of their plans depended on Owen's acceptance of their reasons for coming. *Sedgeworth's lord must never discover the duplicity they were about to engage in.*

Garrick tamped down on his anger and answered, "Our father died in the Uprising. As the eldest, I have taken on the task of trying to salvage what is left of our family's holding. We have sizeable acreage to the north. Our crops are starting to produce again. The Uprising all but decimated our land. How is it that you seem untouched here?"

"I used my head, and I plan to remain untouched."

Garrick wondered, if his father had given in to William the Conqueror would he be alive today? "Our father would have done well to pledge his loyalty to the new king," Garrick said. "He may have lived had he not followed his heart and supported the Saxon people's doomed attempt to regain all they had lost."

With a glance at his brother he added, "At least I have been able to convince Dunstan and Roderick to do so. King William seemed pleased by our efforts; he only took three-quarters of our land." *Instead of all of it.*

Owen nodded and Garrick wondered at the speculative look in the man's eyes. Had Owen had heard of Garrick's reputation, and the rumor that he possessed the strength of three men? The one thing he did know was that Owen thought he had backed them into a corner. Garrick smiled remembering his back-up plan. All he had to do was send word to Lady Jillian, and she would free their brother while he and Dunstan kept Owen distracted.

"Garrick, I would be willing to discuss the terms of your brother's freedom." Owen's eyes hardened to thin slits of black. "I may be persuaded to let him go for a mere one hundred pieces of gold."

Relief, coupled with a feeling of dread, swept through Garrick as his plan came closer to becoming a reality, almost within reach. But gold? He had no coin! Where would he get it? "Your family's name has a price on it?" Garrick asked.

Owen stood and started pacing, "Actually my family's name is worth far more than a mere bag of gold." He stopped right in front of Garrick. "I'm willing to barter if we add an alliance between our families."

Momentarily stunned, Garrick tried to think of where he could get the coin then realized their plans would mesh. This would work so long as Lady Jillian was part of the bargain. Speaking quickly lest Owen name the wrong maid as his intended, "I would ask for the hand of your ward, Lady Jillian."

Owen sat down. Garrick fingered the hilt of his dagger and drew it slowly out of its sheath. He didn't lose eye contact with Owen, so he was certain the man didn't suspect he held the tiny but lethal blade at the ready.

At Owen's continued silence, Garrick became uneasy. He urged, "'Twould join our households. You would be guaranteed my defense of your keep, if the need arose. Our lands would prosper, and I would see to it that no marauding Rebels, nor Scots Reivers, would plague you."

Owen's feral black eyes darted back and forth. Garrick knew his suggestion of bride was not the one Owen expected him to make. He looked at Dunstan. Their gazes met and understanding flashed in his brother's eyes.

"When will you release him?" Dunstan asked in a low-pitched voice.

Owen turned to look at Dunstan. "Soon, very soon. But I need to carefully consider your offer." He paused, rubbing a hand across his chin, "My wife is very attached to young Jillian."

By a ball and chain. The man's wife would have to find another slave to beat her frustrations out on. *Mayhap 'twill not be as easy as I'd hoped.* Thinking of the gold and his choice of bride, he silently vowed, *I'll not leave here without the lass. I gave my word.*

It was time to ask for her help, time to seek out MacInness.

"RODERICK?" JILLIAN'S WHISPERED words echoed in the silence. She called louder this time, "Are you all right?"

"Lady Jillian?"

Relief speared through her, and had her fumbling with the key. "I'll have you out in a trice."

The scraping sound of the key fitting the lock was magnified by the quiet.

Footsteps brushed against stone. He stood before her on the other side of the door. She watched his expression change from one of surprise to one of confidence.

"You've come to take me up on my offer."

Was he daft?

Jillian still could not believe he would go to such lengths to be near her. She had been blunt the last time, refusing his advances, yet still he pursued her.

"We don't have time for talk," she warned, opening the door. "Here put this on and follow me." Draping him in a black cloak, she put a slender finger to her lips. Turning, she led the way toward the darkest section of the dungeon and started searching for their way out. "'Tis supposed to be here, somewhere."

"What are we looking for?"

Jillian jumped at the sound of his voice just behind her. Roderick's warm breath was too close, it tickled the sensitive skin behind her left ear.

The man was making it impossible to concentrate. "Owen's secret bolt hole. Wait, over here...I've found it! I'll have you out of here and on your way before Owen discovers you gone."

Grabbing his hand, she forged ahead, "Quickly, there's no time for explanations. You don't know what Mistress Haldana plans for your brothers." Her belly roiled, thinking of the lady's plans. Roderick had to escape ... now!

Leading the way, crouching low, she swiped at the cobwebs in her path. *Lord, I hate spiders.* Her hands shook, but not from the cold. *What if they got caught? What would Owen do? What would Haldana do?*

God help her, she could not think; her concentration scattered like dandelion seeds on the wind. Tamping down her fear, she thought only of the freedom awaiting Roderick at the end of the long, dark, and damp passage.

Outside the walls of the keep Roderick jolted to a stop, gripped her elbow, and pointed to the lone horse, "Are you not coming?"

"Why would I leave my home?"

His face darkened, "'Tis not truly your home. Maralyne told me everything." His voice gentled as he spoke, "Your father died a hero's death at Hastings."

Tears gathered at the corners of her eyes as betrayal slashed through her. She had told Maralyne's younger sister in confidence. How had Maralyne found out?

"Loughmoe was beautiful," he continued, his words adding to her pain. "Rolling hills of green, broken only by stone walls. Sturdy cottages your father's tenants were proud to call their own."

Jillian could not speak as memories tore her apart.

Unaware of her turmoil, he continued, "Lady Eideanna would be proud, Jillian. You've taken hold of what life has given you and not complained. You toil from dawn to well past dusk." Taking hold of her work-roughened hands, he touched them reverently with his mouth as if they were the unblemished hands of a lady.

"Aye, Jillian, I know what awaits you here. 'Tis no secret, anyone with eyes could see how they treat you. Come with me. I'll take care of you and can promise you a life of leisure."

His words cut right to the heart of her worry. Would Garrick come to hate her for using him as her means of escape?

When she didn't answer, Roderick grabbed her by the arms. "Are you pledged to a man then?"

Her face flushed, the heat of it had her bowing her head to study her worn leather boots. "You know so much about me. Mayhap I should ask you."

He had the grace to flush at her pointed words.

Good. He should be embarrassed.

"Lady Jillian, forgive me. I meant no harm."

His apology came too late to make a difference. His look of admiration confused her. What did he admire her for, speaking her mind? Risking discovery helping him to escape? The stallion pranced before them. The same one the horse thief had tried to steal yesterday, but it was the swiftest one. Would Roderick know? Would he care? She shrugged. He did not have to trust her any longer. All the man had to do was lift himself into the saddle and ride hard for home.

He pulled her close. "Come with me, Jillian." He bent his head to kiss her.

Surprised, she braced her hands on his chest and pushed away from him. "Nay."

Shaking his head to clear it, Roderick seemed stunned that she would refuse him. *It must be a new experience for him.*

But instead of heeding her wishes, he surprised her by bringing his lips down to hers yet again. Anger and frustration combined within her. She lifted her knee and caught him in the thigh, and he grunted in surprise.

"Mayhap you did not understand me," she told him. "I said no. Just as I said no last night when you whispered promises of love through my chamber door."

Tears of frustration filled her eyes. "I'm not interested in your advances, Roderick of Merewood. Save them for Maralyne." Earnestly, she bit out, "You only see me as a conquest, an object of pleasure, not as someone to love, or someone to offer a home and someday children to."

Drawing her shoulders back, squaring them, she wiped the tears from her face. "But your brother Garrick has promised to offer for me and give me all of the things no one else will."

RODERICK IGNORED THE cramp in his thigh, watching her sudden burst of anger spend itself. The pain etching deep lines around her mouth bothered him. But when she turned and ran, he let her go. *She was right. He had only thought of bedding her.*

Thoughts of caressing her creamy skin had inflamed him to a fevered pitch that had him scaling the timbered walls of Sedgeworth Keep searching for toeholds the night before. Not even his brothers knew of his infatuation with Jillian.

He wondered why Garrick offered to wed the penniless ward of Lord Owen. She must be mistaken. His brother's dedication to rebuilding their home would never be swayed by a woman, no matter how lovely. His older brother was predictable to a fault.

He mounted and spurred the horse, riding hard for the shelter of the wood, so close to freedom he could taste it.

The roar of a battle cry startled him. He broke out of his reverie long enough to see a knight on horseback take aim.

Pain seared through his shoulder, immobilizing him. He looked down in disbelief at the arrow buried deep in his flesh. White-hot pain washed over him as blood flowed freely from around the wooden shaft of the unknown enemy's arrow.

Then his world went black.

CHAPTER FIVE

"*J*ILLIAN!*"*

"Hmmm?" she murmured before drifting away again. Back to Loughmoe and her mother's solar. The women had gathered to spin wool into fine threads. Mayhap tomorrow the weaving would begin. While their hands were busy, the women fretted over their children and complained of husbands.

"*Jillian!*"

The unearthly shrieking finally broke through her thoughts, and her hand stilled. Disoriented, she glanced worriedly about her, but she was in the stable, her one and only refuge from the prying eyes of her guardians.

Neither the lord nor his lady would dare to brave the earthy perfume that wafted through it on a warm day such as this. Satisfied that no one intruded upon her solitude, she let go of the breath she held.

"Ah, the melodious voice of my stepmother," she whispered. Stroking the sun-warmed neck of the day-old calf, she crooned, "Lady Haldana likes it not that I take so long at my chores. Shall I answer her summons, or shall I play at being deaf?"

The velvety muzzle of the little cow snuffled at Jillian's cheek leaving a fine sheen of moisture behind, evidence of its affection. Her sigh of resignation blew a faint puff of air against the calf's face. He blinked.

"Lady Jillian?" young Stephan's voice called softly a distance away.

Jillian sighed deeply. "I've been too long at the milking today if they've sent Stephen to look for me. Mayhap the lady of the keep needs a servant to collect fresh herbs for her linens, or someone to replace the rushes that lay at her sainted feet?"

"Milady?"

Stephan rounded the corner and stopped, "Oh! There ya are. Her ladyship's been bellowing for ya." He grabbed her arm and pulled her to her feet. "Please come?"

"In a moment." She smiled, sending him on his way. Once he was gone, she kissed the fuzzy face nudging her. Thinking of the list of chores she'd yet to finish, she sighed. "I hope to be finished by the nooning hour and be back."

Unease skittered through her, thinking of the bargain she'd made with the warrior. She'd been able to deal with whatever Owen and Haldana did to her. "Mayhap 'tis better to stay here than to face the unknown."

Her mind raced along at a frightening speed. Garrick would free her from the life of servitude she led at Sedgeworth, but what of her life at Merewood? Her thoughts stopped abruptly. Wasn't Garrick's character unknown to her?

"Roderick speaks highly of him," she mused. "He treats his servants as well as his crofters, almost like family." *He is a good man,* she thought. *Roderick would have no reason to lie about his brother, would he? Exaggerate mayhap?* The unwelcome thought that Roderick had stretched the truth about his brother and his good deeds did nothing to reassure her.

One last loving stroke and she turned to go.

"BUT OWEN, DEAREST, you said 'twas easy! Simply take them in and wait to annex their land!" Haldana's shrill voice had reached an ear-piercing crescendo, as she stamped her foot in anger. "Well? 'Nigh on three summers have come and gone and still Loughmoe Keep and all its fields lie fallow."

Jillian hid in the shadows immobilized by the brutal truth she had just overheard. Her heart began to pound in her breast as every muscle tensed in anticipation. The need to escape, to run away, overwhelmed her. But the realization she had nowhere to go had her sinking back against the wall.

"Send another missive to the king, Husband!" Haldana demanded. "Loughmoe Keep will be ours. I'll not have our daughters overshadowed by that half-Scots creature a moment longer than needs be."

Jillian slid further back around the screen at the rear of the hall. She fisted her hands tighter in the soft wool fabric of her worn chainse. The insults wrapped around the truth of Haldana's words, arrowed through her. Dear God, she and her mother had been used! Pawns in Owen's bid to take over their home. Had he known they escaped the Normans? Did he have them followed so that he knew when they were ready to give up hope of surviving the night so they'd eagerly accept his offer of help?

"Dear Father in Heaven," she rasped aloud. "Did he tell King William of our indefensibility?" Her head ached as it filled with dozens of questions. Questions she still had no answers for.

The last three years spent slaving for a man, who in all probability orchestrated the end of her former existence, rankled. She had served them without question, thinking she owed them her life, and had come to believe she should accept the punishment Lady Haldana meted out daily as her due. Had it all been part of a grander plan on Owen's part? A plan to gain her family's holding?

Raw emotion clawed its way up from deep within her. Feeling as if she would split in two from it, Jillian fought desperately for control. She breathed deeply; instinctively her lips formed the oft-said words. "Tell me again, Mother, do you still say 'tis God's will that guides our lives? Mayhap 'twas not His will that you follow Father to Heaven so soon after we found this new home?"

No words of love or compassion filled her heart. Her mother's voice was silent. It would be up to Jillian to face the lord and lady who spouted lies as smoothly as Winslow the Scot wielded his claymore. But it had always ended this way, her guardians would say one thing before others, and then in private, Haldana would beat her until she could not stand.

Jillian ran a hand through her hair, hopelessly tangling it. *She could fix it later.* Stepping from her sanctuary, she called out, "Lady Haldana!" Sinking into the expected deep curtsy, her braid slid across her shoulder in a wave of fire. Rising slowly with unconscious grace, she waited for the inevitable tirade.

It wasn't long in coming. If anything, her mistress was predictable to a fault. "You were overlong at the milking, what have you to say?"

"Milady, I—"

Haldana held up a be-ringed hand that showed no evidence of the harsh life of those that served her. "Be silent!" she ordered. "You have yet to complete the day's tasks I have given you, and we have guests for our midday meal. Go to the kitchen at once, your other duties can wait until later." Her eyes narrowed. "And you will finish them."

Forgetting to drop into the expected curtsy, Jillian mumbled a weak reply beneath her breath.

"You will address me with respect." Blue eyes flashed the split-second warning before Haldana's palm cracked against the tender skin on Jillian's cheek.

Taken aback for a second, Jillian saw the hatred in the other woman's eyes as she raised her hand to strike again. Jillian choked out, "Your pardon, milady." Head held high, she turned toward the open doorway, vowing not to give Haldana the satisfaction of seeing how deeply the blow affected her.

The cool morning breeze teased a strand of her auburn hair across the burning patch on her face. Too proud to surrender to the pain and give Haldana the edge she so thrived on, Jillian bent to grab her basket off the stone step and descended into the herb garden on her way to the kitchen.

Breathing deeply she caught the scent of sweet woodruff mingling with thyme and yarrow as the hem of her chainse brushed against the tender blooms, releasing their fragrance.

Closing her eyes, she lifted her face to the warmth of the sun. Her mind drifted off on the faint breeze swirling around her, allowing her to escape all that was painful. *Peace—she always found it here.*

Totally absorbed in her daydreams, she didn't hear anyone approaching until a deep baritone voice called out to her.

"Lady Jillian?"

She tensed and whirled around to face the unknown intruder, but instead found herself looking up into the handsome face of her future husband. *Lord, he was huge!* His form, broad of shoulder and lean of hip, drew her shy gaze. His warrior's build combined with his white-blond hair and brilliant blue eyes left her oddly breathless.

His gaze narrowed, reminding her of the badge of insolence proudly displayed on her reddened cheek. Belatedly, she reached up to cover it.

"Who struck you, lass?" Garrick's voice deepened and grew curiously softer. "It will not happen again. You have my word."

His tone had a soothing effect on her jangled nerves, like a healing balm. He moved her hand, and gently slid his rough fingertips in a wide arc near the edge of the reddened welt. His eyes hardened to a fathomless blue as his gaze came to rest on the stark outline of the handprint marring Jillian's face.

Though his touch had been gentle, she could not help wincing from the pain. She could not speak up and name the guilty party or else she'd end up receiving an even worse fate, a caning with Haldana's favorite switch. She shifted uneasily; her back was not ready for more of the lady's abuse.

"Won't you tell me?"

Bowing her head, she stared at her feet. She just could not feel at ease with him. His first reaction to her bold scheme had been to laugh at Stephan, then later ignore her and walk away.

"Jillian."

She was too embarrassed to look up at him. The Lord of Merewood Keep, her future husband, should not see her like this.

Taking the basket from her clenched hands, Garrick offered his arm. She hesitated, but the knowledge that the arrogant warrior would turn so completely about and treat her as a lady tempted her.

Mayhap he needs me. He must have hated admitting that fact to himself. She had to hold her tongue, lest she blurt out that very thought. Like it or not, they needed one another. Soon they would be duty bound to honor one another for the rest of their lives.

She accepted his arm and told him, "I have duties in the kitchens, milord."

"Garrick," he corrected.

She cleared her throat to dislodge the bittersweet lump of longing lodged there. A lifetime ago she had been treated this way. It brought back memories of happier times.

"As you wish…Garrick. Before I go, I must speak with you privately." She looked over her shoulder and around the garden, relieved to find they were alone.

"Aye, Lady Jillian."

Smiling, she corrected him, "Jillian."

She watched his serious posture relax slightly at the intimate offering of her given name. Would it be too much to hope that he would come to care for her? The emotion flickering across his strong features before disappearing gave her the courage to continue.

"MacInness sent word to you?"

She nodded.

"Have you news of my brother?"

"'Tis done," she whispered. "He's halfway to Merewood on the swiftest horse Sedgeworth has to offer."

Garrick's face hardened, the warrior was back, demanding,

"The one Owen hanged a man for stealing just this morn?"

The angry look she shot him should have singed his hair. It didn't, she checked. "Aye, that same horse. There are no others capable of aiding in your brother's escape. Milord's daughters pamper them with sugared fruits. He would have been caught."

Her look darkened as the stark truth hit her, "You don't trust me." Wounded to the very core of her being, she struggled to hide the hurt Garrick had unknowingly caused, snuffing out the tiny flicker of hope in her breast.

He struggled as if choosing his words with care. "I have learned to hold my trust of those I know not in reserve, until they have proven themselves worthy of it."

His words cut Jillian deeply. "Perhaps one day you'll be able to trust your heart without knowledge of deeds done in support of that trust." Jillian weighed her next words carefully. "But what of your word? Do you intend to keep it?"

Garrick clenched his jaw. Had no one ever questioned his honor before? He didn't like the fact that she would turn his own accusations on him, but could she trust him to keep his word?

"I never go back on my word."

She hesitated; mayhap the fear of what almost happened to his brother caused him to be harsh with her. *Time would tell.* They would watch each other carefully. Bravely she asked, "Will you honor our bargain?"

"Aye, Lady Jillian." He paused and glanced about him, scanning the perimeter of the garden. "Owen has agreed to free Roderick, and granted your hand in marriage, for the price of one hundred pieces of gold and my sword arm in defense of his keep."

Dismay jolted through her. "But he is already free." Owen would never honor his word if he found out his prisoner was gone. She could not expect Garrick to honor his. "Mayhap you should leave now as well."

Garrick grabbed her upper arms and shook her. "I never go back on my word, Lady."

Jillian swallowed audibly and cleared her throat. "How will

you convince Owen to let me go if you've no brother or gold to bargain with?"

"'Tis my concern, not yours. Be prepared to travel to Merewood two weeks hence. I'll see to it that you are freed from your duties."

Free. The word echoed joyfully within her. A feeling of contentment slowly unfurled and spread its wings, ready to take flight. But even as she reveled in the idea, a black thought clouded her moment of happiness. *Why did Owen agree?* Jillian served as personal slave to the mistress of the keep. *Haldana would never let her go.*

Clearing her throat, Jillian dug deep for the courage to ask, "Owen suggested this? Have I no duties then?"

His gaze dipped to the raised mark on her face. "'Twas my decision. Owen will abide my wishes."

Taking a step closer, she tilted her head back to look into her future husband's eyes. His expression was open and honest. She smiled. "Thank you." Turning about swiftly, she missed the look of intense longing that Garrick was not quick enough to hide.

STARING AFTER THE beautiful woman soon to be his wife, Garrick stood with his feet rooted to the spot. She was like no other woman he'd ever encountered. Why had she thanked him? For agreeing to marry her, or for rescuing her from a life of servitude?

Would she ever feel more than gratitude toward him? His gut roiled as a heavy truth hit home. God's teeth, he needed her!

He shook his head at the direction of his troubled thoughts. His parents had not married for gratitude. His mother's hand in marriage had been the price her father had paid when he had lost the siege against Merewood Keep. But his parents had found love, and they had shared so much more. The pain returned sharply as he forced himself to remember the love that surrounded his parents.

Grimacing, he realized the whole time his brain planned to marry for wealth, his heart yearned to find what his parents had shared. Grinding his teeth together, he stalked back to the hall in search of Dunstan.

He found him seated with the Lord of Sedgeworth at the center of a long wooden table laden with a feast fit for royalty. Their gazes locked before Garrick turned to look at Owen.

Garrick nodded at Owen, who glanced at the sumptuous feast before him, ignored it, and bellowed, "Fetch my ward. I must speak with her."

Dipping into an awkward curtsy, the serving girl steadied the large tray she carried. "At once, milord."

Turning to finish serving the guests, the girl realized her mistake when Owen let go a loud curse. She nearly dropped her burden as she fled the hall.

Garrick nudged his brother under the table. Dunstan nodded in silent agreement. Another servant abused, counting his bride-to-be, that made four. Remembering their upbringing, he could not turn his back on it. His parents placed honor above all things. Duty came next. It would be their duty to offer better working conditions to any who sought them. They would offer to take in any abused servants Owen could be persuaded to part with.

Not five minutes later, a disheveled Jillian entered the hall. Wisps of her hair had worked free from the braid held back with a leather thong. Smudges of flour could not hide the still angry welts on her face, nor the swelling of her lip.

Her lip?

Garrick rose from his chair and placed his hands on the table in an effort to still their trembling and quiet his rage. "By all that is holy," he rasped, fighting to keep that rage from boiling over. "Who dared to strike my future wife?"

The room fell silent. He could feel all eyes focused on him. *Let them look.* Straightening to his full height, he let his angry glare sweep the room, letting them all know he was prepared to do battle for his future wife's honor.

Rage simmered to a deadly boil as he struggled with the power of that emotion. Why did it even matter to him? No one deserved such treatment.

Liar, his heart accused. *You care what becomes of the lass.* In a bid to regain his scattered thoughts, he let his gaze drift from the look of boredom on the Lord of the Keep's face, to the handful of servants grouped together. They stood in the doorway watching Jillian with what Garrick could only guess was resignation. Was this a common occurrence? Mayhap all of the household servants were treated badly.

Innocence personified, Owen stood and motioned Jillian forward. She refused with the shake of her head.

As Garrick watched, anger flashed briefly in the depths of her eyes before retreating behind her mask of indifference. *Had she played this game before?* Owen, her lord and protector, feigned innocence of the deed, so who else would have struck her?

"'Twas my fault, milord," she rasped, coming to stand before them. "I tarried too long in answering milady's summons."

Haldana's gasp echoed her husband's. Furious, his wife sputtered, "Owen, how dare you let one of her kind speak thusly."

Hand raised for silence, he waited for his wife to regain her composure.

"I'm certain she is confused," Owen replied. "Jillian, pray explain yourself, then make your apologies to your betters."

The man's gaze leveled at Jillian seemed to unnerve her. She turned and looked to Garrick for support, but he was watching Owen. Garrick's glance followed hers to his right. The look on Dunstan's face told him that his brother was on her side. It seemed all the boost she needed.

As he watched, she squared her shoulders, brought up her chin and spoke directly to her guardians. "I jest not, milady, the proof is still on your ring."

Haldana's gasp of horror only added to the evidence mounting against the lady of the keep. Her hand was no longer milky white, but marred, as was the corner of her wedding ring. Both were crusted with a spattering of blood. *Jillian's blood.* In her haste to preside over the festive meal, the woman had forgotten to wipe away the damning evidence.

Garrick stood, effectively blocking Haldana's exit and chance to strike another blow to the fragile young woman standing before them. Pinning the lady of the keep with his steely gaze, he ground out, "Lady Jillian is no longer yours to discipline. As my wife, she will answer only to me."

Garrick hoped his bride-to-be would not worry overmuch about what awaited her in her new home. He sought to placate the lord and lady of the keep, while at the same time warning them to leave Jillian alone. Out of the corner of his eye, he noted she paled considerably.

He turned his back on Owen and his lady and walked around the table to where Jillian stood. He had to know how she felt. Her cinnamon-colored eyes were so expressive, therein would lie the clue to her thoughts.

Would she still believe his promise of protection? Would she trust him not to take out his frustrations on her once they were wed? Silently urging her to speak with a determined look, he was rewarded when her eyes warmed, deepening to a warm rich brown, as if lit from within.

He gently lifted her hand to his lips and pressed a kiss to each of her knuckles. The skin of her small hand felt cool until his breath warmed where his mouth caressed. Confusion marred her brow. *He had much to teach her.*

He whispered, "Trust me, dear lady." Drawing her to his side, Garrick turned to Owen. "I'll not wait a fortnight. We'll marry this hour."

Owen shook his head. "Our cleric left this morn; the bishop had need of him. There is no one else to record the deed. Father Bernard will return in two weeks' time, the ceremony can take place then."

Garrick weighed the older man's words, finding he did not trust him overmuch, he amended, "Then she will accompany my brothers and me to Merewood. We'll be married two weeks hence."

Owen's shock was palpable. He thundered, "One of your family has already dishonored my good name. How do I know that you intend to carry through with your betrothal promise? What is to stop you from using my ward for your own pleasure before passing her off to your brothers or your household knights?"

Garrick's hands flexed, the need to crush the life from so vile a man nearly overwhelmed him, but Dunstan held him back. "I gave you my word," Garrick bit out. "I will excuse your miserable accusations and conduct this time. Never forget the clemency shown you this day. Such a slur upon my family will not go unpunished."

Garrick reached out to take Jillian by the hand and felt her trembling, "You will apologize for frightening my bride-to-be."

Garrick turned to Jillian. *Trust me*, he willed her with an intense stare. Her eyes answered, but not what he wished to discover.

She's not sure. Again he sought to lock gazes with her, willing her to understand his unspoken message. He wished they were alone so that he could speak freely. *I'll not hurt you, lass. Trust me.*

Jillian swayed as fatigue caught up with her. She was thin, and he wondered if it was from too many missed meals, or too many backbreaking hours of hard work. He would soon find out the whole of it. Then he would repay Owen and Haldana in kind.

Garrick felt her weakening. Before he could act on instinct and sweep her up in his arms, he felt her whole body stiffen to ward off the weakness.

My God, she's courageous. We'll have strong sons. Daughters too…with auburn hair and eyes a rich warm brown.

"Garrick?" Startled from his thoughts, he realized she'd spoken to him and he'd not heard a word.

Looking down into her eyes, he started to drift off again. It was starting to become a bad habit where the lady was concerned. "Aye?"

"I wish to return to my chamber, with your permission, milord." Her face was lined with exhaustion.

"Aye, allow me to escort you." Turning to face the Lord of the Keep, he added, "With your permission, of course."

Owen's eyes narrowed, "Aye, but I wish to speak further of our bargain."

"MILORD?"

As Garrick and Jillian left the hall, Dunstan watched Owen's attention focus on the servant hurrying toward them across the daunting width of the room.

"I must speak with you," he heard the man whisper.

Owen inclined his head slightly to listen. Whatever it was blotched Owen's face with barely controlled rage. Rising up from his carved wooden chair, the man resembled an angry god about to wreak havoc on the lesser mortals.

Those that parted to give him a wide berth shook their heads. Their lord had a fierce temper, and it appeared to be ready to break loose. All eyes were on him, speculating as to the cause of it. Owen spared a glance to no one, leaving the room without looking back.

Dunstan stood and felt all eyes shift from the retreating lord to himself. He quelled the urge to follow and sat back down.

"WHAT DO YOU mean he's gone?" Owen's voice boomed as it echoed off the thick walls of the keep.

"The door to Roderick's cell was locked when I came down to fetch him, but he was gone," his manservant whispered, with a furtive glance about the lower level. "'Tis like he was spirited away."

"Of all the preposterous notions. He was no more spirited away than I can walk through this door." Proving his point, Owen slammed his tightly clenched fist against the heavy wooden door which only hours before held his prisoner.

"MacInness!" He roared. Waiting for his vassal to answer the summons, his face changed from angry red to apoplectic purple.

"Aye?" The burly Scot rounded the corner, joining the others gathered outside the locked door.

"Where is the prisoner?"

MacInness looked questioningly at him before answering.

Owen, well used to the look, waited impatiently for the Scot to continue. He smiled when his vassal attempted to draw out the true meaning of his words.

"Behind lock and key and this one-hundred-year-old, solid oak door."

Grabbing the keys from MacInness's hand, Owen unlocked the door and shoved it open wide. Proof of Revas's claim taunted him. It was empty. Roderick was gone.

"I dinna understand. How could he have escaped?" The tall Scot's amber eyes darkened; his face flushed then promptly drained of all its color.

Owen judged his vassal's reaction to be genuine. MacInness was cagey, but honest to a fault. He knew from experience that the Scot could not be bribed.

"I must return to my guests. Find Roderick. Search the keep, the bailey, and woods. Bring him back by nightfall."

Turning to put the fear of God in his men, he added, "Your very lives depend upon it." Owen turned on his heel and was gone.

Jaw set, eyes focused, MacInness spoke to Owen's retreating form, "Aye, but 'tis the last time I'll do yer biddin'."

Motioning for the men to follow, he headed toward the inner bailey where their horses were being made ready to ride.

CHAPTER SIX

WITH EVERY STEP, Jillian's body cried out from exhaustion. Unable to continue any other way, she leaned heavily on Garrick's arm. She should never have angered her guardians, but what good had hiding behind falsehoods and ignoring her conscience done? The beating would come whether she had spoken the truth or not. The toll she paid for agonizing over her decision was fatigue so great that she stumbled with each step.

"Lady Jillian?"

She looked up into Garrick's face. His worried frown brought a half-smile to her lips.

"Oh!" The sharp sting and hot trickle of blood meant she'd reopened the slit at the corner of her mouth.

Raising the back of her hand to swipe it away, Jillian could not help but cry out in dismay. Her hands were still covered with flour. Heaven help her, she must look a fright. In her hurry to answer the summons from Owen, she remembered brushing her hands on her skirts. Almost afraid to look down, she braced herself and saw the stark white handprints against the worn blue wool. Embarrassment colored her cheeks. Would Garrick be ashamed of her?

Bone-tired, tears filled her eyes, but she blinked them away. Now was not the time to let her tangled emotions take control, she'd weep for days once she got started. She blinked back the tears welling up within her, choking her as she tried to swallow past the lump they formed in her throat.

At Garrick's continued silence, she dared to look up at him and caught the look of admiration in the cool blue of his eyes. *Admiration for what?* The way she had stood her ground earlier, or for not complaining? She was far too tired to reason it out.

An unforeseen and unwelcome thought returned to plague her. He had not come to her aid earlier when she looked to him for support. Instead he had made a show of power in front of Owen, but to what end? She remembered the look he had bestowed upon her in the hall. Was he truly proud that she had managed to brace herself up without his help? Mayhap 'twas the look of encouragement from his brother Dunstan that Garrick had seen. *Mayhap he saw me not at all.*

Tilting her chin up, Garrick dried the tears still clinging to her lashes with a light touch. With the edge of his sleeve, he brushed away the remnants of the flour still dusting her cheek with a touch that belied his strength.

"'Tis an improvement. You're sorely in need of a bath, lass."

The way his mouth curved upward and dimpled his handsome face irked her. Did he find her appearance funny? Would that be the reality of her new life, the butt end of jokes among his people? Outrage stiffened Jillian's spine while her growing temper swept away her fatigue.

All thoughts of embarrassment fizzled out in the fire of her temper. How dare he?

She rounded on him, hands on hips, "I thank you for the escort, *Lord* Garrick, but I need no reminder of my state of disorder. I may not be up to your standards of dress, but at least I am willing to work hard and not afraid to let others see just how hard." Her pike-straight back turned to his face was her dismissal of him. Hand to the door, she shoved hard, opening it wide.

"I'm sorry—" Garrick's words died on his lips.

Jillian turned back to see what had caused his sudden silence. She watched his troubled gaze sweep her sparse quarters and settle in the far corner of the room on the pallet of straw and thin linen covering where she slept. Her eyes followed his to the crudely carved stool and low bench. 'Twas all she had in the way of a table, and she'd had to take on the duty of feeding the swine and chickens to earn that scarred piece of wood. The wooden bowl and the stub of a candle it held were gifts from the few servants who were not afraid to call her friend.

All in all a testimony to her hard life at Sedgeworth. Though sorely abused by her mistress, she'd not trade her few friends for all the fine linens and colored threads that coin could buy.

The frayed linen square lying next to a bowl half-filled with clean water made her eyes fill again. 'Twas one of the last tangible pieces of her mother. She'd gladly take a dozen more beatings a day than to lose the fragile bit of cloth once held in her mother's hands.

Jillian drew in a breath and lifted her chin higher, forcing her spine even straighter. She was not ashamed to live like a servant. It had cost her much to earn the small room above the hall with its rude furnishings, but they were hers. She'd not be pitied for it.

Spinning around, Garrick bit out, "You'll not live as such in my home, Jillian." The reality of her circumstance must have bothered him.

Unsure of his exact meaning, she asked, "To what exactly are you referring, *Lord* Garrick?"

Sweeping his hand about her room left no doubt as to his meaning.

Fighting her embarrassment she said, "'Tis enough for me. I am used to my life here." She swallowed to wet her suddenly dry lips and arid mouth. Her gaze boldly met his. "I'll not ask for any special favors. We made a bargain. We spoke not of luxuries, duties, or expectations, and I'll not pressure you for that which I cannot have."

Her spiking anger fizzled out, leaving her drained. Shaky, she slid wearily onto the stool. Unable to gauge his thoughts, she decided to tread carefully. "I'm sorry, milord. I didn't mean to sound so harsh."

His gaze was intense as it searched hers.

"I am very tired," she said. "You will not find me ungrateful for your offer."

The icy blue of his eyes left her feeling cold as resignation and fear combined within her, roiling in the pit of her stomach. *Can he see what I'm thinking?* Afraid her emotions would be reflected on her face, she rubbed unsteady hands over it.

His silence bothered her. Unwilling to risk showing weakness, she sat quietly, staring down at the floor. The room grew so quiet, she closed her eyes and began to drift off to sleep. His footsteps broke the silence as he crossed the room to where she sat.

"Jillian," he rasped, taking a hold of her work-roughened hands. "Won't you look at me?"

Did she dare? Would he be angry?

"Are you afraid of me?"

Her eyes shot open, looking up at him she shook her head.

He squatted down next to her. "I won't raise my hand to you in anger."

Oddly, his words were just what she needed to hear. He sounded as unsure of her as she was of him. When he spoke again, she was certain of it.

"Mayhap I was too quick to judge that which I did not understand." he paused. "I'm usually a good judge of character."

The look in his eyes swayed her. "Shall we speak of duties now then, or should we wait until such time as you are well rested. You are on the edge of exhaustion." He frowned. "You will not be so again. You have my word."

His speech went right to where her aching heart beat slowly. *He cares.* Though he had not said the words, it was a place to start. Mayhap in time, they would grow accustomed to one another. The promise of life at Merewood, wife to its lord, was daunting but she was not without courage. The hope, rekindled in her breast at his caring words and gentle tone, burned steadily.

With a prayer of thanks to God in her heart, she smiled and said, "Let us wait then … Garrick?"

He nodded, studying her closely. Was he waiting to see if she would change her mind, or was he testing her? She would have two weeks to wait to find out.

"Thank you," he said at last.

THE USE OF his name alone was the key to her feelings. Garrick had picked up on her use of *Lord* when she was displeased. Smiling up at her, he rose slowly to his full height pulling her with him as he stood. Holding her close with great care, lest he add to her injuries, he bent his head and pressed his lips to her brow. Her soft sigh signaled her acceptance of the caress.

Encouraged, he pressed his warm lips to her cool eyelids and the bridge of her nose. The sudden softening of her limbs against him wrought a silent cry from within him. *Could she be the one brave enough to wage war against my demons?* 'Twould be more than he deserved after twice failing his family, nay almost three times. Roderick was still alive, only twice had he failed to uphold his sacred promise to protect his family.

He bowed before the flustered maiden and brought her fingertips to his lips.

"Garrick."

The look of longing playing across near perfect features hit him in the gut, like the blow from a battle-axe. He pulled every muscle taut to keep his knees from buckling. "Aye?" he rasped.

"You'll be missed. Lord Owen awaits your return in the hall."

He smiled down at her tempting mouth pursed in worry. Mayhap their union would be much more than even he anticipated.

"He'll send Winslow to look for you. Please don't let him find you in here."

"Winslow?"

"Aye. MacInness, his vassal."

They were betrothed, soon to wed. He had every right to be with her, but at her pleading look, he acquiesced. "Dear lady, you will bring more to this marriage than the promise of land not yet within my reach."

His gaze swept from the top of her head to the tip of her toes. Knowing its meaning was lost on the innocent woman standing before him, he added, "I'll not give Owen reason to doubt my honor, nor yours."

Her sigh was audible. With the expelling of air from her lungs, she swayed. Her eyes rolled up and her head tilted back.

"God's blood!" He swept her up before her head touched the floor, cradling her close to his heart. Carrying her over to the pallet where she slept, he laid her gently on the rough linen bedclothes. When she didn't move, concern arrowed through him.

Grabbing the linen cloth and bowl of water from her bench, he knelt beside his intended. With deft motions, he dipped the cloth in the tepid water and wrung it out. Gently he touched the linen to her temples, cheek, and forehead, and called her name.

No response.

He called to her again. When she didn't move, his voice became more insistent, "Lady Jillian!"

Still nothing.

Calling on his years in battle, he reasoned out why she still lay unmoving. Remembering he had seen this reaction before, hoping he was right and it was only exhaustion, he bent low over her, checking first for signs of breathing. A faint puff of air stirred the blond lock of hair that had fallen across his brow and stuck to his eyelashes.

"All right then, dear lady. You breathe, time to come back from the darkness whence you traveled."

Taking the now cold cloth and once more bathing her lovely face, he found his hands trembled in his bid to be gentle.

Impatient with the ungoverned reaction to his soon-to-be-bride, he growled low in his throat.

JILLIAN'S EYES OPENED wide at the sound. Confused, she stared at him. Her eyes sliced through the shell that the rest of the world accepted, right to the heart of the man. In one brief moment, she saw the pain and confusion Garrick strove to hide from everyone before the shell to his heart closed over, whole once again.

"You left me, lady."

"Left you?" The lightness of his tone belied the naked pain she had witnessed not seconds before. Did he carry a secret as devastating as hers?

"You swooned, you are exhausted. You'll not slave for Owen or his lady again. I have received his assurances that Sara will take over your duties."

In spite of her tiredness, she shook her head in protest. "I'm sorry, Garrick, but I cannot let her do that. She has duties enough to last from sunup to sundown. Add mine to hers and she'll work the whole day through and into the night."

Garrick stood next to her pallet deep in thought.

Jillian looked up at the huge warrior beside her. *Her husband-to-be.* The words echoed through her entire being. The thought of being at this man's beck and call, keeping his home, serving his men, was daunting. It had been years since she had acted the part of a true lady. Could she rise to the challenge? It would be hard to turn back time, when in her heart she thought of herself as a servant.

She could do it...couldn't she?

When Garrick swept his fingertips along the length of her jaw, caressing it, warm feelings bubbled up inside of her. Holding them close to her heart, she knew she at least would have this much from him to savor later. His touch brought dormant feelings to life. No man had ever made her feel like this. It was as if she was someone fragile to be cared for. Someone who mattered.

What more would possibly be in store for her? What of the marriage bed? Would he be gentle with her?

Though unsure of him, she vowed to do her duty and not hold any part of herself back. She would put her trust, her honor, and her heart in his hands. *Please God, let him be grateful.* Taking a chance and risking her heart, she was willing to give him everything.

Rising slowly on shaky limbs, Jillian reached up and dared to touch the whisker-rough cheek, where his dimple lay hidden.

"Please, Garrick. I'll not make poor Sara's job harder. Speak to Owen, ask that I be able to continue with my duties until it's time to make the journey to Merewood."

Breath held, she waited, trying to guess what he was thinking. His still features gave no sign of his thoughts, but his low rumbled reply made her smile. "You'll not regret your change of mind. Sara and I are grateful."

"Hold, lady. What of your packing? How will you tend to your duties and still be able to pack for the journey?"

The sparking lilt of Jillian's laughter bounced off of the four walls and surrounded him like an embrace.

"'Twould take little time to lay aside what I possess. When my mother and I came here, we had naught but the clothing on our backs. Nothing more. The few things I possess are here." Her hand swept the room. "I'll bring them and that which I came with, the clothes on my back."

The tilt of her chin and blaze of pride in her eyes must have decided him. "I'll speak to Owen." Turning, he started for the door. Opening it, he paused and turned around.

"Should you have need of me, seek out MacInness. He has agreed to look out for you until you travel to Merewood to be my wife. Mayhap I can convince him to serve another master when his service to Owen has ended."

"Aye, Garrick. Thank you."

Her quick agreement seemed to satisfy the man. He closed the door quietly.

Jillian's pent up breath came out in a whoosh with the closing of her door. Straightening her chainse, shaking the remaining flour out of it, she slowly undressed. It wouldn't do to treat her only clothing poorly; she may yet have need of it in her new home. He had not mentioned any new clothing. He seemed satisfied with what she wore.

Troubled by his lack of attention to her appearance, Jillian worried that he would not care how she looked. A dark thought plagued her; mayhap he had no intention of allowing her the privilege of serving him or his men at his table. Would he bar her from his hall? Would he beat her, as she was accustomed to? Holding the sides of her head to still the madness that descended with the close of her door, she sat back down.

"Nay," she answered her own questions aloud. "His own brother speaks of him as if there were no other man with more honor." Trying to reason through her worries, she continued, "He did not lay a hand on me in anger when I appeared in the hall earlier in a such disorder."

Desperately thinking of other signs of Garrick's true character, Jillian reasoned aloud. "His escort was gentlemanly." Her cheeks flamed, remembering the tender way he'd treated her.

Getting down on her knees, she bowed her head to pray.

THE CLOSED DOOR between them was just enough of a distance. His wife-to-be was an innocent. How else would she be able to rouse such feelings within him and not be as affected? Another reason surfaced slowly; was she well versed in the art of womanly wiles? He shook his head, rejecting the idea instantly.

Be not so quick to judge. His father's favorite phrase eased itself into his subconscious mind. More often than not his father had been in the right. His face darkened as he thought of the last decision his father had made—a bad one at that—as vassal, 'twas Garrick's right to lead his keep's people into battle against the marauding Normans. His sire had given his word.

But his father had changed his mind and challenged him to the right to lead their people … and Garrick had lost.

His family had lost far more in that brief battle. Though Garrick would not lead his people into battle, he was left to defend their home. He had failed in that duty as well.

The heavy burden of his ultimate failure to his father, and his duty to protect his family, were his constant companions in the darkness of his troubled soul. Jillian had been a brief respite from that darkness.

He clenched his jaw, fighting to quell the turmoil rioting within him. "She'll not be able to honor her word once she learns the true character of the man she is to wed."

Heading down to the hall, Garrick had no appetite. *No great surprise.* Pausing in the doorway, he scanned the room. Finding Dunstan, he answered his brother's summons with a slight nod of his head.

Garrick sat once more at the long oaken table. One long look at the heavily laden table and his stomach roiled in protest. The variety of fare did naught to change his mind. While the venison looked mildly appetizing, the capon and chicken pies had gobs of fat congealing through the slits of the pastry topping. Platters of sweetmeats and assorted cheeses were just being served.

He had not the stomach for it. Ignoring the veritable feast before him, Garrick found he longed for a taste of the peasant's fare he had grown accustomed to. Fresh vegetables had become a staple in the diet of those living at Merewood. Thinking of the just-picked beans and peas Gertie would be serving with fresh-baked bread, Garrick grew sulkier by the minute. Gert's cooking was far more palatable than the meal before them.

Dunstan shot him a look of impatience. "What ails you,

brother?"

"Naught that cannot be cured by leaving this place." The meaningful look conveyed between brothers went unnoticed by the others gathered for the midday meal.

"You spoke to Lady Jillian?"

"Aye," Garrick said, "'tis done. Our brother is free."

Dunstan looked from the empty seat next to them to the doorway. "Shall we extend our thanks to our gracious hostess in Owen's absence?"

Searching the room for the lady of the keep, Garrick paused. "And where is our host, brother?"

Dunstan frowned. "He disappeared shortly after you escorted the Lady Jillian to her chamber. One of his servants brought him news he liked not." Eyeing the group at large, Dunstan added in hushed tones, "Once he quit the room, I heard voices raised in anger."

A shared look and silent conversation proved that the brothers were united in their thoughts, as always.

"I shall seek out our Scots friend and see that he is ready to take on the task of watching my bride-to-be." Nodding his agreement, Dunstan rose to seek out their hostess.

CHAPTER SEVEN

"**M**ACINNESS!"

He turned around and the head of his Irish Contingent, Patrick O'Malley, called out, "'Tis a black look you've got in your eye."

MacInness locked gazes with the auburn-haired giant. "I've found Roderick."

"Is it bad then?"

MacInness frowned. "It could be worse," he admitted. "He took an arrow to the shoulder. I've had two men move him to Sara's hut…'tis closest to the wood."

Patrick nodded and MacInness knew he wouldn't have to explain more than that. Patrick was more than MacInness's right hand, he was his closest friend.

"Ye ken how long I've served my forty-days for Owen?"

"Well now," Patrick scratched his chin. "Nigh on five times over, I'd say."

MacInness could read the other man's thoughts and knew Patrick would be tallying the number of times he'd come near death. MacInness smiled back, knowing the Irishman owed him his life, at least three times over.

"Ye know I've ne'er trusted him." At his friend's nod, MacInness continued, "Garrick of Merewood has offered me land near a stream flowin' with trout. The land is wide and flat. I'd be able to plant crops enough to help feed half my clan and there's room enough for my Irish Contingent."

MacInness hesitated. He'd not asked any of them. He pushed forward assuming they'd follow him as they always had. "Garrick will be pleased to hire ye all on as well, but if ye'd rather, ye can stay."

"We go with you."

When MacInness nodded, but remained silent, Patrick asked, "You'll be headed north then, to bring them back?"

MacInness was glad that he didn't have to explain. "When my service to the mon is done, and I've delivered Garrick's bride safe and sound to Merewood Keep, I'll be headin' to my Highland home." His brows drew together in a frown.

"What be your worry then?"

He grunted, "My mother maun come willingly, or my wee sisters wilna budge from their home. If the lassies wilna come, my mother…weel now, she's a bit stubborn, set in her ways."

The sparkle of laughter in Patrick's clear green eyes made MacInness's mouth curl up in a smile and admit, "I may have inherited that trait."

The sharp bark of laughter from behind the two men surprised them both and had them spinning about. "Oh aye, you damned Scot, stubborn as an old goat! And now he admits the trait like a woman."

The fist that reacted to the taunt never connected with the younger man's face, he deftly sidestepped the blow.

"Now Sean, you mustn't rile our Scots friend here. 'Tis worried he is about his women folk," Patrick explained to his brother.

Sean's look grew immediately contrite. "Well now, 'tis sorry I am. Your mother then? Is she ill?"

"Nay. Rumors from London say King William heads north to Scotland soon. I wilna have them in the middle of another Uprising. We Scots never give up, ye ken? She'd die before givin' up her home."

"You have a plan then." It was a statement. Patrick and his

younger brother waited patiently for MacInness to fill them in.

"It begins with Merewood. I've agreed to serve Garrick in exchange for land to till, and a home to be built, and he'll welcome ye as well. He's been more than fair in his offerin' to me. I canna let the lass he's to wed come to harm." A quick look at the elder brother confirmed what he had hoped; they were with him. "I trust the Lord of Sedgeworth as far as the keep's bailey and not beyond."

"We're with you." Sean said. "Did you tell Merewood that you have a few more warriors coming with you?"

"Aye, he's wantin' to meet you."

"What of Kelly and Eamon?" the brothers asked.

MacInness's nod settled it. Their future thus mapped out for them, the three men went in search of the rest of the Irish mercenaries. Their new overlord awaited them.

"REVAS!" OWEN BELLOWED his manservant's name with his hands on hips, surveying the room.

When the man hurried forward, he let out his pent-up breath, "Aye, milord?"

Owen glared at the servant. "Has Roderick been found?"

Shaking his head, the man replied, "The keep, the bailey, and all of the huts have been searched." He lowered his voice, "He just disappeared."

Owen held onto his composure by thinly stretched strands, his control tenuous. He knew in his heart the promised bag of gold was beyond his reach. Garrick would rescind his offer of marriage; he would if it were him. His wife would never let him forget they had almost been rid of the chit. Haldana just didn't understand he still needed his ward if he was to claim her former keep.

Emitting a loud groan, he held his head and sighed. "Best

bring Garrick to my chambers; we cannot keep this news from him."

Once the servant left, Owen sat heavily on the stool near the wall. There had to be a way around this current snag in his plans. His mind raced to find a solution without having to let Jillian go.

"'Twould be dangerous for the brothers to travel to Merewood so late in the day," Owen said softly, "Mayhap, they would meet with outlaws on the road—Scots Reivers—and have to fight for their very lives."

The more he thought about it, the more excited he became by his loosely forming plans. Laying a trap for them was far better than to have to bargain with the arrogant young warrior.

"MacInness!" Owen bellowed even louder this time. The tall Scot entered the room, flanked by two of his more troublesome knights. They did not take direction well, only listening to the burly redheaded man who stood not ten feet in front of him.

"Aye?" His Scots' burr was thick and always a bad sign.

When the warrior was angered, his brogue was so thick Owen had trouble understanding him. The only reason he tolerated him was the man's extraordinary skill with his claymore, and the uncanny ability to out-think his opponent.

As the men stood before him, two more joined them, lining up behind MacInness. Now all four of the Irish mercenaries were lined up behind the Scotsman. Owen knew something was up.

Clearing his throat, Owen began, "The prisoner has not yet been found."

Inclining his head, the Scot agreed without words, then turned to one of his men.

Owen did not have time for this. He needed to implement his latest plan as quickly as possible. "I have sent for Garrick. I'll make certain that he'll not break his word to marry my ward or honor his offer of protection."

"But you've no brother to trade," one of the men blurted out.

Owen's gaze held the brilliant green-eyed stare for long minutes before answering, "I have a plan."

He thought he heard his vassal groan under his breath and watched him stiffen his stance. *If only I could read MacInness's thoughts, I'd be able to convince him to leave now and set the trap.*

"Take ten men and follow behind them. As you draw near, split up and hide in the woods. When the time is right, attack from both sides."

The five warriors listened as Owen briefly described his plan to waylay the brothers on their journey home. The men had been silent through the telling, and remained so even while he waited for their ready agreement to his command.

Instead of the answer he expected, the Scotsman bit out, "I have a fortnight left of service to ye. I wilna return. My agreement with ye was for forty days a year until such time as either of us wished to end such service. I do."

Blindsided, speechless, Owen let his jaw drop open. "I pay you well for your service to me."

"Aye, ye do." The tone of the Scot's voice brooked no arguments.

"Then why?" Owen asked. Time was growing short, and he didn't have time for this. He had to waylay the brothers or else his bargaining chip would leave in two weeks' time and his leverage would be gone.

He turned around to glare at the men flanking the Scotsman. "What of your men?"

When they glared back, a thin spiral of unease flickered to life and swept through him. "Well?"

They stubbornly remained silent, their faces carved in stone. Throwing up his hands, he turned once more toward the stairs and shouted for his manservant.

When the mercenaries still hadn't moved, he shouted at them. "What are you waiting for? I have no further need of your services. Get out!"

MacInness took a step closer, folded his arms across his broad chest, and shook his head, "Nay. We'll stay and see our agreements through. None will say we are no' men of our word." With that MacInness and his Irish Contingent turned and were gone.

"Revas!" Owen shouted again.

The servant appeared flustered by the hard look in each of the warriors' eyes as they passed him on the stair.

Hurrying up the last few steps, he answered, "Aye, milord?"

"Fetch Aaron at once," Owen bit out.

Nodding his head, the man trembled before his master's anger, but Owen was too busy planning where to bury the bodies to notice.

CHAPTER EIGHT

"**Y**OU'LL WHAT?"

Owen's incredulity came as no surprise, but it made it difficult to speak to the man.

"Mayhap you didn't understand me," Garrick said quietly. "I expect my betrothed to arrive at my home in a fortnight. Until that time, you will remember to keep your word and not abuse her."

Confusion lined Owen's brow. "But your brother is no longer in my dungeon, are you not calling the trade off?"

"I gave my word," Garrick let his voice ring with conviction. "I have offered for Lady Jillian's hand, and you have given your consent. I intend to make her my wife two weeks' hence."

"I do not understand," Owen wailed.

The man started pacing the confines of the upper chamber, stirring up a small cloud of dust as he pounded the rushes into broken bits, reminding Garrick to change the rushes in his chamber and hall as well. He'd make certain to do that and more before his bride arrived.

"If that is all you wished to speak about then mayhap I could have a word with Lady Jillian before I take my leave."

Garrick turned to leave the chamber, but Owen's question stopped him.

"You're certain you will not change your mind?"

The question had his temper simmering. He tamped down his growing anger. A wiser man would not doubt his word. A glance was all that was required in answer. Owen nodded at the look and led the way to his ward's chamber.

"'Tis doubtful she is awake," Owen lifted his hand to knock on the door.

"Jillian," Owen called out, "Garrick wishes a word with you ere he leaves." Before she could answer, Owen swung the door open.

Fury bubbled up inside Garrick and spilled over, he reached out and grabbed Owen's arm in a grip of iron. "I did not hear the lady bid you enter." His grip and the coldness in his tone were his warning to the man. If he gave in and let go of the tenuous hold he had on the rage seething inside of him Owen would be a dead man.

Jillian struggled to cover herself with the worn linen cover with one hand, while smoothing the wavy mass of auburn hair back out of her eyes with the other. The faint torchlight filtering in from the hallway illuminated her brown eyes, until they appeared round and huge with fear. Her fear slammed into him, twisting his insides into knots. *But did she fear him, or Owen?*

He needed to ease her fears. "Lady Jillian, please do not be alarmed," he began slowly, lowering his voice to almost a whisper. "I wished to take my leave but thought of something else I wished to discuss with you."

At her nod, Garrick picked up the stool and brought it closer to her bed of straw. Looking over his shoulder, he pinned Owen with a glare. The man obviously intended to linger in the doorway. Garrick stared at him until he backed out of the room.

"I'll be right outside if you need me, Jillian," Owen said before softly closing the door.

The need to follow the man and pound on him for being insensitive surged through Garrick. God's teeth, the man was dense. He turned back around. "I have news." He rested his elbows on his thighs, and clasped his hands, waiting for her to ask him why he was here.

She finally nodded and he noticed her face mirrored the white linen sheet she clutched to her breast.

"Aye, milord?" Jillian whispered.

"Garrick." He needed to remember to be patient with her if he hoped to soothe her fears and regain her confidence.

"Aye, Garrick," she rasped.

He had to fight against the urge to smile. She wanted to trust him. "Owen knows Roderick is missing," he lowered his voice, not wanting to be overheard. "They've searched the keep and the bailey but have found nothing."

She nodded and looked down at her hands.

"Owen seemed surprised that I would still honor my word to take you to wife." He waited for Jillian to look up at him before continuing.

When her eyes met his, he finished, "I always keep my word. I thought you should know that I mean to honor my pledge. You will come to Merewood in a fortnight as planned. MacInness will escort you with a contingent of four men. They will be staying on at Merewood as household knights as MacInness has agreed to be vassal to me."

"Lord Owen doesn't know I helped set your brother free. If he finds out..." She breathed out slowly. She'd been holding it too long. He waited while she took another deep breath and steadied herself.

"Did Owen agree Winslow would serve you? What about his pledge to Sedgeworth?"

"I have taken care of the matter. You'll be well guarded while you remain here." He hoped she trusted him. "Do not forget what I said earlier. MacInness and his men will protect you. He'll get word to me should you have need of me."

Her gaze met his.

Neither one of them mentioned the fact that since Roderick was no longer a prisoner, the need for the two of them to wed no longer existed. He'd prove to her that he'd keep his word. She had kept hers.

Rising to his full height, he looked down at the small bundle on the pallet before him. She looked more like a child than a woman grown, and the need to protect her filled him.

He bent and placed a chaste kiss to her forehead. "All will be well. Trust me." With that he was gone.

"Heaven help me, Garrick of Merewood," she whispered, "I know not why, but I do." Laying her head down, she was fast asleep in minutes.

>>>><<<<

THE ROAD AHEAD lay deep in shadow. Pools of moonlight shimmered on the ground in spots where the trees were thin. The evening breeze rustled faintly through the supple green leaves blending with the call of night birds winging high overhead.

"Why did you give Owen your word to marry his ward?" Dunstan asked. "'Twas only our plan to free Roderick."

Garrick wished his brother understood. He listened as the night quieted, leaving only the sound of the breeze whispering through and around the forest.

"Mayhap your plan included only freeing our brother, but I gave Lady Jillian my word to marry her if she aided our brother in his escape." Garrick saw his brother's confusion and it irritated him.

"Though we did not leave the keep side-by-side, without Lady Jillian's timely assistance, he'd still be under lock and key."

Dunstan muttered something under his breath before adding a reluctant, "Aye."

A faint rustling off to the left had Garrick's heart pounding double-time. He reined in his horse and whispered, "Don't move."

Dunstan froze waiting for his brother's signal, his hand on the hilt of his sword.

Garrick tilted his head back and bellowed the ancient Saxon battle cry. An echoing cry resounded as knights on horseback crashed through the brush on both sides of the road with their swords raised high.

Steel met steel, clanging loud as thunder. The warriors tested their mettle again and again. Sparks flew as their blades hacked fiercely, their intent deadly.

They were outnumbered. Six knights moved to close the circle they were quickly forming around Garrick and his brother.

"Your back!" Dunstan bellowed, bringing his sword down. It connected with sinew and bone, slicing cleanly through it. The enemy knight fell off his mount, dead. Sword raised once again, Dunstan successfully held the next warrior at bay.

The battle raged, sweat stung his eyes, but if he lifted his arm to wipe it away, the enemy would have the advantage. Garrick blinked and wondered how his brother fared. He needed to hear the sound of his brother's voice to be sure he was still alive.

"Dunstan?" His split second of emotion cost him dearly. The familiar cold heat of his enemy's blade burned through the flesh of his arm as it sliced clean to the bone. He drew in a deep breath, blocking out the pain. Deftly switching hands, he ignored the warmth of his life's blood flowing unchecked from his sword arm.

"Behind you," Dunstan huffed.

Back-to-back, the brothers created a deadly arc with which to swing their blades. From this position, given their fighting abilities, they were nearly invincible.

Garrick's sword swung with deadly accuracy, as he decreased their enemy by one more. The fight, now evenly matched, turned in their favor. The other knights sensed their failure and fled.

Turning around and grabbing hold of his brother, Garrick stopped him mid-swing.

"Father taught us to fight face to face, never their backs."

Breathing heavily, Dunstan sheathed his sword and asked, "Who were they?"

"I don't know." He worried about the identity of their attackers, but the need to reach Merewood and find Roderick far outweighed that worry.

"Are you hurt?" Garrick asked, concern lacing his words.

In answer, his brother snorted, "Nothing that Gertie cannot fix with her herbs and threads. And you?"

Garrick felt his head grow light. "The same," he lied. "Let's ride." He would find out who laid the ambush, but the loss of blood wreaked havoc with his head; 'twas spinning. The wound was bleeding profusely. He leaned precariously toward his brother before righting himself.

"Where are you hurt?"

Dunstan would know it was bad, since Garrick could not hold his seat in the saddle. "My arm," he rasped. "Wrap it...above the wound," Garrick motioned toward his belt.

Dunstan grabbed a hold of his brother's sword and unwound the thin strip of leather from Garrick's belt that held the sheath to his brother's sword to his belt and fashioned a tight knot above the wound. The flow of blood eased almost immediately, and Garrick braced himself to ride the last few miles home.

The shouts from above the newly laid wall roused Garrick from the brink of semi-consciousness. Holding his fist up and bringing it down to touch his heart, Garrick signaled the guard. With the temporary barricade removed, the brothers rode into the lower bailey.

THE WORLD CAME sharply back into focus with a stab of pain. Roderick's hand shot out and grabbed a fistful of shirt.

"Have a care, laddie," a soft Scots burr warned, "he'll miss a stitch."

MacInness. Roderick groaned. He was well and truly caught. He'd been so close to the wood, freedom just two strides away.

"Easy lad," another voice warned. "'Tis almost done."

"You slept through the worst of it."

Roderick struggled to open both eyes to see who spoke and just where he'd ended up.

"'Twas a neat slice you made, Sean."

Roderick's head swam. *Sean? God's blood, had he ended up a prisoner of MacInness and his mercenaries?*

"The blade so clean and hot, the shaft came out with just a flick of the wrist."

Roderick's stomach protested at the thought of Sean's hammy hands using a dagger on his shoulder to cut an opening to push the shaft of the arrow all the way through. He broke out into a heavy sweat.

"When am I going back?"

"We should be able to get ye to Merewood on the morrow," MacInness answered. "We've work to be done first."

Roderick struggled to sit up. "You'll take me to Merewood?"

"A fine job of it ye've done, Kelly," MacInness praised while the man tied off the last knot and sliced the excess thread with his dagger.

MacInness turned to Roderick. "We've no time to escort ye home tonight. I've got to see to milady Jillian's safety now that your brothers have gone home."

He couldn't contain his shock. "You're not going to send me back?"

MacInness stared at him and shook his head. "Rest well." He pushed Roderick back down on the pallet and called out, "Sara!"

"Coming."

He recognized Jillian's serving friend as she parted the curtain separating the small sleeping area from the rest of the hut. She carried a steaming bowl in one hand and a hunk of bread in the other.

She smiled down at him. "'Tis broth. You'll need strength for your journey."

Roderick watched her. Up close she was a striking young woman, more than just a face in the shadows coming close only when dutifully summoned.

She slid a hand around his back and helped him to sit up. Dipping a hunk of bread in the broth, she held it to his lips, urging him to bite it.

"That's it," she crooned, "easy now."

"Well, now," MacInness said with a grin, "we'll leave ye in guid hands, laddie."

With a nod to his men, they filed out. At the door, MacInness turned and warned, "Trust no one but Sara. They've given up the search for the moment, but come the dawn…"

Roderick understood. He nodded, his mouth too full to answer.

"'Til tomorrow then." The Scotsman turned toward the woman. "Thank ye, Sara." With a bow, the Scot was gone.

"Eat up now, milord," Sara urged with a dimpled smile.

"Ahhh, and what a feast for the eyes," he said capturing her fingertips and the broth-soaked bread with his lips.

She gasped.

He smiled.

⟫⟫⟩✦⟨⟪⟪

THE SOUND OF voices raised in argument woke Jillian from a troubled sleep. Sitting up, she pulled her knees close to her chest and cocked her head to the side. Eavesdropping had become a way of life and because of it, Jillian usually found out how the course of her life would flow. Slipping from between worn linen sheets, she shivered. Cold, she wrapped her cloak about her. Worried about being heard, she tread barefoot down the rough wood steps, careful lest they groan and give her away.

"'Tis not possible!" a deep voice shouted. "Merewood cannot have outfought six armed men."

A fist slamming against wood was immediately followed by the sound of crockery breaking. Jillian jolted to a halt. Only one person in the entire keep had such a volatile temper. Owen.

Hiding in the shadows with her back flattened against the wall, she finally dared to draw in a breath. She strained to listen, though it was quiet in the great hall beyond the door. Uneasy with the lack of sound or movement, she decided to take a chance and move close. Carefully sliding her foot to the side, she gained a few more precious inches closer to her goal.

"But milord," a nasally voice whined, "they fought like demons. We had no choice but retreat."

Aaron. Her heart lurched. She would recognize the dishonorable knight's voice anywhere.

"He defeated four of my best knights and you let him escape?" Owen sounded incredulous.

"Nay. I left my mark deep in his sword arm. If he doesn't bleed to death, he'll never lift it again."

"Nay." Jillian slapped her hands across her mouth.

The door to the hall burst open, rocking back on its hinges to bounce closed behind the three men.

Oh Lord! They'd found her. She could only stare back at the murderous expressions each man wore. Fear chilled her to the core. Not daring to take her eyes off the angry group of men, she reached a hand out to steady herself, while the other clutched her great-grandmother's amber pendant.

She backed away until the wall stopped her. The impact knocked her forward, and she landed hard on her knees.

Then the wall spoke, "Lady Jillian."

Winslow?

His men came running out from the semi-darkness and stood behind the warrior. With a gentleness that belied his size, Winslow MacInness reached down and helped her to her feet, then promptly shoved her behind him.

Jillian started to protest, but the dark looks stamped on each of the warriors' faces warned her to be quiet. She could complain later.

Swords raised, two of the men stood guarding her, waiting

for their leader's command. The grim expressions on their faces promised pain.

"What goes on here?" MacInness asked.

Jillian prayed the Lord of the Keep would not cut them all down where they stood.

"'Tis none of your affair."

Jillian grew uneasy in the silence. The Scots warrior stared at Sedgeworth's lord.

Owen's gaze swept the three warriors before him. He opened his mouth to speak, but closed it as two more knights arrived. Peeking from behind her brave guard, she recognized the two warriors as part of Winslow's elite guard. The icy claws clutching her heart eased enough so that it began to beat more normally.

Their overlord glared at the group of silent men. When he finally spoke, he sounded resigned. "So that's the way of it?"

MacInness nodded. "Ye've no reason to complain of my service before this night. Lady Jillian is my responsibility from this moment forward until she is safely delivered to her new home."

MacInness looked over his shoulder at her and frowned. She wondered what the look meant, but was too busy shifting from foot to foot trying to ease the dull throbbing in her bruised kneecaps.

Turning to glare at the three men who now stood frozen on either side of Owen, MacInness warned, "Ye wilna harm one hair on Lady Jillian's head." He locked gazes with Owen, "Ye ken?"

She'd never seen her guardian speechless, but he was now, with his head bobbing up and down in silent agreement.

"Rouse your lady's servants. We'll be needin' lots o' hot water for Lady Jillian's bath." Not sparing her a glance, still glaring at Owen, she was startled when MacInness added, "Have her fetch one of Madelyne's gowns. 'Tis beyond time the poor lass is treated as she deserves."

Jillian opened her cloak and looked at her worn shift. She couldn't remember the last time she'd been offered a new gown. No, she shook her head, that wasn't right, she did remember. It was a gown of soft pale green that her father told her complemented her dark brown eyes.

When she looked up, the Scotsman's gaze met hers. He seemed to be waiting for her to do something. She had no idea what he expected of her. She whispered her thanks, but it was for far more than the hot bath and promised gown. She'd be under his protection and that in itself was freeing. The prospect of something to wear that would not shame her new husband brought a warm smile to her face.

"About Merewood," Owen began.

Her smile evaporated. How could she have forgotten what she'd overheard, even for a moment! "Winslow," she whispered, moving closer to his side, "I need to speak with you … alone."

With a final glare in Owen's direction, he turned and led her up the stairs.

Halfway to the top, she rasped, "I must get a message to Garrick."

He shook his head and she fell silent, knowing the risk of being overheard was far greater here than in her chamber.

In the privacy of her chamber, she relayed what she chanced to overhear. "Owen spoke to someone in the hall. Garrick and Dunstan have been ambushed." Tears welled up in her eyes, but she blinked them away. "Garrick's been hurt, nigh unto death."

Needing something solid to hang on to in order to reassure herself she was doing the right thing by trying to help her future husband, she grabbed the warrior's huge hand in both of hers and squeezed hard. "You must go find out what happened. Please?" she pleaded. "I must know that he lives."

He stared down at their joined hands for a long, intensely quiet moment. When he finally looked up at her, she knew her trust would not be misplaced. He would do as she bid.

With a nod, he turned and introduced his warriors to her. Kelly and Eamon would stay behind to guard her, while Patrick and Sean accompanied him on a midnight ride to Merewood Keep.

CHAPTER NINE

"WHY AREN'T YOU resting?" Roderick asked. "Didn't Gertie bring you warm ale and honeyed bread?"

Garrick turned to glare over his shoulder at his youngest brother, then turned back to the job of supervising the finishing touches to the new stone curtain wall that would enclose their keep. He was in pain and knew it showed. Old Gert had told him he looked like the walking dead. *I'm not dead... yet.*

"I could say the same for you, brother." Garrick bit the inside of his mouth to keep from lashing out at him for taking such a chance with his life. Didn't Roderick understand how precious his brothers' lives were to him? The threat of losing him had been like a dagger poised, ready to cut out his heart had he been too late to save him.

One look at his youngest brother's eyes told him what he had feared; the lad did not understand. He was too young, too reckless and wrapped up in himself to question his own mortality. 'Twas Garrick's fault Roderick failed to take life seriously. He had tried to make up for the fact that their father was gone, and as a result he had been too lenient in his youngest brother's discipline. Was it too late to make up for that too? Mayhap a heavier hand would be needed to bring him back around.

"Your stay in Sedgeworth's lower levels seems to have taken its toll."

Roderick shrugged.

Too preoccupied to pry conversation from his youngest brother, he asked, "Can you ride?"

"Aye."

Garrick leveled his gaze on his brother's shoulder. On cue, Roderick lifted it up and down. *Stubborn lad. He'll do.*

"I must send you to Fitzrandolph's holding to act as emissary and announce my betrothal to Lady Jillian."

"What about the heiress?"

"I've made no promises, nor broken any vows." He regretted not having been able to negotiate a marriage contract with Fitzrandolph. His daughter's dowry would have paid for the construction of a new hall, and repairs to most of the crofters' homes as well. Not to mention the livestock he would not be getting now.

Roderick spoke up, "Jillian is a fine woman. You'll wed in a fortnight, then?"

Garrick clenched his jaw, thinking of the sprightly maiden who seemed so fragile, yet courageous. "Aye."

She seemed helpless, yet had been bold enough to stand up to her tormentors, and to him. He could not decide what to make of her. He detested confusion and indecision in any man, but loathed it to the point of violence in himself.

Roderick must have sensed the end of his brother's patience. He nodded and headed toward the stable.

"He'll be all right," Dunstan said, coming up behind him.

Garrick looked over his shoulder and nodded. Dunstan fell into step beside him, and they walked to the hall.

"I am counting on his charm to smooth the way." Thinking of Fitzrandolph's disappointment he added, "He had plans for my sword arm." Garrick flexed the stiff limb and groaned.

"Are you certain you will not change your mind and bring Roderick back? Jillian would understand your need to marry Beatrice for her dowry."

Dunstan had unknowingly given voice to the traitorous

thoughts swirling in Garrick's head 'til it ached. "For that reason alone, I cannot go back on my word," Garrick said. "Lady Jillian's offer of assistance came at a time when we had no hope at all of reaching Roderick before it was too late."

He wondered if Owen would have acted honorably and freed Roderick in exchange for his ward's hand in marriage and the promised gold. His gut roiled and his head began to pound knowing the man was not to be trusted.

They owed Roderick's life to Jillian. The steely edge returned to Garrick's voice and with it his resolve to honor his word. "How can you even suggest a refusal on my part now?"

Instead of answering, Dunstan asked, "Are you certain you know what you are getting into? 'Twould not do to have you go into this marriage blinded by mere beauty," Dunstan grinned.

Garrick stared out across the bailey and thought of his betrothed. "Aye, she is that." Disbelief speared through him, thinking of the woman who had sent her bodyguard to make certain he was safe.

Dunstan bit back a chuckle. "Your vassal seemed surprised to find you not dead."

"My bride-to-be was obviously worried she would remain as servant in that household." Once he'd uttered the words, he knew them to be false. *The lady cared.*

When Dunstan spoke, Garrick knew he had not fooled him. "Whatever you say, brother."

Garrick's impatience grew; time was so short. "See to the preparations in the hall. I'll not have my bride arrive only to be scared off by cobwebs and old rushes."

"Do you think so little of her, then?"

Pausing, Garrick remembered the sight of an auburn-haired angel with huge cinnamon brown eyes silently asking him to trust her.

"I am afraid that I am beginning to think too highly of her for my family's good."

Anger flashed in Dunstan's eyes. "God's blood! Your family is not marrying her. *You are.* We will not have to bed her. *You will.*"

Garrick was taken aback by his brother's impassioned speech.

"We do not have to look upon her face day in and day out for the next fifty years. *You do.* Mayhap you need more time to reflect upon your decision to marry." Dunstan turned on his heel and strode out of the empty hall, leaving Garrick to wonder why anyone thought he had had a choice at all.

"LADY JILLIAN," SARA called out.

Turning, Jillian waited until Sara caught up with her. "Have I forgotten something?"

"Oh, aye," her friend beamed.

Resigning herself to the fact that another lecture awaited her, she waited for Sara to fill her in on what she'd done to displease their mistress this time.

"You forgot to tell Kelly and Eamon that you would not be going to the smithy after the noon hour today." Sara's laughter was one-sided.

"Oh, Lord. How could I have forgotten?"

Mortification swept through her. Lord above, she tried not to be difficult, truly, but she simply could not accustom herself to reporting to the man.

Though his protection freed her from worrying about the inevitable beating she would receive at the end of the day, she had yet to grow comfortable approaching the knight with her daily list of duties. Especially when the knight ofttimes frowned and questioned the length and number of them.

But Garrick of Merewood was a warrior to be reckoned with, and to be under his vassal's protection not only freed her, it healed her. The bruises on her face were mere shadows under the cream of her complexion. The welts on her back, from the heavy switch Haldana used twofold on Jillian and her mare, were no longer raised and swollen. She had much to be thankful for. Trying to concentrate on what Sara was saying, she pushed her wandering thoughts aside.

"Aye, Jillian," Sara agreed. "He was most upset. He fears that you are more of a job to watch over than he bargained for."

Jillian missed the glint of laughter in Sara's eyes. The other woman's words cut right to the heart of Jillian's latest fear. *Mayhap Garrick would feel the same way.* Would she be all that Garrick bargained for in a wife? Would she remember how to be a lady when the time came, or had she been too long a servant?

Her thoughts must have been written clearly on her face; her friend grabbed her hands.

"Don't worry about MacInness," Sara whispered. "It was a jest." Sara squeezed Jillian's hands briefly then let go. "You are all Garrick could hope to find in a wife. No one can run a household better. You have a light hand with the servants, and a big heart."

Jillian looked out over the bustling scene in front of them. Servants rushed from one task to another. At midday, no one would dare be idle, lest Owen bring them to task for slacking off in their duties.

Sara's eyes narrowed. "I'll wager you have even gone so far as to forgive your guardians for their part in your miserable life here, haven't you?"

Jillian could not meet her friend's intense gaze. Why bother to hide the fact especially now that that Sara knew she had. Owen and Haldana were weak in spirit, so she unselfishly prayed for their strength. "If I weren't so clumsy that I—"

"You are not clumsy!" Sara's voice grew cold with anger. "'Twas just an excuse for Lady Haldana to take out her frustrations upon you for having a more beautiful face than any of her daughters."

Sara grabbed Jillian and pulled her aside. "'Tis past time someone told you." Lowering her voice so as not to be heard, she began, "In the three winters you have spent here, not one offer has been made for any of their daughters."

Jillian stared at Sara. "I don't understand. They have had plenty of visitors."

Sara's gaze locked with Jillian's as she told her, "They all offered for you."

Jillian's belly iced over. She couldn't think. Her eyes grew round and very dark. The pain of remembered beatings now made sense. She had helped serve meals to guests in the hall. The beatings had been the most severe after their guests had left. At the time she could not remember doing anything wrong.

"I never knew. I would not even think to encourage any of the knights who graced Sedgeworth's table!"

Sara's eyes filled with sympathy. "You cannot help but attract attention. You are very beautiful, Jillian."

Jillian shook her head, but Sara continued undaunted, "'Tis the beauty of your spirit, and the joy you find in living. Even though Owen refused all offers for your hand, the suitors kept coming back again and again. Why do you think young Roderick kept returning to the hall?"

"To see Maralyne."

It was Sara's turn to shake her head. "The irresistible part of your charm is that you do not know how lovely you are."

Jillian fell silent. She didn't agree. Only her father had seen the beauty inside her, even when she'd been awkward, all limbs and freckles. He thought her a rare beauty, but her father was supposed to think that, wasn't he?

She worried over what Garrick's reaction would be had the cut on her mouth not healed straight. Somewhere in the back of her mind, the thought held that he would not have cared, but she worried just the same. Thank goodness it had healed without a mark.

UP AT DAWN to rouse the lord and lady, Jillian's days passed quickly, filled with so much work she barely had time to rest before rising to start all over again.

The day of her journey to Merewood approached finding her rail thin and bone weary. She knew the bluish circles under her eyes accentuated her tired features because Sara told her every chance she got.

It was all she could do to lift the small satchel of her belongings and tie them behind her saddle. She fumbled with the knot, but her tired hands refused to obey. A deep voice offered assistance. She turned around hastily.

"Worry not lass, I can carry your pack." Patrick's bright green gaze held hers long moments. She hoped he had not guessed the truth of how exhausted she was, or why. Groaning inwardly, she knew she was in no condition to journey more than one-half mile, let alone the two-hour trip to Merewood Keep.

While she struggled to hide her condition from the warrior, he ordered, "Wait here."

Nodding required far too much effort, Jillian offered a half-smile instead. Grimacing, the warrior stalked off.

At the door to the stable, MacInness was engaged in a heated debate with his overlord.

"We'll no' wait for ye. The lass is near to droppin' right now. How do ye expect me to make the lass wait another hour while yer daughters pack the rest o' their fine clothes? I wilna do it. Follow along later."

Turning away, MacInness spotted his friend stalking toward him, anger punctuating his steps.

"She's not fit to travel," Patrick ground out. "What ails the lass? I thought you said Owen promised not to abuse her with added tasks. I know she left the hall early every night. I followed her to her chamber door myself."

MacInness agreed with the warrior. "She did leave the hall early every night."

"Well then, what is wrong with her?" Patrick demanded.

MacInness smiled at the man's concern for their mistress.

"I've just spoken with Sara. It appears Owen and his lady had threatened to beat Sara if the extra jobs they assigned were not done to their satisfaction. Apparently, our new mistress snuck out of her chamber in the middle of the night to finish whatever task remained undone."

Patrick appeared thoughtful. "'Tis a loyal woman Garrick is getting. I hope he values her as he should."

"Weel now, we'll just have to see that he does. Ye ken?"

"Aye, you soft-hearted Scot."

⇝⫸✕⫷⇜

MacInness lifted the exhausted woman and settled her in his arms atop his own mount. There was no way around it; he'd have to carry her all the way to Merewood. The journey would be twice as long if they fashioned a litter to pull behind them, or if they used a wagon. Besides 'twas too dark to watch over her. His new overlord would not forgive him if his lady came to harm on their journey. *Nay,* he qualified. He would never forgive himself if anything happened to his mistress.

Giving the signal to ride, a raised fist, MacInness and his Irish Contingent rode away from their past without regret. The future, still a rosy glow on the horizon, held the promise of a better life for them all.

"Garrick," Jillian whispered snuggling against MacInness's chest.

MacInness stiffened only just now realizing how he truly felt about her. Looking down he saw that her eyes were closed. He hesitated; in her present state, she'd probably never realize that it was not her future husband that held her close. A branch reached out to snap in her face. He brushed it aside. "Aye, dear lady?"

"I was afraid you would change your mind," she confessed to the broad chest she leaned against. "I'm clumsy...I daydream," she further admitted. "Lady Haldana oft complained ... 'specially about my mother's gifts," she added sleepily.

Confused, MacInness prodded her to explain. "Gifts, lass?"

"Mmmm, my mother's."

He wondered if she feigned sleep. "But what are these gifts mistr—dear lady?" He almost slipped and gave away the necessary deception.

"My mother had the most glorious auburn hair … true beauty … not me." Jillian sighed and frowned in her sleep. "Haldana is right…I am coarse…ugly."

MacInness wished he had the lady's lying white throat in his grasp; he'd strangle the old harpy.

Settling closer against the man holding her, Jillian breathed deeply, "I'll work hard … you'll not be ashamed of your home. I'll take good care of you. Don't send me back, please?"

The exasperating woman fell back into a deep slumber with her questions unanswered. As they rode on, MacInness thought about all she had said. He knew about the beatings and diverted attention away from the lass as often as possible, but knew she was at Haldana's mercy whenever he was away from the keep.

Should he tell Garrick about their strange conversation? He sighed. On the off chance that Lady Jillian remembered it, he'd have to.

"MacInness?" Sean called out, riding back from his position in the lead.

He saw the concern on the other knight's face and instinctively tightened his hold on his mistress. "Is there trouble?"

The warrior shook his head. "The keep is just beyond that stand of trees. You can see it on the rise." Sean's face looked bleak as he added, "'Tis naught but a shell of a home."

MacInness knew the state of Merewood Keep, but hadn't confided such in his men. "We've five more strong backs and willin' arms," he said slowly. "It wilna be long until it's put to right."

He had taken a chance that his men would rally around him upon first glance at the keep and question him later. He began to dread what they would have to say.

Sean rode back to the front, taking the lead position and hailed the guard posted atop the new stone wall. Raising his right fist, as MacInness instructed, he then touched it to his heart.

The silent party rode ahead through Merewood Keep's new gates, ready to embrace their future.

CHAPTER TEN

"WHERE IS LADY Jillian?" Garrick demanded of his vassal.

"Lower your voice, mon," MacInness growled.

Taken aback by the order, Garrick was stunned into silence. He watched the warrior shift in his saddle and draw back his plaid. Lady Jillian lay sleeping, safely tucked in his vassal's arms.

"The poor lass is exhausted. If I let her ride, she'd have fallen off her horse."

One look at her and Garrick knew the Scot was right. "My thanks."

Opening his arms, he accepted his new responsibility from the arms of the man who'd sworn fealty to him. Garrick had a feeling his decision to trust MacInness and his group of mercenaries would prove to be the first of many changes that would better their lives at Merewood.

Jillian did not waken, but to Garrick's surprise, she reached up and placed her hand over his heart and left it there. Then the lass did an odd thing, she smiled in her sleep. 'Twas as if the steady beat of his heart comforted her.

Deeply moved, he looked up and noticed the men gathering around him were smiling.

"She's a bonny lass," Patrick offered.

Sean nodded. "And loyal."

Garrick turned to leave.

"She'll work herself into a fever," Kelly warned.

Eamon grunted, "She thinks she's clumsy."

"Aye, men, but she's wrong aboot that," MacInness pointed out.

"She's not ugly," Patrick couldn't keep from saying.

Stunned by the one-sided conversation going on around him Garrick stopped mid-stride. Turning back around, he pinned Patrick with his ice blue gaze and ground out, "Who said my wife is ugly?"

Patrick looked first to his brother Sean, then to their leader. At MacInness's nod, Patrick confessed, "Lady Jillian. She told MacInness."

Turning to face his friend, he added, "You'll have to tell him; he's a right to know what she thought she was confessing to himself." Pointing at Garrick, Patrick shrugged his shoulders, turned and started walking toward the stable.

Garrick could not understand Patrick's seeming lack of respect. Truth be told, none of the men seemed to be paying any attention to the fact that he stood before them, his bride-to-be in his arms, waiting their further explanations for their bizarre comments. His vassal and the men under him should be waiting for Garrick to leave before walking away. They should wait to receive their orders, whether they be from Garrick or MacInness.

Dunstan clapped a hand to his shoulder. "I'll see to their mounts," and grinned, "mayhap your lady would prefer sleeping on a bed." Smiling, he followed behind the escort party, whistling softly.

It was then it hit him. MacInness and his men acted just like his own brothers. Garrick shook his head, they'd be loyal to their last breath. God help him if they disagreed with him, he'd never hear the end of it. A breath away from shouting at the group that they should stand and wait for their orders, he remembered Owen and how he treated his household knights.

He would do well to recall the reasons MacInness and his small contingent of men were now serving their allegiance to him. Sighing, he knew he'd have to try to live with their seeming lack of respect in exchange for their undying loyalty.

Garrick crossed the near-empty bailey and ascended the granite steps of his keep. The echo of his booted heels rang out in the silence as he crossed the massive width of his hall. Making his way up the stairs, he shifted his burden slightly, to accommodate his added width in the narrow hallway. Making his way through the upper level, he stopped before the rough-hewn door to his chamber.

Jillian cried out in her sleep. Acting instinctively, he drew the tip of his finger across her brow and down her cheek. Amazingly, she settled back into oblivion. The woman puzzled him, he decided as he laid her on the soft bedding. A whisper of lavender rose to greet him as he knelt on the edge of it. He would have to thank his mother when she arrived. Her influence remained still.

He thought of the hall below him, though under construction, 'twas sparkling clean. There were herb-filled rushes scattered across the stone floor. With each step, the soft scent of herbs rose up to mingle with the stronger scent of fresh-cut pine from the newly planked walls. He was proud of their progress.

Earlier in the day, the mouth-watering aroma of freshly baked bread had made his stomach rumble with impatience. Their cook, Gertie, was a wonder. Loyal to the bone, she had returned to care for her lady's boys. Flexing his arm, he winced. Aye, care for them she did.

"Garrick, where are you, lad?" Shaking his head, he answered the summons, "In here, Gertie." It would do no good to correct her. At eight and twenty he was no longer a lad, but she was too old and set in her ways to listen. After all, she had helped raise him up from a babe. He supposed he owed it to her perseverance in that regard not to demand she change her ways at this late date.

"Is she still asleep then?" Gertie's brow knit in concern. She reached out to touch the back of her hand to Jillian's forehead. "No fever." Gertie's loud sigh revealed much.

She seemed to fret over her new mistress. Garrick was more than pleased. If Gertie accepted her so easily, then their lives would continue on as before. Wouldn't they?

"Nay. But I will find out why she sleeps like the dead. That brawny Scot has a lot to answer for." Garrick strode out of the room without a backward glance.

Gertie chuckled, "Well, now, you poor thing. How did he come to care for you in such a short time? Old Gert will just have to make sure he continues to feel that way." Smiling to herself, she drew up the extra blanket and tucked it around the tiny woman.

"You're naught but skin and bones," she exclaimed. Shaking her head, she added, "We'll fix that soon enough." One last reassuring touch to Jillian's brow and she quietly closed the door.

GARRICK STOOD, HANDS clenched behind his back. His new vassal stood facing him, mimicking his posture. Dunstan stood to Garrick's left, while Patrick and Sean flanked MacInness on either side with Kelly and Eamon standing directly behind in a show of support.

"I'll have your explanation for Jillian's state of exhaustion now, MacInness."

He wasn't long in responding, "Weel now, the lass is a mite stubborn."

The need to protect his bride unnerved him. "Lady Jillian will be treated with respect from this moment on." When no one spoke he shouted, "Do you understand?"

"Being stubborn *is* a compliment, ye daft mon." Amber eyes shot fire at his accuser before MacInness added, "Just how do ye define respect, then?"

"This is going to be a good one, eh, Sean?" Patrick whispered, poking his brother in the ribs. They looked at their cousins.

Catching the glint of humor in Kelly's eyes, Patrick smiled. All hell was about to break loose.

"You pledged your loyalty before me, I'll have your respect as well," Garrick threatened, reversing his earlier decision in the bailey.

"You'd best tell him what you mean, brother," Dunstan suggested.

"What do you mean, what I mean?"

"Respect," Dunstan said.

"Aye," the burly Scot demanded, "just what do ye mean by that, Merewood?"

Garrick's throat tightened in anger, he had to force the words out, "You'll not question my words or actions again. Do you understand?"

The Highlander shook his head. "Do ye really expect me to follow ye blindly without the benefit of my guidance?" MacInness bellowed.

"Aye, you damned Scot," Garrick shouted in the man's face. "I do."

"'Twill be a cold day in hell when I do. My sword is yours and ye'll have my loyalty and my strength as long as I still breathe," his vassal vowed. "But I canna let ye go into battle blind. If I think ye're daft, mon, ye'll no' wonder long."

Out of the corner of his eye, Garrick saw Patrick grip his sides and realized the man was laughing!

He looked at Dunstan; his own brother could not seem to keep a straight face. His gaze followed Dunstan's and settled behind him on the Irishmen, who looked about to burst.

Anger, raw and hot, had him reaching for the hilt of his sword only to be stayed by his vassal.

"Dinna ye ken that I have given ye the best of me?" MacInness rasped, "I'll no' let anythin' happen to that brave lass ye're to wed. Yer home wilna be safe unless me and mine are watchin' over it." Going down on one knee, MacInness ended his speech with his right hand fisted over his heart. "A mon canna ask for more than the loyalty of those before ye."

Garrick's anger abruptly left him. 'Twas obvious the man would protect Jillian, and their home, to his last breath. How could he continue to argue with that? Was it really all that important that the Scot bow before him, waiting with bated breath for Garrick to utter some inane instructions that were of no consequence other than to let everyone know who was in charge?

Be not so quick to judge. His father's voice admonished from deep inside of him.

"Rise." Garrick touched a hand to MacInness's shoulder. "'Twill be difficult for me, but I value your pledge more than my need to spout authority." Turning around he called out, "Gertie, bring mead. We have need to quench our strong thirst!"

Loud guffaws of laughter rang through his hall as goblets were raised. Garrick smiled; the laughter had been missing far too long.

Seated at the end of the long oak table, he looked benevolently down the length of it. Dunstan sat among the men now loyal to Merewood. He watched as his brother smiled at something that had been said. *A jest, no doubt.* The knights, who sat drinking deeply of Merewood's fine mead, seemed unable to speak without riling one another with taunts and cryptic remarks.

Intrigued, he watched trying to figure out why. Suddenly he knew the answer: *camaraderie.* MacInness's men shared what had been lacking since the fall of his family's keep. Searching his brain for a clue as to where it had gone and why it still lacked among his own men, Garrick happened upon a black thought. *Mayhap 'twas his leadership.*

He poured every ounce of his strength and every waking hour into making the vision of rebuilding his family's fortune and home a reality. How then could that squelch feelings of unity among his men?

His gaze settled on his brother, staring hard into the profile he knew so well. What was it about Dunstan that bothered him of late? His head hurt from trying to piece together just what it was, when out of the blue it hit him between the eyes with the force of a well-swung mace. 'Twas his brother's constant badgering to let the past go, his ceaseless pleas to look to the future, working with what they still possessed—the strength of his proud people combined with the fertile ground upon which generations of his father's people had lived before them—generations that had withstood the onslaught of both Picts and Vikings alike.

Thinking of the proud race from which his mother's people had sprung, he realized war could bring about change that would benefit even a conquered people. Hadn't his father taken a Viking bride after defeating her own father's attempt at laying siege against Merewood Keep? Their equally proud bloodlines had mingled and produced three strong sons. Each different in their own right, but bound together by the unbreakable bonds of brotherhood.

Offering up a silent prayer that Roderick would be successful on his journey, he broached the subject that had been weighing heavily upon him since the arrival of his bride-to-be.

He waited until there was a lull in the conversation and asked, "Why is Jillian nigh unto illness with exhaustion?"

MacInness stayed his hand, tankard halfway to his lips as he grinned. "Weel now, didna I tell ye she was a mite stubborn?"

Laughter rang out loud among the men seated drinking deeply of Merewood's smooth heady brew.

"You mentioned it." Garrick's teeth ached from clenching them together in an effort to restrain his anger. It would not be easy to let go of the tight hold he had over the keep and its fighting force. But he needed MacInness and his men, therefore he had to try to understand them.

MacInness finally took pity on him and answered, "She left the hall after the evening meal each night."

"We followed her to her room and stood watch at her door all night, every night," Patrick said.

"How were we to know, she slipped out of her window onto

the vines and climbed back down?" Sean demanded.

"To finish Sara's tasks," Eamon added.

"Sara's?" Garrick asked.

"Yer lady chanced to overhear Owen threaten Sara with a beating if she didna finish her day's tasks. Lady Jillian couldna stand for anyone to suffer as she had."

Their gazes met and held, and MacInness continued, "I'm sorry we didna know what she was up to. We wouldna let her work herself to the bone like that, ye ken?"

Garrick reached across the table and grasped MacInness's hand. "I understand. Thank you."

And perhaps he did for the first time. He too had worked himself to the point where he nearly dropped in his tracks. He would do anything for his family and his people. *Anything.*

No further words were needed. Garrick had accepted MacInness as his equal before his brother and MacInness's men. Change had come to Merewood, and with it the lessening of Garrick's heavy burden of responsibility carried too long alone.

'Twas past time to bring their mother home to stay. Confident she would be safe, he made his decision. Should her sons be unable to, MacInness and his men would guard his mother with their lives.

CHAPTER ELEVEN

DOZENS OF HOOF beats, accompanied by an equal number of voices, roused Jillian from a deep sleep. Heat poured off her in waves. Stretching, she groaned, aching from head to toe. Forcing herself to rise, she walked to the window and looked down upon the chaotic scene unfolding in the inner bailey.

Though nearly dark, the party from Sedgeworth Keep had only just arrived. The chatter of excited female voices drifted upward on the evening breeze. Snatches of conversation danced on the wind just out of reach. For once, Lady Haldana wasn't complaining. Yet. Five of her guardian's most trusted men stood helping Owen's daughters dismount. In a flurry of softly colored wool and snow-white linen, they were set on their feet. Jillian sighed wistfully at the sight of such beauty side by side.

The eldest, Maralyne, was just one year older than her. At eight and ten, she had developed into a beautiful young woman. Her alabaster skin, unmarked by freckles, or bruises, was the young woman's best feature. Next to her stood her younger sister, Maryon, another with perfect skin and hair the color of flax. The twins, Meredyth and Melanye, were identical down to the flecks of gold in their sky-blue eyes.

Last, but certainly not least, stood Madelyne, Jillian's one friend among them. Though only five and ten, she had all of the grace her oldest sister had tried to acquire these three years past, though Madelyne's was natural.

Awed by the sight of them standing shoulder to shoulder, 'twas difficult to imagine how any man could pass by such quiet beauty and not be affected by it. Why then hadn't Roderick offered for one of them? And what of the score of wealthy and powerful men who visited Sedgeworth in the last few years? Why hadn't one of them taken one of the sisters to wife?

Had Sara been right? Was Jillian the reason for this oversight of such grace and beauty? She shook her head. 'Twas just not possible. Who would turn away from such beauty in favor of a mean servant such as herself? *Garrick had.*

But why? her conscience asked.

His honor, her heart answered. *You saved his brother.*

Roderick told you his oldest brother was honorable above all else. *But was it just honor?*

Duty, her heart cried out. What cold companions would they be in their marriage bed? Jillian could only help but wonder.

Tearing her eyes from Owen's daughters and the knights fawning about them, she counted twenty more knights. Owen had departed from his home well protected. Scanning the scene once more, she realized Owen had obviously given in to his daughters and allowed each of them to bring a trunk. Given the size of their trunks, that meant five additional packhorses to stable and feed.

Jillian shifted and groaned. There was no hope for it, time to go below and help smooth the arrival of her guardian's family. She refused to let the burden of their sheer number rest solely upon her intended.

Her legs trembled as she descended to the hall below. Slowing her pace, Jillian controlled most of the shaking, hoping no one would take note of it.

Standing in the doorway to the hall, hand to her throat and heart in her eyes, Jillian stared at the tall warrior placing a log on the fire. Garrick stiffened only once before laying the wood in place. 'Twas the only indication his sword arm still pained him.

While he stood watching the brazier, she remembered what Winslow had told her about that night. He hadn't wanted to tell her about the ambush, she'd had to pry it from his lips.

She smiled remembering his reaction to her threat that she'd tell Maryon how he secretly pined for her if he didn't tell what happened that night. The man had actually shuddered and gone pale. Strange, she hadn't believed Sara when Sara had told her of Winslow's dislike of Owen's second oldest; Jillian thought Maryon was so pretty.

Poor Winslow took her at her word and told her of the treachery abounding that moonlit night a fortnight past.

She stared across the wide expanse of the hall, her thoughts jumbled with past conversations. A sharp bark of laughter brought her sharply back to the present in time to see Garrick's tunic stretch taut across the massive muscles of his back. The sudden urge to knead those knotted muscles to ease the tension caught her by surprise.

She had never thought of touching a man before. Why did Garrick have such a strong effect on her? Would it always be so?

Garrick looked up and caught her staring at him. "Lady Jillian." Crossing the room in swift strides, he took her by the arm, leading her to a chair by the open fire pit he'd been tending at the opposite end of the room from where the men sat at the table drinking.

He bent close to her and asked, "Are you well?"

"Aye," she managed, wondering if his concern was false.

Not wanting to attract undue attention, she placed her hands in her lap, hoping he wouldn't notice how they trembled. But by now her entire body was weak with fatigue and the room had grown sharply colder, even though she sat next to the blazing fire.

She watched him take note of her trembling. Hoping to distract him, she asked, "Owen has arrived. Have you not gone to greet him?"

"I let Dunstan act as host, 'tis fitting is it not?" The dimple in his cheek deepened as grinned. "Do you think Owen will feel slighted?"

"Aye, milord."

"Garrick," he corrected.

"Aye, Garrick, but what of the horses? Have you enough grain to feed them?" When he continued to stare at her, she blurted out, "Would you like me to draw water? I would like to help."

"Jillian dear, how are you?" Owen had come up behind them and now watched her expectantly. A shiver wracked her body and he smiled. She did not trust the man.

"Fine. I have been well received in my new home, as will you be." Turning to speak once more to Garrick, Jillian ignored the cold sinking into her limbs.

"Jillian?" Madelyne's voice came from far away. Before she could answer, the room blurred before her eyes. Shaking her head, refusing to give in to the fever burning from within her, she prayed her vision would clear.

Garrick reached out and placed a hand on her shoulder. "You are not well."

"'Tis but a chill, the room has gone cold."

Garrick slid his hand down to her elbow, helping her up out of the chair. "Let me help you upstairs."

Jillian looked up, confusion warring within her. Used to being abused, she didn't know how to react to kindness. "I can walk."

When she swayed, Garrick bit out, "'Tis clear you cannot." He looked over his shoulder and called out, "Gertie."

The room fell quiet as the woman rushed to his side.

"I was expecting this," she said touching a hand to Jillian's forehead. "'Tis naught but a chill, she'll be good as new in a day or so. You leave everything to Old Gert."

In danger of falling over, Jillian grabbed a hold of Garrick to steady herself. He surprised her by sweeping her into his arms and carrying her from the hall. She felt the muscles in his wounded arm contract, enabling him to accept her weight without an outward sign of weakness. But her fear of what would happen once they were away from prying eyes was greater than her concern for his comfort.

"I'm not ill," Jillian explained as he walked. "Just tired. Can you not see that?"

➤➤➤❮❮❮

GARRICK IGNORED HER continued protests, listening instead to Gertie as they ascended the stairs. He placed Jillian once more in his bed. Standing back to allow Gertie room to minister to his lady, he was struck by the overwhelming feeling of rightness. *She belongs here, in my bed.*

They would do well together. After all, no sacrifice was too great for his family. *Sacrifice?* It would be no sacrifice at all to take Jillian to wife and have her warm his bed.

A small voice beckoned him from within. But what if she hadn't helped to free Roderick? What if her family holding were not part of the bargain? Would you still take her to wife?

His guilt-ridden soul cried out to be freed of its burden.

Shaking his head, he told the still small voice inside him, nay. He would marry only to help his family. If there was no gain, it mattered not how much he cared for Jillian; he would not marry her.

If Jillian could not help him, he would have to ignore the feelings of longing burning within him. Every time those cinnamon brown eyes held his gaze, heat seared him, lighting a fire that threatened to blaze out of control. Awed, he realized he'd never felt anything like this before.

A shake of his head cleared it. Thank God he would never have to worry about setting Jillian aside. Because of her bravery, his brother was alive ... free. They had but to petition King William for her family holding and it would be theirs. Hadn't Owen assured him it would be so? His family's fortunes would soon be solidified and their land annexed to Jillian's fertile holding, Loughmoe Keep.

Their livestock would breed, their crops multiply, and Merewood's people would again prosper. Construction on the keep would be complete by winter, but he'd changed his mind not to wait until then to send for their mother. It was time. Lady Eyreka would return, bringing her own special brand of unconditional love to surround and support her sons.

Half my debt is nearly paid.

Looking down at the fragile young woman who now lay in a deep sleep, his concern deepened. "Is there naught you can do?"

"'Tis but a fever. I must fetch my basket of healing herbs. Just keep a cool cloth to her brow. Aye, like this." Taking his other hand, the older woman gave him the bowl of now tepid water and a soft cloth.

"Dip the cloth like this in the water. Wring out most of the water, but not all," she instructed him. "That's right. Now gently bathe her face and neck until the cloth is warm to the touch."

Frustrated at Gertie's assumption that he lacked the skills to tend to his lady, he barked out, "I know what to do."

She took his gruff comment in stride. "I'll be back soon. 'Tis your job to keep her cool."

Garrick grimaced, "Aye." His fingertip grazed the gentle curve of her eyebrow; 'twas soft as a feather. Gliding the cloth across her forehead again, he checked the cloth for heat. It felt dry—hot. A touch of his fingertip to her cheek had her groaning aloud. He drew his hand back; it burned like a hot coal!

He dipped the cloth in the water again, his worry growing as she began to move her head from side-to-side on the pillow, trying to avoid the cold cloth.

Did she wrestle with her own demons?

He would have to find out. Garrick continued to stroke her face and neck with the damp cloth, slowly easing the heat from her. By the time Gertie returned, Jillian had stopped thrashing about and lay very still.

"How is she?" Gertie laid her basket on the table next to Garrick's bed.

"She's stopped fighting me," Garrick grimaced.

"Aye, that is a good sign." Smiling down at him she added, "Your mother will be pleased to learn you have grown into such a caring man. One not too proud or busy to care for the sick."

Nodding toward the door, she said, "We've shown Lord Owen and his family to their chamber. They may not be too happy having to share, but 'tis necessary. Dunstan is settling the men-at-arms in the lower level." Gertie bustled about the room. "What a crowd they make. I'll need a hand caring for Jillian if I am to feed them."

Garrick turned back around. "Find someone else," he said. "I must speak to Owen."

"Send your vassal up," Gert said. "I'm sure he can handle the task."

Garrick glared at the woman.

"Scottish women are fierce in their defense of their men." Gertie paused breaking into a broad smile., "Well 'tis only right, their menfolk treat them as equals. But I'm certain 'tis the rumor I heard just last month from my brother's wife, Mary Kate, she's Scots you know. Well, to hear Mary Kate tell it, the rugged men from the Highlands are the very devil in bed."

"Enough!" Garrick bellowed. "You'll have me addle-brained for sure if you continue squawking on about the mating habits of your kin." Hands fisted on his hips, Garrick glared down at his housekeeper.

She had the temerity to smile.

"Fine, you win old woman. I'll send MacInness up. See that he understands how to care for my wife."

Gertie burst out laughing. "Oh lad, you're not married yet. She's not even your bride."

In the quiet that followed, Jillian spoke softly, "Is he gone then?"

Gertie looked down at the flushed woman. "You're awake?" Her brow wrinkled when she asked, "Why did you let him think you were out of your mind with fever? 'Tis a cruel game you play."

"'Tis no game." Jillian's face lost all expression. "I had the fever once, three winters past." She turned haunted eyes toward the older woman. "The mistress did not think me truly ill. She took a switch to me. Only when I fell unconscious with the complications of the fever and the whipping did she let me lie abed."

"But lass, Garrick would not beat you. He's never raised a hand to any of the servants here. His mother would have his head on a pike had he or his sire dared to strike a woman." Gertie's gaze searched Jillian's. "What is truly the matter? You can tell me."

"I am afraid."

"Of Garrick?" Gert sounded incredulous.

Jillian nodded. "He was so angry when he carried me out of the hall. I thought I had pushed him too far. I did not know what he would do."

Gert gathered the slender woman close to her ample bosom and stroked her hair. "There now, you did not know the master is a man of honor. How could you after spending three years in purgatory?"

When Jillian stiffened, Gert continued, "Rumors of the Lord of Sedgeworth's temper have even reached us here. He has no honor. You'll come to trust the master in time, you'll see."

The tension left Jillian as Gert's strong hands massaged her neck and shoulders. When sleep came, she welcomed it.

MacInness looked up as Garrick entered the room. The bond that had started forming after their argument held. Garrick knew the moment MacInness understood, without words, that something was amiss. The warrior crossed the room and met him at the base of the staircase.

"What's wrong?" MacInness asked. "It isna yer lady is it?"

"'Tis the fever. Gertie is taking care of her now, but I need to settle some unfinished business with Owen, and I need someone to care for Jillian while Gertie prepares our meal." Garrick gave him a bleak look.

"So ye thought of me?"

Shrugging, Garrick answered, "We have no other servants here yet." Taking a deep breath, he continued, "For some reason, Gertie suggested you. You'll have to ask her why."

I'll be damned if I'll tell him, Garrick thought to himself.

Something flickered in MacInness's eyes. "Just tell me what to do. I'll care for the lass."

Somehow, this time, MacInness's familiar way of speaking of Jillian soothed Garrick. He knew the man could be trusted to care for her as if she were his own wife.

"Wife," he muttered aloud.

"What's that?"

"Nothing." Garrick promised himself to look into the matter of a wife for the Scot—soon.

⊱※⊰

"YE'LL BE ALL right, lass." MacInness wiped the heat from Jillian's brow again, patiently wringing out the cloth and moving on to her flushed cheeks, he repeated the motions. He had watched his mother caring for the sick of their clan, time and again. She had been a great healer; mayhap he carried the skill.

The cool soothing strokes roused Jillian from her deep sleep. Half awake, she muttered, "Mother?"

Startled, he wondered how to answer her. Bending close he whispered, "Nay, lass, 'tis yer guardian angel. Now close yer eyes and sleep."

The closing of the door startled him. He had been concentrating on the task at hand and hadn't heard it open.

Turning around, he glared at the man standing there.

Aaron stood in the doorway. "What do ye want?" MacInness glared at the coward Jillian had run from in terror a fortnight ago.

"Lord Owen sent me to check up on his ward. I'm certain he'll be pleased to learn that you have come to care so deeply for her. I think I'll just mention how tenderly you are ministering to her *every* need."

The way Aaron stressed the word every made MacInness's gut roil; he knew what the man implied.

Furious, he stood up. "You'll no' repeat any such thing ye wee vermin."

In the face of the Scot's anger, the smaller man backed away until he was pinned up against the door. His hand reached to push it open, but he didn't have the speed of the enraged Scot.

MacInness wrapped his hands around the man's throat and lifted him up off of his feet. "Ye'll tell yer master I have been tendin' to Lady Jillian. She has the fever."

Shaking his head, the man agreed.

"Ye'll no' tell him anythin' more. Understand?" When he did not answer, MacInness squeezed the man's throat.

"Aye," Aaron rasped out.

Satisfied, MacInness loosened his grip and watched the man crumble to the floor in a heap. He returned to his vigil at Jillian's bedside. A loud groan and closing of the chamber door told him that the man had gone, and Owen would hear what MacInness wanted him to.

"Garrick?" Jillian called out weakly.

"Soon lass, yer mon will be here soon. Rest now, there's a brave lassie." MacInness heard the door opening this time. Not bothering to turn around he spoke.

"No' again. Didna I tell ye what to tell yer lord? Do I have to throttle the life out of ye before ye listen?"

"I'm quite sure I understand your meaning. Especially the part where you wish to strangle me."

"Garrick." MacInness spun around, the wet cloth still dripping as he clenched it in the hand fisted at his side.

"I thought you were Aaron come back to..."

"What?" Garrick's voice was deadly soft.

"Yer lady called out for her mother. I leaned close and told her..."

"Go on," Garrick urged.

MacInness flushed to the roots of his bright auburn hair. Each and every freckle stood out against the color. "Well, I... That is..."

"Just what *did* you tell my wife?" Garrick bit the words out while a new and unfamiliar emotion ripped through him.

"Haven't I told you, lad? She's not your wife yet." Gertie rushed in through the open door and pushed the men aside to get to her newest charge. "Your meal awaits you below stairs. Do go away, your loud voices are disturbing milady."

Thus dismissed, the warriors glared first at one another and then at the formidable woman tending to their lady. Shrugging, Garrick advised, "We may as well listen. She never backs down unless she is willing."

"Sounds like my own dear mother," MacInness added smiling.

"Now there's a brave woman," Gertie chuckled.

MacInness turned around, a comeback on the tip of his tongue, but Gertie cut him off. "Go on with you. Supper's getting cold."

Closing the door, Garrick stood blocking the way. "Well?"

"Let it go mon, 'Twas nothin'."

"Well then, it wouldn't hurt to repeat what you told her, would it?" The unwanted emotion still clawed at him while he awaited the Scotsman's answer. For some reason, the thought of anyone near his bride-to-be filled him with rage. A stranger to jealousy, he did not take it well.

"Ye're verra determined. If ye must know, I told her 'twas her guardian angel and for her to go to sleep."

Garrick had not expected such a sentimental reply from the

battle-hardened warrior. He was stunned. It was something his mother would have said to soothe the worry away. The poor thing didn't have a mother; somehow Garrick sensed her need for the comfort his vassal's words would no doubt have given her.

Taking a deep breath, he inclined his head. "Let's not keep our guests waiting." Slapping the tall Scot on his back, he led the way down to supper.

Chapter Twelve

Two full days passed before Jillian was allowed to rise from her sickbed. Dunstan and MacInness kept the guests busy enough to prevent any disagreements from breaking out, while Gertie kept anyone from entering Garrick's room where Jillian rested.

She had just pulled the chainse over her head when she heard a woman's voice call out. "Garrick!"

Jillian had to see what new female called to her betrothed. She stood on tiptoe and peered out of the window. A beautiful woman sat atop a magnificent steed.

Swallowing her gasp of shock, Jillian stared down at the sight. Garrick strode down the keep's stone steps and across the bailey. He lifted the woman down off her horse, swinging her around. "Mother, I can't believe you're really here."

Mother? Jillian mouthed the words before sinking to her knees, her hands covering her gasp of surprise. The voices still carried in through the open window, but she no longer listened. Shocked to the core at what had just happened, she tried to reason why she had reacted so strongly to the sight of another woman in Garrick's arms.

She was jealous!

Shaking her head, she said, "In order to be jealous, I would have to have strong feelings for him. I don't, do I?" Sighing, she realized it would be a falsehood to say that she did not care. She had fallen for Garrick of Merewood like a catapulted rock. That first glimpse of him weeks ago had turned her head and lightened her heart. Her life had not been the same since that day.

Pain filled her at the thought of their bargain. "He loves me not. 'Tis his code of honor and duty he'll satisfy by taking me to wife." *My land is what he's after. I'd do well to remember where I stand in his life.*

Checking her appearance, Jillian smoothed her hand down one sleeve of her cream colored bliaut, frowning at the frayed edge. Looking down, she ran both hands from her waist down over her hips, trying to smooth it into place. There was no help for it, the fabric was worn, but at least the garments were clean.

The entire time she lived at Sedgeworth, Owen had not seen fit to have any garments made for her. Mayhap Garrick would not see the need either.

Her shoulders slumped and for a brief moment, she indulged in a bout of self-pity. Then, with an inner strength that would have pleased her mother, Jillian pushed her worries aside and readied herself to meet Garrick's mother. She quickly finger-combed her hair, braided it, and tied it back with a leather thong.

The water in the pitcher next to the bed was still warm, she poured it into the ceramic basin. Reaching for the fine linen cloth lying next to it, she carefully picked it up and marveled at its softness. Such luxuries had not been hers, since before she had lost her home. For a brief moment she reveled in the feeling that she was being treated as the lady of the keep.

Mayhap he will come to care for me. Jillian silently prayed that he would. Without Garrick, she could not hope to regain her family home. She needed a man with enough intellect to sway their king, but he also had to convince their ruler he could rebuild Loughmoe Keep to what it once was, a fertile holding which collected high revenues.

Garrick was a strong warrior. He would defend the land to his last breath, to his last drop of blood. Of that Jillian was certain.

Surely, the improvements he had made at his own keep would be enough to convince King William.

But her feelings toward Garrick must be set aside, otherwise they would distract her from her goal. She owed it to her parents' loving memory to regain all they had lost.

A single tear of frustration spilled over her bottom lash and followed the curve of her cheek. The land meant everything to her father. He died defending it at the bloody battle of Hastings, leaving her poor mother to defend their keep with but a handful of knights. When the Normans came, they had no choice but to flee. To stay would have meant certain death. They would have died in the forest had the Lord of Sedgeworth not taken them in.

Thinking back over all that had happened to her in the years since that time, and what she had recently learned, she wondered if they should have taken their chances in the forest. The agony of her parents' deaths remained fresh. Their memories were all she had left. Mayhap with her husband's help, she would regain a piece of her parents' legacy.

"Father always said the best memories were carried in your heart, but once we regain Loughmoe, I'll have more than memories."

The soft tapping at her door brought her out of her depression. "One moment," she called out.

The swishing of skirts outside her door made her pause in fear. Heaven help her; do not let it be Garrick's mother. Jillian's gaze swept the room, taking in her choice of clothing. Neither gown was fine enough to receive such a lady in her home. *'Tis not my home, yet.*

Running a hand over her hair, checking the braid, she shook out her skirts, braced herself, and opened the door.

"Lady Jillian?"

The woman who stood before her was beautiful. Her white-blonde hair was braided and wrapped around her head. She wore a chainse of the palest blue wool, a fine white bliaut underneath. A golden girdle accentuated her slender waist. But it was the woman's clear blue eyes that held her entranced. She was struck by the realization that Garrick had his mother's eyes.

"Aye," she replied.

"Thank Odin, and the good Lord." The woman grabbed her close and hugged her. "We have so much to talk about. Garrick can be rather closemouthed about his feelings. Have you two had a chance to get to know one another yet? Have you decided where to plant the herb gardens? What about children?"

Jillian's mouth hung open at the barrage of questions that were rapidly fired in her general direction. She didn't even attempt to answer any of them. She merely waited for the woman to slow down long enough to get a word in edgewise. Waiting like a hawk ready to pounce on unsuspecting prey, she saw her chance when the woman paused to draw a breath.

"I'm sorry, but I didn't hear you mention your name," she added politely.

"Oh, my dear, my name is Eyreka, Lady Eyreka to most. But my closest friends call me Reka."

Jillian smiled at the warmth in the older woman's manner. She hadn't felt so welcomed in a long, long time, and she needed a friend desperately.

Lady Eyreka's gaze never left Jillian's face; she flinched under the close scrutiny. Thinking the woman would make a comment about her state of dress, she was not prepared for the woman's next statement.

"If you promise not to let my son know where you heard it, I'll tell you my pet name for him when he was but a boy."

She watched Lady Eyreka pause and smile. "Ricky. I used to call my son Ricky. Of course, as he grew to be such a large man, early on, it became apparent that he no longer wished to be known by that name. Still, sometimes…" Her smile told of happy memories.

Jillian wondered what had happened to Garrick's father. Why had their mother, who obviously loved her sons, left them to fend for themselves without someone to run their household? Nay, that was not quite true, she had met Gertie and liked the housekeeper very much. There had to be more to the story. She was certain of it.

"Lady Eyreka," she began.

"Reka, please," Garrick's mother offered.

"Reka, how is Garrick this morning? I'm ashamed to admit that I have not been up these two days past, otherwise, I would have been there to greet you when you arrived. Is he well? How are Dunstan and Winslow? Is Roderick back yet?" Jillian found that she too had the ability to fire questions without coming up for air.

⤜⟫⟪⤛

THE LILTING LAUGHTER filtering out of the open door beckoned to Garrick and his shadow, MacInness, who now stood waiting impatiently for one of the women to take note of their presence.

Crossing the threshold, Garrick took Jillian's hands in his own. "Jillian, you are well?" His gaze raked her from head to toe. Finding nothing amiss, he turned to MacInness. "She's fit."

"Of course I am," Jillian grumbled, not caring to admit just how ill she had been, or how difficult she had been while fighting the fever.

At his mother's look, he explained, "She's had the fever for the last two days. Without the help of my vassal, MacInness, I never would have been able to care for her while overseeing the preparations for our vow taking."

"'Tis a pleasure to meet ye, Lady Eyreka." The Highlander bowed low over the lady's hand. Looking up he smiled across the top of her head to where Jillian stood.

"Ye look fit, lass, are ye up to this?" He could not keep the anxiety out of his voice.

"I'll be fine, thank you, Winslow. Mayhap I ought to see just what is left to be done for the feast."

"Let me lend a hand, Jillian. 'Twould not be wise to overdo your first day up." Taking the younger woman by the arm, the two descended toward the hall where frantic voices had almost reached a crescendo.

"That will be my guardian, Lady Haldana. She doesn't deal well with servants. You will try to understand," Jillian pleaded, "won't you?"

"Of course, my dear. Lead the way, there is much to be done."

When Jillian turned back to ask Garrick a question, she caught the odd look on both men's faces. She wondered just what had been going on while she lay abed. The tone of the raised voices had turned to anger. She rushed out of the chamber toward them.

"'Tis a blessin' that yer mother arrived when she did. Owen's lady is enough to drive a saint to an early grave," MacInness said.

Garrick nodded. "My mother will see to it that all will be in the ready. Have you spoken to Madelyne about the gown yet?"

"Aye, she was hoppin' on one foot in her excitement, claimin' to own just the thing. 'Tis a fine thing at least one of Owen's daughters treats her well. Why don't ye want Lady Jillian to know aboot it?"

"I have seen what little she brought with her. Her clothes are old and frayed." He clenched his jaw to contain his growing agitation. "I did not know how to broach the subject. 'Tis a woman's task. Haldana should have seen to it."

MacInness agreed, "Aye, mon. Owen's witch of a wife all but dressed her in cast-offs, hoping to discourage any suitors from looking beyond the rags she ofttimes wore."

He watched the two women disappear from view. "Her spirit is just as bright and pure as the day she arrived half-carryin' her poor mother across the stone steps of the hall." The Scot's amber eyes narrowed as if he pictured the scene in his mind.

"The rain had been coming down for three days, when the master arrived home with two wet and muddied waifs. We all thought they were to be servants. What a scene Haldana made when the lass lifted her face and dared to tell the woman not to lay a hand on her mother. She asked for no help caring for her mother, though 'twas clear to all the poor woman was dying. The lass had courage even then at four and ten."

Clearing his throat, MacInness walked down the stairs to the suddenly quiet scene below, Garrick hard at his heels.

⁂

"WHAT DO YOU mean, I've been relieved of my obligations to this dear young woman?" Haldana demanded.

"You must be exhausted from your journey and should be resting," Eyreka said.

Jillian stifled the urge to smile. Lady Eyreka had just arrived and had not stopped to refresh herself. She wanted to press the woman to at least change out of her dusty clothing, but knew that regaining control of the hall was more urgent. It was more important to soothe the ruffled feathers of Jillian's guardian in order to get her above stairs and out of the hall.

"I am quite fatigued," Haldana admitted.

"Well then, Garrick, be a dear and show Lady Haldana to her chamber." Lady Eyreka shepherded Jillian out the side door, leaving her son to do as she suggested.

With MacInness's help, the hall was emptied of females in short order, leaving a blessed silence that the men appreciated.

"I'd never thought that old harpy would leave," Patrick groaned.

"Wouldn't take a hint she was not wanted," Sean told them.

"'Twas obvious your housekeeper fairly itched to take a gag and wrap it around the woman's evil-tongued mouth," Kelly added, as Garrick returned.

"Too bad Gertie didn't let us have any fun. 'Twas certain sure that the witch would not have remained had she known what we…"

"Eamon," MacInness warned.

"Well, it worked before…"

"Dinna even start." MacInness gave him a look that brooked no arguments.

"She screeched loud enough about needing to be alone to rest. I thought she would enjoy a few hours alone below stairs, 'tis just like a tomb."

"Eamon," his brother Kelly warned.

"Well, if I wasn't afraid she'd wake the dead…"

"Aneuch," MacInness bellowed.

"Oh, aye, you damned Scot. Have it your way, but I still say 'twould have been far better to have her locked below stairs bound and gagged."

Kelly knocked his brother off his feet to silence him before their leader had a chance to cuff the man with the back of his hand.

Shaking his head, Garrick sighed. The peaceful existence he had been hoping for did not appear to lie around the corner just yet.

"Garrick," Dunstan called out as he joined the men in the hall. "Mother asked if we had any heather."

"Heather?"

"Aye, white heather. She mentioned something about it being good luck and needing it for a wreath."

"Ah, for my bride." A gleam of anticipation lit his face. His bride. The thought warmed him.

"Take Patrick or Sean to the south meadow. There should still be some blooming."

"'Tis funny, Mother swore you would know where it grew." Dunstan stopped in his tracks. "Why is that?"

"Father used to have me go and pick some to surprise her." Garrick smiled. "I used to lay it on her pillow on my way to bed, and swear the next day I did not know how it got there."

Reliving the memory, Garrick unknowingly showed a part of

himself he thought buried long ago.

"He loved her," Dunstan said quietly.

"Aye, that he did."

"Mother would want no less for each of us, brother."

Garrick shook his head. "Let it go. I have chosen the path to my future." Drawing within himself to hide the hurt, Garrick left the hall in search of the missing cleric.

CHAPTER THIRTEEN

"**'T**IS THE MOST beautiful gown I've ever seen." Jillian's voice lowered to just above a whisper as her fingertips caressed the soft wool of the deep-green chainse she wore. Only a touch to reassure herself that it wasn't a dream anymore, and she feared to snag the lovely cloth with her rough hands.

"You are beautiful," Madelyne sighed, fastening the braided green and gold ribbons of the belt into a loose knot at Jillian's waist, leaving the streamers to hang down the front.

"Lord Garrick will be pleased to look upon so fair a maid. He is fortunate to take you to wife," she added.

Jillian's throat closed. *Wife.* Her mind rebelled, thinking of her new lord and master. Then she reasoned it was simply part of their bargain. Digging deep for courage, she added, "I hope to please him."

"You'll blind him with your beauty," Gertie's voice rang out across the room. She stood in the doorway, a simple wreath of white heather in her hands. Holding it out, she said, "Lady Eyreka made this for you. 'Tis a symbol of love."

Madelyne placed the wreath on Jillian's head and stepped back.

"Perfect. You look like an angel."

"Nay," Gertie smiled. "She looks like the queen of the fae-ries."

Jillian bowed her head to hide her flaming cheeks. Her hair slid around her shoulders, enveloping her. She grabbed a strand and stared at it. It did not hold the beauty of Owen's daughters' flaxen tresses. Her color was bold. Though it forever set her apart from the other Saxon women, she treasured it for what it truly was, a gift from her Scots mother and her grandmother before her.

Jillian smoothed her gown one last time. "Is the green all right, then?" she asked hesitantly.

Gertie smiled at her while a deep voice called from the open doorway, "The green gives you color. It adds peaches to the cream of your face and throat."

Jillian blushed at Winslow's appraising look. To cover her nervousness, she attempted a teasing reply, "I hope you fixed enough food, Gertie, Winslow sounds hungry to me."

"Are ye ready then, Jillie lass?" the tall Scot asked softly.

Jillian stood rooted to the floor, the past crushing in around her. Breathing was difficult. Finally, she managed to drag the badly needed air into her burning lungs. *He couldn't know. Winslow would have no way of knowing Father's pet name for me.* She hadn't even told Lady Eyreka, though her heart longed to share it.

Her hands shook, and it took all of her will to control their trembling as she reached for the amber charm. When her fingers touched the cool stone, she calmed instantly.

The necklace had been a gift from her mother. Before that it had belonged to her grandmother, and so on, back for generations too far to recall. The oval piece of amber had a Celtic cross carved on one side and runes on the other. 'Twas rumored to hold magic. The runes inscribed read:

ᛗ (Mannaz) ᛉ (Algiz) ᛏ (Tiwaz) ᚷ (Gebo) ᛚ (Laguz)

Part of the magic was due to the ancient promise that whoever possessed the amulet *Mannaz*, would be protected *Algiz* by both the gods and a great warrior *Tiwaz*, they would form a partnership *Gebo* and their union would flow, be fertile *Laguz*.

Jillian held on to the amulet now, hoping that Garrick would be her warrior and that the ancient gods, who had forged the amulet would bless their union with fertility.

"'Tis time." Madelyne led her down the stairs to where her future was about to unfold.

⟫⟪

"SHE'S ONE OF them," Patrick whispered, crossing himself.

Sean paled. "Aye, 'tis certain she's too beautiful to be one of us."

"One of who?" Garrick asked, distracted by the fey creature slowly making her way across the broad expanse of his hall.

"The *Tuatha de Daanan*: children of the goddess, faeries," Eamon answered for his cousins, who were now speechless in the face of such beauty and purity of spirit.

"A wood sprite mayhap, her coloring mirrors those of the forest." Shaking his head at such fanciful thoughts, Garrick added, "I've held her in my arms, she's a flesh and blood woman. Make no mistake of that."

"Aye," agreed MacInness. "She is that."

The green goddess of jealousy reared her ugly head at the Scot's ready agreement. With tremendous effort, Garrick concentrated on schooling his features to show an outward calm. No one would guess the extent of his inner turmoil, and the way his gut roiled, at the thought of anyone other than himself touching the maid before him.

Sensual visions of the coming night, Jillian with her fiery waves spread upon the linen of his bed, had taken over his brain, bringing it to a fevered pitch. He had to regain control. 'Twas either that or excuse himself to dunk his head in a bucket of ice-cold well water.

Looking at her now, he berated himself; it would not do to feel too strongly about the woman he had to wed. After all, theirs was a marriage arranged for freedom, Jillian's, and a dowry not of gold, but honor, his. She loved him not; she only needed him to help her escape from her hard life and to fulfill her dream of regaining her family home. They had yet to speak of duty and expectations. Such talk would come tonight in the privacy of his chamber over a goblet of warm scented wine.

The gleam in Garrick's eye had little to do with thoughts of duty. It had more to do with the beautiful woman who had reached his side and laid a hand on his forearm.

"Garrick?"

Her trembling sent a surge of protectiveness rushing through his blood. "'Twill be over soon." Hoping to reassure his bride, he covered her hand with his. The tremulous smile of thanks lighting her face was more than worth the effort it cost him to appear unaffected by her presence.

Garrick's brothers stood behind him, ready to make formal declaration of his worldly goods and assets. Saddened with the notion that his lady had no blood relatives to do so for her, he still glimpsed behind his bride-to-be, knowing one of his vassals would speak for her. He was surprised at the sight of MacInness and his men standing behind Jillian as her family.

A final glance about the room satisfied him that all was in readiness. Owen's cleric had come to act as one of the witnesses and to record the marriage contract. Grimly, he realized that the more witnesses, the better. He would have no one gainsay him on the fact that he had wed the maid standing next to him. He did not trust Owen's family to truthfully speak on his behalf, should the day ever come that the validity of their marriage be questioned.

With a nod, Garrick took hold of Jillian's small hand. Dunstan strode forward and cleared his throat to speak.

"My brother brings to this marriage, Merewood Keep and the lands immediately surrounding it as far north as the stream, west to the edge of the third fallow field, thence east to the edge of the forest, and south to the rock wall."

When he paused, Jillian looked nervously about. Garrick could sense her unease. He brushed a wavy lock off her brow and smiled down at her. Jillian's response warmed him tenfold. Her smile was so brilliant he missed half of what his brother continued to list.

"...eighty knights, fifty men-at-arms. Three mares, one stallion, three cows, one bull..."

He lost his train of thought again as his lady tightened her grip on his hand. Whatever else Dunstan had said went right over his head. He glanced over his shoulder to where the cleric's hand practically flew across the piece of parchment in his haste to record what little he had to offer.

MacInness stepped forward and cleared his throat. "The lass, my Lady Jillian, brings her beauty, strength, spirit, and seeds of the next generation to grace this mon's home. May he come to ken the true gift he is gettin' this day."

His voice seemed to catch before he could continue. "With it a bolt of finely woven blue cloth, a set of twelve carved wooden trenchers, three ewes, and one ram." Throughout his recitation, his eyes never left Owen's face.

Jillian's gasp of surprise was audible. She looked first to Winslow, who was smiling broadly, then to Garrick, whose gaze was fixed on his vassal with a look that silently questioned. But MacInness had turned to stare at Owen, who looked as if he had swallowed salted fish that had not been properly soaked to remove all of the preservative.

She started to speak, but Garrick silenced her with the pressure of his hand, as if not quite understanding how or why it happened, she had come to the marriage with a dowry. Her expression brightened and her eyes filled up. She looked over her shoulder and smiled at MacInness.

But MacInness was not finished.

"I canna tell ye exactly, but when the king reinstates

Loughmoe Keep to its rightful inheritor, Lady Jillian will be bringin' with her that fertile holding and all lands there and aboot it." His hand to his heart, he spoke reverently. "Lastly, I give my word of honor to protect the lass with my life."

Turning to look behind him, he nodded to his men who, one after another, repeated their pledge to honor and protect the new lady of the keep.

Bewildered, Lady Jillian dared a furtive glance at her former guardians who stood red-faced, but silent. Garrick wondered if her reaction was due to the pronouncement that Winslow and his Irish Contingent were pledged to Merewood Keep, or was it the part about her family home?

He was nudged. With the exchange of lands and goods having been duly recorded, it was time for him to pledge himself to Jillian.

"I vow to protect that which is mine from this day until I breathe my last, and so say it before these witnesses in the eyes of God." His gaze held hers while he silently asked, *Can you love me, lass?*

Jillian's lips slightly parted, her gaze transfixed on his face. Was she thinking of the repercussions just now? Did she realize what he was offering her? Then she blinked, twice.

"I, too, vow to protect that which is mine." She smiled at him, sealing her promise. "I willingly agree to bring forth any babes the Lord blesses us with and to love them with all my heart." He searched her eyes. Deep in her soul, her silent plea surfaced: *Please, let me love you.*

Garrick breathed a sigh of relief, "'Tis done." He touched the tip of his forefinger to her chin lifting her sweet lips. He touched them gently at first.

She was here. She was real.

The kiss became more demanding as his passion flared high, burning brightly. His bride melted against him, her curves filling the hollows of his body.

Breaking away before his will left him completely, Garrick

smiled down at Jillian. Her eyes were glazed over, and she seemed incapable of speech. It was a boost to his male pride that his kisses had such an effect on her. Aye, she'd warm his bed and bear his children. His seed would take hold this night, that he vowed. *Mayhap she is the one.*

"Lord Owen," a voice shouted above the cheers of the guests.

"Aye," he answered.

His manservant rushed over to him, explaining, "A messenger has arrived from the king."

The room fell silent. Expectancy filled Garrick's chest. That the king would reinstate Jillian's land on this day was great luck. There was no doubt in his mind that she would be more than willing in his bed once he held Loughmoe within his grasp.

He turned, his lips broadening into a smile and saw Owen's pale face flush crimson. The man visibly struggled for composure; his anger was a living, breathing omen.

"The king did what?" Owen thundered. "'Tis not possible, I specifically requested that I be named—" Owen stopped, whipping around to meet Garrick's gaze, "I must speak with you privately."

He placed a swift kiss to his bride's brow and said, "Follow me."

The silence that followed the men out of the hall was broken by muffled crashes of wood splintering. "Nay, Merewood, you do not understand!" Another crash, this time it sounded like metal smashing against stone. "I have no control over our king's mind."

MacInness and his men ran to avert further destruction, pushing the heavy door wide open.

Garrick had one hand wrapped around Owen's throat, pinning him to the wall. "You said 'twould be mine. I say you lied."

"I never actually said that it would be."

His fingers tightened, "I should kill you for that."

Garrick's plans for a well-mapped future evaporated. A shaft of pain lanced straight through the middle of him. He had been joined in wedlock to a woman who could bring him nothing—his people would starve!

She knew. Jillian must have known of the king's decision. 'Twould explain her eagerness to wed him. It had nothing to do with regaining her home. She knew it was not possible. God's blood, had she used him as her escape from an intolerable life of servitude? His head began to pound; there would be no coin, no livestock, no land. His heart whispered to him that he had not been betrayed, it whispered of love, passion, and healing.

His vision blurred until he saw only deception. Denying the voice, he squeezed harder. His fingers ached with the effort. A sudden sharp pain at the back of his skull released his grip on the neck he sought to break.

The haze cleared. "Dear God, will I ever be forgiven?" Garrick was surprised to find himself surrounded with his arms restrained behind his back.

"Forgiven for what?" MacInness asked, giving a nod signaling his men to release Garrick.

His head throbbed like it had been cleaved in twain, while his heart ached for all that it had hoped to possess. The promised love lying just within reach, dangling in front of his face, had been snatched away. God forgive him, he had no choice but to honor his first vow, for the good of his family and his people.

He had to set aside his bride.

Bone deep sorrow was followed by intense pain as the emotions crashed through to his breastbone. He had no choice. Denying his thoughts, refusing to acknowledge the unfamiliar feeling that grew insidiously there, he steeled himself to speak.

"King William has just granted Loughmoe Keep to Henri du Guerre."

Not waiting for the news to take hold, he went in search of his bride. Jillian stood waiting beside his mother, the wringing of his bride's hands her only outward sign of emotion.

Bile rushed up his throat as Garrick faced her. Never before had he broken his word. His honor was all to him. That he had to do so now nearly drove the breath from his chest and life from his heart. But his vow to love and honor her came second only to the vow he had pledged three years past; when his own life's blood mingled with that of those that had fallen protecting his keep.

Clenching his jaw, he bitterly blamed the woman standing before him for her part in his betrayal. He swallowed the bitter taste of it and lashed out at her, "You knew of the king's decision to award your land to du Guerre. I never would have had the chance to fight for that which was already lost. Would I? You lured me to Sedgeworth with the promise of aiding my brother. That's when you sank your hooks in deep, speaking of legacies lost, a story so like my own that I could not refuse."

Her eyes grew round with what, fear? He steeled himself not to care. Unmercifully he continued, "You deceived me and you cared not that you secured my help with false promises. Deny if you are able that you knew nothing of this," he challenged.

He waited for Jillian to answer the charges he angrily hurled at her, knowing in his heart, he was not yet capable of listening.

She stood silent; chin held high, back straight.

Anger forced him to do what he must. His grand plans to secure wealth and position for his family and prosperity for his people had gone so far awry, naught could be done to straighten them. His final failure loomed before him, taunting him. He would never be the same caliber of warrior as his father. His mind rebelled as his heart cried out for one last chance to set to rights the ruins of his family's life. Garrick would forsake all his hopes and dreams to turn back the clock to relive those last few days before the Normans had stormed across Northumbria, crushing all who dared to oppose them. Had he known his father would break all bargains in a bid to lead his keep's people into battle, he would have used all manner of tricks to best his father in single-handed combat.

His wisdom came from the past. He did not know his father would rather die than let his eldest son take his place leading their people against the Normans. Nor did he realize that by challenging his father to fight for the right to lead their people, he had forced his father's hand. Addison had used the techniques he learned while fighting in the Highlands. Garrick never stood a chance against the awesome combination of his father's superior strength and the crafty maneuvers. His thoughts shifted back to the present.

His bride stood before him unconsciously assuming an all too familiar pose, one of defiance. Garrick had used a similar one when the superb fighting force of King William's men had splintered through Merewood's wooden palisade. His determination had gained him naught, save the tremendous blood loss that accompanied the gash in his side and the wound at his temple.

His chest constricted with pain. He would never be able to forgive himself for leaving his keep indefensible. He would carry the burden of his father's death and the loss of their home inside him always. The only way to live with his conscience would be to continue to rebuild Merewood and restore it to its former glory. With his mother once again safe within its walls, all would return to normal.

Jillian's treachery cost him dearly. He must break his vow to her in order to regain all for his mother, his brothers, and his peoples' children … rail-thin, ragged children who constantly cried out in hunger. He would do whatever necessary to feed his people. They depended upon him; they were the future of Merewood Keep. He could not let them down again.

He turned toward his wife and held out his arm. She lay her fingers lightly upon his arm. He could feel her fingers trembling. Ignoring it, he escorted her to the wedding feast.

The gaiety that had surrounded the newly wedded couple dimmed as news of the king's proclamation spread. The wedding celebrations continued, though subdued.

After what he deemed to be a proper amount of time for the guests to enjoy the feast, he leaned towards his wife. The time had come to confront her. "I would speak with you privately. Now."

Jillian nodded.

Once in his chamber, he turned to face her. She obviously waited to hear what he would say to the untimely news. Would she finally speak and offer proof of her innocence? They faced one another in silence.

"Stop wringing your hands." She jumped, startled by his harsh tone, but obeyed, dropping her arms to her sides.

Struggling to keep the hatred from his voice he asked, "Have you betrayed me, wife?"

The color completely drained from her face; her eyes widened with shock. With all his heart, Garrick wanted to believe her shock was genuine and that she played no part in the treachery surrounding him. He stepped closer, towering over her. He had to ask, he needed proof. He had to know!

"Did you and Owen plan to entrap my brother? Did he tell you to send word to me with your grand plans of marriage in exchange for my brother's life, when in fact he was simply held prisoner for show?"

Hand to her throat, she backed away a couple of paces. "Nay. It was not like that!"

He glared at her. "How can I trust you? Where is the proof I seek?"

⸫⸫⸫⸫⸫

SOMETHING HARDENED INSIDE her at his words. She spoke as if to a child, "I cannot give you the proof you so dearly seek, milord. I have but my word. You have to trust me." Even as she said the words, she knew he would not be able to do so. He was a warrior, a leader of men. Proof of deeds done were as necessary as the vows behind them.

Her eyes filled. Her entire future with the man before her depended upon his decision here and now.

"I must weigh your words against what has passed here today. Until such time as I have come to a decision, you will remain here in my chamber."

Turning on his heel, he slammed the door closed without a backward look. Her husband of but a few hours was gone, the back of his head a forewarning of things to come. Jillian hugged her arms to her body to drive away the chill that had taken root in the very marrow of her bones.

She had traded one form of prison for another. Her jailer, while fairer of face, was far stronger than Haldana. She dreaded the thought of the beating that would surely follow. Sinking to the floor, she wept bitterly.

GARRICK COULD NOT bear to see her naked pain. For a split second, he doubted that she was aware of the fact that her land had been awarded to a Norman baron. But his pride was great and his honor had been destroyed by the woman who had stood before him quietly refusing to show proof of her innocence.

No one contradicted his order to keep Jillian from his sight. In fact, no one spoke to him. One by one, his family and guests left the hall, their unuttered censure of his conduct hanging thick in the air, choking him.

Someone coughed. Looking up at the sound, he saw MacInness watching him closely. "I had no choice. I have to be certain."

"No choice? Ye didna have to accuse her of such treachery, mon."

"I never said—"

"'Tis your silence, mon, it reeked of accusation. Have ye any proof? Dinna ye see her pain? Ye gave her no choice. She's smart enough to realize that ye wouldna believed her had she spoken the truth while starin' God himself in the face!"

"You don't understand," Garrick rasped, "I've failed, again. I have to set her aside and find another wife. One whose dowry can rebuild—"

"'Tis sorry I am that I didna ken the true manner of mon ye are. I'll see to the lass's protection then I'll finish my service to ye. Ask no more, ye're no' deservin' of it."

The sharp edge of his vassal's words cut deeply. Garrick buried his face in his hands. No one understood. The decision had been taken from him three years ago when their keep's defenses crumbled. Those that survived the Norman onslaught had nearly starved that first winter. The years in between had been little better.

He could not confide in his brothers. The responsibility was his and his alone. From the moment his father fell in battle, Merewood Keep and all the burdens it entailed rested solely upon his shoulders.

If he appeared self-serving, concerned with rebuilding and the coin involved, then so be it. It was but a small portion of the guilt he would live with the rest of his life.

Chapter Fourteen

"**I** WILL NOT have it!" Lady Eyreka shouted.

Gertie shook her head at the volume of the argument that had been raging for the last half-hour. The tide had turned, with Garrick losing ground quickly. His mother was in the right and he knew it. All he had to do was admit it, stubborn lad.

"Need I remind you, Mother, I do indeed have the right to treat my wife any way I choose. I choose to leave her locked in my chamber. Her treachery has cost this family everything." His face darkened with barely concealed anger.

"You cannot condemn her. You have not yet let her speak. Mayhap she is innocent." Her voice had dropped to a normal level.

When he remained silent, she turned to face her son. "I know you are possessed with the rebuilding of Merewood. I take full blame for that. I never should have agreed to stay away while you tried to straighten out your life here. Had I known you would heap more blame upon yourself for something you had no control over, I would never have gone.

"I beg you now to speak to Jillian. Hear her out. Mayhap you will come to know her, trust her."

"Trust her? She deceived me from the start."

"Did she? Listen to yourself, Son, you are grasping at straws. You cannot change the past or undo that which has been done.

The future is yours to do with what you will. You do have control over the rest of your life. Give her a chance. Together you two can build a future that will survive. William is a fair king, he is not too quick to condemn, and neither should you be. Judge not, my dear son." She whirled away from him and quit the chamber.

His mother's words tumbled around inside of him until he thought his head would split. She was right. God's teeth, was the woman never wrong? He could not undo the past, but his words and deeds could have a definite effect on the future. But 'twas not just his future. So many others depended upon him.

Pacing in front of the newly finished south wall, he stopped to get a handle on his rising temper. He let himself be distracted by the quality of the workmanship. The planks that made up the wall were well matched and fitted tightly together. They would fare much better this winter, but what of the crofters in need of new thatching? He would have to see to those repairs soon.

Looking around, he saw his home taking shape. It would soon be done. Work had accelerated under the direction of MacInness and his men. The workers toiled from dawn 'til dusk, stopping only to refuel their tired bodies.

Garrick winced as he slowly rotated his shoulder. His sword arm was unbearably slow to regain its mobility. The daily practicing in the open bailey had gone a long way toward strengthening his left arm, but it would take months to build it up to the strength necessary to wield the heavy broadsword with accuracy.

He descended the steps into the sunlit bailey. Five of his knights were engaged in hand-to-hand combat with mace and hammer. Several others were battling with shield and broadsword. He watched MacInness put them through the paces, while off to the left, he watched Patrick instruct more of his men taking turns making a pass at the quintain. His defenses had not been this strong since the Uprising. Garrick felt a surge of energy pulsing through his veins. He needed the outlet physical exertion would bring. Aye, he thought to himself, 'twould do him good to take out his pent-up rage on the practice field.

Starting with the very basic strengthening of his arm, he hefted a large stone in his hand and lifted his arm parallel to the ground. The burning sensation sweeping up from his wrist all the way to his shoulder caused the sweat to bead up on his forehead and the back of his neck. With slow, controlled movements, he repeated the exercise.

After what seemed like an eternity, he lowered the rock and unsheathed his broadsword. The weight of it pulled the newly healed scar tissue holding the muscle and tendons together. To give in to the pain would have been glorious, but Garrick had never done so before. He would not start now.

"Milord?" Garrick whirled around to face the one brave enough to approach him. No one, save his mother or Gertie, had spoken to him these two weeks past.

MacInness stood stiffly at attention waiting his lord's acknowledgment. Garrick lowered his sword. "Aye?"

"Dunstan reported that the north fields have been cleared, readied for planting. The blacksmith's hut and the tanner's are to be thatched on the morrow."

A sigh escaped before Garrick could stop himself. All proceeded according to plan. Everything that could be accomplished, using what building materials already existed on his land, had been done. 'Twas almost finished. The crofter's huts were being repaired and plans for an early harvest would be well under way by the time he returned from his audience with the king. The harvest would be a small one; not nearly enough, but better than nothing at all.

His head reeled with imagined repercussions to the request he would dare put to his king. Would William grant it to him? Would he intervene with the church court and help him secure the annulment he sought, or would he simply refuse to see him, leaving Garrick no alternative but to set his wife aside. Could he set her aside, breaking his vow before God and man?

Rubbing a hand over his heart, he was surprised to find that it ached, deeply, telling him his plans were wrong. Nothing could replace what his family had lost; nothing would bring his father back from the dead. Mayhap 'twas just his wishful thinking spurring him onward toward the end of his quest.

Lost in thought, his mind wandered toward the chamber where his wife, nay bride—he had not been able to bring himself to consummate the marriage—slept. His distrust of her would not allow him to let down his defenses enough to approach her as a husband had every right to. It would be like sleeping with the enemy. There was no proof of her innocence, and the damned woman still refused to answer his accusations.

Best to think of the coin he would gain once he remarried. Coin that would secure livestock, grain, and a better supply of food than his people had seen these three winters past. He had to put his own wants and needs aside. As lord and master of the keep, hundreds of lives depended upon his ability to provide for them. If their meager crops failed again, like last year, his people would starve. He could not live with himself, knowing his people's children were cold and hungry.

Would that he were a simple man, one that served a master such as himself. Then he could claim Jillian, as a husband should, without the worry and heartache he alone as Lord of the Keep suffered.

JILLIAN SAT IN the room that had become her own since the day she wed Garrick. The pain of his accusations had not lessened though a fortnight had passed. He did not trust her. He thought she lied.

Fear of the unknown washed through her, leaving her knees weak. Would he set her aside? Would she be forced to go back to live at Sedgeworth? Nay. That would be intolerable. Somehow she would convince Garrick of her innocence and remain his wife. *But how?*

Thinking back to her guardian's actions after learning of the king's decision, she shuddered. Owen and Haldana had gathered their daughters together and left for London within an hour of the messenger's announcement. They must have had grand plans of introducing their daughters at Court. Hoping, no doubt, to arrange a marriage with Henri du Guerre, the new Lord of Jillian's family home.

Garrick avoided her. Though he told her he would think about what to do, he had not approached her since that day. Shame had been her constant companion. What good was her word when no one trusted her to keep it? The man she had come to care for believed she planned to entrap him, and would use her body to entice him with the lure of her family holding as bait.

Didn't he understand she wasn't like that? No man had ever made her feel even a small portion of what Garrick could accomplish with a look. She had never lain with a man. How had he come to the conclusion that she had? Was it her words, her lack of manners? What had she done to convince him of her guilt?

"Mother, what can I do?" she silently asked. "He cannot wait to rid himself of my presence." Bowing her head, she fought the heartache and the debilitating pain accompanying it. Though tears burned behind her eyes, she refused to give in to them. It was useless, they would solve nothing, but to add a shade of red to the black circles 'round her eyes.

The answer came to her while she prayed; her mother's oft-spoke words: *Be as yourself, my child. You have much to offer a man. Courage, spirit, and love. Garrick will come to love you for yourself. Patience.*

"Lady Jillian," Gertie called, knocking on the door, before opening it.

"Aye," she answered weakly, watching the door slowly open.

"Are you well, child?" The concern in the housekeeper's voice touched a chord deep within her.

"As well as can be hoped." She massaged her aching forehead.

"We wish a word with you."

Jillian was startled to find not only Gertie, but Lady Eyreka as well, waiting to enter her room.

"Pray, enter." She motioned toward two small chairs with cushioned seats and backs.

Once the women were seated, she pressed them. "What can I do for you?"

Clearing her throat, Lady Eyreka spoke, "Gertie and I have thought long and hard about your situation here. We are both of the same mind. Garrick cares for you."

Jillian shook her head violently, denying it.

"Please, hear us out before disagreeing," Eyreka pleaded.

She watched them, but said nothing.

"Garrick is readying the keep for his journey to London. If he were to see how well you run his household, mayhap, he will postpone his journey. Is it not worth a try?"

Jillian considered the possibility.

"Give him time, my dear, he has lost so much."

"And have I not also lost everything I hold dear?" Her frustration rose giving way to anger. "My father died at Hastings, leaving only my mother, myself, and a few housecarls to defend our home. We were no match for the Normans when they arrived to crush those Saxons brave enough to rise up against them."

Jillian's face twisted in anguish as she was caught up in her dark memories. "We had to flee our home and hide in the woods. We had no one. Every last one of our household knights were cut down."

Dry-eyed, she recounted that black night three years earlier when her world had come to an end. "Their blood slickened the stone steps of my home. My mother suffered from shock," she rasped, "and never recovered. She was not strong enough to face life without my father. 'Twas up to me, but even I could not save her."

"After we escaped, we waited in the wood just west of our home. We lived off the forest for a week before Owen found us." Her hands closed into fists as she shouted at them, "Don't you see? I had no choice! My mother was starving to death. The loss of our home was the final blow. Without Loughmoe to remind her of Father, her will to live vanished. 'Twas naught else to be done. Owen's offer of shelter seemed our last chance."

Eyreka's eyes glistened, as did Gertie's. The young woman before them had been wronged in the past and stood wronged yet again.

"Jillian, please hear me out," Eyreka pleaded. Not waiting for agreement, she continued, "Join us below stairs. Cook is waiting for instructions for the midday meal. The rushes are littered with bone and remains of the evening meal. Someone must see to their care. Herbs must be freshened."

"But why haven't you seen to this?" Jillian asked.

"Garrick must see you in the role of mistress before he leaves. You can make a difference in his life here. Please try. He knows it not, but he needs you."

Her clear blue gaze added yet another plea. Garrick was her son. Unless Jillian misunderstood, Eyreka was asking her to do all in her power to save him from himself. How could she say aye? How could she say nay?

"Why is he so obsessed with rebuilding? What happened here that scarred him so?" Jillian waited expectantly for the riddle to be solved.

"Mayhap 'tis best if you put your questions to my son."

After a brief silence, Jillian agreed. "Aye, but will he afford me the opportunity to speak with him? I am little better than prisoner here."

"How can you say that? Are you not well fed? Is the gown you now wear not of the finest wool? Do you not sleep on finely woven linens?" Eyreka's point hit home.

"But I am not free to go about as I please. I am kept under lock and key with a guard by my door. Is it not enough that he intends to set me aside? Must he twist the blade of distrust so cruelly?"

Jillian's heart wrenched with pain at the thought of Garrick's promised retribution. She had been filled with renewed hope after their first meeting. He had been attentive and caring. But his mother was right, though the weight of impending disaster crushed in upon her, she owed Garrick something for taking her out of purgatory.

"Ask Garrick to explain why he torments himself with burdens from the past. I will arrange a meeting. My son will do this for me."

Jillian trembled, thinking of the upcoming confrontation that was now unavoidable.

"Are you afraid of him, then?"

Her mind raced down the dark tunnel toward the unknown. *Unknown.* Aye, that was all that she feared. Her only memories of Garrick were solicitous. He had never raised a hand toward her in anger. His hands had been gentle the time she had awakened from swooning. Straightening her backbone, she stood before Lady Eyreka and answered.

"I do not fear him. I'll accompany you. There is work to be done and though I may not be for long, I am mistress of this keep. Shall we start in the kitchen? Mayhap Cook has some thyme to add to our evening stew?"

The three women hugged one another, drawing the inner strength necessary to go on. The one who could save the heir to Merewood was willing to try against all odds. Surely God would aid them in their quest.

"OPEN THE GATE," a guard announced from atop the curtain wall. "Roderick's back."

Roderick and his escort of three stout looking men-at-arms

rode into the open bailey. A shout from one of the upper windows of the keep hailed him.

Raising a hand to deflect the midmorning glare, he looked up, but saw no one. He dismounted and led his horse to a much-improved stable. The side planks that had been broken were replaced. The reinforced stalls were now occupied with prime horseflesh. Obviously some things had improved with his brother's marriage.

"I trust all went well at Fitzrandolph's holding?" Garrick asked.

"The Lady Beatrice was not unaffected by your announcement, but I managed to smooth over her ruffled feelings."

Roderick's broad grin suggested another conquest in the name of love. But Garrick had more weighty problems on his mind; the possibility of covering up another of his brother's indiscretions would have to wait for another time.

"Do you think she would consider me as husband?"

"Husband? Did you not bid me tell her of your marriage to Lady Jillian?"

"Aye." Pain knifed through Garrick. Cinnamon brown eyes and fiery waves beckoned to him. The promise of passion unfulfilled taunted him. God's breath, would he never rid his mind of her presence?

Not knowing of any way around it, Garrick decided on the direct approach. He told his brother all that had transpired during his two-week absence.

"Jillian would not betray you," Roderick said angrily. "Do you honestly think the almighty Owen of Sedgeworth would confide in a woman, one he considered less than a servant? Have you gone mad? What would Jillian have to gain by such treachery?"

Roderick's heated response had been no less than Garrick expected. His brother put his life at risk once for her; obviously there was a connection between them. "She would gain a way out of bondage, free to live the life of a lady."

Garrick paused before adding his strongest argument, "She would gain the sword arm of a warrior intelligent enough to bargain with his king for her land. One strong enough to defend it."

Unnerving silence met Garrick's ready answer.

The sorrow-filled gray gaze that met his own put a chink in the armor of his indifference. His youngest brother had their father's eyes. It was their father he imagined looking at him now.

"I say that you have become so blinded by your obsession that you are about to throw away the only chance at true happiness you will ever be granted." Roderick's level gaze held, while Garrick's wavered. "What has Jillian said to the charges against her?"

Uncertainty knifed through Garrick. *Mayhap he had misjudged her.* Unable to look his brother in the eye, Garrick answered his feet. "Nothing."

"Nothing? Did she not defend herself?"

Garrick hesitated. "I did not give her the chance. We have not spoken since the wedding feast."

Roderick charged his unsuspecting brother and knocked him right off his feet. Pinning him to the straw-covered stable floor, Roderick demanded, "Why? What has she done to you to deserve such treatment? Did she not fulfill her agreement? Am I not alive because of her intervention?"

Raw anger surged through him, a living, breathing emotion. The frustration of the past weeks erupted from deep within him. Garrick violently twisted the upper half of his body and flung his brother across the width of the stable.

Roderick landed hard against one of the old walls, cracking it. Before he could shake off the aftereffects of his flight, Garrick was on him. Pummeling him.

Roderick fought back with an intensity that surprised them both.

The bucket of water dousing them with its icy coldness had the desired effect. They both turned to leap on the intruder, but they were not fast enough. MacInness and Patrick held the raging bull that was Garrick, while Sean and Kelly pinned Roderick against the floor. Eamon stood at the door to the stable smiling, holding another bucket full of water.

"Are ye ready to listen, mon?" MacInness shouted into Garrick's face.

Silence.

"'Tis no' bad enough that ye locked yer bride in her chamber, but to lather yer own kin when he only just arrived home from doin' yer biddin' is beyond what a mon has a right to do."

Garrick could feel the clenched muscle in his jaw tick in reaction to the Highlander's impassioned speech. He held onto his temper, and with great effort breathed deeply to try to cap it off.

"Mayhap our fearless leader is in a temper because it's guilt he's feelin'," Sean suggested.

"Oh, aye," Patrick agreed. "His bonny bride has been locked away for a fortnight. Her winsome ways have not had a chance to soothe the beast."

"Not that she would," Eamon bit out.

"Enough," Garrick bellowed.

"Nay, mon. It wilna be enough until ye speak to yer bride. Hear her out. She deserves better treatment from ye, and I mean to see that she gets it." MacInness's fist was a hair's breath away from Garrick's nose. He counted twenty freckles on the man's brawny knuckles.

From the corner of his eye, he noticed Roderick had been released, though Sean and Kelly still flanked him.

"Lady Jillian deserves better than you, brother. I'll return to Fitzrandolph's holding after I speak to Jillian. If you do not wish to remain wedded, who am I to stop you? I will offer myself in your place. Mayhap she agreed to wed you, Garrick, but she told me 'twas only because you asked. Had I not suggested otherwise, she would have wed me."

His vassal helped him to his feet. "'Tis no shame upon ye that ye no' want to bed any other than yer bride. She's a beautiful woman, lovin' and warm. Make her yer wife. Can ye no' find it in your heart to at least listen to what she has to say? Ye'll no' regret it. There's a fire burnin' inside her. Do ye want another mon to set it free? I couldna."

The wily Scot's words hit home. He had been tormenting himself with the image of Jillian lying in his bed, her long auburn waves wrapping around him as her slender limbs entwined with his own.

Would she willingly accept him after the accusations he hurled at her? Would she fight his right to bed her? Those questions and more raged through him, but the most important one of all nagged at him, taunting him. How could he bed her one time and walk away?

If he honored his second vow, he would forsake the first. How then would he feed his people come winter?

God help him, he had not the answers.

CHAPTER FIFTEEN

THE HEAVENLY AROMA of fresh baked bread wafted in on the breeze wending its way under the door to the hall. Garrick paused to breathe deeply, then pushed it open. The sight greeting him closed his throat with emotion.

The stone floor had been swept clean of the old rushes and fresh ones lay strewn about. As he stepped into the room, the pleasant fragrance of herbs teased him. Though he could not identify the scent that rose to greet him with each new step, he definitely appreciated their addition.

The hall had been rearranged. The long table that used to stand at the center of the south wall now stood out in the middle of the room at one end. Benches were placed at intervals along the empty length of the wall. A grouping of chairs had been placed near the brazier at the opposite end of the room from the table.

Though the walls were bare, Garrick knew his mother would begin sewing another tapestry; her hands were never idle. The state of the hall was a good sign. It meant his mother had forgiven him.

Garrick's brow furrowed at the thought of his bride waiting for him above stairs. For the first time in his life, he actually considered putting his own needs before that of his people.

Gertie's voice mingled with softer tones drew his immediate

attention, and then he saw her. "Lady Jillian."

Betrayer, his mind screamed. *Innocent,* his heart cried back. The war going on within him threatened to tear him apart. He had to speak to her—listen to her. She had never done anything to warrant his charges against her. It had been his own guilt speaking. Looking down into her angelic face, it was hard to hold out against her.

The past two weeks had gone by swiftly, though he had not set eyes on her, she had been in his thoughts. The never-ending list of tasks left unfinished each evening. Each dawn bringing another day filled with the backbreaking chore of setting to rights a home left too long in ruins. Not only coin was required, but a score of men who accomplished much in one day.

Now as Garrick looked upon his bride, shame for breaking his vow to her, and for accusing her without proof, battled against the worry that his people would starve. He was a man tormented. He glanced at his mother and realized there was wisdom in his mother's order to hear Jillian's side of the story. He nodded to her before turning his attention to his bride.

"You are looking well, Lady Jillian."

She stared up at him.

Sweeping a hand around him, he said, "The hall looks fine."

Still she didn't speak. "Jillian," he tried again.

"I would have a word with you, Son." Lady Eyreka's tone brooked no argument.

"Later."

"Nay, Ricky, now."

At the use of his boyhood name, Garrick turned to stare down at the woman who gave him life. Her eyes flashed blue fire, though she smiled sweetly. Threads of the past wrapped around his heart, memories of his mother looking lovingly at his father drifted across his mind. He had taken it all away from her. He owed his mother whatever she asked.

"Aye, Mother, now," he relented. Mayhap someday he would be able to fully atone for his past sins. It was best to start now, it was sure to take a lifetime.

They left the hall by the side door and walked through the newly weeded herb garden, down past the kitchens where the savory aroma of rabbit stew mingled with the fresh green scent of spring.

Eyreka stopped beneath the base of an oak tree. Turning around, she looked up at her eldest son.

"You must speak to Jillian. You know I cannot countenance the treatment you have meted out. 'Tis a cruel punishment to cage one so full of life as her. She grows restless with the lack of duties, pale from lack of sun."

Drawing herself up, throwing her shoulders back, Lady Eyreka locked gazes with her son. "I asked her to join me in the hall where she would act as mistress of the keep."

"Do not add to her grief by letting her have a taste of such power. 'Twill only be taken away."

"So you have a care for her feelings then?" She pressed him.

He shrugged, he did have feelings for her. "'Tis unfair what you ask."

Hands clasped behind her back, Eyreka paced beneath the tree. "Can you not tell her what is in your heart? She is willing to assume her rightful role as mistress. Jillian is more than able to care for your home and more."

"Our home, Mother," Garrick added quietly.

"Nay, 'tis your home now, Son. You and Jillian will fill it with the sounds of love and laughter. Addison would have expected you to step into his role as Lord of this Keep. You have come a long way toward rebuilding; don't stop just short of the real goal. Secure our future. Give me grandchildren."

His heart answered immediately, but his vow to help his people held out against his mother. "I will consider it." Garrick made his way to the stable with long, purposeful strides.

SORROW ETCHED YET another line near her mouth. The weight of it made smiling impossible. But for now she was free. She hoped there was enough time to prove to her husband that she knew nothing of Owen's plans. She was innocent of the blame heaped at her door. There had to be a way to show Garrick the truth. She knew he had to be able to hold the truth in his hands. To see it for himself.

Her aching heart twisted painfully as the answer made itself known. *Her home.* The answer was so simple she almost passed over it. It was a last resort, and mayhap the king would not even grant her an audience, but if it would clear her of all charges in her husband's eyes, it would be worth the agony she would live with for the rest of her life if the king agreed.

"Lady Jillian?" Gertie came up from behind her, concern marring her usually placid features.

"Let's see to the serving of my husband's men. They are working down by the smithy's hut. Send someone to fetch them."

That command given, Jillian felt a small surge of satisfaction. At least she could care for the knights who slaved to rebuild Merewood. God willing, Garrick would need them to rebuild Loughmoe. If only she could be there to see it happen. Shaking her head, she realized that if she continued on her present path, that day would never come.

The days flowed into one another, an endless stream of sameness that would haunt Jillian for a long time. Each day, she sought out her husband to speak to him of her possible solution to their problem. Was it not enough that she be willing to give up everything for the man? Could he not spare her a moment of his time so she could tell him so?

After a fortnight of trying, she accepted the fact that he had no desire to speak to her alone. Did he have second thoughts about the hurtful accusations he hurled at her?

"Nay," she answered aloud. "My husband cares naught what becomes of me. So long as he rebuilds his home, he will be happy. 'Twill be the loss of my family holding that 'twill cut more deeply than the loss of an unwanted wife."

Fingering the amulet that lay cool against her chest, she choked back the tears threatening to fall. Her grandmother had been wrong; the amulet did not protect the wearer from harm. Her warrior had forsaken his vow. There would be no partnership, no children, no future. Mayhap the magic of the ancients was too weak to find its way to her.

FOR THE FIRST time in her life, Jillian was ready to admit defeat. The loss of her parents and their home, and the subsequent life of drudgery that followed, had been far easier to bear than the unwanted beginnings of love that had blossomed only to wither and die at the first sign of adversity.

Lord, help her, she did not want to care for Garrick, but his gentle treatment and promises of a future together bound him to her. She wanted to hate him for locking her in her chamber, but she could not. During her time alone, her mind had accepted what her heart could not. Her own father would have acted the same way. Too many instances occurred pointing the finger of guilt at her. A man of logic would not be able to see it any other way.

"Jillie lass, where are you off to?"

Winslow's brogue soothed her, while the concern filling his amber gaze left her feeling unsettled.

"To tend my...er milord's herbs." She hoped Winslow would not notice the slip of her tongue. One of the first duties she had taken over since gaining her freedom was that of tending the kitchen gardens. The herbs now grew unhampered, the weeds choking them long gone. When working the soil around them, she had thought of them as her own. It was only temporary. By the end of the harvest, she would be gone.

The warmth of Winslow's large hands around her own

caused a shiver to dance up her spine. Looking up, she saw more than she wanted to. Her husband's vassal was not trying to hide his feelings from her. His amber eyes grew molten with each ragged breath he drew.

"Please, don't…you cannot care for me," her voice broke. "I belong to another."

"Nay, lass. Ye belong to no mon. The lord of this keep sleeps with his men in the lower level. 'Tis no' a secret he plans to set ye aside." He stopped to catch a crystalline tear with the tip of his finger, while his thumb wiped along her lower lashes capturing still more tears.

"Dinna cry for the mon. He's no' worth it."

Tears of frustration let loose at the kind words spoken by a man who had done more than protect her; he had given her his friendship. She didn't pull away when Winslow drew her against his massive chest. She buried her face in the soft linen of his shirt, as if hiding from the world in his arms would make it all go away.

"There now, lass, go ahead cry if ye maun. 'Twill be all right."

A strong hand brushed the hair off her forehead, while the other held her close.

Jillian had not been held like this since she bade her father safe journey on his way to fight alongside King Harald, six long years ago.

Her tears stopped long before she pulled out of the warmth of his embrace. A dull ache started behind her eyes and spread across her forehead to her temples. She knew she had to lie down before she fell down.

"Thank you for caring about me, Winslow. It means more than you know. I haven't made many friends here—"

Winslow's lips silenced her. They were warm, tentative at first, then more demanding as he pulled her closer still. But his kiss did not ignite the same feelings Garrick's had.

Pulling away, she placed a hand to his chest.

"I'm sorry, Winslow," she said shaking her head. "I don't feel that way about you. Besides, I'm married."

"Only on paper, lass, no' in deed."

The suggestion that she had not been with her husband to seal their vows brought the blood rushing to her face and neck. Embarrassment coupled with the shame she felt.

"'Tis between Garrick and me what goes on in our married life." The stricken look he gave her made her pause. She did not want to hurt Winslow's feelings; she cared about him. But he deserved the truth.

Reaching up to stroke the side of his face, she spoke softly, "I have come to care a great deal for my husband. I would not do anything to forsake the vows we took before God. Even if he intends to take another to wife after setting me aside, I would still honor my vows. Can you not understand?" she beseeched him.

"Aye, lass, I do. Garrick does no' deserve yer loyalty. He has done naught to. I wilna try to change yer mind, though I think I could be verra persuasive."

The wicked look in his eye suggested things Jillian could only speculate about. Somehow she knew he just might be able to change her mind. 'Twas that very thought that scared her the most. It must have shown on her face, he backed away to a more respectable distance.

"I wilna press ye again. Know that I am yer servant. Dinna worry when I am with ye, lass, I'll be there to protect yer honor. I'll no' take it away. But know this, 'twould be easier to cut the heart from my breast. I canna help myself, ye are everythin' I want in a wife."

Dropping her hands, he searched her eyes one last time. Jillian could not bear to meet his gaze. She looked away. When she turned back, he had gone.

The sound of a heavy footfall had Jillian whirling back around. Guilt for letting Winslow embrace her made her uneasy. But she was alone, with only the quiet of the gardens surrounding her.

The warmth of the sun beat down upon the firmly packed

dirt path she followed between the herb and vegetable gardens. Jillian surveyed the neat rows of beans and peas. Spiky green sprouts had proudly unfurled tiny green leaves just last week. Kneeling down beside them, she touched the tip of her forefinger to a small leaf.

Its life was still so new; the hardships would be many. Mayhap a cold rain would come to beat down upon the small plant, or a fortnight without any rain at all. An insect may decide to make a meal of the succulent leaf, or mayhap wait until the bean had already formed and grown plump before attacking the plant. Just maybe, the plant would grow big and strong and produce crisp, juicy green beans.

The longer she knelt, the more possibilities swirled around in her head. She likened her life to that of the young sprout; her life had been full of hardships. The cold rain of death had beat down upon her. She lost her father, then her dear mother. Replaying the last few years of her life, she thought of Owen and Haldana as black insects come to attack her, to cut her down before she had fully realized her destiny in life.

Her small, rough hand reached up to touch her cheekbone. 'Twas a miracle that it hadn't shattered under the continuous blows Haldana had inflicted. Mayhap her life was not over, mayhap like her strong plants, she was meant to blossom and grow to maturity. Her woman's curves were gentle, not yet full blown. But her eyes were old. They told of sorrow and loss, and the strength of will to go on. 'Twas just possible that God had brought her all this way toward a life filled with love, laughter, and children so that she would look within herself for the strength to stand up for herself and claim them.

The first few drops of rain fell gently on her bent head, soothing her. Each drop massaged her scalp with silvered fingers of water. Lifting her face to the cool sprinkling of late-spring rain, Jillian closed her eyes and let it soak her. As it seeped in it renewed the dryness of her soul, replenishing her.

Her face wet, her body soaked, Jillian finally rose and bid

good-bye to her green garden friends. She was not afraid of Garrick, nor was she afraid of life. Feeling renewed and willing to take life head on, she went in search of her husband. It was time to settle things her own way.

CHAPTER SIXTEEN

"JILLIAN." THE INSISTENT pounding on her door woke her from a deep sleep.

"Aye?" she answered, her voice husky with sleep.

"'Tis Garrick."

Her hands flew to her mouth a heartbeat too late; her gasp of shock was audible. *What did he want?* She had been trying to get her husband alone since that day in the garden, but he had been avoiding her.

"Jillian?"

The stark reality of her husband pounding on her chamber door in the middle of the night was sobering. Pulling the covers up to her chin, she called out, "Come in."

The door opened swiftly and closed quietly. The man who stood before her looked haggard, from either too much work or lack of sleep. If the rumors circulating the keep were true, it was likely to be both.

"I must speak with you." He absently ran his fingers along the scar that crossed his brow down to his temple.

It wasn't new, did it still pain him?

Jillian waited for him to say something. His intense gaze had her wondering if he could read her thoughts. Her husband definitely worried her.

"At times, I am too quick to judge," he rasped. "Mayhap even condemn those who are truly innocent."

His clear blue gaze seemed to search her face for signs of what she was thinking. She fought to keep her expression blank.

"In the weeks since we wed, I have watched you. You rise at dawn each day to see to the breaking of our fast. And though there are others to see to the chore, you help haul water from the well. Food is prepared and spread before us in a veritable feast day after day. The sweet smell of fresh bread wafts through the lower hall where it waits, prodding my men and myself to rise. We all know at the end of our days' training, though we be too tired to lift our arms, we will be well tended and fed."

He may have avoided speaking to her, but he had not ignored her presence. "You care for those about you, dear lady. The wound in Eamon's thigh healed with no fever. Though the gash be deep, there was no infection." The look in his eyes softened. "Eamon and I thank you."

Her breath hitched and caught in her chest, the sound of it rattling when she could finally let it go. "Milord—"

"Garrick."

Not ready to be back on such familiar terms, she ignored his plea to do so. "Milord, I only do what my mother taught me. To run your household, caring for all of those who dwell within. Your men are no exception. If they are not well fed, how will they be able to lift their broadswords in defense of our home?"

She could have bitten her tongue. Dear Lord, had she said *our*? Hoping her husband had not noticed, she continued, "Besides, Gertie has far too much to do to tend every wound your men inflict upon one another. She is overworked."

Jillian knew the woman didn't need her help as much as Jillian needed to provide it, thereby making her presence at Merewood matter. "I am only trying to alleviate part of her load. She has labored long and hard for your family and deserves a lightening of the burden for her years of service."

Jillian had let the covers slip from her hands as she rose to confront her husband. She stopped when they were toe-to-toe, belly-to-hip and cheek-to-shoulder. His warmth radiated through the thinness of her cotton gown, while his scent pervaded the air around and between them. It was clean and spicy, tinged with a hint of body-warmed leather. She closed her eyes, sighed and leaned into him.

GARRICK PULLED HER close, holding her in a grip of iron. He leaned down to rest his face in the softness of her hair. The scent of wildflowers teased him until he lifted his head. With his knuckle, he nudged her chin until she looked up at him. He gave in to need and pressed his lips to hers.

Easing a step back, he saw her eyes mist over. *Would she cry?* She stood straighter and he knew she wouldn't. His control was slipping with each deep breath she drew in. Her curves taunted him, tempting him to fit his hands around her waist and pull her close.

For long moments they stood facing one another, Garrick wished he could read her thoughts. He needed to do something to distract himself from the temptation before him. He started to pace. It didn't help. He stopped in front of her. "Jillian... I cannot..." shaking his head, he tried again, "I've never wanted a woman the way I want you."

But I cannot have you!

To his horror, his eyes welled up; he turned away from her. "My vow of honor to my family and my people came first. I'm sorry, but it must come before all else." He lifted his shoulders and let them sag back into place. "My people..." spreading his hands, he swallowed the tightness in his throat so he could speak, "... will starve."

She stared at him, and he rushed to say, "I know you do not understand," he paused again. "I am grateful for all you have done for my family and our home, but I have no other choice but to journey to London three days hence."

ONCE AGAIN, AN oak door stood between them as a barrier. His head pounded as the blood that surged violently through his body cooled. He cared about her, more than he realized. In spite of his vow to his family and their people, he was afraid he cared too much for the bride he could not afford to keep.

He'd never felt this way toward any woman; he had not lied about that. He had to get away, to clear his head and think. It hadn't been enough to simply avoid being near her. She not only transformed his home, but his life as well and that scared him to the very depths of his being.

He shook his head as he walked away. God's breath, the woman sang when she cleaned, hummed when she cooked. He had come upon her performing both tasks, captivated by her lilting voice. When he asked why she'd been doing either task, when he had Gertie and other servants to perform such menial duties, she said she didn't mind the chores and enjoyed helping.

Another memory was tugged from the shelf in his brain as he remembered the soft touch and angel's face that tended the infirm or injured Gertie had not the time to care for. Aye, he thought, his wife was a complex woman.

The crofters loved her, everyone who met her loved her. *As does that damned Scot I've assigned to protect her.* It was past time to tell her that he had seen her in his vassal's arms. That he watched her pull out of them too, professing her love for her husband. The direction of his thoughts bothered him, as his heart badgered him to recognize what was staring him in the face.

"King William must grant me an audience. Merewood will not last the winter without the added stores a wealthy wife would provide."

Garrick strode down the steps and through the quiet hall. He needed to find MacInness. Patrick was in the hall and reminded him, "He's to take over the watch from me. I suspect you'll find him cuddled up to a warm, soft body right about now." Amusement glinted from his eyes.

Garrick clenched his teeth. "Which serving wench is he with, then?"

"Well now, I don't rightly know if it be a wench he's with. I said he'd be cuddled up next to a warm, soft body, 'twas you who suggested it be a woman." Patrick laughed out loud at his own jest.

"Where is he?" Garrick bit out.

The look in Patrick's eyes hardened as he said, "You'll find himself in the stables currying down his mount."

Garrick turned on his heel and stalked outside across the moonlit bailey toward the stables. Soft torchlight glowed warmly when he opened the door. The scent of fresh cut hay mixed with horse manure, blending together to form a familiar odor that surrounded him, comforting him, as he stepped in through the opening.

True to Patrick's prediction, MacInness stood with his back to the door brushing down the powerful black horse he called Duncan. Garrick's own mount nickered to the left of him, catching the scent of his master.

He cleared his throat. MacInness whipped around and stood silent for a moment watching him, waiting for him to speak first.

Garrick decided to get right to the point. "I'm leaving for London three days hence. I trust that you will watch over my wife while I am gone."

"Have ye made her yer wife in deed, then?"

Garrick's hands itched to punch the man in the face, but he fought to control the murderous bend his mind had taken at the Highlander's words.

MacInness paused then shrugged. "Will ye be gone long, then?"

"As long as it takes to be granted an audience with our king."

The Scot took a threatening step closer and got right in Garrick's face, shouting, "And what in God's name do I do with her when ye come home, freed from yer vows, sportin' another wife on yer arm? I wilna hurt her, mon. I'll wrap my hands about yer scrawny throat first!"

"I would like to see you try."

Both men stood like two rival dogs with the hair on their backs bristling, standing on end, teeth bared, ready to pounce, the air surrounding them was thick with tension.

Duncan pushed his muzzle into the small of his master's back, as if to knock some sense into him. The spell had been broken. Both men realized now was not the time. *Later.*

"I'll send word as soon as the king comes to a decision. Until then, guard her with your life."

"She'll no' suffer at my hands, that I pledge on my sword and in the name of my Clan."

Garrick nodded, accepting the oath.

⋙✦⋘

"BUT, FATHER, WHAT will Jillian do if Garrick sets her aside?" Owen's youngest daughter seemed frantic at the thought of her friend coming to such an end after the promising beginning when she had wed the Lord of Merewood Keep.

"'Tis not your worry, Maddy dear." Owen reached a hand out and brushed a stray white-blonde wave off his youngest daughter's face.

"But, Father, will she come back here?"

He watched her blue eyes fill with tears.

"Nay. Your mother will not have her back under our roof." Tilting her chin up, he said, "I have enough to do planning marriages for your sisters. You do understand since they are older I have to see them settled first?"

At her nod, Owen patted her hand. "Well then, I'm to meet our new neighbor, Henri du Guerre."

"Has he Loughmoe Keep, then?" Madelyne asked.

"Nay, but he soon will. 'Tis past time to join the others in the hall. Tell your sisters to make haste."

CHAPTER SEVENTEEN

T HE TENSION CLOUDING the air of Merewood Keep and its people cleared with the parting of their lord. The last few days had proved to some that their lord was a hard taskmaster. To others, it showed what heartache could do to a strong man.

Jillian stood atop the wooden walkway of the curtain wall. Sorrow filled her heart as despair weighed her down. Her husband had been gone just one day, and already she fretted about the inevitable end to their brief marriage.

What would she do? Where would she go?

The next few days did little to calm her down, or to convince her he would turn around and come back for her. By the end of the first week, she became frantic with worry and on the very edge of sanity. She had to take back control of her life.

"Reka," Jillian spoke softly to Garrick's mother, "I must ask your help."

"What is it?"

Jillian looked over her shoulder; but they were alone in her chamber.

"Will you accompany me to London?" she blurted out.

Eyreka looked stunned. "London?"

"I have decided if Garrick wants my land badly enough, then I shall do all I can to see that he gets it. Mayhap if the king agrees, I will be allowed to remain his wife."

Eyreka's eyes filled with tears at the whispered words. "Why would the king rescind his decree that du Guerre should have your land? What will you offer?"

"I cannot tell you." Jillian's throat tightened. "Please do not ask." Her mind had worked long and hard on a solution to her problem. She hoped once she was able to offer Loughmoe Keep to Garrick he would say the words she wanted to hear. He would tell her he cared. The attraction between them, his gentle touch and tender kisses, had been his unspoken promise of caring. He just didn't realize it yet.

The only answer that kept recurring was a simple one. Somehow she had to convince the king to give control of her family holding back to her. It was the only thing she could think of that would convince Garrick he could keep his vow to his keep's people and to her. She understood he needed the coin a wealthy wife would bring.

"Who will escort us?" Eyreka asked, "Winslow?"

Jillian hoped Garrick's mother would agree without having to confide the whole of her plans. "I asked Roderick to accompany us. He has agreed, and promises to have ten men ready to ride just after dawn tomorrow." Hesitating, she asked, "Are you certain you are up to the trip? You seem very tired lately."

Touching a hand to the younger woman's shoulder, Eyreka smiled. "Your concern warms my heart almost as much as your willingness to help my son." Her blue eyes swept across Jillian's face. "When will you admit to your heart that you love my son?"

"Love him?" Jillian choked, "I don't... that is, what I mean to say..."

"Aye, dear, you love him and it warms my heart. We had best be going if we are to be ready for travel at first light."

A heady warmth suffused her entire body, but she couldn't let herself admit the words her heart longed to acknowledge...not yet.

True to her word, Lady Eyreka was waiting the following morning with only a small bundle. Eyeing the size of the pack,

Jillian smiled. "We both have the same idea of traveling light."

Smiling, Eyreka motioned to the door. "We had best be on our way. 'Twill take nearly a fortnight to travel to London."

Roderick stood ready to help the women mount. Ten immense knights were saddled, ready to go at his command. With a flick of his wrist signaling their departure, the party cantered out of the bailey as the first faint rays of sunlight peeked through the dusky rose–colored clouds.

They rode until the sun had risen high and bright overhead. After a brief meal and much needed rest, the party resumed their journey. At dusk, Roderick drew his horse up alongside of Jillian.

"We'll stop here for the night," Roderick announced to the group.

Jillian spied a stream through a break in the trees. Her eyes lit up. The cool water would feel wonderful. Turning around, she beckoned to her escort. "Tell Reka I'll be back...there's a stream—"

"Wait," he interrupted, "you should not venture anywhere alone." His warning warmed her heart, but she didn't believe it necessary.

Looking up into Roderick's eyes, she saw them soften. And knew he'd give in. "All right then, but you'd best be careful. I'll send mother to you."

Jillian did not intend to miss out on the brief reprieve she had been granted. She ran toward the stream, paying little heed to the stones scattered across the path. The shock of pain slicing through the sole of her foot sank in too late. The damage had been done.

When Lady Eyreka found her, Jillian was hobbling slowly toward the water. Shaking her head, the older woman sighed as she helped Jillian over to the moss-covered bank and sat down. Jillian gingerly removed her torn leather boot and shredded hose. The arch of her foot was bruised and bleeding.

"Poor dear," Eyreka soothed, "we best wash the dirt from it."

Jillian edged closer to the stream and let Eyreka bathe her foot in the cool water. "I was in a hurry."

"And a lot of good it did you," Eyreka said, washing the wound, and tearing a strip of cloth from the bottom of her bliaut.

"I'm sorry."

Eyreka wrapped it around Jillian's foot. So far, their journey had been uneventful; Jillian hoped this was not a portent of what was to come. Deep in thought, she did not hear the twin snapping of twigs nearby.

The tree branches whistled softly as they sliced through the air crashing down on their unsuspecting heads.

⇒⇒⇒⇐⇐⇐

"JILLIAN AND MY mother should have been back by now." Roderick scanned the stream bank in the distance then turned back around to face his men. "I'll go and find them."

He returned alone, rasping, "They're gone."

"Any sign of Reivers in the wood? Rebels?" one man asked.

"Nary a sign of life…man nor horse," Roderick added.

"'Tis like they were spirited away," another said.

Looking at the men surrounding him, the seriousness of their situation hit him. Roderick felt a clawing hand rake his insides. He drew in a ragged breath. "God help us they've been taken." The deep-rooted fear clutching his belly did not ease up. "Search the area by the stream again. If no trace is found, we head back to Merewood for help."

⇒⇒⇒⇐⇐⇐

JILLIAN WOKE TO darkness and pain. She thought to touch the lump on the back of her head, the source of her pain, but her arms were numb. A thread of fear began to unravel within her as she realized her arms were bound behind her.

Opening the other eye caused a sharp pain to lance through her skull. Her dire situation came clearly into focus. She was

164

trussed up like a fowl on a spit and in an unfamiliar section of forest. Rallying her rapidly dwindling courage, she started to talk to herself.

"You've truly made a muddle of things this time. Your husband is in London waiting to annul your marriage, while you've taken matters into your own hands and what happens? You're being held prisoner by heaven knows whom." Her head ached like it had been split open and her foot throbbed miserably. Forcing herself to look over her shoulder, she was just able to see the bottom of her foot. She shuddered; the makeshift bandage wrapped around it was covered in blood, and encrusted with dirt.

The rustle of leaves warned her someone was coming. Shutting her eyes, she lay still. Dear God where was Lady Eyreka?

"Wake up!" A large, booted foot poked her ribs too sharply.

"Ouch."

"Ahh, Lady Merewood you're awake. Sit up wench. I'll untie you. We're hungry."

Jillian looked closely at her fair-haired captor. She didn't recognize him or the ugly purple scar running the length of his cheek ending under his left ear.

Don't let him frighten you. "I don't know you," she said slowly.

"Aye," he answered gruffly. As the large man bent over her to untie her hands, she got a good whiff of him and stiffened.

"Offended by my tender touch? Don't worry…we'll all be getting a turn having you after you've tended the camp."

His lecherous comment left no room for speculation. His evil laugh made her skin crawl. As he loosened the knot, his words rang through her aching head. Finally her hands were free, but the feeling hadn't returned to her arms. She must have been tied up for hours. Terror washed over her leaving her weaker than she already was. The last thing she remembered was sitting on the stream bank with Lady Eyreka. Where had they taken her?

Trying to focus on something other than her fear for Garrick's mother, her tired mind conjured up an image of clear blue eyes. Thoughts of Garrick gave her inner strength. Her fear evaporated, settling her jangled nerves.

The overpowering stench of the man untying her ankles made her gag. With a will of iron, she swallowed the bile surging up her throat.

"Follow me."

She ignored the pain shooting up from her foot and followed. Eyreka sat in the clearing near a dead fire and an empty cooking pot. One look from her assured Jillian she was no worse for the blow to the head they had both suffered.

Watching their captor retreat, Jillian blurted out, "Reka, praise God you are all right."

Garrick's mother gingerly touched the base of her skull and winced. "The back of my head aches."

Trying to make light of their desperate situation, Jillian mumbled, "It must be very hard to find someone to cook for them. Mayhap they should try asking instead of beating women over the head with a stick." Her attempt at levity fell flat.

"Jillian," Reka whispered, "I know that man over there." Reka pointed toward a tall man standing in the center of a group of ragged warriors.

"Who is he?"

"Harald the Saxon. My dear Addison fought with him in the Uprisings. No one saw or heard from him after Addison died. We all assumed him dead or taken captive."

"But what does he want with us?" Alarm took hold of her.

"He knows who I am. Harald is a shrewd man, you can be sure he knows who you are too. 'Tis why we've been taken prisoner."

"Best get to building the fire, wench," the man with the scar yelled from across the clearing.

Not wanting to attract undue attention, the women quietly searched the area for kindling.

The crackle of their small fire warmed them. "Where did you learn how to do that?" Eyreka asked.

"My father used to let me travel with him when I was younger. We'd make camp in the wood, not far from home mind you, lest my mother worry." Jillian smiled at the pleasant memory. "If we are going to keep the flame burning, we must find larger pieces of wood," she added.

The two women combed the immediate area, gathering wood while they quietly talked. Jillian lifted the hem of her once-pale-blue chainse and filled it with larger pieces of dry wood. Her bliaut caught on a briar and tore.

While she struggled to free the cloth, the reality of their circumstances descended upon her with a swiftness that took her breath away. Tears clogged her throat, but she would not give in to them.

'Tis my fault we were captured.

Looking for a way to keep a lid on her fear, she began instructing Eyreka in the tending of the fire. Then she lugged the iron pot to the stream. Feeling sluggish, she felt a wave of heat pulse through her. The pain in the arch of her foot was almost unbearable. The added weight of the iron pot made it next to impossible to walk. Tucking her skirts up under the leather belt slung low on her hips to keep them from getting wet, she bent down and filled the pot half-full of water.

When she returned to the fire, she was surprised by the small supply of vegetables waiting there. "Will there be meat to add to the stew?" she asked.

A man with a patch across one eye glared at them. "I'll be back with a couple of rabbits, but you'll have to skin them yourself."

Eyreka shivered, obviously dreading the task to come. While they waited, they washed and cut up two large heads of cabbage, then peeled onions and shelled some early peas.

"I don't suppose they've any herbs or spices hidden about." Jillian laughed nervously trying to cover up her flagging courage. Stirring the rapidly warming stew, she was totally unaware of the tension forming between the rebels in the camp. Neither woman had any idea that they were being discussed in great detail.

"WHEN DO WE get a turn at the wench, Harald?"

A few of his men turned and added a chorus of enthusiastic ayes.

"Not until we receive the ransom."

"But that could take weeks," one of the rebels groaned.

"I'll bet she's a hot one," the man with the eye patch said.

Nodding their silent agreement, Harald's men champed at the bit, waiting for their first taste of the creamy-skinned beauty bending over her task of skinning rabbits.

Harald stood up, his very presence commanding everyone's attention. "No one takes the wench before I do. She'll do her fair share of work first. By the time I'm ready for her, the wench will beg me to take her. One look at her and you can tell she is not used to toiling over a hot fire. She'll be in my tent by morning," he bragged.

"But what about the ransom?" one of the rebels demanded.

Harald threw his dagger into a tree next to the group of men gathered, waiting to state their reasons for being allowed to be first with the prisoner.

BLISSFULLY UNAWARE OF the stir she caused, Jillian wiped her hands on the tall grass near the ring of stones that kept her fire contained. She started gutting the next rabbit. Skillfully slicing them up, they were in the pot simmering in no time. Pride and Lady Eyreka kept her going, though she be bone tired and nearly frightened out of her wits.

"Mayhap, they'll leave us alone if we can prove our worth as cooks."

Clinging to that hope like a lifeline, the women concentrated on serving the stew. The men gulped it down, leaving the huge pot empty. They had eaten it all.

"I should have thought to set a small portion aside for you."

"And what about you?" the older woman asked gently.

"I don't think I could eat." Her head pounded and her stomach roiled in protest. *Mayhap 'twas the blow.*

Sighing, she lifted the pot and trudged back to the stream. After rinsing the pot, she scrubbed it with some loose sand. Finished, she straightened up and dizzying waves of heat swamped over her. Bending back down, she cupped her hands full of water and drank deeply.

"'Twould have been a blessing to eat, or rest." A small nagging voice inside her made her sit down and carefully unwrap her bandaged foot. The site of the dirt-encrusted bandage sickened her.

"Mother would have had my head if she could see the mess I've made of it."

Too late. The damage had already been done; the gash in her foot was filthy and had a yellowish cast to it. The skin surrounding the wound was an angry red and hot to the touch. Silently she wished for her basket of healing herbs. The only thing she could do now was to clean the dirt out as best she could.

Making her way slowly back to camp, she was relieved to see Eyreka resting near the fire. Her eyes were closed, but slowly opened as Jillian drew near.

"Your face is flushed," Eyreka said. "Here, sit down and let me take a look at your foot."

Jillian sat beside her and confessed, "I wasn't paying attention. There was dirt in it. I washed it in the stream just now, but it's infected."

Eyreka's brow furrowed as she inspected the injury. "I'll rewrap it for you—we cannot take too long or we'll draw their attention." She quickly wrapped Jillian's foot.

"Thank you. I am so tired, and my head aches—" The fever

that had been slowly burning all afternoon spiked, and Jillian fell unconscious to the ground.

The rebel leader came running. "What did you do to her?"

Eyreka gasped, "You arrogant boar, I was not the one to strike her down from behind with an oak branch."

Harald stepped dangerously close to Lady Eyreka, but she did not back away.

"What ails the wench, Harald?" one of his men asked.

Turning toward the still form of their captive, the rebel leader walked cautiously over toward where she lay in a crumpled heap. Nudging her with the toe of his leather boot, he spoke. "Up, wench, 'tis time to see to my needs. I said up."

Grabbing her by the hair, he roughly pulled her into a semi-reclining position. Watching her slide bonelessly back down into a prone position, he swore colorfully. Thinking to demonstrate his power over their captive, he grabbed her by the chin. Hot dry skin burned his fingertips. He released her.

"God's blood. She's on fire!"

The raucous cries from his men stopped him from crossing himself. As the cries and protests of his men grew louder, Harald shouted, "Silence!" His voice boomed across the camp. The quiet that followed was sharp in contrast.

"Alan, you have the gift of healing. See if you can find out what ails her 'Tis the sleep she's in that seems unnatural."

"I'll see what I can do." Turning back to Eyreka, he asked, "Will you help?"

The plea in the proclaimed healer's voice seemed to soften her stance. "Of course."

He bent down to examine the unconscious patient, while Jillian remained blissfully unaware of her predicament. The men stood in a circle around her as their healer probed and prodded trying to find the source of her fever.

After what seemed like an hour, but was only minutes, he slowly stood. "I cannot find the source of her fever—the bandage she has on her foot is clean."

"It should be, I wrapped it up myself," Eyreka said.

The grumbling started slowly and built to a crescendo, the men could not seem to agree whether to wait for Jillian to awaken from her swoon to take what they felt was their due, or to take turns while she lay on her back oblivious to all.

Lady Eyreka's horrified gasp echoed through the camp. She crouched down beside her daughter-in-law, shielding her.

As if she could feel the turmoil flowing between the leader and his men, Jillian tossed and turned in her fevered state.

The flash of the amber pendant around her neck stopped them. Harald bent down on one knee to have a closer look in the firelight. Grasping the amulet, he turned it over. One side was etched with a cross, while the other had an inscription on it that he could not decipher.

The longer he held the pendant in his hands, the hotter it grew. Not sure if she were bewitched, or the devil himself, Harald dropped the object that burned him. It settled against her creamy skin, giving no indication that it burned her. But the proof had left its mark on Harald's palm.

Shaking his head, he stood and spoke to his men. "No one touches her. I'll have your vow on it."

At his threatening stance, legs braced apart, his sword lance-straight and eye level, his men gave in.

Each in turn cast one last lustful glance at the tasty morsel at their feet, before grumbling and turning back to their duties. Satisfied, the rebel leader nodded once to their healer and strode toward the icy stream.

Eyreka hugged Jillian close and wept.

CHAPTER EIGHTEEN

GARRICK'S HANDS SHOOK with the force of his anger. They had Jillian and his mother. The proof was clenched in his hands. He silently damned the Saxon rebel leader and his own brother for allowing the women to be captured in the first place.

"Is there a reply?" the young man asked.

Garrick was already plotting the rebel's slow and painful death while trying to keep his feelings of fear for the women at bay. "Who gave this to you?" Garrick demanded.

"One of the kitchen servants."

"A name, give me a name!"

The messenger shrugged. "The wench got it from one of the stable hands."

Garrick rubbed his throbbing temples. Harald was as silent moving as ever. It was why no Norman ever captured him. The man lauded as brilliant when they fought against the invading Normans was now reviled. When Garrick found Harald, he would kill him. It was no use asking any more questions. No rebel would have dared to enter the castle. Only a friend of a friend of the notorious rebel would. Damn the man for his cleverness.

"Milord, the king wishes a word with you," a page summoned him.

The king finally had time to see him and all he could think about was the dire news he had received. God help him, he had to set thoughts of Jillian and his mother aside and make ready to see his king.

KING WILLIAM LEANED forward. "I understand you wish to set your wife aside, Merewood." The king raised his hand and Garrick forced himself to remain silent. "And that you have received a ransom note for your wife and mother." King William leaned forward anticipating Garrick's reply. "What shall you do about it?"

'Twas no use to deny it. The king already knew of its existence and Garrick's desire to set Jillian aside. "I will answer it."

"Have you the coin demanded? What of the head of cattle? Are your people prepared to brave the harsh northern winter with no grain?"

Garrick clenched his jaw to keep from blurting out if it had not been for King William, he would have plenty of coin, cattle, and grain.

He swallowed his pride and answered, "Nay, Sire. Mayhap Harald will receive something from me, but 'twill not be what he is expecting."

"What have you planned?" his king demanded, pounding his fist on the arm of the massive oak chair he held court in. He was a large man, imposing when angry.

But Garrick did not fear him. Besides, he was too busy planning his revenge to notice his king's anger. A plan was already loosely forming and it was time to put it into action. "What will you give me for the capture of Harald the Saxon and his rebel force?"

"Impossible. My own army tried to flush them out of the woods to no avail." Raising an eyebrow in question, the king waited.

"I grew up in those woods," Garrick answered. "If they are in hiding, I will find them. I stake my life on it."

"And so you shall." The king fell silent, as if considering Garrick's boast. "Your word that you will bring the rebel leader and his men to London."

"You have yet to name the reward for his capture," Garrick smoothly added.

"Your word first."

Going down on his knee, Garrick bowed his head. Placing his hand over his heart, he vowed, "I will bring them to London and justice or die trying."

Satisfied, the king smiled. "In return, you shall receive grain to feed your people through the winter, a head of cattle for each rebel brought in, plus 100 pounds in gold for Harald the Saxon, but he must be alive to collect your gold."

The reward was staggering. Garrick bit back the shout of joy ready to erupt at the naming of such wealth. *Wealth*, his brain screamed…he could feed their people. The skeletons of his people spare with flesh and cloth, that had haunted his sleep for weeks now faded as relief swept through his soul. He would not have to set Jillian aside; she could still be his wife. His heart lightened with the realization that he could keep both of his vows.

"Sire, about my wife and her holding—"

"Aye, Loughmoe, I know what you will ask. I have given it some thought, but wish more time. Her family's holding could be rich again with the right man managing it."

"But," Garrick began.

"Go to Northumbria, bring back the rebels." The king ended the audience.

With a heavy heart, Garrick returned to his chamber. He had not secured the king's word to grant him Loughmoe Keep, nor did he tell the king he had changed his mind about setting Jillian aside now that he had the promise of the reward for bringing Harald to justice. Throwing his few tunics into a satchel, he went in search of Dunstan. His mother and his lady wife were in need of rescuing, there was no time left to bargain for Loughmoe Keep.

"God, let me not be too late," he prayed.

⟫⟫⟪⟪

"WE HAVE TO stop!" Dunstan cried out through the driving rain. His shout was softened by the wall of water falling from the leaden sky. Mud, three days deep, tried to suck their horse's legs out from under them. Lightening flashed, spooking the wearied mounts.

Bending low to whisper in his stallion's ear, Garrick soothed the wild-eyed, black beast. Once he had him calmed, he answered, "Make camp ahead, near the break in the trees." He pointed to a spot a hundred feet farther up, what in drier weather would be called a road.

"'Tis no use to push ourselves too close to the limit. We are four days away from Merewood."

"In dry weather, brother," Garrick reminded him.

"Mayhap six days, then."

"Aye, and reason enough to push on. We leave at first light."

The mud-spattered band of warriors rode into Merewood Keep five days later on the brink of exhaustion. MacInness was there to greet them.

Garrick bit out, "Where's Roderick?"

"He's only just returned."

MacInness faltered in his bid to speak, and for the first time had trouble meeting his overlord's gaze. "I have news, mon. Bad news and I dinna know how to tell ye."

"That whoreson Harald sent his ransom demands to London." Garrick finished for him.

"London? But they've only been gone three days. 'Tis at least four and ten to cover that distance. I dinna understand," the Scot muttered.

"Harald must have been watching the keep for the last few weeks. One of his spies would have been able to pass on the gossip of the keep easily enough. He knew weeks ago I was going. The clever bastard must have taken a chance and sent word of the ransom before Jillian and my mother were even captured."

His vassal's worried gaze met his own. "I canna bring myself to say it."

"I know, but I can. 'Tis beyond clever Harald's plan. It borders on madness. God's breath! How can I outthink a madman?"

Both men fell silent, each lost in the turmoil of their own grim thoughts. Leading the horses into the dry stable, they rubbed them down.

When the horses were contentedly munching on sweet hay, MacInness spoke again. "I know a mon most think mad." Wiggling his eyebrows for emphasis, he continued, "'Tis two day's ride to his home. If ye maun leave before then, I could catch up to ye."

Though silent for a while, Garrick finally nodded. "Aye, Take Eamon and Kelly with you, I'll need Patrick and Sean with me."

"About Jillian," MacInness began.

"The king is still deciding." Garrick was not ready to discuss his plans or the bargain he struck with his monarch, not yet. At the moment, all that mattered was getting the women back, safely.

"What will ye do when ye find them?" his friend asked.

"I will see that justice is done."

"Aye," MacInness agreed. "Cut them down where the Sassenach dogs stand." The Highlander was rapidly warming to the topic. His eyes glittered. "Ye plan to skin them?"

"I said I would see justice done. I will bring the prisoners to London to stand trial for their crimes. Kidnapping is just one of them."

"Aye, and treason." The man's smile was deadly. "I wilna be missing their execution. 'Tis not often a mon is drawn and quartered."

"You Scots are bloodthirsty." Garrick smiled.

The big man grinned. "Aye."

Shaking his head, Garrick tried to get control of the conversation before MacInness sidetracked him again.

"What is this madman's name?"

"Iain. They call him black hearted. But he is no more so than any other good clansman whose family was slain in a border raid. He has no kith nor kin; no woman of his own." Pausing to frown, MacInness added, "He has no fear. He's nothin' to lose and less to gain. 'Tis an honor to die in battle. Iain plans to die honorably."

"Bring him back then. We'll meet on the road south in four days' time."

"Aye."

"WHAT DO YOU mean you won't pay?" Gertie planted her hands on her hips and glared at him.

"Where would I get the coin?" Garrick's mind was a whirlwind of black thoughts, the longer they delayed leaving, the worse it would be for his wife and mother.

"I don't care where you get it from, just get it and bring milady and Jillian back here where they belong," his housekeeper nearly shouted.

Closing the gap between them, he laid his hands on her square shoulders. He could feel the trembling even through her considerable bulk. His gaze sought hers. "Worry not, Gert, I will bring them back. Would you pack some provisions for our trip?"

She let go of her anger with a visible shudder, and finally agreed. "Some of my oat cakes and bread?"

"Wrapped tight. We may be in for more rain."

"Milord?" One of the stable lads stood in the doorway to the hall wringing his hands, his gaze darting about. Garrick recognized the lad as one of the servants they'd brought back from Sedgeworth Keep. "Aye, Stephan, what is it?"

The boy looked up beseechingly, his eyes clouded with unshed tears. "Bring Lady Jillian back safe, please?" He sniffled and toed the ground with his scuffed boot. "She treats me like I's someone special, lets me help her brush down your horses. I promised to watch over milady. Bring her back so's I can?"

The boy's fervent speech cut a path straight to Garrick's heart. "Aye lad, I'll bring her back."

Walking across the bailey, he was stopped by the blacksmith. "Milord?"

Though the man had gone gray, he was as broad as an oak, just as he had been when Garrick's father was lord. He wondered what the normally silent man wanted. Time was growing short. "Aye?"

"Bring milady home safe. Her way with herbs healed the burn on my arm. See?" The man shoved his elbow under Garrick's nose.

With a nod Garrick continued on his rounds. The whole time cataloging away the countless demands from his people to bring back his lady wife. Not one of them seemed to doubt that he could do it. They simply wished he'd get it done. He was stopped by five more of the keep's people before he finally made it to the kitchen where still more waited to speak their piece.

"We miss your lady singing while we work. 'Tis like we lost a bit of sunshine now she's gone."

'Twas the truth. Her presence in his home was like a bright ray of sunlight in the cold corridors of his battered soul. He pushed aside his feelings of betrayal at her hands once and for all. The overwhelming affection and acceptance of his people only added to the depth of what he was beginning to feel for his bride.

During the time they spent apart, he had come to carefully replay the events of the recent past. He spun them around in his head again and again, until both his heart and his mind accepted her innocence. Freed from the hold his anger had upon him, emotions he'd never experienced before washed over him. He missed Jillian. He needed her in his life, but was afraid he'd be too late to tell her of the love growing in his battered heart.

Would she forgive him for his error in judgment?

The fact that his keep's people felt the same way about Jillian reinforced the urgent need to bring her safely back to Merewood. He needed to tell her how he felt.

"Milord?" Gertie's kitchen helper stopped him this time.

"Aye, Bess, after I bring her captors to face justice in London, we'll be home."

"That he will, Bess. Worry not," Gertie handed him a sack of food for the journey.

Taking Gertie by the hand, he promised, "We'll be home soon. I expect the fatted calf when we return."

"If the hunting's good, mayhap a venison pasty."

"Venison pasty?" Dunstan winked. "For the road? Gertie you are too good to us."

"When you fine hunting men bring me a deer," Gertie sniffed. "I'll be fixing you that pasty."

Roderick was unusually quiet standing next to his brother. One look at his haunted eyes and Garrick could feel the pain his brother tried to hide. He was moved, his youngest brother may not be the same caliber of warrior as the rest, but he was not without honor. His brother had failed to safely deliver Jillian to London. Which had him asking, "Why was our mother traveling to London with Jillian?"

"Was Jillian a prisoner here, locked in an ivory tower?" Roderick poked him in the chest. "Was she not free to come and go as she pleased? Were you afraid she would embarrass you by following you to London, brother mine?" The anger behind his words struck Garrick with the force of an unseen blow.

"Nay, she was not—"

"I saw how you treated her, brother. God's teeth, I would never have expected my own brother to treat a woman so foully. Did she complain that the keep was not to her liking? Was it the food? Mayhap 'twas the amount of work heaped upon her slender shoulders?"

"It was not my idea."

"I should have taken her away with me while I had the chance," Roderick ground out.

"Roderick," Dunstan warned.

"Leave off. I'll speak my mind to this dull-witted boar of a brother." Getting right in Garrick's face, he shouted, "Are you so without human emotion that you could set aside the loveliest woman God ever made in favor of the cold companion wealth would have you seek?"

Garrick's temper was but a hairsbreadth away from erupting into a rage of volcanic proportions. He didn't have time for explanations. Grabbing his brother by the front of his tunic, he shook him hard. "We're wasting time."

Garrick's throat felt like it was being squeezed closed. *He had to find them, time was running out.* The woman he had unwillingly given his heart to needed him. The black hole in his chest, where his heart should be, lay open and bleeding. Jillian held his heart in her tiny work-worn hands.

By all rights, she should feed it to the wolves roaming the perimeter of his lands near the edge of the forest. Dare he hope that she'd continue to care for his heart and offer her own in return?

While Garrick's soul writhed in pain, his body calmly walked back out to the bailey where his horse was tethered. Slinging the sack of food in front of his saddle, he untied the reins. Swiftly mounting, he set off, leaving his brothers to follow.

CHAPTER NINETEEN

"**T**HERE NOW, JILLIAN, easy."

Her mother-in-law's voice seemed to come from a great distance. Licking her lips, she tried to form the words to answer her, but the fever would not let her speak, or open her eyes. Jillian felt as if she were being bathed with tongues of fire, enveloped in heat so intense, it made her eyes burn and her head pound.

Relief came, in the form of a cool wet cloth, in answer to her unconscious prayers. She quieted.

"HAS SHE NOT wakened?" the rebel leader asked, concerned now that one of his tools for controlling the Lord of Merewood Keep may not live to satisfy his ends.

"Nay," their healer answered.

Harald was growing more worried by the moment. The Lady of Merewood needed to be alive if Owen were to play his part.

"I thought you knew what to do for fever." It was nigh onto two weeks that she lay in fevered state. By all rights, she should have died. Nothing Alan did seemed to ease the sickness that gripped the lady who would keep him free from the bonds of a king he refused to swear fealty to. She had to live, the fate of his rebel force depended upon it.

"JILLIAN." THE CALL came as barely a whisper.

"Have they gone?"

"Just as you knew they would. How can you be so sure of their movements?" Lady Eyreka was clearly baffled.

"'Tis been two weeks. I listen. I watch. Something inside sends a flicker of warning through me." Sighing she sat up and stretched her cramped arms overhead. Rolling her shoulders and head, she loosened the rest of the kinks lying still for hours on end caused.

"'Twas an ingenious plan to feign sickness. How much longer do you think their healer will believe it so?"

"I don't know."

Eyreka sat back on her heels and smoothed at the wrinkles, now a permanent part of her woolen chainse. Though she be worse for the wear, her mother-in-law was still every inch a lady.

But her question plagued Jillian until she thought to go mad. Though she lay on a soft bed of moss and green leaves, she could not relax; to do so would make her vulnerable. Her body cried out for sleep, and she was near collapse from the stress of the deception they played.

How soon would the healer catch on? When would he reach out with a wet cloth to soothe her fevered brow and notice healthy-colored skin lying beneath the thin layer of the ash-paste she had applied? When would he arrive ahead of schedule and catch Eyreka fanning Jillian's face with a piece of burning bark to heat it?

Moving closer, she huddled next to Eyreka, drawing needed strength from Garrick's mother. Every muscle in her body ached from both her recent illness and the ever-present threat of danger that had become their way of life.

"Close your eyes," Eyreka said softly. "Sleep."

Jillian yawned. "'Tis my turn for watch."

"I slept soundly last night," Eyreka told her. "If you sleep now, you may take the next two watches in a row."

That sounded wonderful to Jillian. "Mayhap, I'll teach you another of Father's survival skills." Smiling she closed her eyes and breathed deeply, falling into an exhausted sleep.

The rough shaking woke her from a nightmare, thinking she was being held down by one of the rebels, she kicked hard trying to loosen the bonds that held her.

"It's me," Eyreka whispered in her ear.

Jillian relaxed. "I was dreaming."

"I know, but Alan's coming with another poultice for your fever. We've no time to wave the heated bark by your face. What can we do? He'll be able to tell this time."

Jillian's mind raced, but could think of nothing. A quick glance across the camp made her sigh with relief. The rebel leader pushed the healer, while shouting obscenities at him. It would give them a few more moments reprieve. When she paused to listen, snatches of the argument came through clearly, and with it a name…Owen.

Her breath froze in her lungs, pain searing through her leaden chest. Lord help her, was he behind the kidnapping? It all made sense. Owen wanted her land, and that was the one truth she had heard him speak.

"Reka, have you any ash left?" Jillian's voice was edged with desperation.

The older woman nodded. "Lie still, whilst I sprinkle it on your face."

"My neck too, hurry." They needed more time to uncover the real reason behind their abduction. While she was no longer fevered, she knew she was not strong enough to chance escape, yet. Grabbing a hold of her grandmother's necklace, she closed her eyes and prayed to God first, then entered a plea to the ancients for protection from evil.

Eyreka's hands shook as she smoothed the ash across Jillian's brow, hoping that from a distance it looked to be soothing touch, when in fact she had missed a spot with ash in her haste.

"Lady Eyreka," Alan's voice sounded curt, though his eyes were full of sympathy.

"She's cooler, but won't waken." Hoping to confuse the man with symptoms, she added, "Look at the black rings round her eyes, she's so thin."

Real tears welled up in her eyes looking down at her brave daughter-in-law. Why could her son not be here to see what a strong woman he had wed? Thickheaded man—he needed her.

Jillian felt the strength in the hand lying against her forehead. An idea leapt into her weary mind. Would his soul be as caring as his healer's heart? Could he be talked into helping them escape? But what would they offer in return? Protection from the Rebels? Sanctuary at Merewood, or mayhap a chance to utilize his skills in the art of healing? It was but a faint hope, and little more than the prayer ever on her lips, but she had to try.

"Lady Eyreka, please bring more water back in this. I'll use up what is left here," Alan's voice sounded more gruff than normal. Jillian's ears picked up on what her eyes could not; one week of feigned illness had made it a necessary habit.

"I'll be back, Jillian, dear," Eyreka said before she could stop herself.

"She can't hear you." Though but a statement, the underlying question lay behind it.

"'Tis true, but I feel better trying to talk to her, mayhap soon she'll wake up and answer."

Jillian prayed desperately, that the healer believe Reka's obvious lie.

"She's gone, Jillian. No one else is near. Won't you speak to me? Please?"

Involuntarily, her lashes fluttered. She started to sweat, cold and clammy moisture pushed its way to the surface of her skin, and she could feel clumps of ash forming on her face and neck.

Cool water bathed her cheeks. She could hear the music of it being sloshed about by the capable hands of the man who had cared for her unfailingly for a fortnight. Shame suffused her pale face until it bloomed with color.

"Aye, that's it, lass. Open your eyes, now. I'll not hurt you."

The truth of his words sounded in her brain, ringing as clear as a newly hammered bell. Her curiosity may be the end of her yet, but she would brave the consequences.

The face that came into focus was strong of cheek and jaw, and though not shaven, 'twas clean and smiling. Her fear must have shown in her eyes, he spoke quickly to reassure her.

"On my word as a healer, I would do naught to harm you, lady." He looked over his shoulder before turning back to her.

"You have no reason to believe me, but I am not one of them. They forced me to join them. 'Twas late winter when five of them stormed into my home, pulling me from my bed to tend their wounded leader."

"Why did you not fight them?" Jillian could not hide her need to know.

"I did." Alan's eyes grew dark with emotion. Brushing the hair back from his temple revealed a jagged scar that ran from that point, through where his ear should have been, disappearing to a point beyond where she could see.

Jillian shuddered.

"Aye, lass, 'tis not pretty, but 'tis my own badge of courage."

Feeling the need to explain, she hastened to speak. "Nay, 'tis not the sight that leaves me weak, 'tis the deed behind it."

Reaching up she traced the length of the scar with her fingertip. Taking his hand in both of hers, hope gave her strength. Trusting in her instincts, she blurted out the escape plan that suddenly burst through her. "Help us, Alan. If we can reach Merewood, I know we'll be safe. I have friends there who would listen. They would soon come to know you for the man you are, not the man you would have others believe you to be."

Something akin to hope flickered in Alan's eyes. Jillian felt it catch hold of her too, as the renewed emotion sparked within her breast. She had faith in the man beside her. When he moved to capture her hands in his, their gazes locked. His silent promise was enough for her.

"Nay!" Eyreka slumped to her knees, dropping the pail of water she had been carrying.

"Reka, 'tis naught to fear." Jillian's eyes shone with admiration looking up at the man beside her. "Alan will aid in our escape. He'll be coming with us."

A long and silent pause fell upon the trio as each took the other's full measure.

"Well, then, if he betrays us, we'll just have to slit his throat," Eyreka boasted.

Jillian grinned. Her mother-in-law was terrified, but tried to mask it with threats of revenge. Pride flowed through her, bearing love in its wake. Aye, she thought, she loved her husband's mother as if she were her own.

"Have you any ash left?" Alan asked.

"Ash?" The two pretended not to understand what he was asking.

"Aye, ladies, we need to wipe Jillian down with more ash after we blot her face with a dry cloth. Harald plans to try a hand at healing since I have failed to bring his captive 'round." The deep lines of a frown marred Alan's otherwise smooth forehead.

"Reka?" Jillian prompted.

"I have some stored in the hollow of that tree." She pointed to a tall oak a few feet away.

"Get it then. We've no time to waste." While she ran to do his bidding, he spoke to Jillian, "You're a brave lass, Lady Jillian. You must remain so if we are to escape from here."

"With your help, we can leave during the change of the rebel's watch."

A brow lifted in question, he asked, "What do you know about their watch?"

"That it changes thrice in six hours, rotating between the man with the purple scar, the one with the eye patch, and the fat one with no teeth." Shuddering at the combined unwanted vision of the men, she grabbed at her necklace again. The smooth amber stone felt cool to the touch, soothing her while a mysterious throbbing pulsed from where she held it straight up her arm. Strength flowed through her.

It was then she remembered the legend of the amulet. Somewhere in her heart, she knew it was not false. Her grandmother had been right. The strength of ancient warriors flowed through her blood. As she grasped the stone, she felt its power surge through her.

She was the warrior—she would save herself! The powerful combination of her Celtic pride and wisdom of the ancients swirled through her blood.

If Alan had seen anything out of the ordinary, he did not speak of it. He seemed to be waiting for her to speak.

Carefully testing the deep waters of newly acquired wisdom, yet untapped, she said, "Come check on me during the first change in watch. Eyreka will pack the rations she has stored away this week past."

"Rations?" He was clearly amazed.

"We have not been idle."

"'Tis the truth. I suspected you were not truly ill, but I was not certain until today. Lady Eyreka is a wonder with ash and water."

"Thank you, Alan," Eyreka spoke up as she returned to the group with a small bundle of leaves clutched tightly in her hands. Opening it, she carefully dipped her fingers in, scooping up the powdery fine ash to smooth once more on Jillian's face and neck.

"Let us hope that Harald will also continue to believe me ill."

"What next?" he asked Jillian.

"I cry out in pain, and you come back to tend me."

Shaking his head, Alan disagreed. "If you cried out, I would not be able to keep Harald away."

Eyreka's hand stilled for a moment before continuing to smooth the ashes into place. "A diversion then." She knew not what, but between them they would think of something.

"Aye," he agreed.

"Mayhap, Alan could start an argument between the two men standing watch," Eyreka said quietly.

"Brilliant," Alan beamed, rising to his feet. "You two are not timid women." He offered a hand first to Eyreka, then Jillian, helping them to their feet.

"'Tis the truth." Jillian admitted. Changing the subject, she asked the one question burning within her, "Why did you not try to escape before now?"

His face darkened. "They laid torches to my home while I lay slashed to the bone bleeding. I had nowhere to go, no hope of freedom if I did escape. Who would believe I was forced to join the rebels? Our king's spies are many, I would have been strung up and hanged before I could prove my innocence."

No one contradicted him. They all knew 'twas the truth.

"Until tonight, then," Lady Eyreka vowed.

"Wait." Jillian laid a hand on his sleeve. Turning back around, his gaze bore deeply into her own. What she saw there surprised her. Raw passion and pure unadulterated need. It lasted only a heartbeat, before it vanished, leaving only a look of concern. Had she truly seen it at all? She wondered.

"Aye, Jillian?"

"Will we escape on foot?"

"I think 'tis best. We may not get far quickly, but we will have the ability to hide. Horses cannot climb trees."

She laughed at the thought. "All right, then. On foot."

Taking a step closer, she searched his eyes for a clue as to what she thought she saw earlier. There was nothing. "Have a care, Alan."

"And you, lass."

Something tugged at her heart watching him go. His broad back strained under the fabric of his tunic, he was no small man.

Though a healer, he nearly equaled the size of her warrior husband.

Garrick, her heart cried out, but her mind overrode the plea. Her husband was not here, and even so, he believed she betrayed him. The pain of his accusation had cut deeply. Why could he not be more like Alan, who truly saw her for what she was? A woman alone, depending on her wits to get by. Heaven help her, there was no time left for thoughts of her mule-headed husband.

She was grateful to Alan for his help. It accelerated their plans to leave by a week. If either she or Eyreka faltered he would be there to lend a hand, or a powerful shoulder, to lean on. They had an ally, a friend hidden among enemies. She hoped to God it would be enough.

⇛⇛⇛⫷⫷⫷

"THEY HAVE BEEN through here, recently." MacInness sounded positive. The proof lay embedded in the loamy soil on the path, at least ten horses had passed through earlier that day.

"Is Garrick tryin' to avoid ye, mon?" Iain inquired.

"Nay, he wouldna do that. I trust him." MacInness said nothing to back up his reasoning, his opinion spoke for itself.

"I canna understand ye trustin' a Sassenach like that, but 'tis enough for me that ye do," Iain added quietly.

MacInness cupped a hand to his ear. "Hear that?"

Nodding his head, his friend put his heels to his mount's sides. They galloped across the clearing and hid in a thick copse of fir trees.

Nodding to Iain, MacInness gently stroked his hand down the star on Duncan's muzzle and placed his hand over the horses' nostrils, speaking quietly to him. Iain did the same with his horse.

A group of six mounted knights cantered into view on the far side of the clearing then slowed their horses to a walk. They appeared to be searching for something, or someone.

"I wouldna want to surprise our friends too soon," Iain warned, when Winslow made a move to let go of his horse.

"They wear Owen's colors." Though not common practice, all knights serving the Lord of Sedgeworth wore black tunics with red armbands.

"That Sassenach dog ye used to serve?" his friend prodded him.

"Aye."

"I dinna think they be here as a welcomin' party. They look to be ready to fight."

"Let's follow them, I dinna trust them, ye ken?"

MacInness's amber gaze riveted on the group of knights he knew only too well. They were Owen's elite force, those chosen for duties done behind the veil of darkness.

CHAPTER TWENTY

"**T**HAT'S THE THIRD campsite we have found in two days."
Dunstan's face settled into grim lines with their continued failure.

"We are closing in on our quarry." Garrick's voice was filled
with certainty.

"Have you heard from our Scots friend?" one of his men
asked.

The hoot of an owl echoed softly through the dense foliage,
strangely out of place in the mid-morning light.

Patrick broke into a broad grin. "'Tis himself."

Sean gave the answering call, while the others slowed their
horses to a stop, waiting.

The parting of tree branches was their first sign of MacInness's arrival. He moved like a predator, swift and quiet.

"You've finally come back then, you damned Scot," Patrick
chided his friend.

"I've brought company with me." Grinning, he motioned to
the shadows behind him. Iain, the man they'd waited for, pulled
his horse up alongside and nodded his shaggy black head in
greeting.

Eyeing him, Garrick took the man's measure in a heartbeat,
and found himself silently agreeing with his vassal. Iain was the
man they needed. It wasn't so much the man's appearance—the

side of his face and his neck were badly scarred—it was the quiet control emanating from him that commanded the men's attention. Here was a man that exuded power. A man others could follow. Definitely a man Garrick needed on his side.

It seemed Iain had been taking Garrick's measure as well. A nod in MacInness's direction proved Garrick's theory. He let go of the breath he held, realizing that he too had passed muster.

"We've been following Owen's men," MacInness said.

Garrick's face lost all expression, becoming a mask of control. Rage simmered to the boiling point. *Owen.*

The silence of the woods enveloped them. Rubbing a hand across his face, Garrick quietly spoke, "It all makes sense now. Owen has much to gain by detaining my wife. Mayhap he is hoping I will speak to the king, knowing full well that William will not change his mind about her land. He thinks I will set Jillian aside. That would leave only one man standing between Owen and Loughmoe Keep. Henri du Guerre."

"The baron has not taken a wife as yet," Patrick said.

"Do you think Owen plans to push one of his whey-faced daughters on his new neighbor?" Sean asked.

"Now, Sean," Eamon began, "not all of his daughters are pale-faced wenches. Maryon has the face of an angel."

"And the tongue of a viper," Kelly added, laughing.

"Aneuch," MacInness bellowed. The group surrounding him fell silent at his command.

Iain spoke up, "They moved northward at the fork in the road just over the ridge. We had best be going."

Garrick gritted his teeth, readying himself internally for battle. He felt it in his bones—just hours away. The silent column of warriors kept up a fast pace, gaining back precious time as their quarry's trail lay before them.

"We're gainin' on them," was all that Iain would say.

Eamon signaled and rode ahead, returning a short time later with news. "They've stopped to water their horses at a lake just ahead. If we move quickly, we can take them."

Garrick shook his head. "If we attack them now, how can they lead us to the Rebel camp?"

"We take turns following close," Garrick said. "Patrick, you and Sean ride ahead."

Looking over his shoulder, he took in the sullen form of his youngest brother. "Roderick, ride with them."

His brother's face lit up, and for a moment, Garrick saw a man possessed. But his expression changed back to a stone-carved stillness.

MacInness looked at him, but Garrick shook his head.

By dusk, the small group rejoined the hunting party with the news that Owen's men had made camp for the night. They could do naught but wait and follow at daybreak.

"Dunstan, you ride with Iain and Kelly before first light. I want one of you to ride back and let us know when they break camp."

"Aye."

"MacInness and I will take the first watch."

Thus assigned, the men settled down for a brief respite from their quest.

An hour past dawn Dunstan stormed back into the camp at a full gallop. "They're gone. Iain and Kelly are following them, they ride to the north."

With a fist raised in the air, Garrick signaled to his men to mount up. Having broken camp hours before, they easily caught up to Iain and Kelly farther up the road.

"Send someone back to check on the wagons." He turned to face his vassal. "Time to put our plan into action."

Garrick turned to face his brother. "I'll need four more men if we are to fill each and every barrel."

Roderick motioned to four of the men-at-arms riding with them. The knights followed him back the way they had come. With any luck, the wagons would catch up this evening.

JILLIAN COULD HEAR the hoof beats growing louder. "Please God, no!" Since their escape, they expected to be recaptured daily. She was tired and afraid, but for Eyreka's sake, she could not give in to either emotion.

"This way." Alan pulled both women into the hollowed out bottom of a half-dead oak tree. It was damp from recent rain and filled with an earthy-smelling rot, but it offered both shelter and a place to hide.

Frantically gasping great gulps of air after their last sprint, Jillian tried to speak, but ended up shaking her head. Huddled together, in the warmth of their friends' arms, she finally relaxed.

They had been on the run for two days now, just out of the rebels' reach. So far they had out-run and out-hid them, but the rebel band drew ever closer. She didn't know how much longer they could hold out. Eyreka grew weaker by the day.

Jillian knew her mother-in-law was stout of heart, but not as young or strong in body. She watched as her mother-in-law's steps dragged as she tried to pull her body along. She knew when Eyreka was finally too tired to run anymore. Jillian had survived on sheer determination, now even that dwindled rapidly.

Their meager store of rations would have fed the two women for at least five days or more, but the three of them had gone through the food in just two days' time. Alan's great size needed more than a woman's small appetite to fuel his body. But she did not blame him, 'twas not his fault. They never would have made it this far without him.

The first day on foot, she had suffered from a cramped leg. Alan's sure hands had rubbed the knot from her calf so they could move on. By the third day, Eyreka showed signs of weakening. Alan had taken over her turn at the watch. He wouldn't hear of dividing the time with Jillian. He took the two watches in stride. Even though a prisoner, he fared much better physically than either of the two women.

Mayhap men were stronger. She shook her head, mayhap men were stronger when on the run being chased by a band of rebels.

They were the prey: cold, tired, and hungry. The rebels were the hunters: heated by their anger, rested and fed. The odds were not in her party's favor; their time would soon be up. Jillian knew it in her heart, as surely as she knew that she still had so much left to do in her life. She wanted to set things right with Garrick before she died.

Her heart was his. Even if the king would not grant her request to reinstate her land, mayhap he would change his mind and give it to Garrick, if Garrick were free to take a Norman bride.

Her heart twisted in her breast. The thought of him with another woman caused a shaft of pain to arrow through her. But he was not hers to love, though she would wish it with all her heart. She knew from that first day he had more than his own needs in mind.

Watching how he interacted with his people, she knew he was a man who placed others' needs before his own. He was responsible for hundreds of crofters in addition to his family and the knights who served under him. Though his eyes may have glowed with the depth of emotion she wanted to test, her heart told her to face the truth of it. Garrick was a man who held honor and duty above all things. He was honor bound to rebuild the lives of his people.

Her breath hitched in her chest as she held back tears. Though he may have wanted her, though she could feel the air between them crackling with passions barely held in check, she knew he would never give in to them if it meant forsaking his word. It was his bond and all he had left of value to give anyone, and he did not give it lightly.

While she lay there listening to Eyreka's shallow breathing, she marveled anew at God's hand in her life. She had lost her own mother, but had recently found the mother-of-her-heart. Merewood Keep and its people made her feel a part of their lives. She had a place now, a home. Though she would gladly give it up if it would help the man she loved, she truly hoped that God would let her stay just a little bit longer. Worry ate at her insides until she could not be silent.

"Alan," Jillian whispered.

"Aye?"

"What's to become of us?" Her concern grew with each day on the run, as had their friendship.

"I don't know, but don't give up hope yet. You've given it back to me. I never thought to be free again, until you were taken captive."

She could not see his face clearly in the dim, small space they occupied. But she could feel his strength, and she fed off it.

"It means much, being free," she said with conviction.

"I'd give my life rather than be taken prisoner again. Now that you have helped me taste freedom again, I'll never go back. I'm ashamed now that I had been weak enough to let myself remain captive."

"But you were hurt," she protested.

"Jillian?" Eyreka called weakly.

"Right beside you. Rest now, 'tis my turn at the watch." Stroking the older woman's brow, she fell silent until she heard Eyreka's breathing even out.

"We leave at first light, lass, rest now."

"But 'tis my turn to—"

"Nay." He pulled her into his arms until she felt warm and protected. She fell asleep dreaming it was Garrick's arms around her, his cheek resting on her head.

"DID YOU COUNT the barrels?"

"Aye, brother," Roderick called out across the camp, "twelve."

Two wagons stood hitched and ready to go. The massive bulk of the horse teams chosen to pull the wagons stood chafing at the bit, their hooves pawing the ground.

"Iain?" Garrick called.

"Ready."

"MacInness?"

"Stop wasting time, mon. Ye know we're all here, like the horse team, champin' at the bit ready to fight. We dinna want to miss them."

Garrick's jaw tightened at the reminder that he had taken too long already, but he had to be sure his plan was flawless. Both his mother's and Jillian's lives would depend upon it.

Taking one more trip around the wagons, he knocked on the barrel closest to the back end of it.

"Ready," came the muffled reply from within the wooden depths.

Satisfied at last, he raised his fist into the air one last time. Three separate parties rode out, each one determined to make their part work.

CHAPTER TWENTY-ONE

JILLIAN'S GAZE MET Alan's. His eyes flashed with righteous anger. The raised broadsword hovered for a brief moment in time as her cracked lips formed around the unspoken word—*no!* The sword sliced down in a cruel arch parting sinew from bone, blood from tissue. The warmth of Alan's blood splashed on her face.

Her stomach rebelled. She fought to control the spasms, but the horror of his death was too much to bear. She retched until the meager contents of her stomach had emptied, all the while tears streamed from eyes too shocked to register what lay before her.

Eyreka's voice drifted through the haze that had suddenly blocked her vision. It was growing dark … blurry … and a thousand bees swarmed in her head.

"God in heaven, Reka, he's dead. 'Tis all my fault."

In one blinding instant, her mind and her vision cleared. The brave man she had coerced into helping them escape lay in a mangled heap at her feet. She had never imagined death to come so swiftly, nor so brutally. The image of his body hacked in twain would be with her forever. Alan had given his life for their freedom, and she would carry the guilt of his death to her grave.

She could take no more. Without a sound, she fainted dead away.

"Halt!"

Garrick kept his gaze on the man with an eye patch as he rode into the encampment.

Heeding the warning, he slowed. Every muscle stiffened ready to pounce as soon as the wagons following close behind rolled into camp behind him.

"I seek Harald. I have brought the ransom demanded."

A tall warrior strutted out from where he stood watching the progress of the party. He stood legs apart, arms crossed across his broad chest.

"You have found him," the man boldly answered.

"Where is my wife?" Garrick demanded.

"Someone will take you to her after I have inspected the wagons. John?"

A lanky man with greasy hair strode forward to grab the reins out of Garrick's hands. But he out-maneuvered the man deftly, with a foot to the middle of the man's chest, he shoved, propelling him backward.

Five rebels immediately swarmed around him, yanking the reins from his hands.

"Now then, Merewood, perhaps we shall begin with that first barrel over there."

"'Twas not part of the bargain. Where are my wife and mother?"

"The bargain is now mine to make, you have no say in how I execute it. John, get up."

A woman's shrill scream of terror echoed through the camp, an eerie silence following in its wake. Fear sent shards of ice down his spine; he knew that voice.

"Mother!" Garrick bellowed. He was a man possessed, she was somewhere nearby being tortured. He had to get to her! Leaping from his saddle, he took the two closest men out with his feet. The third he knocked down and used as a stepping stone to outrun the other two. Still he followed in the direction of the scream.

He found her kneeling beside a pile of rags, sobbing.

The rags moaned and his mind dimly registered the fact that it was his wife who lay bruised and bleeding, bound and gagged. He must have whispered Jillian's name; his mother turned to look up at him.

His bellow of outrage sounded close enough to the battle cry he was to signal his men with. Back in the clearing, a dozen armed warriors sprang up from inside the barrels where they had been hiding, waiting for his signal.

The loud clanging of steel upon steel filled the forest glade. Shrieks of pain alternated with the clash of weapons. The scent of fear mingled with the smell of blood. It blocked out the clean fresh scent from a recent rain wafting through the trees as if the battle raging were of no earthly consequence. The sun angled high overhead, its warmth touching down through the gaps in the trees.

The rebels fought with deadly intent; they outnumbered the smaller fighting force by ten, but Garrick's men were fighting to hold onto their way of life. They were fighting for honor, duty, and the lives of two women who made a marked difference in their bleak warriors' existence. Righteousness strengthened their sword arms, steeling their resolve to arise the victor.

With God on their side, and the aid of a canny Scot and his Irish mercenaries, Merewood and his men overpowered the weakening rebel force.

He ordered the prisoners bound. MacInness saw to the detail. Returning to his mother, he knelt with her at Jillian's side. Unacknowledged emotions raged through him; they were too close to love for his comfort. He tamped them down, striving for a measure of control that he did not feel.

"What happened?" His voice broke over the question.

"They beat her," she said simply.

"Why? What did she do?"

"Do? You believe she has done something to deserve this treatment?"

Before he could answer, his mother continued, "I have never met anyone more courageous than Jillian. She was unafraid, even when they executed Alan—" This time, Eyreka's voice cracked. Unable to continue, she broke down and wept.

Pulling her close, Garrick tried to make sense out of what his mother was trying to say in the midst of great gulps of air and jags of tears.

MacInness caught his eye. Garrick motioned for him to join them. When he did, Garrick turned his mother over to his vassal's capable hands.

Bending down, he brushed a wisp of hair off Jillian's forehead. His stomach flipped; the bloody, jagged split of skin had been hidden by her hair. Ignoring the acid roiling in his gut, he took his time checking for obvious injuries before looking for hidden ones. Her face was a mass of tiny cuts and odd shaped bruises. Her bottom lip was split and bleeding. Aside from the gaping cut on her forehead that would have to be sewn back together, the only other major wound appeared to be the twin bruises on her sides. The size of a man's footprint.

His wife had been kicked—repeatedly. He silently vowed to kill the man responsible. He hoped her ribs were not cracked beneath the bruises; any sudden movement could cause her further injury, even death. The thought speared through him right to his aching heart. Though he had tried to hold back the feelings and deny them, he could not. They existed and the need to tell Jillian he loved her filled him. But before he could, he had to see to her injuries and get the women to safety.

He turned to face his men, "Find out who did this." He paused, then ground out, "If Owen is behind this, he won't live long enough to be afraid of me."

"I still say we should skin them," MacInness countered loudly to Iain.

The sharp intake of breath to his left satisfied the Scot that his threat had been loud enough to be overheard, and feared.

"We need hot water, hot enough to cleanse wounds," Garrick bit out.

He worked silently, efficiently with what little supplies they had. He tore a wide strip of linen from Jillian's bliaut. Though the hem was in tatters, the rest was in one piece and was cleaner than any other cloth to be found in the camp.

While Patrick and Sean took turns at watch, Eamon built a fire to heat the water. Kelly seemed to be knowledgeable as a healer, and Garrick had him help alternately soak the deep cut across her forehead and pat the lesser cuts dry.

Having nothing else available, he carefully removed the thread from the sleeve of Jillian's gown in one long strand. He then lowered it into the boiling water, leaving it to soak. While he waited for the thread to be ready, his men rifled through the campsite and found passably clean thin strips of linen. Careful not to pull too tightly, he wound the strips around Jillian's middle to protect her battered ribs.

That done, he sat back and looked around. His eyes met with a bright amber gaze. "I need help," he simply stated.

"Ye have but to ask," MacInness replied.

"I need a steady hand to help hold her down. If she wakens…" Garrick began, but couldn't finish the thought.

MacInness placed a hand on his shoulder in a silent show of support. "There isna anything I wouldna do for the lass."

Carefully threading the needle he had found lying among the thin strips of linen, he heated it in the fire, then began the slow process of stitching the wound. Jillian murmured incoherently but blessedly did not wake. Sweat poured down his temples as he worked. Each time the needle pierced her broken flesh, bile surged up his throat, burning it.

With each tug on the threads, the wound closed a little bit more and his stomach settled—halfway there. Praise God, she lay unconscious. Garrick knew he would not have been able to stitch the wound had she been awake watching him. Finally, the deed was done. Covering the stitches with a piece of boiled cloth, he wrapped it around her head a few times to ensure the bandage would not move.

"'Tis done."

"Aye, mon, ye did well." MacInness nodded.

"I hope 'twill be enough. It's too soon to tell. Now we wait."

"Wait?" Dunstan asked coming up behind the two men.

"Aye," Garrick answered, "for the fever."

For three days while the others stood guard and tended camp, Garrick ministered to his wife. He bathed her face and neck constantly trying to bring down the fever gripping her fragile body. Twice daily, he tried to force broth down her parched throat. While tending to his wife, the overwhelming need to tell her he loved her swept over him. She had to recover soon, so he could tell her how he felt.

Deeper still were the familiar feelings of failure, of making decisions that had devastating effects on those he was responsible for—those he loved. It was his fault his bride lay semiconscious, burning with fever. His decision to set her aside must have forced her to follow him to London. Though he was still not certain why she did, he blamed himself nonetheless.

A fierce surge of protectiveness welled up within him. She was still his wife, but for the first time in his life, Garrick did not know what to do. All his life he made decisions based on the needs of others. He wanted to take her back to Merewood, where she would be safe, but he had to press on to London. He could entrust her safety to MacInness, but what if something else happened to her? He'd never forgive himself. Better to keep her close at his side.

A lifetime would not be long enough for her to forgive him. Now that his heart had convinced his head that he truly loved her, would they be destined to part? By God, he would change their destiny if he had to. But he would have Jillian as his wife.

"Please...for the love of God, no!" Jillian thrashed about in unnatural sleep, fighting an unknown enemy.

Taking her firmly by the shoulders afraid she'd add to her injuries, Garrick held her down but she did not stop. She became more agitated, crying out for help. At the end of his patience, he grabbed her, pulling her tight against his chest. She melted into his arms and a blessed silence followed.

"Is she still feverish?" MacInness sat down near Garrick.

"Aye." Pain and uncertainty swirled round inside him until his head ached from it. The look in MacInness's eyes told Garrick how much he cared. Garrick had long grown used to his vassal's feelings for his lady wife—in fact he depended upon them.

"I do not know what more I can do for her," he confessed.

"Well now, ye shouldna keep the worry all to yerself, mon. Get some rest, ye look like the verra de'il."

"She's my wife. I'll take care of her."

"Do ye really care what happens to her, then?"

He swallowed against the lump of emotion lodged in his throat. "She has to recover, there are things I need to tell her. Wrongs to be righted. I—" Garrick could not continue.

"Let me watch over her for a while. She's stronger than most from what yer mother tells me."

Taken aback, Garrick realized that he had not spoken to anyone in the last few days. He rubbed his face with his hands. His time had been spent bathing the pale, thin face of the woman who had taken hold of his battered heart with both hands.

"Have a care with her," Garrick warned, "she's so fragile."

"At first glance ye maun think so," MacInness said, "but I canna agree. It takes a woman of uncommon strength to stand up to a bunch of rebel cutthroats protectin' those she loves."

As Garrick went in search of his lady mother, he had a premonition that he would not like what he was about to find out.

CHAPTER TWENTY-TWO

"HAS THERE BEEN no word from Harald?" Owen asked, starting another lap around the cold stone floor.

"When we left, Harald's men were winning," one of his knight's answered. "Mayhap the battle turned in his favor." The man shifted his weight from one foot to the other under the fierce scrutiny of his lord's black eyes.

"Take three men and find out what happened," Owen commanded. "My entire winter store of food is out there sitting in those barrels…go and get it!"

His man stared at Owen open mouthed, then finally asked, "The ransom was for Sedgeworth?"

Owen glared at the man. The swish of steel being drawn out against leather was his answer.

"Aye, milord. At once."

"HOW IS THE she?" Eyreka asked.

"No greeting for your son, then?" he countered.

She glared at him. "I've nothing to say that has not already been said. I cannot agree with the path you have chosen, but it is not for me to tell you how to live your life. Your father and I taught you all we knew about love and life while you were young. How you could turn your back on it all is beyond me."

"I've done naught to deserve your condemnation, Mother. I have used all Father taught me well."

"Oh, aye, in battle then, but what of the things that really matter? A chance at happiness, with a wife who will love you, bear your children to carry on our proud blood?" Eyreka's eyes were empty, near soulless, searching his face for the answers she sought.

"I used to think rebuilding would somehow make amends for all of the wrongs that I had done. Now I realize it was just an excuse to hold onto the hatred." His eyes softened. "Since Jillian has come into my life, with her warm smile and gentle ways, our home has regained a measure of its happy past. If she'll give me the chance, I plan to make it up to her."

"Is there room in your heart for love, then?"

He nodded.

His mother wrapped her arms around him and something shifted inside of him and broke free. As he held her, his mind sorted through past conversations stored away in his memory. Gradually, bits and pieces of his brother's words came back to him. Dunstan did not want to be part of Garrick's decision to marry wealth. He told him he should marry a woman with a pretty face and warm disposition. Roderick blamed Garrick for hurting Jillian beyond repair, had in fact even vowed to marry her once Garrick set her aside.

Lady Eyreka eased back and locked gazes with Garrick. "'Tis time you listened to what happened." She poured out the story of their capture and Jillian's bravery and ingenuity. Then Eyreka told of their escape with the help of the healer, ending with their recapture and Alan's brutal execution.

"Why is it that you are unharmed?" He needed to know.

"'Tis yet another of your wife's brave deeds. She fought our captors tooth and nail when they let it be known that Alan was to die. She went wild," she rasped. "I was afraid they would kill her.

'Twas only when Alan pleaded with her that she calmed," Eyreka's voice broke with emotion, her eyes glazed with the remembered fear.

"You see, it was Jillian's bravery and need to be free that inspired Alan to aid us. He had been captured himself. He bore the scars of his abduction."

Tears streamed down Eyreka's face. "He told Jillian he would rather die fighting for his freedom. He felt he was less of a man, having given up the fight for freedom too easily the first time. Though she calmed, she still tried to stop them from killing him."

Garrick watched his mother close her eyes and swallow hard. "And?" Whatever she knew had to be beyond horrible. He could see it on her expressive face.

"While two rebels held Jillian's hands behind her back, four others held Alan by the hand and ankle on either side. They were face to face when he died."

Garrick pressed her for more. "How did he die?"

"God help us, they cleaved him in twain from his neck to the belly. Jillian was so close, his blood spurted in her face."

The agony his wife and mother must have suffered was beyond comprehension. No stranger to battle, he knew the effects some suffered from the carnage. His heart ached, thinking of what his gentle wife and mother had witnessed.

Staring across camp over the top of her head, he spotted his brothers. Motioning to them, he waited until they had joined him before speaking again to his mother.

"I cannot fathom the pain you must be suffering, Mother, but I must ask you something that may cause you more."

A nod of her head appeared all she could manage in the way of a reply.

"Where is the body?"

Lifting a quaking arm, she pointed toward a shallow ravine a hundred yards away.

"Dunstan, Roderick, stay with our mother. I have one last duty before we break camp."

Gritting his teeth, stiffening his spine, Garrick walked over to where Alan's body had been dumped. In reverence for the brave man, Garrick buried him in silence, a prayer in his heart that God take care of the man's soul.

Twelve rebel prisoners, bound and gagged, were loaded into the now empty wagons. The only evidence of their being in the clearing, were the bits of broken barrel lying scattered on the ground.

Though it would have been better for Jillian to be carried on a litter, it would take too long. He held her in his arms, praying she would survive the journey. They had to reach London to deliver the prisoners.

By the afternoon of the second day, Jillian's fever broke. "Milord?" She croaked out the words.

"Jillian."

Shaking her head to clear it she asked, "When…?"

"How do you feel?" His words seemed to confuse her.

"You want to know how I feel?" Her brow puckered, then she frowned and asked, "Why?"

"Why what?"

"Why do you want to know how I feel?"

His clear blue eyes were filled with compassion. "You are my lady wife. I care."

Jillian turned her face into his chest. "Wake up," he heard her say into his tunic.

"Where is Reka?"

"My mother is well, though worried about you."

"She should not be concerned about me."

"You have had wound fever for five days and nights."

With her pale face turned upward, she appeared lost and uncertain. Garrick was moved. All that he had learned of his wife should have been a surprise to him, yet somehow it was not. She had braved certain beating at the hands of her former guardians to free his brother. Yet again, she braved such treatment when she sought to save her friend, Sara, who had been threatened by

Owen and his wife. Jillian was not without courage.

He would not give up his wife. Though the battle was yet to be waged, he now must face Jillian. He had to prove himself in her eyes in the battle to win back her trust.

Gently, he traced the line of one eyebrow, then the other, repeating the caress until Jillian's eyes closed. Bending down, he touched his lips to hers with a whisper of a kiss.

Her eyes flew open, her gaze capturing his. With the tip of his finger, he explored the contours of her lovely face. Caressing the line of her cheekbone, he frowned at the yellowed marks she bore there. He traced the jagged scar on her forehead with his eyes, infinitely sorry she suffered, then pressed his lips to the edge of it tenderly. Her eyes slowly closed, and her breathing deepened. His wife had fallen asleep in his arms. It was a start.

"Garrick!"

He looked down at his wife, but the shout hadn't woken her. "Problems, Iain?"

"Nay," the Scot answered, "but we've a rough section of land to cover ahead."

"See that three more men flank the wagons," Garrick answered. "We've come too far with the prisoners to lose them now."

"MacInness and I will relieve his Irish friends," Iain said.

Though the wagon jolted over the rocks and holes ahead, all of the prisoners remained inside them. At dusk, they made camp. Exhausted, Jillian slept through the meal. Her sleep was obviously disturbed, she cried out once again. Garrick was the only one able to calm her, and as before, only when he held her.

They covered half the distance to London and still Garrick had not progressed any further in his bid to win his wife over. Because she was exhausted, he just couldn't bring himself to bring up the subject of their marriage. Thinking of the tale of their capture and imprisonment, he wondered if she feigned sleep? He could not tell.

One thing was certain, his wife was wreaking havoc with his

control, and she knew it not. Mayhap when they reached camp this evening, he would put his plans into action. He would woo his wife until she would see that he had changed his mind—he would never let her go. He hoped she would come to care for him.

CHAPTER TWENTY-THREE

JILLIAN WOKE REFRESHED for the first time in days. She opened her eyes trying to remember where she was. Her thoughts were fuzzy, and a feeling of dread burned within her. Something was not right and would never be again. Try as she might, she could not quite put her finger on it. Sitting up was a challenge, but she managed it.

The tantalizing aroma of stew drifted past her nose, her stomach rumbled, loudly. Frowning, she could not recall the last time she had eaten.

Seeing Eyreka sitting near the fire, she rose and crossed the small grassy space between them. She felt out of touch. Had she been ill that long?

"Reka. Where are we?"

"Thank the Lord you are up and about." She hugged Jillian.

"I don't remember much after…"

"You slept. We are three days outside of London." Nodding her head, she continued, "My son intends to bring the rebels before King William to answer for their treasonous acts."

"But the penalty for treason is—"

"I know what it is," Eyreka interrupted. "But it is far kinder than what Winslow and Iain had in mind."

"Iain?"

"Aye, he's Winslow's friend. Some call him mad, but I think

not."

Jillian's stomach growled loud enough to be heard.

Eyreka grinned. Rising she filled a bowl with simmering stew from the large pot. "Eat slowly," the older woman warned, "you're not accustomed to food as yet. This will put meat on your bones. You're much too thin."

While Jillian sat and ate, Eyreka filled her in on their journey southward.

Jillian asked, "Has Garrick said anything about what he intends to do with me once we arrive in London?"

"My son no longer confides matters of importance to me."

Jillian could not decide if she saw hurt in his mother's eyes, or irritation. She felt compelled to try to ease some of Eyreka's burden, lighten her mood.

"Mayhap he needs to be encouraged to open up to you, Reka. People change, he has carried a great many burdens these last years. It is not always easy to speak of what is closest to your heart." Jillian's own heart was breaking, thinking of the promise of love within her grasp, a love that was not meant to be.

Eyreka seemed to sense her need to talk; she drew Jillian closer to her side and waited.

"I am ashamed, Reka."

"Of what?"

"I am afraid."

"Everyone fears something," Eyreka soothed, "'tis natural."

Chin up, Jillian met Eyreka's level gaze. "What do you fear?"

"Being alone." Her eyes softened as she continued. "I loved Garrick's father with my whole being. When Addison died, a part of me died with him. Separately we were two very different people, but when joined together we formed one perfect person. I'll miss him always."

Jillian's eyes filled. "My parents shared a love such as that. 'Twas beautiful the way they were together. At times, they were at odds, but then all be forgiven and forgotten."

Looking her mother-in-law in the eye, she confessed, "I am

afraid of what I will become after Garrick sets me aside. Where I will go? What I will do? I have no family, no home, no dowry."

The pain that came with admitting her fear spread through Jillian's being, numbing her with its intensity. She did not feel the warmth of the hands holding hers, nor did she see Eyreka's smile.

"Would you go back to Sedgeworth?"

"And willingly become a victim of Owen's machinations? The object on which Haldana vents her frustration? Never. At one time, I thought I deserved to be beaten. I no longer do."

Smoothing the hair off Jillian's pale forehead, Eyreka spoke softly. "Don't fret over what you cannot control. It will all come aright. Besides, you are not alone, you have me."

"Not once your son marries again."

"You are still his wife." Eyreka turned her head away, to hide her tears of joy. She would not spoil Garrick's news. Besides, she was not going to smooth the way for her son one bit. He dug himself into the hole he was in, let him claw his way up and out. Her daughter-in-law's love was worth the fight ahead.

Though it pained her greatly, Jillian smiled.

"There ye are, lass." MacInness smiled, slow as molasses and warm as sin.

Her pleasure at seeing him again was genuine. "Winslow!"

"I am glad to see ye up and aboot. Have ye any pain left?"

Touching the scar he stared at, Jillian denied that she did, covering the wince she felt with a grin. "I'm fine. Is there anything amiss?" She grew oddly restless under his intense scrutiny.

"Nay, I canna believe ye're standin' before me. When we found ye, death shadowed yer face." Giving her a hard look, he continued, "Ye're a foolish woman trying to escape from Harald. Brave, but foolish."

His reminder of the horror of their recapture seeped upward from the hard pain clenching in her belly, and held her with icy fingers of dread. What little color she had, drained from her face, leaving the fading bruises and puckered stitches glaringly obvious.

"Sit," MacInness commanded roughly.

She had no choice; her legs had gone to water at the knees. Rather than embarrass herself by falling down, she folded her legs beneath her and sat back down on the grass.

"Have you a cup of water, Lady Eyreka?" the tall Scot asked.

Reaching for the cup being handed to her, Jillian saw the quicksilver flash of loving concern before it was hidden behind his mask of control. It warmed her heart to know that he cared for her. It gave her hope that she was loveable and maybe someday she'd be able to convince Garrick to care for her as deeply.

Droplets of water softened her dry lips as she drank. The coldness of the icy stream water refreshed her. Closing her eyes, Jillian gathered her fleeting thoughts, bundling them together in a bid to control them. When she opened her eyes, she was alone.

"Thank you," she whispered into the silence. She did not want to have to remind Winslow she was a married woman. His argument the last time had been very persuasive. But her loyalty to her husband would not be swayed. Mayhap 'twas time to find out Garrick's plans for her.

She found him easily. Only two other men stood as tall or broad, and they both had flaming red hair. Singling him out, she advanced slowly, rehearsing what she would say until she thought she had the way of it.

"Milady." The men surrounding her husband seemed surprised to see her. Was she not supposed to be among them? She had not noticed their reluctance to be with her before. Their reaction confused her, until each one started to speak.

Kelly stared at her, then said, "She looks pale and should be lying down."

She felt the corner of her mouth curve upward.

"Shall I carry her back, then?" Sean asked, his eyes glimmering a bright green.

"I canna see what all the fuss is about. The lass isna fallin' down. Besides, she looks fit to me," Iain added staunchly.

Jillian smiled.

"She's been through hell and back, you damned Scot. I'll take her back to lie down." Patrick's voice brooked no argument, but he got one anyway.

Hands on hips, eyes flashing, Jillian let all of them have a piece of her mind. "I can see my own way about camp. I'm no frail creature needing to stay put while others about me work their fingers to the bone seeing to my comforts."

Though her head ached from raising her voice, she did not back down. "I've come to help, you bunch of daft men. I won't have Lady Eyreka slaving over the lot of you."

Garrick's reply was as smooth as newly churned butter. "My lady mother has not lifted a finger here, other than to tend you when I took the watch."

The implication that he had tended to her left her mouth dry and her thoughts jumbled. "I, that is, what I mean to say—"

Garrick approached her cautiously, as if he were afraid she'd bolt. His men alternately frowned, then smiled, grumbling to themselves as they disbursed quietly, leaving them alone.

A breeze stirred the supple young leaves that formed the green canopy overhead. The call of a jay startled her.

"'Tis naught to fear, Jillian, you're safe with me."

Looking up into his crystal blue eyes, she believed him. Though his face appeared hard, mouth set, his eyes told their own story. Desire flared briefly before settling down to a simmer of affection.

Jillian was confused and afraid what she saw was her mind playing tricks on her.

Garrick reached a tentative hand to her. She did not resist. His touch warmed her chilled flesh, suffusing her with feelings of contentment. Her breath hitched in her chest as she allowed herself to be led through a break in the trees to a sunlit spot on the edge of a meadow.

"'Tis good to see you up. I was afraid you'd arrive in London still fevered."

Do you care?

"I know not what you are thinking, but the look on your face tells me you do not believe me."

She shrugged. "How did you find us? How long have we been here?"

Garrick looked away from her for a brief moment. "The rebel's trail was not hard to follow. 'Tis near a full fortnight we have been traveling. We will reach London in a few days."

"What then? Will you hand me over to the king?" Her sudden burst of anger surprised her, but was unable to stop herself. It was her fear talking now.

"Nay, I..."

Before she would let him speak, the fear gave way to anger. "Have you another wife picked out, then?" she interrupted. "I am sorry that I do not have more fine clothes to give her, but the few that I have were left behind when we were captured."

Garrick grabbed her by the arms and shook her. "I've not looked for another wife."

The thought of another woman being wife to her husband, receiving his tender touch, made her heart hurt and her head pound. "I promise not to get into any more trouble between here and London. You'll have plenty of time to look for a wife when we get there."

A wicked gleam shone from her eyes. "What type of woman are you looking for? Fair, dark? Mayhap you should weigh her purse before wasting your precious time courting her."

Her well-aimed barb must have struck a nerve. Her husband's jaw flexed and his eyes cooled to an icy blue. So, she thought, he can be pushed into a temper. And now I know the right buttons to push.

"Well, if you've nothing further to say, I'll be going. I'm sure Dunstan or Winslow will let me know how I can help out. In the meantime, your mother and I will come up with some suitable ideas of a wife for you."

It was the perfect exit line. Let him have a brief taste of what she had felt after their wedding. She almost walked away, pride intact.

Hands clamped around her waist in a rock-hard grip. She was whirled around and crushed up against his massive chest with such force, the air whooshed out of her lungs. When his lips descended, she was still struggling to catch her breath.

Jillian sagged against him from the lethal combination of lack of oxygen and his bone-melting kiss. Her plan to prick his temper had worked, only it backfired. He was not acting like a man filled with dislike for her. Nay, he was a man filled with passion.

"I don't need a wife," he bit out in between mind-numbing kisses.

"But you have one," she managed to say when she got her wind back.

"That I have." Garrick rained fiery kisses across her cheek and along the line of her jaw. The trail of heat left behind burned.

The last time he had kissed her, he shared his plans to leave. Fear that he would do so again shook her to the core of her being, giving her the strength to push him away.

"I will not be used only to be discarded once you have found your heiress."

"God's blood woman, do not persist in your taunts."

She fought Garrick's hold on her and pushed out of his arms. Blinded by tears, she ran across the meadow, until her lungs burned and her body ached. She could not see clearly where she was going, or where she had been. Realizing the futility of continuing, she crumpled into a heap under a tall weeping pine tree. The soft carpet of needles beckoned to her, releasing a clean pine scent when she sat on them. Physically exhausted, emotionally depleted, she let herself be lulled to sleep.

She did not stir when gently lifted, nor did she waken while being carried back to camp.

CHAPTER TWENTY-FOUR

"GOD HELP US, please don't kill him!" Jillian cried out from her tortured dreams.

"Easy, love. I'm here." Garrick's deep voice soothed her.

With her face tucked into the crook of his neck, her arms wrapped tight around him, Jillian finally let go of the horror her dreams held.

The feather-soft kiss to her brow, accompanied by a shake to her shoulder roused her from a deep sleep, ending her torment. She groaned struggling to open her eyes, trying to brush the sleep from them. She was so tired; she fell back into a deep, dreamless sleep.

When she woke, her head felt heavy again, as it had of late. She didn't sleep soundly anymore; the nightmares would not let her. It was the same dream, night after night. She and Alan stood facing one another, the sword would rise above his head, and then she would scream, remembering the cold-blooded brutality she alone was responsible for.

Finally able to focus her eyes, she was startled to find she was being observed very closely by not one, but three of her husband's men-at-arms. Their hulking forms sat in a semi-circle around her, watching her. They looked so intent, so serious, she had to smile. When she did, they smiled back.

"'Tis well ye look this morning," Winslow complimented

her.

"She looks like she slept in a—" Iain's comment was silenced by his friend's elbow.

"Didn't you sleep at all, milady?" Patrick asked. His eyes filled with worry.

"I think so. Why?" Jillian began to suspect Winslow lied about her appearance.

"'Tis the black circles round yer eyes, lass," Iain said. "They make them look twice as swollen."

"Aneuch," Winslow warned.

"Oh, and why don't we just tell her how fine she looks, when ye know 'tis a lie," Iain bit out. "The lass needs sleep, good food, and a warm bed, and mayhap a wee bit of attention from that brick-headed husband of hers, then she'll look better."

Jillian burst into laughter. The musical sound of it filtered through the clearing. "Winslow, you've not been honest with me. Have you?"

Clearing his throat, he opened his mouth to speak but no words came out. The poor man turned a brilliant shade of red before pushing to his feet and stalking away.

"Well then, Iain," Jillian stood up, "mayhap a splash of stream water would set me to rights."

"I dinna want ye to get your hopes up, lass." Iain and Patrick rose to their feet. "I canna imagine how it would help." Patrick shoved at Iain this time. Iain shoved back.

Sensing a grudge match was in the making, Jillian stepped between the men, effectively stopping it. "It's all right, Patrick. I understand what you and Winslow are trying to do, but perhaps 'tis best if I hear the truth rather than something to simply make me feel better."

Her smile went a long way toward softening the angry warrior.

"We only mean to protect ye, milady."

She laid her hand on his forearm. "I know, and I thank you for it. Please let Winslow know how I feel."

A curt nod indicated he would do as she asked, but she could tell he wouldn't like it. Turning to face the burly Scot, rumored a madman, she grinned. "So, icy water would not help."

"Och no. I meant what I said before. Ye be needin' rest lass, lots of it. Ye've no' been eatin' right. Yer clothes are hangin' loose. Yer tired. It shows."

Iain's concern was covered up by his gruff comments, but she could sense beneath the surface, 'twas just as strong as Winslow's or Patrick's. She wondered yet again, what secrets were buried in the man's past that had others labeling him mad. She had a feeling that it had to do with a great deal of pain, both physical and emotional.

"I'll keep it in mind." Over her shoulder, she said, "Mayhap the water will wake me up."

Iain's loud laughter rang through the campsite, causing heads to turn in their direction. "Ye've got spunk, lass. 'Tis why I like ye."

Smiling to herself, Jillian wondered if she had enough spunk to make her husband change his mind about her. She couldn't seem to help herself where Garrick was concerned. From the first he affected her balance. At one time, she thought it was purely a reaction to his warrior's build and handsome face, but after spending time at his home she realized that was only part of it. The way he made her heart pound and breath sigh, longing for him to kiss her again had her tumbling head over heels.

The way he cared for and about the people who depended upon him had her searching her heart for reasons to keep him from setting her aside. That she wanted him in spite of his lack of need for her was proof that she had lost her heart, as well as her mind.

Kneeling in the spongy moss lining the bank, Jillian dipped her hands in the water. 'Twas clear and very cold. Leaning over, she splashed her face and neck with its icy freshness. Shivers of pleasure gave her goosebumps. Eyes closed, she reached behind her for the linen towel she had placed there. Her hands reached and searched, but to no avail.

"Looking for something?" The depth of Garrick's voice added another layer to the gooseflesh covering her arms, though not from the cold…it was from the heat in his voice.

Jillian's eyes popped open and focused on the face not two inches from hers. His hot look had her tingling from head to toe. "Aye," she choked on the word, frantically trying to think.

At last her brain remembered where she was, what she sought, and whom she was with. "I cannot seem to find the drying cloth I brought with me." Deciding to do without, she shook her hands to quick-dry them, then smoothed the rest of the water droplets from her cheeks and chin.

His nearness made her uneasy.

"Allow me." The deep, seductive timbre of his voice seemed to reverberate through his massive chest. Garrick took his time gently wiping the rest of the water from her face with the soft cloth she'd been searching for with swift, deft motions, not one wasted.

Jillian could not have moved, or protested, if her life depended upon it. She was mesmerized by her husband's touch. *Her warrior husband*, she thought, *tall and proud*. His white-blond hair and ice-blue eyes were a testimony to his heritage; there had to be Viking blood mixed with the Saxon. Coupled with the mere sight of him, she was nearly incapable of speech or movement.

"'Twould not do to have you fall ill so soon after your recovery, Jillian." His gaze riveted on her face, slowly caressing it with the warmth of his penetrating gaze.

She trembled as his tender perusal heated her blood, igniting tiny flames, as it sped through her veins. Everywhere his intense gaze touched she burned, and there was naught she could do to control it.

Garrick reached out a hand to help her to her feet. They stood no more than a breath away from one another. His eyes locked with hers. She was powerless to move. He had a control over her no one else ever would. Whatever he wanted, she would let him take. Nay, she'd hand it to him on a hammered silver platter.

He bent his head to sip from her lips. Soft, urgent kisses that built in intensity and length. Dazzled by him, she gave in to need and kissed him back with a boldness that made him groan. Caught in a state of semi-awareness, a dream-like world where everything was surrounded with a soft filmy haze, she felt the searing brand of his hand on her knee through the fabric of her gown.

Her head cleared instantly. Next, he would tell her he was leaving, and she didn't know what to say to him that would make him change his mind and stay.

"Garrick, please stop," she pleaded.

His labored breathing and harsh sound from deep in the back of his throat told her how hard it was for him to do as she asked.

He scrubbed his face with his hands and closed his eyes. When he opened them, they were dark with intensity. "Why did you pull away?"

Tears clogged her throat, making speech difficult. She shrugged.

He grabbed her close, and demanded, "Tell me."

"I cannot."

"God's blood, wife. Why not?" His shout hurt her head.

"I am not your wife."

"You are."

"Nay," she shouted back this time. "You've not seen fit to make me your wife in deed. I am a wife in name only. And I shall remain thus." Fear curdled her stomach, then lay there making it sour. She had no means with which to defend herself against her warrior husband. More than that, she had not the right. Hating her helplessness, she lashed out at him. "I'll not let you bed me only to leave once you've replaced me." Her dark eyes were mirrors reflecting the pain that clutched at her soul.

"One day a man will want what only I can give him. Me. When that man comes along and wants to take me to wife, I'll go with a clear conscience and a glad heart, knowing I've saved the best of me and not given it away in the heat of passion."

Garrick's hands dropped from her arms, freeing her. Still he held his anger and his tongue.

Jillian didn't think it was possible to hold more hurt in her heart, but she was wrong. What she was feeling now eclipsed what she felt when Garrick shamed her by refusing to consummate their marriage, threatening to set her aside. She turned and fled.

Alone she dropped her head into her hands and prayed, "Help me, Mother. What shall I do?"

⟫⟫⟫✦⟪⟪⟪

GARRICK LET HER go. He wanted to tell her he'd changed his mind, but he sensed that her anger would not let her believe him.

After what seemed to be enough time to let her reason it out, he followed her. He found her sitting beside the stream with her head tucked into her bent knees. He thought she was weeping, though she made no sound. Needing to tell her of his new plans, he called her name, "Jillian?"

When she looked up, his gut twisted. Stark pain left shadowed lines of hopelessness etched upon her beautiful face. To know that he was the cause of such pain added yet another black mark on his soul. He didn't know what to say to her, where to begin to apologize for hurting her. *Would she believe what he had to say?*

In the end, he turned from her, walking back to their camp. "MacInness," he shouted. "Dunstan."

"Aye?"

"Brother?" Dunstan's face mirrored MacInness's concern as they stood before their overlord.

Garrick knew his temper was high. 'Twas all he could do not to strike out with his fists to cool the rage that boiled inside of him. She wanted him, but couldn't trust him. Years of training took over. He reined in his black thoughts and crimson rage with every shred of control he could muster, wiping all trace of emotion from his face.

"Make ready for the last leg of our journey. The rebels will not remain docile much longer. I've a bargain to keep."

"Bargain?" MacInness echoed. "With whom?"

"'Tis none of your concern." Garrick's clipped reply seemed to bring the Scotsman up short. For once, the man remained silent, lifting a brow in question.

His brother, however, would not be left in the dark. Dunstan asked, "What bargain? Have you made plans for your wife, then?" His stance became rigid. "If not, I will take her to wife myself."

"Well now," MacInness drawled, "if memory serves, 'twould make that three offers for yer lovely bride. How will ye decide who gets her, then?"

"I will decide my own future." The husky reply coming from behind the men shocked them as much as it did Garrick.

Chin raised, she glared defiantly at him. "I am not without means, and will have a say in what is to become of me."

"But ye've no family, lass," MacInness reminded her.

"No dowry," Dunstan further commented.

The hair on the back of Garrick's neck bristled at the look in her eyes. Whatever she planned, he was certain she would accomplish it. He had seen that look thousands of times, facing an enemy in battle. *Kill or be killed.* All of a sudden, he was afraid to ask just what she planned, and afraid not to.

Thousands of questions danced on the tip of his tongue. He wanted to ask her what she would do. How she would secure a future when she was a woman without means. On the heels of those questions lingered a dozen more, all centering around his need to profess his growing love for her. He had never felt like this before and didn't know how to handle these feelings—let alone give voice to them. In the end, he decided to wait. He barked out the order, "Pack your things, Jillian. You ride with MacInness."

Taking one step closer to the maid who ignited a fire in his gut and love in his heart, he waited for a touch, a word of explanation.

Jillian's whispered reply was barely audible. "I am ready." She walked stiffly to where the horses were tied.

She refused to confide in him. Could he blame her when his trail of broken promises followed in her wake? He had sworn to protect her, and he'd failed.

The hand on his arm gave him a start. A look over his shoulder at MacInness did nothing to ease his conscience.

"I canna think the lass would have anythin' of value hidden away at Sedgeworth, and I wilna believe if she had any coin she would keep it from ye. It maun be somethin' ye have yet to grasp."

"Mayhap the ride will loosen her tongue." Garrick hoped it would. "'Twill be a fair distance before we stop again."

"I will do my best to get the lass to open up. I'm verra good at talk."

"Aye." The half-hearted attempt at a smile felt stiff to him. He hoped no one would try to get him to talk on the ride ahead.

"THERE'S NOTHING LEFT of the barrels, milord," Aaron dutifully reported. "We've brought the pieces with us for your inspection."

"Nothing? No salted pork? No grain? Nothing?" Owen was incredulous. Not only had the women escaped from the rebels once, but twice. Worse still, no ransom had been paid. Nothing had been gained for all of his planning.

"That was to be our food for winter," he ground out between tightly clenched teeth.

"But milord … there was no sign of spilled meat, nor flour. Not a trace."

"What of Harald?"

"There were signs of battle, low hanging branches broken. Dirt churned up."

Owen's eyes narrowed. "Anything else?"

"Aye." The man hesitated.

"What then?" Owen demanded. For all his girth, he was apt to move quickly.

His man-at-arms stepped to the side in a bid to avoid his overlord, leaving his back protected by the stone wall. "Three freshly dug graves."

"And did you not think to uncover them?" At Aaron's grimace of disgust, Owen asked, "How else are we to know the outcome of the skirmish? I need those supplies, and I need to know what happened." Leveling his vassal with a look, he added, "Do not fail me."

CHAPTER TWENTY-FIVE

"HEAR THAT, LASS?" Winslow cocked an ear, listening intently.

"Nay," Jillian stubbornly refused his latest attempt to draw her into conversation.

Doing so for the last hour had the base of her skull pounding. It was her own fault, she thought, the poor man was only trying to be nice to her. Deciding to lower her guard and cool her temper, she tilted her head to listen and heard the high keening call of a hawk screeching for its mate.

Mate. The word haunted her. Deep inside her a voice whispered, *Garrick's the one.* I'm not sure if he wants me, her mind stubbornly answered the voice. *Talk to him, give him the chance to explain.*

While her mind tried to work out the plan that she had formed, their journey progressed ever closer to London, the place where her love for Garrick would be tested. If she should succeed, she would be able to gift him with the one thing he desired above all, material wealth for his family and his people. *If she failed…* She would not even consider the ramifications should she not be able to convince the king.

What of your vows? Her conscience spoke again. Unwanted tears clogged her throat. Unrequited love took hold of her heart and squeezed it.

"He'll always be the husband of my heart."

"A lot of good that will do ye on a cold night," Winslow retorted.

Aghast that she had spoken her thoughts aloud, she turned away to hide her flaming cheeks. Forcing her tears back with a will of iron, she pasted a false look of contentment on her face and stared ahead. There was no going back, only ahead.

Lady Eyreka and Winslow had tried to force Garrick and Jillian together, but to no avail. Her husband could not seem to hold a conversation for more than a few moments, and only if it entailed the most impersonal of topics. Still recovering from the ordeal of her capture, Jillian decided 'twas best to keep quiet.

Garrick maintained a distance between them for the rest of the journey, only speaking to her when courtesy demanded. His questions were never more than cursory. How had she fared that day? Was she hungry? Cold? Tired? Never offering to delve deeper into the hurt wrapping itself around her heart. Was it because of the heavy burden he carried, bringing the rebels to justice? Or something more?

By the time they reached their destination, Jillian was more than ready to petition the king. She had to end the tension existing between Garrick and herself. He was so preoccupied; he didn't notice she had drawn within herself.

The echo of hoof beats pounding against stone jarred her from her semiconscious state. *They had arrived.* She looked to the ramparts where armed guards watched their slow entry with undisguised interest. Odd, not one of them demanded their group halt.

"Why are the guards ignoring us? Shouldn't they be asking who we are and what we want?"

Roderick moved his horse closer and answered, "We are expected." Nodding over his shoulder, he glared at the group of closely guarded prisoners.

Jillian didn't need to follow his gaze to look at the rebels, she'd never forget them. But now that she was so close to her goal, the prospect of speaking to the ruler who'd ultimately been responsible for the loss of her home and way of life made her stomach roil and fingers of dread slither up her spine.

Misunderstanding her unspoken fear, Roderick reassured her, "The king has waited a long time for this particular group of rebels."

Mayhap the king knew something of Garrick's plans and would be willing to share a bit of that valuable information with her once she made her offer.

"Take the rebels to the dungeons." Garrick's voice cut through the stillness around them.

As if by magic, his words brought everyone in it back to life. People called loudly again from one side of the bailey to the other, their voices carrying across to her. "…I hear he's gonna hang them all!" one of the men unloading a wagon filled with hay called out.

Horrified at the prospect of more death, she listened to the rest of the conversation.

A burly man tossing a bale of hay onto his back called out, "They're to be drawn and quartered."

Every ounce of spit dried up in her mouth as she watched the men haul the hay into the stables.

A contingent of soldiers arrived to escort the prisoners. Two barefooted young boys pushed and shoved one another across her line of vision on their way toward the well.

She was so caught up in the activity and snippets of conversation she didn't realize Garrick stood beside her until his strong hands encircled her waist. Warmth filled her at his touch.

Did he realize the effect he had on her? She dared a glance at him through lowered lashes as he lifted her from the saddle and set her gently on the ground. When she looked up, his gaze locked on hers. Passion and desire swirled in the pale blue depths as he stared at her lips.

She stared back, wanting, nay needing him to take her in his arms and kiss her. Had she lost her wits? Her heart bled for him, but she knew 'twas not meant to be. This one kiss may be the last one they shared.

He tightened his grip and bent his head.

"Garrick!"

He blinked and the stark warrior's gaze returned. Garrick eased back, nodded to her, and dropped his hands.

The tingling sensation of being so close to her heart's desire made her head swim. Locking her knees to keep from falling, she managed to hide the fact that she'd nearly fallen on her face. Lord, she was weary.

Determined now more than ever to follow through with her plans, Jillian breathed in a deep calming breath, drawing on her inner reserves. She had a meeting to arrange, and though her ultimate goal may have changed, her purpose had not altered. 'Twas time to act.

Hours later, all of her eagerness began to wear off as the evening's feast drew ever onward. One platter followed another as their appetites were tempted with an assortment of delicately cooked fowl and meat. Sweetmeats, cakes, and cheese accompanied the spiced, and honeyed wine. Her body cried out for nourishment, but her stomach wouldn't hold more than a mouthful or two.

"You must eat to keep your strength up," Eyreka chided.

"I'm not as hungry as I had thought." Pushing herself away from the still-full trencher she tried to smile, thinking of the unfortunates who would benefit from her lack of appetite. At least she hoped most of her meal would be given to the poor as was the custom, and not to the dogs lying on the rushes at her feet, ever vigilant in their bid to appease their hunger.

Midway through the meal, she noticed the late arrival of a small party. Her hands clenched the goblet she held tighter. Owen and his family! *So they were still here.* 'Twould bear watching, remembering the mention of his name while she and Lady Eyreka were held captive.

She nudged Eyreka with the toe of her slippered foot. Their

eyes locked for a heartbeat before the lady looked in the direction Jillian nodded. A look combining both hatred and pain crossed the older woman's face, then she turned back with a look of warning.

Jillian acknowledged the look with a slight nod and dipped her hands in the herb-laced water bowl to remove any trace of the meager attempt she made at eating. Drying her hands on the cloth provided, she waited for the meal to end. It seemed an interminable amount of time had passed before the king rose, signaling that the meal had finally ended.

Upon rising, the king beckoned to Garrick, who sat on the other side of his mother from her. Her husband rose and made his way to his sovereign's side. She watched him walk away, hoping she'd not seen the last of him or else she'd never be able to explain why she'd pushed him away.

"Do you think he noticed Owen?" Eyreka asked.

Jillian shook her head. "I'm not sure. Owen and his family are seated on the far side of the room." Pausing, she leaned closer to Garrick's mother. "Shouldn't we be more concerned with whether or not they saw us?"

Eyreka didn't have time to answer as Garrick's brothers were ready to escort them back to their chamber.

"'Twas a fine meal—" Roderick began, only to be interrupted by his brother.

"Did you see Owen and his family?"

A meaningful look passed between the brothers before Roderick spoke. "I noticed, but what good would it do to mention the obvious? One look at Lady Jillian is enough to see that she too is aware of his presence."

"What business does Garrick have with King William?" she asked. "Does it have to do with the Rebels?" *Or the end of our marriage?*

Dunstan's eyes were filled with understanding, which warmed her heart, while at the same time, the fact that his eyes were the exact same shade of Garrick's totally unnerved her.

Why couldn't I feel something for Dunstan? He's more steadfast in temperament and actions. Merewood's people need him to aid in planning, planting, and harvesting. But unlike his older brother, he's not ultimately responsible for their people's lives.

She searched her heart and his gaze for a portion of the feelings she had for Garrick. 'Twas not the same. She cared about Dunstan, but Garrick held her heart, and was the man she loved unconditionally.

The full weight of that realization struck her hard in the chest. It was the first time she acknowledged her true feelings. Heart in her eyes, she met Dunstan's gaze.

He cleared his throat. "So that's the way of it, milady?"

"I would welcome an offer of friendship." She hoped he would not turn his back on her.

He didn't. Taking her hand in his, Dunstan brought it to his lips. His breath across her skin warmed it, but no answering call swept up through her being, threatening to take control of her mind, body, and soul. She smiled, though it didn't quite reach her sorrow-filled eyes.

"I know our brother meets with the king to report on the capture of the Saxon Rebels," he admitted, "but as to any other reason…" He shrugged. "I have no idea."

Desperate to push him to see if he knew but didn't want to confide in her she rasped, "I was hoping to find out how much longer I had before your brother ends our marriage."

"Now, Jillian, dear," Eyreka said, putting her arm around her, "you do not know for certain that it is inevitable."

Acute sorrow swept through her. "I do know that unless I am able to convince the king otherwise, Garrick will soon be free to marry another." The silence that followed her comment was palpable.

"And just how do you plan to change the king's mind?" Roderick demanded.

"Aye, Lady Jillian," Dunstan looked ready to explode, "how?"

Looking from one brother to the other, she realized they were more like Garrick than she'd thought. Mayhap it would be best to tread carefully and mind her words.

"The less you know," she said, dropping her voice to just above a whisper, "the safer you shall be." The uneasy feeling of being observed through the second half of the meal returned. She darted a quick glance around her expecting to see Haldana glaring at her, but the woman was nowhere in sight. Their small party was the only one about. A shudder worked its way up her spine.

"Has someone threatened you?" Dunstan demanded. "I'll deal with him myself." The middle brother placed his hand on the hilt of his sword.

"Who threatened the lass?" Winslow bit out.

Spinning around to face the warrior, Jillian felt her skin grow clammy with fear. He hadn't seen Haldana, had he?

An inch away from her he stopped and demanded, "Well?"

Her gaze met his. Anger, hot and deadly emanated from her protector. Rather than hold his gaze until she confessed each and every thought running through her brain, she looked down at her gown, picking at a fold, giving it her full attention.

The rough fingertip beneath her chin redirected it. "How can I protect ye from harm if ye wilna help me to do it?"

The plaintive plea in his voice tugged at her heartstrings, but she could not give in. Why depend on people who wouldn't be there when she needed them?

"Who threatened ye?" he repeated.

"No one." The lie slid off her tongue easily.

Her Highland protector clenched his jaw with enough force to crack all of his teeth. He was as mad as a rabid dog.

"I'll find out, milady," he vowed, "and God help the mon responsible. I'll skin him alive."

Judging from the look on his face, she didn't doubt for a moment he would do just that.

Eyreka intervened, placing a hand on the Scotsman's forearm. "Thank you for the escort, Winslow dear," she soothed. "Will you be guarding us tonight?"

His gaze broke away from Jillian's, though it appeared to be killing him to do so. "Aye."

Jillian wondered if he would choke on his tongue in an effort not to bite it off.

"Don't trouble yourself, Winslow," Jillian hastily added. "We will be perfectly safe. Go and get some rest."

He moved with lightning speed, grabbing her by the arms and forcing her to look up at him. They stood toe-to-toe, chin to chest. For the first time since he took over the job as protector, she was uneasy.

"Ye wilna step from this room," he ordered. "I'll have yer word on it, Lady Jillian."

It was telling that he didn't call her lass. Mayhap she would have to forego her plans to seek out the king. Amber fire lay banked, waiting for her agreement, or mayhap the excuse to break free and burn all in its path.

Bravely meeting his commanding gaze, she gave her word. "I'll not leave this room—by the door."

Immediately his grip loosened, and he stepped back. She smiled at his relief, almost feeling sorry for the man. She hadn't promised to stay; she'd only agreed not to use the door.

⋙✳⋘

JILLIAN BIT BACK another cry of pain as her already raw knees scraped the outside wall of the castle for the umpteenth time. Eyreka's head poked out the window yet again. "Are you all right?"

She swallowed hard, and answered, "Aye."

There was no other way out of their chamber; she had to be patient and pay better attention to the sway of the rope and the closeness of the wall. "Just a little more rope, a little bit lower now, and I can jump to the ground."

"Be careful."

Smiling up into the darkness, she promised. *Lord, please let me land without breaking a limb.*

The bedpost they had tied the knotted bedclothes to, held fast as she was lowered to within ten feet of the ground.

Now, or never, she told her quaking limbs.

Now!

She let go of her lifeline and landed on her feet with a bone-jarring thud, then promptly fell onto her backside. She gasped, drawing in a deep breath at the sudden stinging sensation numbing her legs and back.

"Jillian?" Eyreka's voice reached her.

"Take the sheets back in and untie them," she managed. "Hurry!"

Once Garrick's mother was gone from view, she stood up, groaning in pain. Taking a few tentative steps, she was able to loosen the cramps in her legs, and those in more embarrassing places.

"It didn't look that far down," she mumbled to herself. Too busy trying to rub the numbness and pain from her bottom and back, she didn't see the guard approaching until her body collided with his.

"What's a pretty lass like you doing alone on a night like this?" The soldier's tone was liberally laced with undisguised warmth.

Momentarily speechless, she stared.

The warrior looked her up and down, and his gaze grew hotter. Self-conscious, Jillian raised her hand to her hair. It had come out of the braid and was curling about her face and throat. A hand to her shoulder told her it was bare. The chainse had slipped off her shoulder. Jerking the material back up onto her shoulder, she stammered. "I … I'm Lady Jillian of Merewood—"

"Garrick's wife?" he interrupted.

"Aye, but—"

"Come with me." He grabbed her arm and held fast escorting her through a nearby door. They made their way through the maze of torch lit hallways stopping before a heavily guarded door.

"Your husband is still with the king, but I am sure he would want you with him." The sadly misinformed soldier stood ready to knock on the closed door.

Before he could, it opened wide, and Garrick backed out of the room. Her breath caught in her throat at the sight of his broad back outlined with the bright light from the room.

She panicked. *He can't find me here!*

The guard was temporarily sidetracked by whatever was going on within the room. She took advantage of the guard's lapse and darted into the shadows down the darkened hall.

"Lord Garrick, your wife is here—" The guard turned around, but she was already gone.

"Jillian? Impossible, she's in our chamber sleeping. Is something amiss?"

The guard shook his head. "I must be mistaken, but the woman, wench, had the look of your wife about her." He ventured off down the darkened passageway looking to the left and then the right.

Garrick turned and headed toward his chamber, and the woman he needed to hold. He had news he wanted to share with her. Preoccupied, he didn't see the wraith-like shadow creeping back toward the king's chamber door, but he must have felt her presence as he called out to her, "Jillian," his voice was hard as stone.

Her hand dropped and she grimaced at the censure in his voice. She turned away from the door, so close to reaching her evening's goal. "Aye?"

"I'll have your explanation now." He stood rooted to the floor, his stance battle-ready. The look in his eye brooked no arguments.

Hope speared through her like a well-sharpened battle lance. Mayhap now was her chance. If he wanted an explanation, she'd give him one. "May I speak with you in private?" Jillian did not want to disclose her evening's activities within earshot of anyone save her husband.

Garrick practically dragged her down yet another unfamiliar section of hallway. Throwing open a massive door, he pulled her into the room. After a furtive glance down the hall, he shut the door behind them.

Silence engulfed them, sealing them off from the rest of the occupants of the castle. Though the room was lit by the soft glow of a torch on the wall, Garrick proceeded to light the candles lining the table by the bed.

Jillian noticed his hands shook. *Why?*

"Sit." As she settled onto a cushioned chair near the cold brazier, he seemed to steel himself.

Garrick got right to the point, "Is he dead, then?"

Baffled, she asked, "Is who dead?"

"MacInness. It's the only possible explanation for you to be sitting before me so obviously abused by a man. MacInness must be dead. How did it happen?"

She barely managed to contain the giggle of mirth bubbling up inside her. "Winslow is fine. As a matter of fact, I am fine."

His intense gaze turned bitter cold as it locked with hers. "Never fear you cannot trust me with the truth, wife. I took a vow to protect you, and I mean to follow through with that vow."

Her temper flared burning brightly as he turned colder. Her voice broke, "What of honoring the vows of marriage we spoke before God and man?"

Garrick opened his mouth to speak then changed his mind, locking his jaw down tight.

The hope that sprang to life in her breast only a short while ago shriveled up and died a slow and painful death. "I see."

"You cannot possibly begin to understand," he bit out, "I have given my pledge to speak to no one." His hand reached for hers. "Can you not trust me?"

Jillian wanted to believe, to trust, but she had things to do before she could answer him. She blinked at the moisture pooling in her eyes and shook her head.

Going down on his knees before her, he took her hands. She stared down at their joined hands. His were scarred, twice the size of hers but they enveloped hers with a warmth that suffused itself all the way to her bones.

"There are things you don't know about me," he hesitated, "things I have done in the past that would shock you to the point where you would revile me."

Cupping his cheek in her hand, she lightly stroked his jaw. "'Tis not possible." Compassion for him swirled through her. Had he no one to confide his fears, no one to soothe away the hurt she sensed went right down to his soul?

"Then why can you not trust me?" The hurt in his eyes mirrored the pain she now felt.

Moved, she asked herself the same question. Could she trust him? Glancing down into his clear blue eyes, she nodded. "I want to trust you."

He reached for her hand. It was that easy. Two lost souls reached out for what each thought they were unworthy of seeking. *Forgiveness. Acceptance. Love.*

A tentative bridge was crossed in that brief span of time. Blessedly their souls beckoned, their hearts trusted, and their minds opened.

The overpowering need to set him at ease so he would be able to trust her filled her. For a moment she didn't know how to get him to do so. Closing her eyes, she prayed for guidance.

The answer filled her entire being. In order to get him to trust her, she had to trust him by unburdening her own heavy heart. "Much has been done to me since the death of my parents. Those who would call themselves my guardians took out their frustrations on me. Their children treated me lower than a servant." Fierce Celtic pride surged up from within her. "I am not afraid of being beaten," she rasped. "I have survived worse."

Searching his face for a spark of understanding, what she saw stole the heart she so closely guarded. Naked pain and longing were etched across his handsome brow and suspicious moisture clouded his beautiful eyes.

He understood, shared her pain, and thus her heavy burden.

"I cannot change the past, but I can change the future." He pressed his lips lightly to her hand, brushing them reverently across one knuckle at a time before straightening up, not letting go of her hand.

"The first part of my plan has been successful. The king promised to bestow a reward upon me for the capture of the rebel prisoners."

"What kind of reward?" Her interest was piqued.

"Grain to feed my people through the winter."

"That is beyond wonderful! Gert will be so happy!"

"That's not all," he said. "He's promised one head of cattle for each man brought in, though he did not say when we would receive this reward."

The enormity of the boon hit her. Merewood's people would not starve this winter. She silently rejoiced for Garrick. Though it would cause more unrest, she had to tell him about her guardian's part in the abduction, but he was so happy, she didn't want to destroy his moment of sheer elation.

While she waged a silent war with how to break the news to him, Garrick stroked the palm of her hand, drawing circles between the patches of work-roughened skin, eliciting tiny shivers.

Her heart recognized they were destined to be lovers, and whether or not they would remain married, she knew in her heart her fate lay in her husband's strong hands.

Struggling to still her racing heart, she was finally able to speak coherently. "There is something that you should know, husband. While your mother and I were held captive, I heard Owen's name mentioned more than once. It had something to do with the ransom they were asking."

When he remained silent, she asked, "Was it difficult to come up with what he demanded?"

"Nay."

She sighed, "Praise God for that. I will see to it that you don't ever regret paying it."

"I didn't pay it." His voice was clipped, curt.

"Then how were we freed?"

"Your father was a great warrior, was he not?" His shift of topics worried her.

"Aye."

"Then he knew of the Trojan Wars."

She nodded, waiting for him to continue. When it became apparent he was finished speaking, she prodded him to further explain. He told her of the ingenious Greek plan to gift the Trojans with a huge wooden horse.

She nodded. "My father told me the Greeks gained entrance into the city of Troy with their gift."

Garrick seemed to be waiting for her to say more, then shrugged. "We had two wagons filled with barrels. They were to be filled with the ransom of salted meats and grain. But when we drove them into the rebel camp—"

"They were empty," she asked, "weren't they?"

He shook his head. "Each contained a warrior." Garrick described how his men had hidden until he gave the signal then they leapt out of the barrels surprising the Saxon Rebels.

Pride filled her, but she still wanted to know about the ransom. "Why did you not want to pay?"

"'Twas not a matter of want," he said through clenched teeth. "I had it not."

Understanding added one more link to the chain binding them together. Each had used their wits to bring about the safe return of his mother, a woman dear to them both. Though Jillian's attempt had failed, it ultimately aided Garrick's successful capture of the rebels.

The tentative beginnings of trust blossomed between them. Their gazes met and held, understanding followed. When Garrick opened his arms, she flew into them.

CHAPTER TWENTY-SIX

HIS ENVELOPING WARMTH spread through her like a welcoming burst of sun after weeks of rain. Garrick buried his face in her hair, breathing deeply. A euphoric sense of happiness took hold of her. Reveling in his embrace, she trusted him, giving herself over to him fully, for the first time.

As their lips met, barriers of distrust melted. The tender way he kissed her reinforced her belief in him.

Slowly, he lifted his wife into his arms and carried her over to the bed. As gently as he could, he laid her on top of the linen bedclothes. Gazing into the cinnamon depths of her eyes, humbled by the unspoken promise of forever, he was lost.

JILLIAN MOANED WITH pleasure. Garrick was making her feel things she hadn't known were possible. With each rub of his tongue, each deep pull of his mouth, her body arched and writhed. Her woman's core wept with pleasure as her husband built a fire that burned hot and fierce.

Her passion cooled as he slipped her chainse and bliaut over her head. When she would have pulled back, he paused, meeting her gaze, silently asking for her trust. Incapable of speech, Jillian nodded, giving it to him. In response, heavy, callused hands stroked every inch of her. Garrick unleashed the passionate side of her he must have sensed lay just beneath the surface.

Jillian pushed his tunic up and over his head and ran her hands up and down the taut muscles across his back and chest. Then it was her turn to rain hot, moist kisses on his face and neck, until he arched and writhed under her awkward, but loving, hands.

Pulling free of his braes, he settled between her legs, drew in a deep breath, and paused. "I don't want to hurt you."

"You won't." The lie slipped off her tongue. She knew there would be pain, but she needed to mate with this man more than she needed to draw in her next breath.

He groaned and eased forward, every muscle in his upper body straining to hold back.

"Garrick, please?" she begged.

He was huge, and it started to burn, but she wanted him. Needed to be his wife in all ways.

She called his name one more time, and it was as if something broke inside of him. He surged forward, plunging deep inside Jillian's welcoming warmth. Her hips rose to meet each hard thrust, again and again, until they were at the brink of a precipice.

"Love me," he rasped.

"I do," she groaned.

They were lifted high above themselves, muscles clenching and clinging, not yet willing to let go.

Jillian's orgasm slammed into her. Garrick felt her body tense then go slack, and he followed her into the madness, emptying himself into her with a shout.

The candles had long since gone out; the torch burned low. Velvet darkness swirled around them. Held close in Garrick's arms, Jillian fell into a deep, dreamless sleep.

THE KNOCK AT the door roused them from their love-induced sleep. She felt the bed move, but wasn't ready to get up. She rolled over, ignoring Garrick's soft command to wake up. She heard the musical splash of water and knew her husband must be washing.

"Jillian." Garrick nudged her gently.

"Mmmm?"

"Wake up." This time Garrick's lips brushed the edge of her ear.

She rolled over onto her belly, tangling herself in the linens. His sharp intake of breath instantly cleared her mind. *Her scars!* She tensed, waiting for him to acknowledge them.

He pressed his lips to her back, tenderly, as if the scars were newly healed. His tender touch spoke volumes. Holding her bliaut to her, he rasped, "Here, put this on."

"Garrick! Open up," a deep voice demanded from the other side of the door.

His eyes mirrored his sorrow at the visible proof of the beatings she'd suffered through.

"Open the door, mon," MacInness called out. "Lady Jillian is gone."

Instead of answering, he stepped closer and spun her around. His warm lips touched the worst of her scars and all of her doubt fled.

"Garrick!"

Words were superfluous. He pressed his lips to the nape of her neck and turned her back around so he could kiss her mouth. He slid the garment over her head and called out, "Enter."

"Milord, 'tis yer lady wife. She's…" MacInness stopped dead in his tracks and swore. His gaze swept over her sleep-tumbled hair. She knew she must look a sight, but could not help that, or the smile bubbling up inside.

"Well, now, 'tis about time." His broad grin flashed at her.

Could he tell from her smile she and Garrick spent the night making love? She shook her head, it just wasn't possible.

He turned back to Garrick. "Yer mother is near mad with fear. She keeps tryin' to tell me somethin' about the window."

Jillian coughed to try to cover her laughter.

Garrick shot her a look that promised retribution. "Mayhap my wife would like to tell us how she came to be in this part of the castle last night?"

"I canna understand why ye dinna ask last night, mon."

Garrick's jaw tightened then relaxed as he smiled at her. "We were trying to settle other matters." His gaze locked with Jillian's. The beauty of last night's loving came back full force, distracted she didn't notice both men were now glaring at her.

"Well, Jillian?" Both men asked simultaneously.

Looking from one to the other, she finally noted the black looks each was sending her. There was no hope for it; she would have to confess. "I climbed out the window," she decided not to tell of Eyreka's part in the scheme.

"But that's twenty feet off the ground!" Garrick boomed. Agitation, evident in the deep lines of concern, bracketed his mouth.

"Ye could've been killed, lass! Have ye no concern for those who care about ye? What would Lady Eyreka have thought?"

"Who do you think held the rope?" she muttered under her breath.

"Rope?" Garrick took a menacing step closer, Winslow hard on his heels.

Chin up, eyes blazing, she closed her mouth, refusing to say anymore. Her mutinous expression must have warned both men off, for the moment.

Garrick was the first to sigh and take a step back. "Go and tell my mother that Jillian is with me."

Jillian could feel the blush heating her face, as she added, "And that the fall didn't do any serious damage."

As soon as the words were said, she could have kicked herself. She closed her eyes and counted to ten. When she opened them, her husband and his vassal stood hands on hips just a few inches away.

"'Twas not so far to the ground. I'd rather not discuss it right now." Turning around, she thought that would end it. She was wrong.

Two strong hands gripped her arms and whirled her around. Ice blue eyes flashed a warning effectively silencing her. "How far was it?" Garrick bit out through clenched teeth.

Swallowing the lump of fear that rose in her throat, she managed, "Only ten or so feet."

"Leave us." Garrick's voice had gone suspiciously soft. Without another word, the tall Scot retreated.

"Why?"

"I'd rather not say."

Pulling her closer he glared her into talking. "I wanted to speak to the king."

"I had just been to see the king. What possible business could you have with him?"

She could not meet his eyes. If she told him now, would he go into a rage before listening to why she wanted to meet with the king?

The inner war she waged with herself must have shown on her face. Garrick stroked first one eyebrow, then the other, then drew his fingertip down the bridge of her nose. Dear Lord, she loved him. 'Twas not such a hard decision after all. Hadn't she trusted him with her heart last night? "I know that you wish to end our marriage, but I don't."

"Jillian, I don't—"

She wouldn't let him finish. "I must now ask you to trust me. I cannot say just yet what I have planned; to do so would jeopardize everything. Please, Garrick?"

They stared at one another; finally, he broke the silence between them. "I trust you. You have never gone back on your word. You are more honorable than I have been," he rasped. "But you don't understand, I do not wish to end our marriage."

Jillian threw herself into his arms, kissing him with desperation.

"You'll tell me as soon as you are able?" he asked.

"Aye, husband."

He put his arms around her, holding her against his heart. "Who else knows of your plans?"

"Your mother," she sighed snuggling against him. "Can you arrange a meeting with the king? The sooner I see him, the better. We do not know why Owen is here, so we can only assume 'tis not to our benefit."

He traced the line of her cheek and jaw with a fingertip. "You are a rare woman. Not only brave, but wise as well. I don't know that I deserve you, but I will do all in my power to see you safe and happy."

"I'll speak to William this afternoon, when I am to meet with him again. Can you be ready by then?"

Love flowed through her. "Aye." She could still not fathom the fact that he had not shunned her for the ugly scars crisscrossing her back. He'd kissed them, cementing her decision to trust him. A wondrous thought filled her. *What if their night of loving produced a babe?* She placed a hand on her belly.

When she looked up, Garrick was staring at her hand, she wondered if he too wanted a babe, but was too shy to ask.

Her husband's expression changed to one of resignation. "We had best go to the hall to break our fast. I promised MacInness we'd meet early. We have to find out what Owen is up to."

Making their way back to the hall, Jillian felt the warm cocoon of Garrick's love surrounding her. She had promised to trust him, and in return, Garrick had given his word to trust her. Lord willing it would be enough.

Eyreka rushed forward to embrace her as they entered the hall. "Thank goodness you are well. How's your—"

Jillian shook her head to cut her off and whispered, "I'll tell you later."

They smiled like two conspirators, causing Garrick to raise an eyebrow over their quiet conversation, but he did not pursue it.

"Mother, would you mind if Jillian kept you company in your chamber until this afternoon?"

"But we planned on touring the castle."

Garrick shook his head. "I must meet with the king. You would be safest in the chamber."

Jillian soothed the older woman, "We shall see the gardens later. Garrick has much to discuss with our king. Besides, I've given my word to trust him. Can you not do the same?"

Eyreka smiled at her words. "Aye, daughter. I can."

"No climbing," Garrick warned out of the side of his mouth.

"Of course not," Jillian huffed, "after all, I gave you my word."

"Best you remember it." His words were sharp, but his look told her he too would be thinking about her while they were apart. The look of love passing between them was a healing balm that soothed their ravaged souls. The first step had been taken. God willing, she would be able to convince the king. Then she and Garrick would have it all.

CHAPTER TWENTY-SEVEN

"YOU HAVE KEPT your word and brought Harald the Saxon and his band of rebels to London. You shall have the promised grain and coin when you leave. The cattle will be coming from one of our estates to the west."

Pausing as if for effect, King William then broached the subject of Garrick's marriage again. "Now about your wife. We have decided to set her up in an abbey until we have the church court look into your circumstances. Then I shall see if your new neighbor Henri du Guerre would be willing to marry her."

The words cut through Garrick, shredding his soul to ribbons. "Sire. You cannot."

"I understand that you are grateful, Merewood, but do not overstep your bounds gainsaying your king." The low tone the king used belied the anger suffusing his face with color.

"You did not give me the chance to speak before I left to bring in the rebels. I no longer wish to set aside my wife."

The king's eyes narrowed. "Your wife. I thought you had not consummated the marriage."

"My wife and I came to an understanding; the marriage has been consummated."

Rubbing a hand across his brow, the king grew thoughtful. "This presents a problem, I have already spoken to du Guerre. He believes Lady Jillian to be a virgin, that the marriage was never consummated." His voice elevated as his temper rose. "I have given my word,"

Not wanting to anger his liege further by professing his love for his wife, Garrick instead broached the subject of her meeting with the king. "Lady Jillian seeks an audience with you as soon as possible."

"What does she wish to discuss?"

"I believe our marriage," Garrick lied.

"Bring her back here before we sup. I'll speak with her then. I would advise you to keep your distance from the lady until we settle the matter of her holding."

Nodding his head in silent agreement, Garrick returned to his chamber. He couldn't believe his king's ready agreement to meet with his wife, but he was worried about du Guerre. The king was a man of his word. How would he be able to convince him to go back on it?

JILLIAN WRUNG HER hands from the moment she learned of her appointment until she was shown through the door to the king's chambers.

A servant motioned for her to be seated and for Garrick to leave. Though she longed to have him stay, 'twould be much easier to speak her mind without his presence.

"Now then, Lady Jillian, what do you wish to discuss?" the king asked from his seat in the center of the room.

Jillian felt that she was at a distinct disadvantage seated at the floor level rather than on the dais, but she was prepared to fight for her rights. It didn't matter where she sat. "The ownership of Loughmoe Keep."

The king remained silent for a long time, his large hands steepled together. Finally, he asked, "What concern is it of yours who owns Loughmoe?"

"It belonged to my father and my father's father before him. My family has tilled that land for generations. No one else could possibly love the land as I do."

"Loving the land and making it profitable to your king are two distinctly different matters."

"I have watched how my husband cares for his land and his people. You would find no better lord to run Loughmoe."

"I have already spoken to Henri du Guerre, he is to take control of the holding." King William looked her in the eye as if to challenge her, "He needs a wife."

Jillian felt the bottom drop out of her world. Her head began to pound, and her palms grew sweaty. Deathly afraid of his answer, she rasped, "Whom did you have in mind?"

"You."

Bright spots swam before her eyes, making it hard to focus. Heat suffused her body, then fled, leaving her stone cold. Gripping the arms of the chair, she rallied bravely to regain control of her traitorous emotions. "I already have a husband."

"Who seeks an annulment," he countered.

Pain left her bereft of speech. Oh God, she had been a fool. She could not believe their joining meant nothing to him. It had to be a lie. Nay, her heart refused to believe the king. But why would he lie to her?

"But I thought—"

"You thought?"

The calm tone and level look only added to Garrick's betrayal. The wound cut her so deeply no threads would ever hold it together. Pride was all she had left.

"Lady Jillian?" William's eyes searched her face, looking for a sign as to what she was thinking.

"I thought, that is we..." She could not think, let alone speak of last night without dissolving into tears, which she refused to do. In the midst of her suffering, a bleak thought speared through her. What would happen to those back at Merewood if the grain and cattle were delayed, or diverted on the way to Merewood

Keep? She needed to ensure they received the added wealth of her land. She could not turn her back on them. Though only for a short time, they had been a family to her and treated her as one of their own. She owed it to Garrick's people to ask one more time.

"Sire, is there no way to change your mind?"

The speculative look in his eye did not bode well, of that she was certain. The long silence that followed wreaked havoc with the tenuous hold on her control.

"Mayhap, after bringing the rebels to justice, I should grant the holding to Merewood. What say you, Lady?"

Eyes bright with hope, she answered, "He would rebuild it back to its former glory, Sire. The people would respect him."

She had to give Garrick that much, though he played her false, he would never do anything to hurt the people who depended on him for their livelihood.

"If Merewood were to marry a Norman woman…" the king began, "mayhap I will find somewhere else for du Guerre to live. But if du Guerre is difficult, and he holds me to my word, would you marry him if I granted your wish and gave Merewood the land?"

Jillian froze in the chair, eyes wide in stark terror. She knew then she would never live at Loughmoe again. It had been an unrealistic dream to picture a life there with Garrick. Besides, he didn't want her. What truly mattered was that someone would care for her family's land. Garrick was that someone.

She loathed the idea of marriage to anyone other than Garrick; she loved him more than life itself. But it would be selfish to put her wants and needs before the good of so many. Hundreds of his people could be fed and clothed this winter and the next, and the people of Loughmoe would have food to eat and grain to plant come spring. 'Twould be a small price to pay, giving Garrick his freedom so that he could marry another, a woman who had the means to rebuild both Merewood and Loughmoe. The loyal people of both holdings would not suffer further. 'Twould be her gift to her parents loving memory, restoring their home. Though she would never live there, it made a difference that Garrick would.

"Aye, Sire." Jillian rose slowly and moved to the dais. Sinking into a deep curtsy, she waited until she was bid to rise, then took her leave.

The moment the door closed behind her she started trembling. The uncontrollable shaking made it impossible to walk, so she sank to the floor and waited for the reaction to pass.

While she sat, she thought of all that had transpired. Had Garrick truly asked the king to intercede with the church court and seek an annulment? Had he told the king of his earlier plans to set her aside?

He couldn't have, could he? There must be another explanation, one she couldn't quite grasp. *Garrick would not betray her that way.* There had to be more to the story than their monarch let on. Mayhap he was testing her loyalty to Garrick? With that thought in mind, she rose, albeit still wobbly, and walked back to their chamber.

"Jillie lass, are ye all right?" Winslow's voice seemed distant.

She shook her head and struggled to put one foot in front of the other. Strong hands pulled her through the open doorway and pushed her into a chair.

Jillian felt cool water lapping against her lips; she drank deeply. As she became more aware of her surroundings, the room gradually came into focus. Garrick stood on the left side of the chair and Winslow to the right.

"What happened?" Jillian's brain was fuzzy, a delayed reaction to her meeting with the king.

"I left you alone with the king," Garrick said slowly. "When I arrived to escort you back here, you were already gone." His concern seemed genuine. But was it?

Bits and pieces of her audience came back to her,

"We spoke about Loughmoe."

"And?" Garrick waited expectantly.

"He agreed to give it to you." She did not add, only if Garrick either married a Norman woman, or she agreed to marry du Guerre.

The look of joy on her husband's face took her breath away. He had been through so much because of her, what right did she have to make demands upon him now? If her father had lived, he would have given the land to them anyway, she was his only heir. She decided to hold off asking him if what the king said was true, if he had asked for an annulment.

"She needs to rest," Eyreka said, shooing the men out of the room. "I'll stay with her." The sound of the door closing echoed in the quiet.

"Tell me the rest," Eyreka softly commanded.

When Jillian opened her eyes, the look of concern on her friend's face was endearing. She would miss Reka.

"The king said Garrick wants to set me aside."

"You cannot believe—"

"In return for granting the land to Garrick, I am to marry Henri du Guerre," the last words came out in a rush.

Eyreka hugged her tight to her chest, cursing her son for his timing and her king for using two innocent people as pawns in his bid to claim all of England for his followers.

"Are you going to tell my son the rest of the king's decree?"

"Why should he be concerned, when he is getting all that he wished?"

"Because he loves you," Lady Eyreka calmly explained.

Jillian sniffed back a tear. "He could not wait to be rid of me."

"If he wanted to be rid of you, why would he go to the trouble of rescuing you when we were held captive?"

"You were held captive with me."

"Why did he stay by your side 'til you wakened from the fever?" Garrick's mother insisted.

Jillian shrugged. "He felt guilty."

"Why didn't he leave you to wander the halls of the castle?"

"'Twould have caused talk. Besides, he needed to find out what the king had to say," Jillian reasoned.

"What will you do?" Eyreka's voice was breaking.

"I will do what my king wishes." *Though I may die inside.*

⇶⫷

MacInness stood in the buttery, behind the partition separating the pitchers of wine and mead from the great hall. He could hear Owen speaking to one of his daughters. Listening intently, he strained to hear their conversation.

"Father, is it true? Will Jillian have to marry Henri du Guerre?" He recognized the voice as Owen's youngest daughter, Madelyne.

So that's the rumor circulating around the castle and what is wrong with the lass! Garrick needed to learn of this. Pausing before turning to go, he listened closely.

"A wise person does not go against his king's wishes."

"But what of Garrick?" Madelyne's concern for her friend seemed real.

MacInness remembered that the two women had been friends, before Jillian married and moved to Merewood Keep.

"He will be allowed to set his wife aside, then he will be free to marry again." Owen's voice was tinged with anger.

"What if Henri were not free to marry Jillian? What would become of her?"

"The king would probably send her to an abbey until he found someone suitable to marry her."

Owen answered a summons from across the room. MacInness heard him say, "Find your sisters and be seated, daughter. I must speak with Aaron." Owen's voice faded away.

MacInness thought he was alone, until he heard Madelyne whispering, "I'll not be used like a bargaining chip to bring two plots of land together as one. I'm not a Norman...I'm a Saxon woman with rights," she said in a low voice, "and I'll not be set aside like Jillian."

His fists clenched at his sides, MacInness waited for the

sounds of her retreat.

"Mayhap Henri will not mind some company this night."

The Scotsman nearly swallowed his tongue at the implication he heard in Madelyne's seductive tone. 'Twas time to search out Garrick. With what he had learned earlier from Lady Eyreka, and what he had just heard, they had much to plan if they were to save Jillian from her good intentions.

"MILORD OWEN!" AARON hailed his overlord.

"What news have you?" Owen demanded.

"We found naught but broken bits of barrel." Hesitating, he added, "the graves contained Rebels."

"Merewood must have taken the ransom back with him," Owen muttered aloud.

The warrior shook his head. "I overheard one of his men bragging about the battle."

"And?" Owen demanded.

"His men hid in empty barrels. Once they were inside Harald's camp, they sprung their trap. There was no ransom." Aaron waited for his overlord's reaction. He was not disappointed.

Owen hurled his goblet against the wall, denting the metal beyond repair then drew his sword and slashed the tapestry hanging on the wall over the bed.

Aaron watched the two pieces drift gracefully to the floor, never to be whole again. *Like the man buried by the ravine.*

In a bid to calm his liege, Aaron spoke. "Rumor has it Lady Jillian is to wed du Guerre in a bid to regain Loughmoe."

"The selfish little whore," Owen hissed. "Wasn't it enough marrying Merewood?"

"But you said he would set her aside. How could it be enough?" Aaron's confusion was evident.

"Loughmoe should be mine. William gave his word."

"I thought you said he was *considering* granting the land to you," Aaron said.

"'Tis the same thing." Owen stopped mid-stride, openly glaring at his vassal as if daring further comment.

"Milord?" His manservant interrupted the heated discussion.

"Aye?"

"'Tis the Lady Madelyne. She's not in her chambers."

The speculative expression Owen wore changed to one of satisfaction. His recent conversation with his youngest replayed in his head. Her concern for Jillian, her worry over Henri du Guerre…

"Du Guerre!"

"You think she's with du Guerre?" Aaron stood ready to act with his hand on the hilt of his sword.

Owen rubbed his chin, his eyes half open.

"Lord Owen, about Madelyne," his servant began.

"Mayhap my daughter is ready to make an alliance. Aaron."

"Aye?"

"Post a guard outside du Guerre's chamber. See to it no one leaves, or sees you there."

CHAPTER TWENTY-EIGHT

"HAS THE KING changed his mind?"

Jillian struggled to hide her distress from Eyreka. A second audience with the king had not changed his mind.

Jillian shrugged. "He maintains our agreement will stand." Though her eyes burned, she refused to give in to the tears closing her throat.

It had been weeks since the king had made his decision known to her, and announced it to those at Court. To her intense dismay, Henri du Guerre pursued her wherever she happened to be. In order to avoid contact with the man, she had taken to hiding in the chamber she shared with Garrick's mother.

To add to her pain, her husband began avoiding her. Too ashamed to face him, she knew it was better this way. After all, he must know by now she was to wed another.

The king demanded her presence in the hall tonight. Did he know she was hiding? There was no hope for it; she could not ignore a royal summons to dine.

"There must be something that we can do. Some way we can change his mind," Eyreka maintained.

Their eyes met. "You are a true friend, Reka. I would go mad without you." Twin drops of sorrow escaped from the curve of her lashes before she could stop them.

"I have made peace within myself," she said, wiping the tears away. "I did all that I could to regain my parents' home; they would be pleased that a warrior such as Garrick will be the one to rebuild Loughmoe. Those that are left working the fields will have an overlord who will care for them, about them, and Merewood Keep's people will thrive." As if trying to convince herself, she added fervently, "'Twas the only choice."

"What about you, dear? What about what is right for you?"

"I cannot have what is right for me."

"Mother. Lady Jillian," Dunstan's called from the hallway.

"We're coming." Eyreka answered, opening the door.

"How do you fare, Jillian?" Dunstan's concern was evident. His gaze met hers, and she knew her bleak expression left no doubt as to how she was feeling.

He offered his arm to both women and without another word escorted them to the evening meal.

"I have asked to speak to King William," he confided, pulling the chair back for his mother. When she was seated, he did the same for Jillian. "I do not think the marriage he plans is in your best interest." Placing a hand on her shoulder, he leaned down to add, "I have spoken to my brother, 'tis not as it seems. He never sought to—"

"Lady Jillian," Haldana interrupted, "how lovely you look tonight." The false note in Haldana's voice cut through Jillian's haze of pain. Her eyes darted to Dunstan's face, searching for a clue as to what he had been about to say, but he turned away from her when Lady Haldana arrived.

"And you, milady." The polite reply through stiffened jaw nearly did her in. But a loud commotion coming from the dais caught everyone's attention. The spacious room grew oddly quiet, belying the large number of nobles in attendance.

"I demand satisfaction," Owen thundered. "He ruined my daughter!"

Jillian saw Madelyne, standing beside her former guardian. A sideways glance at Lady Haldana revealed nothing. The woman's face had a serene look plastered upon it.

Dunstan nodded to his older brother who sat across the room from them. Jillian tried to guess what he and Garrick were trying to communicate but couldn't. She gave up, though she could not tear her gaze away from Garrick.

What did he no longer plan to do? Her mind plagued her with possibilities. She jolted at the cry of outrage erupting from somewhere to the left of her.

She leaned closer to Eyreka, noticing Garrick's mother's eyes seemed bright with emotion. "What did Owen say?"

"It seems that your royally appointed husband seduced young Madelyne. Her father is demanding they marry at once."

Du Guerre marry Madelyne? The idea glimmered like a beacon at the end of a long, dark tunnel. It would be the only way out of marrying the man herself. *But what of Loughmoe?*

"Henri, what have you to say to the charges brought before me?" the king demanded loudly.

Madelyne stepped forward boldly and spoke in hushed tones. Whatever she said made the king smile, while her father turned purple with rage. Owen raised his hand to strike her, but he never delivered the blow, du Guerre stopped him.

"'Tis the truth." The man's stance was threatening as he clamped his hand tightly around Owen's forearm.

King William stood facing the room, a large goblet raised high.

"Send for the cleric." The king's gaze connected with Jillian's. "We're to have a wedding."

Jillian could not seem to catch her breath. The king's announcement drove the air from her body. Seeing her distress, Eyreka pounded her on the back until Jillian realized what the woman was trying to do and breathed out.

"DEAR GOD IN heaven," Jillian rasped, "I'm not ready. I thought I would have at least another few weeks to prepare."

Her terror-filled gaze sought that of her husband. He had risen up at the king's command. Pain mirroring her own slashed across his handsome face.

He loves me!

But it's too late.

Someone had taken hold of her hand in a grip of iron. Distractedly, she looked from her hand up into the face so close to her own.

"Winslow?"

"Aye, lass, dinna be afraid. 'Tis not what ye think. I canna say anymore, but trust us."

"Us?"

"Your husband and I, lass."

With that he was gone.

Swallowing to ease the huge lump that had formed moments before, she focused on the dais, waiting for the king to beckon her forward.

A TRICKLE OF sweat ran down her back, though she was cold with fear.

"What are they doing?" Eyreka asked motioning to the group of men forming behind her eldest son.

"I'm not certain."

Garrick stood grim faced, feet apart, flanked by his brothers. Behind him Winslow and the O'Malleys, his Irish Contingent, stood in silent show of support. Half of them stared at her, while the other half stared at du Guerre.

Jillian had no idea what was about to happen, but every one of Garrick's men stood with their hands on the hilt of their swords, battle ready.

The cleric arrived in a flurry of activity, robes flying out behind him as he rushed up to the dais, ready to record the union.

King William stood and motioned for silence. He turned and looked directly at Jillian.

She froze, never more frightened in her life yet grasping the feeble straw she had just been handed. *Trust us*. She met the king's gaze, forcing a smile to her lips. He nodded.

To her shock, Henri du Guerre was joined to Madelyne of Sedgeworth. They were to leave at once for their new home, Loughmoe Keep.

Before her mind could recover from that announcement, she was summoned to stand before her monarch. Moving on leaden legs, she did as she was bid.

"Lady Jillian, circumstances have necessitated our bargain be changed. Garrick has changed his mind. He no longer wishes to annul your marriage."

Her legs shook, and her body trembled. Refusing to hope, she waited for him to continue.

"It has long been my intention to install a Norman baron at Loughmoe. Henri was instrumental in taking the keep during the Uprising. 'Twould have been my first wish to see you married to du Guerre as you had bargained."

Garrick spoke then. "What was the rest of the bargain, Sire?"

Jillian could not meet his eyes, though she could feel his gaze searing the top of her bent head.

"You would have received Loughmoe."

"I am not Norman by birth." Garrick appeared confused.

"Aye. But you have more than proved your worth to us by bringing the rebels to justice. Your loyalty is known to us."

The revelry behind them grew loud enough to hamper conversation.

"Enjoy the feast. Do you return to Merewood, then?"

"Aye, Sire. My wife and I shall leave on the morrow."

"Then you and your lady wife may retire to your chamber to make ready." With a wave of his hand, they were dismissed.

Taking Jillian's arm, Garrick led her around the edge of the crowded room and out of the great hall. Pulling her into a deep alcove, he wrapped her in his embrace. His lips sought hers, desperately, as he realized how much they had to be thankful for.

"Thank God I have been given another chance, Jillian. Mac-Inness told me what the king tried to do. But my hands were tied—I had to wait until the right moment."

"After I had been given in marriage to du Guerre?"

"My men were ready to take action."

Jillian's heart clenched at the thought of the blood that had nearly been shed in the name of love. Thank the Lord it had been averted in time. "Then you didn't tell the king you wanted to set me aside?"

"Weeks ago, yes. But that was before—"

Stricken by the knowledge that he had at one point sought an annulment, she rasped, "Before what?"

"Before I tended your wounds, before I learned of your brave deeds...before I fell so deeply in love with you that I may never recover."

His lips touched hers tenderly, leaving no doubt that she was well and truly loved.

Her throat was so tight, she could not speak. As her love for him radiated from deep within her, she hoped he could hear the truth pounding in her heart.

"There are things you should know about me." If the set of his jaw were an indication, she would not like what he had to tell her. "Come."

Jillian willingly followed.

When they were alone in his chamber, he took her into his arms and kissed her tenderly. His kiss so sweet it brought tears to her eyes.

"You were willing to give up your family home for me. The value of such a gift is beyond price."

"I would give anything to see you happy."

"But your land? And at such cost." Jillian felt the hard edge of his temper as he continued. "You would marry du Guerre?"

"The king said you still planned to set me aside."

Garrick's ire left him at her words. She saw the softening around his eyes and mouth. "He did not tell you I had changed my mind?"

"Had you truly?" Even though she already knew the answer, she could not stop herself from asking just one more time.

"Jillian, I asked you to trust me. Do you?"

Though it was there in her eyes, he asked again. This time she gave him the words. "I trust you."

"I had changed my mind before I found you unconscious at the hands of the rebels."

"Then the night we—"

"Later, love." Garrick lowered his lips to hers.

He'd nearly lost the woman of his heart. The thought nearly immobilized him. One thought seared through him, over and over. He had to seal their vows again. This time, there would be no going back.

"I love you," he vowed, grasping the hem of her gown and sliding it to her waist.

"Forever," she whispered, reaching for his braes.

They were together as one in a heartbeat. Their joining frantic. His rhythmic thrusts matched hers; her moans of ecstasy echoed his.

His tongue urged her higher, while her hands stroked him upward. With each plunging motion, their love was cemented, their hearts nearly bursting with it, until they were at the edge of the summit.

She looked into the bright blue depths of his eyes and surrendered body and soul. They climaxed together, plunging into the abyss of darkness at the edge of sanity.

CHAPTER TWENTY-NINE

THE PULL ON her hair woke her, and she opened her eyes and found it wound around and under Garrick. Jillian smiled at the boyish charm that had settled on her warrior husband sometime during their long night of loving.

She stroked his cheek tenderly, enjoying the vastly different texture of his whisker-rough face. She was still smiling when he opened his eyes. Jillian bent down to press her lips to his.

The insistent hammering on the door was punctuated by the loud use of his name. "Garrick!"

"'Tis past the hour I had planned to rise." Placing a chaste kiss on her forehead, he rose and drew on his tunic and braes before handing Jillian her linen shift.

"For God's sake, mon open the door. We're ready to leave."

Garrick opened the door to admit his grouchy vassal.

In spite of his complaining, MacInness beamed at the pair. "I told ye to trust us, lass."

"Thank you, Winslow, for everything."

"My pleasure, lass."

The men left to gather the rest of their party leaving Jillian to quickly wash and braid her hair. In less than one hour, they rode away from London.

FOR THE PAST week Jillian had not felt well. By the time they stopped for the noon meal, she was so nauseous she doubted she could get back on her horse. Only two days away from reaching Merewood, and she was not certain she could make the rest of the journey.

Shaking off Eyreka's hand, she pleaded, "Just give me a few minutes privacy. I'll be fine."

Jillian hoped no one would follow her. She had yet to confide how she was feeling, wanting only to be sick in peace. When she emptied her stomach of what little she had eaten hours before, she sat back on her heels. Weariness engulfed her. *How will I be able to walk back to the horses without help?*

"Lady Jillian," Roderick's voice called out to her from the other side of the bushes.

"Coming," her voice falsely cheerful to her own ears, but hoped he would not notice.

He seemed relieved when she walked toward him. "Garrick sent me to look for you. He and MacInness are busy scouting the area ahead. When they get back we'll eat."

He paused, taking a good look at her. "You look awful."

She grinned; someone had finally taken her at her word and honestly told her how she fared. "No gentleman would truly tell a lady she looked bad, even if she did."

They laughed. Companionably, she slipped her arm through his, grateful for his strength.

If Roderick noticed her leaning heavily on his arm, he gave no outward indication, merely patting her hand while they walked back through the trees.

Eyreka was waiting expectantly. Her sharply blue eyes bored into Jillian's, demanding to know what was wrong with her.

"Help me unpack the bread and ale, dear."

The mere thought of drinking ale at that very moment turned

her stomach completely upside down. Roderick let go of her as she clapped a hand to her mouth and bolted back through the trees.

He started to give chase, but his mother held his arm. "Give her a few moments, dear. She'll be fine." To his surprise, his mother chuckled under her breath.

"God's blood, Mother, she turned a ghastly shade of green. I must go see what ails her," he protested.

Lady Eyreka held firm and convinced him to wait.

When Jillian returned a few minutes later, no one said anything. She accepted the proffered hunk of bread without a word of protest. Eyes closed, she chewed and swallowed, one small bite at a time, until the entire piece had disappeared.

Eyreka handed her a cup of water, which she drank down, greedily.

"Have you told Garrick yet?"

Jillian shook her head.

"Told me what?" He walked toward his wife.

Taking her youngest son by the arm, Eyreka urged, "Come dear, Jillian has something to tell her husband." Looking over her shoulder, she asked, "Don't you, dear?"

"Aye, Reka."

"Is something amiss? You're pale as flour." Garrick took his wife in his arms and held her close, rubbing a hand up and down her spine. When she sighed, he kissed the tip of her nose and then her mouth. "Just tell me. Whatever it is cannot be so horrible. Tell me, don't hold it inside and make yourself sick over it."

The incongruity of his words caused a ripple of laughter to flow from her. She looked up and smiled. At his look of loving concern, her eyes filled with tears.

"Jillian?" Garrick looked worried.

She smiled. "I have a gift for you."

"Oh?" His voice sounded normal now, more relaxed. "What is this gift? When will you give it to me?"

"Before the last snow thaws."

Garrick was lost in total confusion. Jillian smiled, knowing he would be. "Our babe will be born sometime before the end of winter, mayhap the beginning of spring."

He grabbed her up in his arms and swung her around. His shout of joy brought the others running. By the time they were able to share their news, everyone was hugging Jillian, then Garrick.

"You had best feed my son, wife. He'll need to grow big and strong."

"What if he is a daughter?"

"I pray she has your smile."

His lips met hers, sealing their love with a kiss.

"WAKE UP LOVE. We have arrived," Garrick's whispered words tickled her ear.

"Mmmm."

"Dreaming of me?"

Jillian's eyes slowly opened, bringing the face of the man she loved, the father of her babe, into focus. She thought back over the fortnight they spent journeying home, and the life they now knew lay sleeping inside her.

She sighed, snuggling deeper into the arms holding her close. The stone wall surrounding Merewood rose up in front of them. Garrick raised a fist in greeting before placing it over his heart. The warrior on guard duty signaled for the gate to be opened.

The bailey was soon filled to bursting with people talking all at once. The blacksmith demanded to know why Lady Jillian was not riding her own horse, while Stephan, the stable lad, wanted to know if she would help him rub down the beasts. Jillian's smile was brilliant as the crowd of well-wishers gathered closer still.

Gertie spoke up, "While we are all glad to have you back, I am sure Lady Jillian and Lady Eyreka are tired from their long journey."

Her meaning was not lost on anyone. The people slowly went about their business, promising to stop by and talk to Jillian later.

"Now then," Gertie began eyeing her mistress closely, "is there something wrong? Or do you have good news to be shared with Old Gert?"

Garrick chuckled softly. He slid down from the saddle then turned and lifted his wife gently into his arms. "Aye, you meddlesome woman, come winter's end, we will have an heir to Merewood."

Good news traveled fast, and a barrel of mead was brought out, and toasts were made to the couple, their babe, and to Merewood. Jillian stood through it all, though her limbs were stiff from the long ride. Garrick's people were now her people too. When her husband pulled her close to his side, she went willingly. They had a chance to start over. Nothing could possibly happen to break them apart again. *Hadn't the worst already happened?*

The evening meal continued their earlier celebration. Boisterous toasts rang out through the crowded hall. Jillian's appetite was tempted with lightly seasoned dishes, nothing too heavy, so she would not feel ill.

By the time the meal ended, Jillian leaned sleepily against Garrick's broad shoulder. She roused when he lifted her into his arms.

"Welcome home, husband," she murmured against his cheek.

"Welcome home, wife." His lips brushed lightly across the scar on her forehead. The tenderness of his caress filled her with warmth.

"I love you, Garrick."

CHAPTER THIRTY

"I'LL NOT REST while everyone else works their fingers to the bone feeding the growing number of men that serve my husband," Jillian said, emphasizing her displeasure with the latest stricture Garrick had placed upon her by stamping her foot.

"I'm carrying his babe. I'm not dying!" *He's too protective of me,* she thought. *I'm perfectly capable of carrying a platter with my hands and his babe with my body.*

The young serving woman standing between her and the kitchen didn't move. "Please, milady, you'll ruin this fine day if you anger milord so early."

"Aye, lass. That ye will," Winslow drawled. "'Twould be a pity to waste such a glorious day feelin' so sorry for yerself that ye'd cause yer busy husband worry."

"He's not worried," Jillian pouted. "He likes telling me what to do."

She could feel her chin quiver and tears pooling in her eyes. She blinked furiously to keep them from falling.

MacInness could not have helped but notice her rapid mood change. Lord help her, even she was beginning to grow weary of trying to keep her emotions from bouncing around.

"Aye, he does enjoy ordering small redheaded tyrants about. 'Tis all part of his plan to refine my patience. The more he upsets ye, the more ye lash out at me." His warm look belied his words.

"Ye could drive a strong mon to drink, Jillie lass."

Jillian bowed her head. "I'm sorry. I can't abide being idle, you must understand that." She searched his eyes for a clue as to what he was thinking. They were cloudy, not clear and bright. "What's wrong?"

He swallowed hard and looked away from her, but she could feel his pain.

"I promise not to trouble you anymore today if you tell me what has taken the sparkle from your eye and the spring from your step." She laid a hand on his arm, a silent entreaty, and waited.

MacInness straightened his shoulders and turned back to her, taking hold of her hand. "I canna tell ye just yet, lassie." The faraway look in his eye faded. "It does my heart good to ken how much ye care." He lifted her hand to his lips and placed a chaste kiss upon it.

"Well, wife, I can see you have little regard for my wishes." Garrick's eyes were curiously merry in contrast to his harsh words.

"'Tis not that I try to upset you," she paused searching for the words to explain how useless she felt now that she had no duties. Such a change from the backbreaking work she had grown accustomed to at Sedgeworth. *She felt lost, alone.*

"'Tis good to hear," he replied smugly. "Am I also to assume that my vassal's attentions toward you are not provoked?"

SHE NEARLY CHOKED on her reply, "Attentions?" She could feel her face flush with the anger she tried to control. "You have paid little enough attention to me these weeks past but to order me not to lift anything heavier than my finger." She pointed that forefinger right between his eyes. She could feel her temper simmering and knew she had to let it out or explode.

"Now, lass, 'tis for yer own good," MacInness tried to reason with her.

"Lack of exercise is not good for the babe, nor me. Just ask—"

Garrick swept her off her feet and carried her back the way she had come. His expression grim, but determined. She worried that she had angered him in spite of her decision not to.

He put his shoulder to the door to open it, turned halfway around, and hooked it with the tip of his boot to close it.

"Now then, wife," he said depositing her on their bed, "'tis time to exercise, then you will obey me and rest."

She stood up on the bed, hands on hips glaring at him. "I need something to do." She poked him in the chest, "I'll not sit idly back while the other women do their share of work as well as my own."

His eyes sparkled. "Oh, we'll not be idle." Garrick's meaning was clear when he reached out to pull her clothing up over her head.

"You're just trying to distract me—"

"Is it working yet?" His voice was husky with passion. He laid her gently on her back.

Jillian started to protest, but gave up when her husband's hands began working their magic on her. Her lips instinctively sought his.

"DID THE LASS decide to rest, then?" MacInness called out when Garrick crossed the bailey toward him.

"With a little persuasion, I convinced her she was tired." He couldn't keep from smiling.

His vassal grinned. "A mon has to do what a mon has to do." He turned and shouted at one of the younger knights training, "Not like that, mon, yer opponent will cleave yer sorry head in two."

"Where's Iain?" he asked Garrick.

"Building a fence for the cattle."

The promised reward from the king would be arriving in a few days. *And thank God for it*, Garrick thought. Were it not for the cattle and grain, his people would not have made it through another hard winter.

"I need his help showing these latest recruits how to fight." MacInness looked about him and shook his head; his face lined with worry.

Garrick could tell his friend was worried about something, but he didn't have time to draw it out of the closemouthed Scot. "I'll send Iain to help you train. Dunstan can oversee the building as well as any."

"Aye," MacInness answered distractedly.

"I'll be leaving by week's end to collect the ransom the king has promised our people, can it wait 'til then?" Garrick asked.

The Scot met his gaze and understanding passed between them, "Aye, it can."

Garrick nodded, whatever was on his vassal's mind weighed heavily upon the man. First the delivery of cattle, then he'd see about helping to solve whatever troubled MacInness.

❯❯❯❯❮❮❮❮

GARRICK AND MACINNESS spent their days busily tallying up the list of needed repairs both within the walls of the keep and the village surrounding it. Jillian was tired and irritable. She had not been sleeping well. Her nights had been plagued by the recurring nightmare of Alan's death.

Now that they had established themselves at Merewood, her husband was gone on business that kept him away from her side most days from dawn 'til dusk. She felt more alone than ever before. Though she needed to be around people to keep from going out of her mind, what she really needed was her husband.

She sought out Gertie, hoping to work her way around her husband's edict that she stay abed and let the others run the household. "I think I'll see about the evening meal, Gert."

"You should rest yourself and the babe. Lady Eyreka and I can take care of the household." Gertie steered her back toward the stairs.

Jillian clenched her teeth, hating to feel so useless. She had to be in the thick of things, where she would not be alone with her memories. She didn't want to rest. If she did, she might fall asleep and dream.

"I feel fine, if I could just lend a hand—"

"Off with you." Gertie all but pushed her out of the door and up the stairs.

Jillian slowly climbed the stairs, but before she reached the top step, she knew she had to clear her head. A ride outside the keep's walls just might do it...*if I can elude my overbearing husband.* She cringed. She loved Garrick to distraction, but between his overprotectiveness and his long absences, she was growing more and more restless. If she could only sleep soundly, she wouldn't be so close to madness.

"But, milady, I've orders not to saddle a horse for you." Young Stephan folded his skinny arms in front of him, not moving.

There was no hope for it; she'd have to bend the truth. "You do your job well, Stephan, my husband is pleased." While the boy puffed out his chest with pride, she added, "I'd prefer riding without a saddle anyway."

Jillian led her horse out of the stall, turned over a bucket and stepped up on its back. Stephan grabbed at the reins trying to stop her, but she laughed, "I need the exercise, I'll not ride long." Taking pity on the small boy, she added, "Don't fret, you didn't saddle a horse for me, now did you?"

"But, I don't think milord—"

"You should not try to second guess my husband's wishes." Jillian smiled, waving over her shoulder. *One down,* she thought, *one to go.*

"Lady Jillian?" The gatekeeper's surprise was almost funny.

She smiled. "I need to escape for a little while. I'll be back soon."

"But milord said you aren't to ride out alone," the old man protested.

"Then you'll have to send someone to follow me, won't you?" She waited while he grudgingly opened the gate, promising to send someone after her. Jillian waved and dug her heels into her mount's sides.

The wind whipped her hair across her eyes; she shook it back glorying in her moment of absolute freedom. By the time she heard hoof beats, she had ridden hard enough to grow weary. *I hadn't counted on that.*

"Lady Jillian," MacInness shouted to her.

She looked back at the warrior hard at her heels just long enough to take her eyes off the path she rode. "Aye?"

"Look out!" The warning came a split-second too late.

Her horse stumbled on a root in the path and went down on one knee. Jillian held on, wrapping her arms around the horse's neck.

"Easy, milady," MacInness took her by the arm, "I've got you." He helped her down off the injured horse. After first checking her out from head to toe, he looked at the horse's foreleg. It was swelling and warm to the touch.

"Ye canna ride him back. We'll have to double up." He lifted her up into the saddle and tied her horse's reins to the back of his mount's saddle.

Jillian felt badly; poor horse. She sighed loudly, 'twas her fault he was injured. "I'm so sorry." She felt guilty about the horse hobbling slowly behind them.

"'Tis not entirely your fault." MacInness held her securely in front of him.

"Did I take you away from anything important?" she asked belatedly.

"Aye." His one word answer made her feel even worse. It was not like him to be so quiet. Lost in her own troubled thoughts, she didn't notice that her protector had gone rigid, until he whispered in her ear.

"I saw a flash in the wood to the left. When I jump off, ye ride like the de'il for the keep. Dinna stop until ye reach safety."

"But what—" Her words were cut off by a war cry accompanied by crashing branches and pounding hooves.

"Now!" he shouted, slashing the reins holding the injured horse, setting it free. MacInness leapt to the ground and slapped the rump of his horse.

Jillian had no choice; it was hang on, or fall off. Thinking of the babe, she leaned forward and held on for dear life. The wind whipped strands of her hair across her face. Branches slapped out at her, but she kept her head. *Oh God*, she thought, riding toward the keep, *not again*. Another brave man would have to pay the price for her actions.

Not Winslow.

Dread filled her with an icy coldness that numbed her, until her mind rebelled and broke free. "I cannot let another man die." Jaw clenched, mind set, she squeezed her legs tight to the sides of Winslow's horse and turned back toward the sounds of battle.

MacInness stood within a circle of six warriors, claymore raised high, poised to strike again. His sword connected, the knight groaned before crumpling to the ground, dead. The Scot was so intent upon staying alive; he didn't see Jillian riding toward him. But the others did. When they turned away it gave him the edge he needed. He cut down two more warriors, evening up the battle. *Three to one.*

"Winslow!" Jillian shouted, "On your left!" She veered the horse toward the unsuspecting knight whose back was toward her. His sword was raised above his head, just like her nightmare. Terror pumped the adrenaline through her body giving her inhuman strength.

"No!" she screamed, gripping the reins. Jillian bent low over her mount and rammed into the side of the man. The knight lost his balance. MacInness saw his chance and ran him through with his sword before turning to her. Blood flowed down the side of his face and arm. His amber eyes glowed, fixed on the spot behind her.

"Dinna move," he warned.

She had the sensation someone was directly behind her. Trusting Winslow, she waited until he gave the signal. "Now!" She ducked, but not soon enough. The tip of a blade sliced into the tender flesh at the back of her arm. She cried out in pain.

Winslow's own battle cry was echoed by Patrick's, who rode hell-bent-for-leather toward the last knight, who stood ready to cleave the enraged Scot in two.

While Jillian watched in horror, their movements slowed like in a dream. MacInness dove to the side, avoiding the worst of the blow. The sword caught him in the thigh, but MacInness didn't stop, he reached up and caught the enemy in the throat with his blade.

Bile gushed up her throat at the sight of so much blood. She clamped her mouth shut against the instinctive reaction. Her vision grayed. She grabbed hold of her necklace and asked for strength and courage. "Power of the ancients," she whispered reverently, "help me." She blinked and the grayness mystically vanished.

MacInness swayed, but Patrick reached him in time to steady him, wrapping an arm about him.

"Lady Jillian, you're bleeding." Patrick's expression went from grim to green.

"Is it that bad?"

"Aye. You'll need threads to hold it closed. We'd best get back before Owen realizes his ambush has failed." Patrick looked to MacInness. "Can you ride?"

He shook his head. "I canna feel my arm, or leg."

Jillian could feel herself weakening. "Patrick, help me stop the bleeding, then we'll get him on his horse."

"What about you?"

She could tell the knight was wavering between his duty to protect her and getting her to safety, and the obvious—MacInness would bleed to death before they made it to safety.

"He'll die." It was all that needed to be said. They worked quickly, tearing strips off the bottom of her gown. When their friend's wounds were wrapped tight enough to staunch the flow of blood. Patrick turned his attention to her arm.

"Now you, milady."

"Nay, I'm fine. Let's get him—"

"Sit," Patrick ordered.

Too exhausted to argue, she sat. He ripped one last strip from her gown. It now reached her knees, though at the moment, neither was concerned with modesty.

Concentrating on Winslow, she asked, "Is he all right?" Her eyes were wide with fear for her dear friend. She didn't like the gray cast to his skin. He had lost so much blood.

"We've got to get my healing herbs, mix a poultice—" She stopped speaking when MacInness slumped over, unconscious. "Dear God in Heaven!"

Patrick placed his strong hands on her shoulders. "Lady Jillian, listen carefully. I have to get you both back to the keep now; we cannot delay. Can you ride?"

Her vision wavered, and her legs felt like she was standing knee deep in frigid water, but she nodded. "Aye."

"I'll tie him to the saddle. You sit behind him and hold tight."

"I won't let go," she vowed. She could do it. She had to hang on. Talking to herself helped her concentrate on the injured man before her and not the pain creeping back into her arm.

"I'll follow behind to protect your backs, we've no time to waste."

When she saw the edge of the clearing through the trees, she knew they would make it. Her mind started to wander. She tried to concentrate on Winslow, ignoring the pain, just for a few minutes more.

"Almost there, milady," Patrick called out. "Just a little longer."

Her hands trembled and her arms shook, but she held on for dear life…Winslow's. It was all the incentive she needed. She would protect her husband's vassal to the last ounce of strength she possessed.

CHAPTER THIRTY-ONE

"J ILLIAN."

The voice was insistent, as were the hands shaking her. She groaned when pain sliced through her arm, forcing her heavy eyes open.

"We're safe. You can let go of him now."

Confusion muddled her brain. "Safe?" She licked her dry lips.

"Aye," Patrick answered.

"Thank God." She let go of her tenuous hold on Winslow and consciousness. When she awoke, she was disoriented for a moment before it all came back to her. Her horse stumbling and the war cry and the ambush that followed.

"Winslow—" she croaked out.

"Aye?" MacInness limped over to the side of her bed. He was pale as death, but he was alive enough to glower down at her. "Ye shoulda listened when I told ye to ride for the keep!"

She looked away from the censure in his eyes. Her gaze collided with Garrick's brilliant blue stare.

Her reaction ran the gamut of emotion from shock to joy to sheer panic.

But her husband's look was cold and forbidding. She had saved his vassal's life, why was he angry with her?

"Why did you take a chance with your life and that of our babe?"

Her hands flew to her stomach in fear.

"By the grace of God, you haven't lost it yet." Shock ripped through Jillian. Her stomach rebelled at the thought of losing their babe. She reached for the chamber pot, gagging. Strong arms held her through the worst of it.

"Gert says you're stronger than you look." He looked down at her arm then wiped her brow with a cool cloth. "Jillian?" His voice sounded hesitant.

"Aye?"

"What you did today was foolish," he began.

"I told her to ride for the keep," MacInness interrupted.

Jillian didn't know how to begin to explain that she had already caused one good man's death; she couldn't let another die because of her foolishness. In the face of her husband's anger, the words died on her lips.

"Leave us."

The warrior rose, pausing at the door, he gave her a hard look and left.

"MacInness would have given his life to protect you."

"I could not let him do that," her voice broke. "It was because of my desire to escape your overbearing strictures that led him into that ambush. Had I listened, his life would not have been endangered."

Garrick kissed her brow with tenderness. "I do understand your actions wife, but you are not a warrior."

Jillian's hands sought her necklace and closed around the smooth stone. "Mayhap not in your eyes, husband, but I protect what is mine." Her eyes flashed with conviction, "'Tis men who make war on the battlefields, but ofttimes while they do, their women must wage war while protecting their homes."

She dared a glance at her husband. It seemed impossible but he appeared angrier. Jillian mistakenly thought she had seen the worst of that emotion the day they wed. She was wrong.

She was afraid she had not been able to make him understand why she acted without hesitation. Jillian searched his face for a hint of forgiveness, but could not read his expression. A moan of hopelessness escaped her constricted chest. Suddenly, she was wrapped in Garrick's embrace.

His lips pressed fiercely to her forehead, cheek, and the hollow of her throat where her pulse beat frantically. Her husband pulled her even closer into his loving embrace.

They both fell silent. After a lengthy pause, he spoke, his voice colorless. "When we were in London, I started to tell you about my past."

"But what has that to do with today?" Jillian whispered.

"I killed my father," he interrupted.

"Surely you did not raise a hand to your father?"

Jillian's look of disbelief warmed his heart, putting a crack in the ice around his soul. "I did."

Reaching out to touch his face, she stroked it gently, silently pleading with him to unburden his troubles to her.

"Before the Uprising, I was to lead our people in battle against the Normans. My father argued that he would lead them, but 'twas my place as his vassal. He would remain behind and protect our keep and my lady mother."

His remembered failure clogged his throat, making it hard to speak. The constant feather-light touch to his face and brow urged him to continue. The woman he held gave him the strength to do so.

"My father decided to give me a chance. If I bested him in hand-to-hand combat, I would win the right to lead our people into battle. If not, I would stay and protect the keep."

"Did you win?"

"Nay." Garrick felt the brutal blow to his solar plexus as if it had just happened; he struggled inwardly to regain control of his labored breathing.

"What happened?"

"My father struck the winning blow. He led our people into battle."

"But you said you killed him?" Her confusion was evident.

"Had I not lost the fight with my father, he would still be alive today." *He had said it at last.* After holding it in for the last three years, he had finally admitted his guilt aloud.

"And where would you be?" Jillian's softly whispered question hit him between the eyes.

"Where I should be," was his reply.

"How can you even think such thoughts?"

"I have not finished." He reached deep inside for the courage to continue. "Because of me, our keep fell to the Normans only three of us survived." Garrick waited silently for the condemnation that would surely follow.

When he could no longer stand the wait, he looked up. The tender look of understanding filling his wife's eyes cleansed the first layer of his guilt.

"Garrick. My father died at Hastings 'Twas just my mother and myself left to defend our home when the Normans came through to squelch those who rose up against King William. We were no match for the first wave of Normans, but even if we were, the second wave of soldiers would have decimated us."

"Is that what plagues your dreams?"

"Nay," she whispered, "'tis Alan."

Before she could speak her terror aloud, Garrick took her hands in his and spoke softly, "You gave him back his hope, his freedom. That he died fighting for it was his choice."

"Then can you not understand my actions earlier, I could not live with the death of another good man on my conscience." Her eyes locked with his, willing him to understand. "Life is precious, a gift from God to be treasured. Don't wish it away, hoping to somehow trade places with your father."

Garrick pulled her close and held her against his heart. The balm of her love slowly seeped in, washing away each layer of guilt and hurt that had wrapped around his soul, until it lay fully exposed, yet stronger for having survived the cleansing. That she understood and shared a like pain freed him.

"You did not kill your father. No man can decide for another when it is his time to die. 'Tis up to God. He has our lives planned for us from before the day we are conceived. Though we may think we are in control of our lives, His higher power truly controls us all."

"If you believe that, Jillian, then can you still hold the blame for Alan's death so close to your own heart?"

The truth of his words arrowed through her. Her heart felt suddenly lightened from the heavy load she had carried. "Are you still angry?" she asked, biting her lip.

Garrick pulled her back into his arms and kissed her until her mind was mush. "Aye."

"But—"

"After what happened today, I would think you'd cease to question me, wife." His voice softened, "You could begin by promising to obey without question in the future."

Jillian's eyes filled with love for her husband, as she said, "You wouldn't want me to speak falsely, would you?"

His laughter bounced off the walls and echoed in her heart.

"I love you," she confessed.

"I know," he smiled. At her disgruntled expression, he kissed her and said, "I love you, too."

When he could bring himself to break the embrace, he voiced his worry, "You cannot ride outside the walls again until your guardian has been subdued."

She nodded.

His eyes iced over, his words without inflection, "Owen will pay for his part in the ambush today."

"What will you do?"

Garrick silenced her with a fierce kiss. "The time for talk has passed."

CHAPTER THIRTY-TWO

THE PLAN CAME together with surprising speed. By the time Jillian's head touched the pillow on their bed, Garrick and Patrick headed up the small band of warriors who rode out in search of justice.

After a heated debate, it was decided MacInness's injuries were too noticeable, and their plan called for swift action. If Owen had a clue as to the truth of what happened earlier that day, their plan would fail.

Though MacInness argued admirably, for once he was outnumbered. Even his crew of Irish mercenaries voted that he should be left behind to guard the lady of the keep.

The band of warriors riding to Sedgeworth's gate were of the same mind; all were calm, it would be necessary if they were to succeed.

Pulling up on the reins of his destrier, Garrick called in a voice that rang out clear and strong. "I've come on urgent private business with Owen." He ignored the burning in his stomach that had taken up residence there the moment he laid eyes on his blood-covered unconscious wife.

He had thought them both dead. Shaking himself free of the gruesome memory, he focused on the task at hand. They had a liar to flush out. Once that was accomplished, they would make him talk. Garrick smiled inwardly, knowing he would enjoy applying torture if necessary.

He dismounted stiffly, the strain of keeping his simmering temper in check difficult. He handed the reins to the stable lad, willing his hands to steady themselves. He would not think of his wife, or the gash that ran from the top of her shoulder down along the back of her arm to her elbow. Though he knew Owen had not wielded the broadsword that had laid open her tender flesh, ultimately, he was responsible. *And he would pay.*

Focusing his energy and anger on convincing the lord of Sedgeworth that he did not suspect him of the near fatal ambush, Garrick followed along behind Owen. Once they gained the hall, he and his men were offered a mug of honeyed wine.

When everyone seemed relaxed and at ease, he decided 'twas time to put the second part of his plan into action.

"There was trouble near the edge of the clearing to the south of my land earlier today." Garrick watched his host closely.

"Trouble?" Owen cleared his throat loudly. "What sort?"

Garrick looked to Patrick; the warrior's face was etched in stone, giving away nothing. He knew the pain the man suffered, he had seen the raw emotion on the man's face when he caught Jillian in his arms as she slid from her horse. He would remember always the look in Patrick's eyes when he carried MacInness inside the keep. Though he had never had a friend like that before, he could not help but feel the emotion that tied the two men together.

"We came upon what looked like the remains of an ambush," Garrick told him.

"Remains?" Owen asked, his gaze was dark and deadly.

"Aye." Garrick almost smiled as he drew out the telling of his false tale. "Six knights had been brutally slain and left to rot."

"Six?"

"Aye." He nodded slowly. Garrick felt a warmth surge up within him; he had Owen's undivided attention.

"No survivors?"

"None." Though he was dying to push Owen to confess, he

wanted the man to trap himself.

"Did they wear colors?"

Owen's question convinced him beyond a shadow of a doubt in Garrick's mind. No other group of Saxon knights wore like colors—none save Owen's band of cutthroats—but he played innocent of any such knowledge.

"Colors?"

Owen hesitated for a heartbeat. During that moment, Garrick saw him clearly for the first time. Right through to the man's black, pockmarked soul.

"'Tis something I had seen of late, just a thought…" Owen's voice trailed off to a harsh whisper.

Patrick rose and walked over to stand at Garrick's side. Garrick noticed his agitation, but shook his head hoping to silence the Irishman. Patrick seemed to rein himself in. When Garrick glanced around at the faces of the men flanking him, he knew he had the best of the best. Through some quirk of fate, his wife had brought an elite fighting force with her to Merewood. The men were loyal to the last, but it was their kinship surrounding him, standing there in their enemy's hall that mattered. Their combined strength flowed over him, filling him.

"My thanks for the wine. You had best have a care and remember what happened at Merewood. If you are not careful, one of your family might ride out and befall the same fate as those knights." Garrick paused, rubbing a hand across his chin, he added, "I'll not let my lady wife leave the walls of Merewood until we capture the person, or persons, behind this foul deed and punish them as befits their crime."

He had the satisfaction of watching Owen's face lose all color. His threat had found its mark. Owen was responsible, and now Owen knew Garrick would not rest until justice was served.

CHAPTER THIRTY-THREE

EYREKA BUSTLED INTO Jillian's chamber just after she had risen to break her fast for the day.

"Riders are approaching from the south."

Grabbing her cloak, Jillian followed Eyreka down the stair, through the hall, and out into the bright sunlit bailey. Jillian hailed the guard, "Eustace, can you see who comes?"

"Nay, mistress, but there is a woman in their riding party. 'Tis all I can make out from this distance."

The guards along the curtain wall waited, arrows notched, until the group rode close enough to decide if they presented any danger to the keep.

"Tell Garrick, Henri du Guerre and his lady wife wish entrance to your keep," a loud voice demanded from the other side of the wall.

Jillian and Eyreka exchanged glances; their like minds had them clamoring up the wooden steps of the platform to see over the wall. Standing side by side, they took in the sight below them. Madelyne sat astride a beautiful horse who pawed at the ground impatiently, while to her right, her husband Henri sat atop a black destrier who snorted loudly while being restrained.

"Maddy!"

"Jillian? Are you well? Should you be out of bed yet?" Her friend's concern-wrapped words felt like a warm hug.

"Aye, Lady du Guerre, she should as yet be abed," a deep voice answered from directly behind Jillian.

She whirled around so fast her long hair snapped like a banner in a stiff breeze.

Their gazes locked and held, neither one speaking. Words were not always necessary between them. She sensed her husband's displeasure. Deep lines were drawn around his mouth, forcing it into a grimace. A bad sign.

"Are you going to stand there and glare at me, husband? Or will you bid them enter before I catch a chill standing out here in the wind?"

Her sassy reply brought a rumble of laughter from the solemn man at her side. "Open the gate!" he called down.

Before Jillian could slip out of his grasp, he pulled her close to his side and took hold of her arm. Bending he whispered in her ear, "Lady wife, do not think I shall forget you have disobeyed my wishes after you gave me your word."

Her broad smile should have given Garrick a clue to what she was thinking.

Jillian saw Reka give her son a hard look out of the corner of her eye as they descended the stairs. She would find out why later. As soon as Madelyne dismounted, Jillian took Madelyne's arm and steered her across the bailey to their hall.

"I was worried for you," Madelyne confessed.

"'Tis only my husband who thinks I should be abed. I feel stronger by the day." Looking around for her husband, she added, "He worries about me overmuch."

"Aye, 'tis the way it should be," Madelyne agreed. "Henri could drive me mad with his cautions. Don't ride out alone, Maddy. We have a cook, Maddy, let her do her job."

Jillian laughed at Madelyne's mimicking of her husband. "He cares for you, then?"

Madelyne's smile was blinding. "I love him."

"I didn't know, but am glad to hear you say so." Jillian grew thoughtful before adding, "Does he return your feelings?"

"Oh, aye." The younger woman's face flushed a bright pink.

"Madelyne," Henri stalked over to his wife's side and glowered, "I knew I should have forbidden you to ride out."

"Why is that?" Jillian asked.

"'Tis not your affair, wife," Garrick said softly.

"But she's my friend," she added hotly.

"She is du Guerre's wife," he reminded her.

With a great sigh, Henri answered them both, "She carries my babe, and I'll not let her ride out again until he is safely delivered."

"Oh, Henri," Madelyne laughed softly. "I am fine, mayhap a little tired."

"Come sit over by the fire," Jillian took her by the arm, "and tell me about it."

Garrick offered a mug of mead to Henri. "To fatherhood," Henri toasted.

"My wife doesn't realize her limitations," Garrick complained.

Henri nodded knowingly. "*Oui*, our women are strong willed, no?"

"Aye, they are," Garrick agreed.

Finally, the question that had popped into his brain the moment he looked down from atop the curtain wall and found du Guerre awaiting entrance to Merewood came out, "Why are you really here?"

"Ah, you think I have other reasons for this visit?" Henri nodded. "I have come to cherish my wife, but cannot stomach her sire."

Garrick's eyes grew cold at the mention of Owen. "Then we share similar feelings toward that whoreson," he added under his breath.

"*Oui*. Can we speak privately?" Henri urged.

"Jillian, Henri and I are going to meet with the blacksmith."

"Aye, Garrick." Her puzzled look made him smile.

Once outside, Henri began, "'Twas Owen who led me to

Loughmoe three years past. I was ready to level the home of any traitor to my king. The fact that two women resided alone at Loughmoe tempted me further still."

Garrick's face grew taut, as the rage within him bubbled up.

Du Guerre put a hand out to stop Garrick from grabbing the hilt of his sword. "Hear me out. There is more."

Nodding his head, Garrick released his death grip on the hilt.

"We surrounded the keep, yet the women still escaped. After that I trusted him not. He tried to contact me more than once to tell me he had the land within his grasp, but I cared not. That is not until the night I spent with his daughter."

Henri's gaze searched Garrick's before he continued; "I lost my heart to my Maddy that night. Living with her has changed my view on things."

"Such as?"

"Hating all Saxons. We must learn to live among one another if we are to survive and become a stronger people."

Garrick was moved by Henri's declaration. "Aye. 'Tis as it should be." Pausing, he lowered his voice, "Owen was behind the kidnapping of my wife and mother, and the ambush a fortnight ago."

"*Oui*, this I know. Maddy has recently overheard her father making plans to take back the ransom he was never paid by you."

"He would not dare."

"He would dare much. As much as I love Madelyne, that much I despise Owen of Sedgeworth."

With one hand on his heart and the other on the hilt of his sword, Henri went down on one knee before a stunned Garrick. "I offer my sword in defense of your keep. Together we stand stronger than alone."

Garrick felt humbled by the Norman's words. All that du Guerre had divulged about Owen had not surprised him. That he would pledge his sword to defend Merewood did, but he was wise enough to take him up on his offer.

Reaching a hand out to his new vassal he said, "Henri, together, we shall keep Owen and his band of Reivers under control. With our forces joined, our keeps' people will have naught to fear."

"*Oui*, my friend."

"Aye, my friend." Garrick paused before speaking his inner most thought, "Owen will pay for his actions."

"What do you have in mind?" Henri prompted him.

"Land and wealth is everything to the man," Garrick said aloud, while rubbing his chin.

"*Oui*. That and life at the court of King William," du Guerre added quietly.

"His true nature should be exposed, so all would know him for the coward he is," Garrick stated emphatically. "'Tis time to draw the vermin away from his keep and spring the trap."

MUSICAL LAUGHTER FLOWED out of the open door as Garrick and his new ally returned to the hall. Jillian and Madelyne sat with their heads bowed together, auburn waves mingled with flaxen tresses.

Fire and sunlight.

Garrick felt a warmth rise up inside of him at the sight. Jillian's laughter, her essence, had infused itself into the walls of Merewood. He was humbled that her courage let her forgive him, and with her loving touch, heal him. His hall rang with joy and laughter.

Now he had a strong ally he could count on should Owen decide to cause more trouble. But beyond that, he had made a friend, heretofore an enemy. Their lives were cycling further away from war by the day, back toward more peaceful times.

"You were gone overlong, husband," Jillian teased. "I missed you." She stood on tiptoe and brushed her lips across his cheek, barely catching it in her haste. Garrick pulled her back to him and kissed her deeply, needing to show her without words what her gift of herself meant to him.

When at last he released her, he felt her knees buckle. Chuckling, he wrapped an arm around her waist and led her to an empty chair. Before Jillian knew what he was about, he had settled her down on his lap, resting his hand lightly on the hard mound of her belly. Both watched the babe within it, bounce up and down.

"Milord," she said softly, "we have guests."

"Henri understands," Garrick said, "Don't you Henri?"

"*Oui.*" Surprising a yelp out of his wife, Henri lifted her out of her chair and sat down, settling her down on his lap in one swift motion.

"Mayhap my son and his guests would rather I return another time?" Lady Eyreka suggested frostily.

"Nay, Mother, come and sit. 'Tis past time we got to know our neighbors at Loughmoe Keep."

Turning toward Henri, she asked pointedly, "How is the renovation of Jillian's home going?"

"Nay, Reka. This is my home. Loughmoe belongs to Maddy and Henri."

Looking from her son to her daughter-in-law, Eyreka nodded. "Aye, 'tis your home."

Jillian suddenly felt as if the truth had finally come to her. *Merewood was her home.* It was filled with the people she loved. Within a few short months, their babe would be born in the bed she shared with the man who held her heart. Wrapping her arms about his neck, she laid her head over his heart and listened to the strong steady beating of it.

The Lord had blessed her the day she met Garrick of Merewood. But His blessing did not stop there. He gave her a new mother to love and brothers. She'd always wanted brothers. She closed her eyes and smiled.

CHAPTER THIRTY-FOUR

THE LIGHTNESS GARRICK experienced after unburdening his feelings of guilt remained with him still. Knowing he had a strong ally at Loughmoe added to his feelings of contentment.

Two months had passed since the day he and Jillian bared their souls to one another. Swollen with his babe, he marveled that she grew more beautiful with each passing day.

Looking over at her, pride swelled within his breast for the auburn-haired beauty who captivated not only his heart, but his very being. He saw her frown. "What are you thinking?" he asked.

"MacInnes has been talking about going to Scotland." Worry creased her brow. "He'll have to go, won't he?"

"Aye, love. 'Tis his home. Besides, he will not rest until he is certain his mother and sisters are safe."

"What if it turns into another Uprising?" she asked. "What if the Normans storm through Scotland, laying waste to all in their path?"

"You should not worry about what might not happen wife. It cannot be good for the babe." He placed his strong hand atop her growing belly, then a kiss.

"Do you feel up to a walk this morning?" Garrick asked.

Jillian stood before her husband and tipped her head back to look him in the eye. "But I'll not stop worrying just because we are out walking in the woods."

"The change of scenery will do us both good." Garrick touched the curve of her cheek, marveling at the smoothness of her skin. *His wife.* Her courage and loyalty would rival that of his most trusted vassals. He had been well and truly blessed the day she asked him to marry her.

Walking arm in arm, they followed along the path that wound past the new stone wall of the keep, around to a dense glade. Sunlight filtered down through the trees. Shafts of bright beams shone on the rocks and stumps littering the forest floor.

They walked to the lake and watched the mist rise off the still cool surface. Pulling her closer to his side, they silently paid homage to nature's bounty. The swift flight of a grouse rising from its hiding place startled them both into laughter. The keening sound of a hawk as it split the early morning quiet; they paused to watch it fly.

"Come, I want to show you something." Garrick's face lit up like a boy as he dragged Jillian off the path deeper into the woods.

Lifting a low-hanging branch, he pulled her into a small clearing. A large, flat rock sat in the center bathed in full sun. The air was still crisp with the morning chill, but where the sun touched was warm.

Leading her over to the rock, he took off his cloak and spread it on top of the smooth surface. He reached out and undid the brooch at her shoulder and added her cloak to his. Leaning over, he tested the softness of it with a tentative hand. Smiling, he took her hand in his, leading her over to the rock.

The heady scent of pine filled the air around them as the sun caressed the needles. With as much tenderness as possible, he laid her down upon the makeshift bed.

"Let me love you, Jillian."

Jillian's heart leapt with joy, and she reached up to enfold him in her arms, pulling him down on top of her. Their lips met, the sweetness of the kiss rivaling the sugared cakes he favored.

With slow, sensuous motions, Garrick slid her gown from her

shoulders, baring her creamy white breasts. He dipped his head, drawing her engorged nipple into the heat of his mouth. She wondered if their babe would derive half the pleasure her husband did suckling at her breast.

All thoughts fled as his knowing hands caressed and teased her willing body into a peak of frenzy. She reached up and tried to yank the tunic from him, but had not the strength. Garrick smiled, as if he knew it was the power of his loving that had left her weak.

"I cannot wait—"

Garrick freed them from the rest of their garments. He poised above her as if waiting for a signal from her.

Jillian reached up and took hold of his hips, guiding him home. She rose to meet his powerful strokes, again and again.

He swallowed her cries of ecstasy with his mouth, robbing her of air. Garrick wanted to be gentle with her and take his time, but the overwhelming need to bury himself in her warmth drove all other thoughts from his mind.

Jillian grabbed hold of him, pulling him deeper still. They slipped over the edge of awareness, reaching fulfillment together. As they did, the sun burst in the sky, showering them with sparks of light that danced before their eyes.

Later, as they lay entwined, a blessed peace stole over them, lulling the lovers to sleep. The heat of the sun on her face woke Jillian. She was safely wrapped in her husband's arms, right where she wanted to be. Smiling to herself, she laid the palm of her hand against her belly. The thought of a babe with hair the color of flax, eyes a deep blue, brought tears of joy.

Blinking them away, she buried her face against Garrick's broad chest and listened to the steady beat of his heart.

"Come, Jillian, or we will be missed." Retracing their steps through the trees and back to the path, they walked toward the keep, lighter in heart, deeper in love.

When they reached the path just outside the gate, a voice hailed them, "We searched the keep top to bottom looking for you." Dunstan gave them a censorious look.

"We were not in the keep," Jillian answered sweetly.

"Is there news?" Garrick's voice had gone quiet.

"Aye." The brothers shared a meaningful look.

"You'd best tell me too, Dunstan," Jillian said.

"Aye, brother, my wife is strong enough to bear whatever you have to say."

"Owen has been summoned to London to answer charges that he withheld revenues from the king."

"'Tis a serious charge, is it not?" Jillian asked.

"Aye, love. If proven, he could be stripped of his land, and that is the least of what might happen." Garrick pulled her closer to his side.

"You knew nothing about this, husband?" she asked pointedly.

He shrugged, "Owen cheated many people. We simply made our king aware of Owen's duplicity."

"Well then, we'd best send someone trustworthy to London to be there when it all comes out." She pretended to consider who would be best to go, all the while pointedly looking at Dunstan.

"'Tis the least I could do to ease the mind of my brother's lovely wife." Dunstan bowed low over her hand.

"I'll pack something for you to eat on your journey." Jillian headed toward the kitchen.

⇥⇤

"I HAVE TO go, mon," MacInness stated what was painfully obvious to Garrick.

"I know you do." He slapped a hand to his vassal's shoulder. "God be with you, then. Watch your back. There are those who might not understand."

The two men clasped hands. When they withdrew, Garrick

spoke, his voice rough with emotion, "Take Sean and Eamon with you."

"Take them where?" Roderick asked coming up from behind them, surprising them.

"'Tis not your concern, brother," Garrick answered, ever anxious to protect him.

"When will you stop treating me like a lad of five and ten?"

MacInness nodded his agreement. "Aye…when?"

Garrick sighed, knowing it was past time to give his youngest brother another chance. He knew Roderick still blamed himself for letting Jillian and their mother be kidnapped. 'Twas time to stop holding him back and let his brother redeem himself.

"MacInness rides to the Highlands to be with his mother and sisters. William plans to ride to Abernathy—"

"Does he plan to subdue King Malcolm?" Roderick interrupted.

"I think that is his plan." Garrick was pensive. "It will be dangerous, brother. If you are caught, no one will take the time to ask why you travel with a Highlander. Take every care to come home in one piece." He wrapped his brother in a bear hug, praying it would not be the last time he laid eyes on him.

CHAPTER THIRTY-FIVE

JILLIAN SPENT THE last weeks of her confinement in the warmth of the hall. The keep held more warmth than last year, her husband assured her, but she was still chilled.

Her steps were slower; she knew she waddled like the fat ducks that fed on the grain she loved to throw them. She smiled, thinking of the way they greedily gobbled it up. Her smile faded when she realized, lately, she ate with the same gusto.

A deep ache nagged at her lower back, but she ignored it and bent her head once again to concentrate on the needlework that lay on her huge belly. The linen jumped, she moved it aside and pressed lightly on her belly, smiling. It was a foot, she was certain of it, feeling the shape and angle of a heel. Another sharp pain radiated up her spine. She gasped with the strength of it, dropping her needlework to the floor.

Jillian looked around her to make certain no one had seen her distress, wanting to wait before telling anyone the babe was ready to be born. She retrieved her needlework. Picking it up she marveled at the fact that her hands did not snag on the fine linen. Tears filled her eyes; she had Garrick to thank for that, and more, so much more.

A home. Family. And love, so much love.

Garrick paused in the doorway to watch his wife. She was breathtakingly beautiful to him. The fact that she was heavy with his child made her even more beautiful in his eyes. He frowned when she arched her back as if in pain. He strode over to where she sat, eyes closed, concentrating. "Is it the babe?" he asked roughly.

Her eyes shot open, and the knowledge hit him in the chest. They were the focused eyes of a warrior. She was readying herself for the battle ahead. One hand was gripping the piece of amber dangling from her necklace while the other held tightly to the needlework of which he knew she was so proud.

He could not help himself; he grinned.

"Do you think this is funny, husband?" she ground out between clenched teeth.

He shook his head. "It is a part of life, our life. I plan to see that you deliver our babe safely, so that we can begin work on his brother."

"How can you even think of getting me with child, when I have yet to deliver the one I carry?" she said gasping, breathing hard through another contraction. This one was much stronger than the last. She knew labor would be hard work, but she was not afraid, she was ready.

He took her hands and held them in his strong grip. "I know you're strong lass, a true warrior."

She smiled, he knew just what to say to soothe her.

"You battled to win my heart and heal my soul with all the courage you possess."

"'Twas the sweetest victory," she whispered.

Garrick lifted her into his arms and carried her across the hall.

Gert stopped them at the bottom of the stairs. "Is it time?"

"Aye," Garrick answered.

"I'll fetch my healing herbs and meet you upstairs." The woman practically skipped outside into the biting cold toward the kitchen.

Garrick shook his head; the daft woman had forgotten to put on a cloak. The urge to laugh bubbled up within him. He looked down into Jillian's eyes; she had done that for him. His wife had given his life meaning, filled his home with laughter, but most importantly taught him how to love again.

Moved beyond words, he bent his head to kiss her, and she bit his lip.

The daft man was trying to kiss her while she was struggling to remember to breathe through the pains. When the contraction passed, she looked at his fat lip.

"I am sorry," she said contritely.

"I'm not." His lips sought to kiss hers again.

This time she let him.

EPILOGUE

J ILLIAN STROKED THE soft blond fuzz on top of her newborn son's head. She pressed her lips gently to his brow, inhaling the sweet scent of him. Exhausted, she slumped back against the pillow, and let her eyes drift closed.

"You gave your mother a hard time, son," Garrick whispered to the babe resting sleepily in his wife's arms. "'Tis not to say the birthing was any easier on you." At his words, the wee one scrunched up his face and let out a loud wail.

"There, now sweet babe, mother's here," Jillian soothed while helping him find her swollen breast. He rooted around until he found that which he instinctively sought. Latching on with a vengeance, he suckled loudly.

"Our son takes after his father," she laughed softly.

"Aye, he knows where to find comfort, where to find love."

Their eyes met, filled with an outpouring of love flowing from deep within them both. Their hearts were whole. The icy bleakness surrounding their souls melted in the warmth of that love.

"Dearest Jillian, I shall love you more than yesterday, but less than tomorrow."

"Always, my love," she whispered.

Wrapping his arms around his new family, Garrick opened his heart to the promise of a lifetime of love.

Jillian raised her lips to his and willingly accepted the loving challenge.

About the Author

In case we have not met yet, here is a little bit about me:

I write Historical & Contemporary Romance featuring: Hard-headed Heroes & Feisty Heroines.

I fell in love at first sight, when I was seventeen, with the man who will hold my heart forever. DJ and I were married for forty-one wonderful years until my darling lost his battle with cancer. We have three grown children—one son-in-law, two grandsons, two rescue dogs, two rescue grand-cats, and one rescue grand-puppy.

My Hardheaded Heroes and Feisty Heroines rarely listen to me. In fact, I think they enjoy messing with my plans for them. BUT if there is one thing I've learned in dealing with my characters for the past twenty-nine years, it is to listen to them! My heroes always have a few of DJ's best qualities: his honesty, his integrity, his compassion for those in need, and his killer broad shoulders.

I have always used family names in my books and love adding bits and pieces of my ancestors and ancestry in them, too. I write about the things I love most: my family, my Irish and English ancestry, baking and gardening.

Happy reading!